LEFT BOOK CLUB ANTHOLOGY

LEFT BOOK CLUB ANTHOLOGY

Edited by

PAUL LAITY

VICTOR GOLLANCZ
LONDON

First published in Great Britain in 2001
by Victor Gollancz/Weidenfeld & Nicolson
Imprints of Orion Books Ltd
Orion House, 5 Upper St Martin's Lane,
London WC2H 9EA

A CIP catalogue record for this book
is available from the British Library

ISBN 0 575 07221 0

Typeset at The Spartan Press Ltd,
Lymington, Hants

Printed and bound in Great Britain by
Clays Ltd, St Ives plc

ACKNOWLEDGEMENTS

This is the last non-fiction book to be published by Victor Gollancz – a firm associated with books about politics, especially radical politics, since it was set up in 1928. A Left Book Club anthology, though nothing more than a reminder of Gollancz's own most celebrated venture, seems an appropriate – if wholly unintentional – marker of the disappearance of his name from political publishing in Britain.

Many people have responded to my calls for help. Thanks especially to: John Arnold of Monash University; Bernard Attard of Leicester University; Andy Croft; Jean Eisler; Michael Foot; Paul Foot; Livia Gollancz; Jeremy Harding; William Jones of Cardiff University; Arnold Rattenbury; David Rose; John Sutherland of University College London; and Olwen Terris at the BFI. Thanks also to Sara Holloway, once at Victor Gollancz, Keelin Watson and especially to Ian Preece, my understanding editor at Orion.

and Judith Williams; *These Poor Hands* reprinted by permission of Vivian Davies. The right to reprint *Fallen Bastions* is held by Orion Books. Every effort has been made to trace the copyright owners of *Walls Have Mouths*, *Our Street* and *Out of the Night*; anyone claiming copyright ownership of these books should make contact with the author.

P.L.

CONTENTS

INTRODUCTION

In January 1936, the 'red squire' and super-barrister Stafford Cripps took Victor Gollancz out for lunch. They were joined by the bestselling Marxist writer John Strachey. What could be done, Cripps wanted to know, to revitalise and educate the British left? He was considering a new weekly paper, but Gollancz had another idea – a club along the lines of the successful Book Society, which would sell radical books very cheaply. The first advertisement for the Left Book Club appeared only a month later. It was a call to arms. Political understanding, Gollancz wrote, was a matter of 'terrible urgency at the present time, when the world is drifting into war, and fascism is triumphing in country after country'. The Club's aim would be to 'help in the struggle *for* world peace and a better social and economic order, and *against* fascism'.

The response to the ad was staggering. Two thousand adherents were needed to make the Club work; after only a month, there were more than 6,000. By the end of the first year, membership had reached 40,000 and by 1939 it was up to 57,000; in total, millions of LBC volumes were put into circulation. Today, the Left Book Club is a thirties legend, the definitive symbol of a time when British intellectuals were seduced by Communism and writers skipped off to Spain. In the midst of all the mythologising, however, the books themselves are often forgotten. The hundreds of different volumes published by the Club have long since faded into one another, a long tangerine stripe on the shelf of a second-hand bookshop. This anthology dusts down a dozen or more in order to show what the LBC was about, and why it was such a success.

Robert Graves and Alan Hodge wrote in 1940 that a collection of Club titles was 'an armoury from which a weapon could be selected for argument on any conceivable subject' – from farming to Freud to air-raid shelters to Indian independence. Some of the books were extended news bulletins, others were closely argued treatises; almost all advocated a politics to the left of the Labour Party – there has never been such a powerful force in Britain for the dissemination of far left ideas. (There were, Gollancz said, 'lots of people who want to learn'.) The Club published a few novels, and a small amount of poetry and drama, too. Most impressive, however, was its output of personal political reportage – from Wigan Pier, the Welsh collieries, Shaanxi Province, Barcelona and other zones of crisis in those remarkable years.

Gollancz's scheme was simple. Club members were committed to buying a designated title from his list every month, for a minimum of six months. The books were often specially commissioned for the LBC, but were sold to the general public, at two or three times the Club price of 2s 6d. They were distributed via bookshops and some newsagents. To encourage as many new readers as possible, the monthly choices were supposed to require 'not the slightest knowledge of politics, economics or history for perfect understanding'. Gollancz wanted to create an active political readership, an intellectual Popular Front.

The sales of each of the Club's monthly selections far surpassed those of most other topical books. The print run of Orwell's *The Road to Wigan Pier*, for example, was 42,000; that of his next book, *Homage to Catalonia*, published by Secker, was 1,500. And given that every LBC volume was a guaranteed bestseller, Gollancz was able to attract the most talented authors – Clement Attlee, for example, was delighted with the £600 that *The Labour Party in Perspective* netted him, while Stephen Spender used his handsome £300 advance for *Forward from Liberalism* to furnish his Hammersmith flat with an ebony-topped desk and copper-bowl lamps.

The LBC quickly developed from a book club into a distinctive political movement, as members formed local groups to discuss the monthly choices. By the outbreak of war, there were 1,200 such groups, one in almost every town in the country – they held lectures and 'socials', distributed pamphlets and acted as recruiting centres. Hundreds of press cuttings featuring Club events poured into Gollancz's office in Henrietta Street, Covent Garden each month. The LBC was fast becoming, he said in June 1936, 'a genuine movement of the masses'. The 7,000 tickets to the Club's first national rally, held in the Royal Albert Hall in February 1937, sold out within days: 'From floor to ceiling,' the *Universe* reported, 'the vast auditorium was filled with eager and earnest youth.' After a couple of years, the Club was organising larger anti-appeasement demonstrations than the Labour Party. And, thanks to the groups, it provided a focus for left-wing cultural activity of all kinds – in theatre, film, poetry, travel, music.

'It could only have happened', Strachey said, 'at the present moment.' The Club's first months coincided not only with nervousness at the prospect of another war, but the triumph of the Popular Front in France and, crucially, the beginning of the Civil War in Spain. In Britain, the Tory-dominated National Government was widely disliked, but there was no effective Opposition: the Labour Party was still reeling from betrayal and defeat in 1931; the Liberal Party was in permanent decline. At the same time, a new, radical middle class was emerging – hooked on modernity, often employed by local government and desperate to understand the current political situation, so that something could be done. The popularity of the LBC, and of the new Penguin Specials, published by Allen Lane from 1937, depended on this readership.

With the Labour Party appearing unadventurous and feeble, many socialists looked further to the left. A Marxist view of the world was never more plausible. World capitalism was in crisis – economies crashing, governments toppling, empires over-extended – and most British progressives agreed that it had to be replaced (even Harold Macmillan said as much). The National Government was believed to be running the country in the interests of big business rather than the people. Its perceived origins – the 'bankers' ramp' – offered proof that the City wouldn't tolerate even a meek and mild Labour administration. Neither the 'boneless wonder' Ramsay MacDonald nor his successor as Prime Minister, Stanley Baldwin, provided any answers to the country's economic problems, other than cuts in wages, reduced unemployment assistance and the dreaded Means Test. The aim, it seemed, was deliberately to impoverish the working class in order to limit its power. The imagery of blight could be seen everywhere – dole queues, abandoned docks and shipyards, slums in decaying towns. Baldwin was dismissive of unemployed hunger marchers, but well enough disposed towards Oswald Mosley's Blackshirts. On the horizon, socialists believed, was a very British form of fascism. 'When our labour leaders are interned,' the veteran left-wing journalist H. N. Brailsford wrote, 'our Storm Troopers will not beat them: they will play cricket with them on Saturday afternoons.'

The Government's overseas record confirmed it all. The Hoare–Laval deal which handed Abyssinia to Mussolini was, it was thought, a sure sign that Baldwin was cosying up to fascism. The world was taking sides –

fascist vs anti-fascist – and it was unclear which side Downing Street was on. Britain had done nothing to prevent either the Japanese move into Manchuria or Hitler's seizure of the Rhineland, even though Germany was obviously a ravenous empire sustainable only by a series of military successes – in Austria, Czechoslovakia and who knew where else. It appeared perfectly possible that Baldwin's administration would acquiesce in a fascist war to destroy the Soviet Union. Quickly enough, the death throes of capitalism would lead to war in Western Europe, too, and in a last-ditch attempt to save itself, the British ruling class would opt for militarism over socialism and peace.

The only answer, Gollancz believed, was for Labourites, Liberals and Communists to forget their differences and form, as they had done in France, a Popular Front government to cope with the emergency. This new administration would immediately sign up to an anti-fascist alliance with France and the USSR and stop the dictators in their tracks. The LBC was founded as a means to support this unity campaign. 'We are convinced,' G. D. H. Cole wrote in his monthly choice, *The People's Front*, 'that Great Britain cannot be ranged unequivocally on the side of peace and democracy without a decisive victory of the Left in British politics, and that the Left cannot win this decisive victory unless it is united. There is no time to lose.'

To help him select the Club volumes, Gollancz recruited Strachey and Harold Laski. It was an awe-inspiring trio – the Holy Trinity of the LBC – including as it did three of Beaverbrook's 'four horsemen of the socialist apocalypse' (the other was Kingsley Martin). Brought up in a privileged Liberal household (Lytton was his second cousin; his father edited the *Spectator*), Strachey had been shocked in his youth to learn that workers couldn't afford the things they produced. He became a Labour MP in 1929 and supported Mosley's proposals for emergency measures to prevent unemployment. Having left Parliament in 1931, he was active on behalf of Mosley's New Party. When he realised where that was heading, he took up with Communism, 'from chagrin', he used to explain, 'at not getting into the Eton Cricket XI'. He followed the Communist Party line closely, though he was never a card-carrying member (the Party was too sensible to allow that). Strachey's *The Coming Struggle for Power*, published in 1932, was a godsend for the CP: it made Communism seem practical and logically necessary, not simply dependent on people's better feelings. He was a great persuader, and his ease with theory and smooth prose gave Strachey tremendous influence with leftists eager for a credo – *The Theory and Practice of Socialism*, a monthly choice in 1936, became the LBC bible.

Laski's books were more widely read even than Strachey's. A professor at the LSE, he was also the most popular Labour Party figure outside Parliament. He came from a Liberal family, but found a home on the left of the Labour Party, joining the ILP and, later, the Socialist League. Intellectually unsatisfied, he found that Marxism gave him 'inner peace'. He distanced himself from the Communist Party line, however, and more obviously than Strachey blended his Marxist ideas with liberal sympathies. Laski stood slightly apart from the LBC as well, but Gollancz knew that he commanded great respect. Not only that: he could read manuscripts at an incredible lick (a page at a glance), remembering every word.

Gollancz was himself a committed, impulsive socialist. As a young man, he had 'thrilled' to the Russian Revolution and rebelled against his authoritarian, Jewish upbringing. He set up his own firm in 1928 and by the mid-thirties was already a publishing phenomenon. This was thanks partly to the sleuthing of Dorothy Sayers's Lord Peter Wimsey, but was also the result of unexpectedly large sales of left-wing political literature (Strachey, Cole, *The Brown Book of the Hitler Terror*). Gollancz's volumes were easily recognisable, with their bright jackets and daring typographical design. They were also marketed as no books had been before, with large, brash ads in the papers (one was pulled at the last minute from the *Observer* – the editor, J. L. Garvin, had no time for Gollancz's 'pacifist, socialist ordure'). He was celebrated, too, for his demonic energy. A newspaper profile portrayed him getting through work 'like a destroyer through the sea . . . he guts a 75,000-word MS in 45 minutes . . . often works from 9.15 a.m. to 1 a.m. the next day, and believes he could do four times as much work easily'. This zeal was combined with a self-assurance which slipped easily into arrogance ('I am incapable of error'). He oversaw everything to do with the LBC ('the Club is myself!') and was, Strachey said, a 'generous, emotional, greedy, intelligent, gorgeous and sometimes absurd man'. Aware, perhaps, of his instinctive approach, he was overawed by the tough, scientistic language of the Communist Party and, despite retaining Labour Party membership, was identified as a Communist fellow-traveller, albeit one who always travelled first class. 'I was as close to the Communists', he was later to say of his politics in the thirties, 'as one hair is to another.'

Gollancz was too much of a crowd-pleaser to confine the Club's output to Marxist polemics, however well written. He cast about for political 'narratives of adventure' to put some pace into the list. As a result, the first few monthly choices offered variety and élan as well as topicality. They included a book on the French Popular Front; a study of the future of genetics; two novels – André Malraux's *Days of Contempt*, about a political prisoner in Nazi Germany; and Hillel Bernstein's *Choose a Bright Morning*, a satire on the 'follies of fascism' – and Wilfred Macartney's *Walls Have Mouths*, a 'sensationalist' account of life inside Parkhurst prison, which proved immensely popular.

There was good educational fare, too, of course: the enormous *World Politics 1918–36* by the Communist Party's leading theoretician Rajani Palme Dutt, for example (also available in a special 'Christmas Gift Edition'); and Hyman Levy's *A Philosophy for a Modern Man*, a study of dialectical materialism, which many readers found so abstruse that he had to tour the Club's local groups to explain it. 'It really makes one's hair stand on end', Gollancz said, 'to think that fifty thousand people should be induced to read this book.' Letters from around the country soon let the selection committee know if the choices weren't exciting or accessible enough, though when Gaetano Salvemini's *Under the Axe of Fascism* raised protests from members for being too difficult, Gollancz gave them a ticking off: the Club was 'not just for light entertainment'. One subscriber, at least, was contrite:

Forced to make the choice ourselves
Our rude forefathers loaded shelves
With Tennyson and Walter Scott
And Meredith and Lord knows what!
But we don't have to hum and ha,
Nous avons changé tout cela –
Our books are chosen for us – Thanks
To Strachey, Laski and Gollancz!

Gollancz's strictures made little difference. The most popular books remained those of reportage and memoir – Edgar Snow's *Red Star over China*, for instance, and *American Testament*, an autobiography by the American poet Joseph Freeman, which took in 'bohemian Paris', Moscow and socialist rallies in Berlin. Historical narratives also went down well: A. L. Morton's *A People's History of England* has remained more or less continuously in print since its first publication. Other choices were – as old members cheerfully admit – hardly read at all. According to Graves and Hodge, 'once the books started to arrive each month, it was as difficult to break the habit as to stop paying instalments on an electric vacuum-cleaner or radio set'. To keep up the Club's momentum, Gollancz introduced different types of membership and began to offer 'Additional', 'Supplementary', 'Educational' and 'Topical' books as well as the monthly choice. The administrative complications – Fill out the yellow card, not the green or red! – were blackly comic to the drudges in Henrietta Street.

One aspect of the selection process was never made explicit – the unwillingness on the part of Gollancz, Strachey and Laski to criticise the Soviet Union and its leadership, or to publish anything which would seriously annoy the Communist Party. For instance, a great deal of anguish surrounded the publication of the second part of *The Road to Wigan Pier*, which, with its stinking workers and assault on Marxist intellectuals, was tough for the CP to swallow: Gollancz overruled Party objections in putting out the book, but wrote a special foreword – included in this anthology – which tried to set Orwell straight. Although the LBC was quickly accused of being an instrument of Communist Party policy – letters to this effect were written to the *New Statesman* and other papers – the extent of the Party's control over the Club has been hotly disputed ever since.

It's pretty clear now that it came close to being a 'front' organisation. Gollancz's colleagues in Henrietta Street, Sheila Lynd and Betty Reid, were Party members. John Lewis, who looked after the local groups, almost certainly was as well (though he never said so). And Emile Burns, who had an informal presence on the selection committee, was an assiduous follower of Comintern dictates. In March 1937, Gollancz, Strachey and Burns agreed that all Club groups should include 'one or two good Party members' and that 'existing Party convenors and prominent members should be given the right line'. The Club became a key part of the Party's recruitment drive; the assumption was that, as a result of the political education provided by LBC books, non-Communists would come to appreciate the correctness of the Party's viewpoint. Palme Dutt noted that the Club's 'success and scope, so far from being injured, is probably the greater because it is recognised by the public as an independent commercial enterprise on its own feet, and not the propaganda of a particular political organisation'. (Dutt was the epitome of the calculating revolutionary; accused of having no sense of humour, he replied irritably that he laughed if it was a comrade telling the joke.) Singing 'The Internationale' was discouraged at Club meetings in case it alienated non-Communists. The LBC became, in other words, the key element in the CP's Popular Front strategy.

In theory, the Popular Front embraced all opponents of the Government from dissident Tory to Trot. In practice, however, it was positioned to the left of the Labour leadership and dependent on the Communist Party, which had, on instructions from Moscow, abandoned its earlier strategy of aggressive opposition to social democrats. Labour leaders hadn't taken kindly to being labelled 'social fascists' in the twenties, however, and were now suspicious that the Communist Party was trying to infiltrate and capture all leftish organisations. Despite giving the Left Book Club his initial support, therefore, Attlee, a staunch anti-Communist, wanted nothing to do with the Popular Front or any other CP-influenced initiatives. Yet Transport House also fretted that the Club was turning the new left-wing middle class against the Labour Party and at one point Hugh Dalton suggested to Gollancz that the selection committee should include a couple of representatives of the official Labour view. Gollancz wanted none of it. Eventually, the Labour Party warned its members off the unity campaign. It even tried to set up its own book club, and expelled a couple of local constituency activists because of their membership of the real thing. (There was a Right Book Club, too, administered by Foyle's bookshop; David Low, an LBC supporter, produced a 'Book Club War' cartoon – 'heavy casualties are reported,' the caption ran, 'including 29 unconscious and General Gollancz's spectacles blown up'.)

Although the Communist Party called for a broad church on the left, it reacted strongly to any whisper of criticism from liberals of the regime in Moscow, especially following the show trials of Zinoviev, Kamenev, Radek and the others, which coincided with the first years of the Club. Gollancz was equally sensitive to any criticism of Stalin and was blithely pro-Soviet. On a trip to the USSR, he told the Moscow *Daily News* of the 'real, genuine classlessness' he had seen on his visit, 'a sort of springtime feeling . . . that pre-history is over and history is just beginning'. And in November 1937, when asked by *Cavalcade* magazine to nominate his man of the year, he chose Stalin, who was, he felt, 'safely guiding Russia on the road to a society in which there will be no exploitation'. (After a conversation with the nominal head of the Comintern, he remarked: 'Do you know, Dimitrov thinks of the Left Book Club the way I do.') On discovering that H. N. Brailsford's LBC volume, *Why Capitalism Means*

War, took the Soviet Union to task for lack of personal freedoms, Gollancz pressed him to revise the manuscript: 'My own view is that support of the Soviet Union at the present juncture is (as the one hope of averting war) of such overwhelming importance that anything that could be quoted by the other side should not be said.' Brailsford, a candid critic of the show trials, refused. If the book was published, he explained to Gollancz, 'you'll have an answer to people who say that you only publish orthodox Communist dope'. In the end, only Laski's threat of resignation assured its publication. The political direction of the Club remained unchanged. No work by Stalin's arch-villain Trotsky or his admirers stood any chance of being published (no books by C. L. R. James, for instance), and the panegyrics flowed on. Lion Feuchtwanger's *Moscow 1937*, a 'Topical' offer in July of that year, eulogised Stalin, in Socialist Realist style, as 'big, broad and commanding . . . He walks up and down whilst he is speaking, then suddenly approaches you, pointing a finger of his beautiful hand.' Gollancz was in no doubt that the trials were legitimate and necessary, even restrained. The Club's monthly journal, *Left News*, mocked the stories of torture, truth-telling Tibetan drugs and sexual perversion which explained the bizarre confessions of the victims. There was, Strachey wrote, 'no conceivable alternative' after the accused had told their stories 'but to shoot them'.

Clearly, the god had yet to fail – the formulation 'Stalinism' barely existed – and the disasters of the Soviet Union were still obscured by the glare of optimism. The USSR was the target of fascist threats and was alone in helping Republican Spain – in these circumstances, even those on the left who would have blanched at Strachey's endorsement of the firing squads were unwilling to issue condemnations. All sorts of plausible people (Lady Astor, H. G. Wells, G. B. Shaw, Malcolm Muggeridge) had visited the Soviet Union and reported tremendous improvements in agriculture, schools and hospitals – the USSR seemed to have escaped the world economic crisis, thanks to the Five Year Plan. Even the anti-Communist Hugh Dalton, after his trip there, commented that the Russians were better fed than the unemployed in his constituency. The Webbs' now notorious dispatch, *The Soviet Union: A New Civilisation?* – 'the most preposterous book ever written about Russia', according to A. J. P. Taylor – argued that the Soviet system was in some ways the highest form of democracy so far evolved (it was reprinted by the LBC without the question mark in the title). 'What one saw in Russia,' John Lehmann said later, was 'a welfare state being built up with heady Slavonic enthusiasm'. 'How deeply the Left craved giving the benefit of the doubt to Moscow,' Michael Foot has written. 'No one who did not live through that period can quite appreciate how overwhelming that craving was.'

Despite the show trials, then, Communist Party membership soared in the late thirties. The CP was congratulated for mustering the British Battalion in Spain, and praised, too, for its double-barrelled assault on unemployment and the Blackshirts rampaging through Mile End. Communists seemed, well, up for it. (Wal Hannington, the Communist agitator responsible for the hunger marches, was now encouraging two hundred out-of-work men to lie down in front of the traffic on Oxford Street; a hundred others invaded the Grill Room at the Ritz and asked for tea.) In Harry Pollitt, the Party had a likeable leader of obvious ability – a working-class hero who was one of the best orators of the age. Spender remembered his 'friendly twinkling manner'; Barbara Castle, whose LBC membership was firming up her youthful socialism, found him 'unexpectedly mild and pleasant'.

Since first calling for left-wing unity in the mid-thirties, the Communist Party had also made itself more presentable. Its members – Comrade Denis Healey has recalled – 'started shaving, tried to avoid being drunk in public and played down their Marxism–Leninism'. Koestler later wrote that 'the Communist Party in the West acquired a new façade with geranium boxes in the windows and a gate wide open to all men of good will'. The Party had discovered culture – its newspaper now included a weekly books page and criticism of plays, film and art. Communists even adopted Milton, Cromwell and other darlings of English radicalism.

As a result of all these things, Pollitt was welcoming an illustrious band of intellectual adherents: Auden and Spender took up the cause; Vaughan-Williams abandoned folk music for anti-fascist symphonies. Sylvia Townsend Warner joined the Party simply because she was 'agin the Government'. On the evidence of Philip Toynbee (the first Communist president of the Oxford Union), it wasn't uncommon to learn of socialist viscounts 'folding the *Daily Worker* as their butlers pushed Left Book Club books back onto the shelves'. A Communist of the Popular Front era didn't always correspond, therefore, to the crass, cartoon image drawn in the fifties of a traitorous, philistine dummy to a Comintern ventriloquist; as Arnold Rattenbury has reminded us, there were plenty who were 'happily idiosyncratic'.

Furthermore, for many Communists and for the vast majority of Club members the Popular Front wasn't a manipulative strategy or a sham, but had, in Koestler's words, 'strong emotional appeal, and the recent mystique of a genuine mass movement'. The LBC took off politically because it was the most active and largest organised body working for a united opposition to the Government. Gollancz guessed that only a fifth of his subscribers were Communists or near-Communists – 'I do happen to know my members.' A far larger number of Club enthusiasts expressed allegiance to Labour but thought its leaders were incompetent and ineffectual, offering nothing but polite resistance to a criminal Government: after all, a half of constituency Labour parties voted in favour of a Popular Front. The Club presented itself as a glue binding together different progressives; its groups were encouraged to make contact with trade unions, co-operative societies, the League of Nations Union and other such organisations. The line-up at the major Club rallies looked for all the world like a genuine coalition – the speakers included the Labourites Cripps and Bevan; the Liberals Richard Acland and Wilfred Roberts; the Conservative Robert Boothby; Lloyd George; and, representing the Church, Hewlett Johnson ('that bloody red arse of a Dean', as Pollitt called him). The Club's innumerable smaller meetings, too, provided evidence that the Popular Front transcended divisions between party leaderships, even party politics altogether. Talks were given by – to take a sample – J. B. Priestley, Paul Robeson, A. J. P. Taylor, Quentin Bell, Rose Macaulay, Sylvia Pankhurst, J. D. Bernal, Cecil Day Lewis and Edward Upward.

The majority of members of the Club may have read Strachey's *The Theory and Practice of Socialism* but they had little interest in the manoeuvrings of the Communist Party. Their activism was more about passion and urgency (and perhaps a bit of class guilt) than the formalities of dialectical materialism. It was driven by a sense of duty, a desire to 'do something' and 'to be useful'. Their idea of Communism was probably a bit vague. So while the Club does represent an extraordinary moment in British history when many thousands of members of the professional classes were regularly buying Marxist books, it also fits comfortably into a national tradition of rather hubristic, emotional extra-parliamentary campaigning which goes back to the adulation of Garibaldi in the mid-nineteenth century (and earlier), and forward to CND in the 1950s and 1980s.

The issue that stoked the passions of the Popular Front was Spain. The Club surfed the wave of sentiment and activism which moved swiftly across progressive Britain following Franco's rebellion. Once the fascist powers and the USSR became involved, the complex situation in Spain was easily transformed into a simple struggle of good vs evil: a people's army was fighting for democracy and a classless society. The non-intervention policy of the National Government was denounced as a cynical ploy to assist Franco and Hitler; official lies about numbers of foreign troops and bombers were exposed. The Labour Opposition and the TUC at first followed the Government's lead, and it was this, more than anything, which drove disgruntled Labourites to the left. Gollancz told LBC members that every day 'without some piece of activity' was 'a betrayal' – it was their duty to 'convert laziness and indifference into active enthusiasm'. Holding meetings about Spain was, he urged, 'the first big chance for us to prove that we are, each one of us, missionaries for civilisation'. All of Europe was a 'suburb of Madrid' Strachey said at the first Club rally: 'We do not want to wait until London is suffering the same fate.' The Club's official reports of events in Spain were naturally gung-ho: 'with unexampled heroism, Madrid's defenders have hurled back the onslaught of Franco's murderers'. Very few LBC members knew the unsavoury nature of what was actually going on – Gollancz refused to publish *Homage to Catalonia*, because of its uncomfortable revelations that Spanish Communists, under their Russian-trained commissars, were busy fighting their anarchist allies as well as Franco's troops.

Spain transformed the Club. Meetings were held everywhere, often in combination with Labour constituency parties and Spanish Aid Committees. Some groups constructed motorbike ambulances; others adopted Basque children. There were 'knit-ins' to make clothes for the International Brigades and money raised to send a Club food ship to Spain. As one member from Furness Vale told Gollancz: 'apart from making us read, and think, the Left Book Club is making us "do"!' The books had an impact, too. The December 1936 choice, *Spain in Revolt* by Harry Gannes and Theodore Repard, taught members the background to the conflict and became, one commentator says, 'a kind of Thirties "Lillibulero", which swept young men into the International Brigade'. The poet Valentine Ackland, who travelled to Spain, congratulated Gollancz on publishing the book: 'it supplies us with what we need.' Koestler, who after the publication of *Spanish Testament* was renowned as a former prisoner of Franco, toured Club groups to speak about his experiences and was touched by his audiences' vigorous and uncomplicated support for the International Brigade. Many of the volunteers themselves were Club members. David Goodman, from Middlesbrough, for example, said that his inspiration for fighting in Spain was 'the crash course in political education' he had received from reading his monthly choices. Wally Tapsell, a cockney commissar, asked for his battalion to be sent a hundred copies of the current selection; a few weeks later, the volunteer George Aitkin asked Harry Pollitt to 'be sure to get Left Book Club to send *all* publications'.

The intensity of feeling over Spain goes some way to explaining the cultish fervour of the Left Book Club. Its meetings had, one American observer noted, 'the atmosphere of a true religious revival'. (Malcolm Muggeridge said, more savagely, that Gollancz was greeted by his members with the acclamation due to a Führer.) *Left News* constantly impressed on its readers their responsibility to recruit and evangelise ('Stop Press! One member has just sent in his 14th recruit.') A yellow slip with the message 'PLEASE use this leaflet to get a new member' went out with every book. Adherents were told to put a sticker on their letters, which asked: 'Are you a member of the LBC?' One branch, from Hemsworth, near Barnsley, covered all the surrounding towns and villages with posters ('If you believe in the necessity of maintaining World Peace and defending Democracy, come along and let us hear your views'). Some groups thrived where left-wing politics had barely existed before ('"Lefts" of Richmond and Kew', one letter to the Gollancz offices said, 'had thought themselves isolated until the Book Club came along and introduced them to one another'). Another enthusiastic recruiter who lived in an unnamed 'reactionary town' managed to convert 'two enamelled and trousered lovelies' in a saloon bar, 'two sinister colonels in a railway carriage' and a doctor's 'large and, I had always thought, smug' family. With its Communist cachet, even its button badge and slogans ('a penny a day keeps reaction away'), the Club had a sort of radical chic. It also dealt in big political questions and ideas, not tiresome debates about detail and administration: there were 'a large number of people', Gollancz believed, who would turn up to a Club event but 'never dream of going to an ordinary political meeting'.

Every issue of *Left News* published a list of towns where local groups had yet to be formed. One journalist imagined Gollancz seated at his desk with a map of the country in front of him. Every time the telephone rang, he stuck in a red flag – a new group for Blackpool, another for Manchester, one for Stow-on-the-Wold. (The Club also spread overseas: Paris, Zurich, the Gold Coast, South Africa – Australia alone had 4,500 members and 98 branches.) Most, but by no means all, of the British groups were in the south. Their size varied from a few subscribers in villages and small towns to 500 in cities; the biggest group was in Manchester, convened by the future MP for East Salford Frank Allaun ('never has there been a better example', he later said, 'of a movement catching the tide of popular feeling and simultaneously guiding the direction in which the tide should move'). Smaller groups tended to meet in a member's house, over coffee and biscuits, enjoying, Julian Symons has written, 'the warm sense of shared feelings and common attitudes that keeps all minority movements together'. 'A spot of coffee drinking about half-way through the evening,' Gwyn Thomas from Bristol noted, was effective for 'breaking down shyness'. Urban groups met in a café, bookshop or meeting hall.

Unexpectedly, all sorts of vocational and other specialised groups began to appear: bus drivers, London Indian residents, railwaymen, Clarion Cycle Club members, clerical workers, musicians, civil servants, hospital workers, postmen, architects, teachers (by far the biggest vocational group), City workers, engineers, marionette theatre enthusiasts, sixth formers, bank employees, doctors, lawyers, commercial travellers, journalists, London cab drivers and accountants (who discussed topics such as 'Britain without capitalists'). Among the more prestigious were the scientists' groups, formed in London, Cambridge and Bristol, the participants in which included J. B. S. Haldane, J. D. Bernal, Hyman Levy, Joseph Needham and others. These gatherings addressed such questions as the 'relation of the scientific man to his social milieu' and embodied the optimistic, leftish nature of science in the thirties, with its ideas of nature easily dominated and its belief in scientific planning to solve society's problems. (This sociological fashion encouraged scientists to make all sorts of political recommendations: Haldane, the best-known spokesman for the LBC science groups, toured the country talking about his monthly choice, *Air Raid Precautions*, in which he described his visits to the Spanish Front, exposed the fraudulence of Home Office claims to have protected the population from gas attack and called for the building of deep, underground air-raid shelters in Britain's cities.)

Over forty groups opened special Club premises. The Camden Town branch boasted 'two tables, a typewriter, a gramophone and a couple of banjos', while the centre in Paddington enjoyed easy chairs, committee rooms and a buffet. The less fortunate residents of Wolverhampton had a gloomy loft in a barn, approached by a ladder, in which members gamely played table tennis. 'Brightly coloured Soviet posters' – sunlit tractors and smiling workers – could be obtained free of charge. With or without premises, a bewildering variety of activities were organised by the groups. A Cambridge convenor promised that 'on every Saturday night, some kind of social, film show or sing-song will be taking place. A radiogram has been installed and light refreshments will be available at most times.' In Stepney, the members ran a football club, a gramophone recital circle, a swimming team, PT classes and various educational courses, as well as launching its own inquiry into conditions in the East End. *Left News* said that 'even games, songs and recreation can, and indeed should, reflect and awaken a left-wing attitude to things . . . walks, tennis, golf and swimming are quite different when your companions are "comrades of the left" '. The Weybridge group decided to charter a river steamer for a day on the Thames: 'members were taken to Bourne End, where an excellent tea had been arranged for them at the Quarry Hotel'. Commitment knew no bounds: one plucky member attended a fancy-dress dance with orange cardboard attached to his front and back, and wearing a skull cap with 'Join the LBC' written on it.

It seems he wasn't alone. The novelist Pamela Hansford Johnson, former lover of Dylan Thomas and future wife of C. P. Snow, featured the Club in *The Monument* (1937). Mrs Sellars, a Labour Party activist and local LBC organiser, takes part in a march for Spain ('the proud and lovely ranks of the Spanish flags . . . the streaming purple, magenta and gold'). She is waiting with her children, dressed as Basques, when she hears a 'soaring gust of laughter from the watching crowds as the Left Book Club contingent came up. That's a good idea' – she thinks to herself – 'all those orange books prancing about on legs looking like something out of *Alice in Wonderland*.' Orwell, on the other hand, who grew to despise the Club for its CP connections, was scathing when he featured a provincial LBC lecture in *Coming up for Air* (1939). The audience of 'West Bletchley revolutionaries' includes Miss Minns, anxious to improve her mind, a woman knitting a jumper, two others, sitting 'like lumps of pudding', and a younger woman, 'one of the teachers at the Council School', who is 'drinking it all in'. Then there are 'two blokes from the local Labour Party' who have been 'pitchforked' into foreign politics; and a group of young Communists, 'twitching' to get involved. The speaker is 'a human barrel-organ shooting propaganda'; his message is 'hate, hate, hate'.

The groups made use of two film organisations, Kino and the Film and Photo League, both of which had links to the Communist Party. Kino was formed in 1933 to screen films in unlicensed halls and so escape censorship. It specialised in Russian classics (Eisenstein and Pudovkin) and Spanish films (*The Defence of Madrid, They Shall Not Pass, Spanish Earth*). The FPL distributed short documentaries, such as *Hunger March 1936* and *Dock Workers*, designed to combat the 'lavish and pampered display of the capitalist cinema'. Films were effective propaganda, it was argued, because they struck 'straight home to brain and feeling'. (One popular LBC choice, *Promised Land* by Cedric Belfrage, was a novel about the seedy side of Hollywood – it 'revealed' that the purpose of films made by the big studios was to drug the masses into acceptance of the capitalist system.)

Club members advertised Russian language classes and – to see the socialist experiment at first hand – trips to the Soviet Union. The typical arrangement was a three-week organised tour, featuring daily excursions to the Park of Culture and Rest, giant factories, polyclinics, divorce bureaux, crèches, People's Courts and even a 'prophylactorium' for prostitutes. *Left News* issued a warning that there would be 'a mixing of all classes of passenger' on board the Soviet boats. Other destinations for tours were co-operative farms in Scandinavia and – considerably more appealing – Paris, the Riviera and the Alps: 'enjoy a winter's sports holiday in Popular Front France.'

Like the Fabians and the ILP, the Club also ran weekend and summer schools. A series of weekend events near Hastings was announced in *Left News*: 'The company is left and congenial, the situation delightful, our host is an excellent fellow and a real socialist, the cooking superb and the terms moderate.' Annual summer schools were held at Digswell Park country house. Talks given by 'Sage' Bernal and Tom Harrisson (on 'Mass Observation') were alternated with 'sunbathing in a minimum of clothing in a field of new-mown hay'. The 'steady beat of the radio-gramophone from the big hall' meant that 'in spite of the energy already expended during the day, dancing was not going to stop until "Lights Out"'. The first year the school was organised, Alan Bush, the Marxist composer, and the poet Randall Swingler assembled an impromptu choir to sing 'left songs'. A 16mm film shot by residents at the school that week survives. It's a quaint comedy about the conversion of an upright Tory woman who accidentally finds herself at Digswell Park. After her initial horror, she begins to enjoy herself in such congenial surroundings, reads a book on the position of women in the USSR and dreams of honest labour in the fields working a simple plough. There's plenty of tennis, country dancing and nodding vigorously at lectures – linen jackets and tea-dresses, and Gollancz in a straw boater.

There were also 'distressed areas summer schools', run by a Club enthusiast. One was based in Pontypridd. The idea was that those attending should board with unemployed families, but if that was too bleak a prospect 'alternative accommodation' could be found. Potential signers-up were reassured that the town had 'first-rate tennis, bowls and an excellent miniature golf course'; they should pack overalls if they wanted to go down a pit. The school run in 1937 was judged a triumph: 'the people, *all* the people, were entirely charming. I think none of us could speak too highly of their genuine kindness and simple dignity. Of course, the gap of class difference lay between us and them.'

Notwithstanding the Club's intentions, almost all its activists were middle class. In 1937, Gollancz expressed his concern that, despite such initiatives as stalls at the TUC, the percentage of working-class members wasn't high. A report from a joint conference of the Surrey groups stated that, 'as may be expected, there were few (if any) working-class representatives', though it was hopeful that the situation might be improved if more effort was made 'in areas such as Norbury and Croydon'. Similarly, the press reports of the first national rally noted that it was 'roughly speaking' a 'middle-class one'. Most of the readers of *The Road to Wigan Pier*, one subscriber pointed out, had not made 'living contact with the working class movement'. Gollancz himself was often accused in the press – along with Tom Driberg and others – of being a 'Café Communist' with a narrow circle of acquaintance (to make up for it, he praised his chauffeur in *Left News* for being a good recruiter).

On the other hand, there was a social mix in some of the local branches. One Essex convenor reported in 1937: 'Our group consists of a draughtsman, a doctor of physics, a printer, a dental mechanic, a road mender, a school teacher, a painter, several clerks and sundry others.' Gravesend Club meetings were 'sharply divided socially' and included 'trade unionists and working men either in or out of work'. Working-class Communists (most of them in South Wales and Glasgow) were often members and there were workers' vocational branches, too (one miner from Carcroft told *Left News* that it was difficult to organise meetings with his workmates because of the 'many different shifts'). When James Hanley, conducting research for his book *Grey Children* (1937), visited a miner's house in South Wales he 'noticed one or two volumes of the Left Book Club at the head of his bed. He said he was a member of that, but that he shared his membership with six others as he couldn't afford it himself.'

Gollancz encouraged workers to write books about their experiences but little that he was sent was publishable. An isolated breakthrough was *These Poor Hands*, a memoir by the miner B. L. Coombes, who had already won an essay competition run by *Left Review* (edited by the Communist poet Edgell Rickword) and had a short story published by John Lehmann in his quarterly, *New Writing*. Both magazines were convinced that literature was an agent of social change. The Club's ideas, too, extended beyond the vocabulary of mere 'politics'. The LBC Writers and Readers' Group, launched in January 1938, had three aims: to 'arrive at a clearer understanding of the relationship between literature and society', to 'demonstrate that literature has its basis in the broad masses of the people and is not the exclusive preserve of a privileged section of the community' and to bring 'readers and writers into a closer relationship'. Writers no longer 'glorified in isolation' but looked ahead to a socialist society which would – as Ruskin and Morris had promised – liberate the creativity of all workers. The group attracted support from Rebecca West, Christopher Isherwood and Rosamond Lehmann, among others, but its most active members included Sylvia Townsend Warner, Randall Swingler, A. L. Morton, Edgell Rickword, Alick West, Valentine Ackland and Amabel Williams-Ellis. Regular meetings were held in the top room of the Rosebery Hotel in Newport Street. Talks were given on Jane Austen and Lawrence, among others; Langston Hughes was one of the guest speakers; his theme: 'The Writer in Relation to Social Change'.

The Poets' Group, meanwhile, met in Great Newport Street (its line-up for November–December 1938 was: Montague Slater on 'The Subject Matter of Poetry'; Charles Madge on 'Poetry and Everyday Life'; Louis MacNeice on 'Poetry's Many-sidedness'; Cecil Day Lewis on 'Byron'). It also produced its own small, mimeographed journal, *Poetry and the People* (later renamed *Our Time*), based on the idea that verse, too, should have 'some connection with reality' and daily life. The journal was anything but precious (consider Miles Carpenter's song lyric 'Frankie and Johnnie at Woolworths': 'Frankie was working at Woolworths,/She didn't work there for fun,/When she'd finished in the evening,/She was feeling pale and wan . . .'). Some of the poems were blunt instruments (Jack Lindsay's 'Questionnaire', for instance: 'Do you think, do you feel, do you hear,/Do you smell, do you see?/FRANCO'S MOPPING-UP OPERATIONS ARE PROCEEDING SUCCESSFULLY'). Others, such as Randall Swingler's anti-war satire 'Sixty Cubic Feet', were of a different order.

There was also a professional actors' group, among the members of which were Michael Redgrave, Gerald Savory and Sybil Thorndike ('she was always joining clubs,' Thorndike's son has said, 'for the promotion of every cause from the saving of the lives of multicoloured guinea pigs in Persia to petitioning the Archbishop of Canterbury to lead a delegation to talk to Hitler'). But more important for the average Club member was the LBC Theatre Guild, which encouraged the local groups to stage productions in rooms and small halls and also to act as flying squads, performing plays and sketches at rallies and meetings. Within a few years there were 300 branches of the Guild. It was initially run from the Communist Party-associated Unity Theatre (near King's Cross) and, in effect, became its national co-ordinating organisation, a successor to the defunct Workers' Theatre Movement. Its organiser, John Allen, one of Unity's leading directors, said that the co-operation required to put on a play was 'a splendid lesson in practical socialism'.

By far the most popular play performed by the groups was Clifford Odets's *Waiting for Lefty*, a short agitprop drama about a New York cab strike, which had already been a huge success for workers' theatre in the States. In May 1938, the Glasgow LBC Theatre Guild gave a performance for the Trades and Labour Council – the 2,000-seat theatre was easily filled and several hundred people were turned away. Cecil Day Lewis called for *Waiting for Lefty* to be staged in front of the recalcitrant TUC so that 'its emotional effect' would sweep away 'the sophistries of the Citrines and the Bevins'. Another favourite was Herbert Hodge's *Where's That Bomb?*, about an unemployed mechanic who nearly takes a job writing capitalist propaganda on factory toilet paper. A variation in propaganda-as-drama were the mass declamation poems, most notably Jack Lindsay's *On Guard for Spain* ('What you shall hear is the tale of the Spanish people./It is also your own life./On Guard, we cry./It is the pattern of the world today'). This was recited by up to six people, sometimes dressed in International Brigade uniforms; it usually ended with audience and actors together shouting, '*No Pasaran!*' 'When we did *On Guard*,' one activist has recalled, 'the impact was almost always enormous . . . I saw people in tears even at the mention of the name of certain Spanish towns, even just the list of names could achieve that, because they knew what had happened there.'

Even when, in 1938, the Aragon Front began to collapse and it became clear that the Nationalists were winning the Civil War, the Spanish cause continued to inspire the Left Book Club. It was only gradually replaced as the focus of the Popular Front campaign by the need to attack appeasement as the worst way to prevent war (though the word 'appeasement' itself had no negative connotations at the time). Gollancz knew that the LBC had, despite its success, made little impression on the Government and was increasingly frustrated by his inability to transform the Club from a thriving minority organisation into a genuine mass movement. As a result, he began to favour the distribution of anti-appeasement leaflets on a massive scale. Ten million flyers protesting against the granting of belligerent rights to Franco were distributed in a few days; and during the Sudetenland crisis, he called with such urgency on the group convenors to distribute his leaflet opposing any sell-out to Hitler that half a million copies were on the streets the day the printers delivered them. There were other achievements besides the leaflets and huge rallies. Gollancz managed, for example, to obtain a share in the control of Cripps's Popular Front weekly, *Tribune*. And a by-election victory in Bridgewater for the 'Independent, Progressive' candidate Vernon Bartlett owed something to the activism of local LBC groups (Bartlett was invited to stand by Richard Acland and Cresswell Webb, vicar of Oare and a Club subscriber).

By this time, however, Gollancz was having second thoughts about the Club's political direction. The catalyst was Munich. Presented with the immediate prospect of war, he lost some faith in the Communist Party argument that Britain under the National Government was barbarous and fascistic, and began to argue that, if it came to it, even a non-socialist Britain would be wholly justified in fighting against Germany. He became sensitised to the 'immensely valuable liberties' – 'tolerance, the open mind, freedom of thought and discussion' – which were enjoyed in Britain, whatever its faults. As a result, he also questioned his defence of 'the suppression of these things in the Soviet Union, on the ground that a socialist society cannot be brought into being except by means of a dictatorship'; he no longer felt able to argue that the end justified the means.

Gollancz was swayed, too, by the growing realisation that the Communist Party had a controlling influence over many Club branches and had, in effect, turned them into what one convenor called 'bastard CP locals'. A number of these groups, Gollancz discovered, had abandoned discussion altogether and opted for direct action (chalking slogans on the streets, and so forth). Everything, he said, had taken on too much of a 'King Street tinge'. In response to complaints from Pollitt about the new tenor of his editorials in *Left News*, he said the Club could no longer be relied on to peddle Party doctrine. (To demonstrate this, he commissioned the veteran liberal Leonard Woolf, a critic of the show trials, to write a monthly choice attacking all totalitarian regimes: on publication, *Barbarians at the Gate* provoked many Communist resignations from the Club.) At the same time, Gollancz continued to demand a peace alliance with the USSR as the best way to avert war.

The Nazi–Soviet Pact, signed on 23 August 1939, put an end to that. It was a moral and intellectual earthquake in the life of all Communists. Their prodigious investment in the USSR as an ally and a socialist ideal had been betrayed. With war imminent, most of the Henrietta Street publishing operation was evacuated from London to Gollancz's country house. Sheila Lynd and Betty Reid were asked to run the LBC groups from there. Having consulted with Pollitt, they refused. Lynd announced that she was 'sick of putting up with lectures about the stupidity of the Soviet Government, and scoldings for not believing they have gone into isolation'. Reid said the Club would be impossible to hold together if it was 'entirely dependent on one man . . . who may at any moment decide that the whole thing has been wrong . . . and that it should swing behind the Government'. Their first concern in helping John Lewis build up the LBC groups, they said, had been the usefulness of this work to the Communist Party.

Days after the Pact was signed, war broke out. Gollancz supported it as an anti-fascist war, and could claim consistency in doing so – the Club's warnings against Hitler were finally being listened to. At first, the Communist Party took the same position; then, having heard from Moscow, it changed tack and came out against an 'imperialist war'. Strachey toed the line and the Club hierarchy was split. Gollancz grew incensed when he found out that the Party was turning a number of LBC groups into 'Stop-the-War' committees. John Lewis was sacked.

The valiant days of the Left Book Club were now over. Gollancz maintained some enthusiasm for it. He was determined to continue circulating large numbers of progressive books and, in any case, the Club was, he said, 'an integral part of my publishing business' (though the expense of subsidising the various Club activities meant it had never made him much money). On some occasions – during 1942, for instance – he was convinced that it could regain its pre-war popularity (he thought of changing its name to 'The League for Victory and Progress'). Membership in wartime had fallen to 15,000, however; after the war, it fell again to 7,000. A potential lease of life was granted in 1946, when Laski arranged for the Club to provide educational material for the Labour Party – now in Government – but Gollancz rejected the deal. He had had enough; the Club was finally wrapped up two years later.

But although the LBC had failed to bring in a Popular Front government and failed to prevent war, Gollancz's efforts had not gone to waste. It was 'the unorthodox political education of the Left Book Club', Bevan said, which 'prepared the way' for the Labour victory of 1945. Richard Crossman was similarly convinced that the Club helped bring about the 'psychological landslide to the Left' which ensured an election defeat for Churchill. The millions of LBC books in circulation, and the thousands of Club missionaries who could talk about them, had exerted an immense influence in wartime. A Captain Smith wrote to Gollancz in August 1945: 'The Labour Party's magnificent victory at the polls is due in very much greater degree than has been recognised to the work of ex-LBC members in both forces and factories. We have good reason to be proud of our contribution.' John Lewis, who had lectured in the Education Corps and the Army Bureau of Current Affairs, discovered that many other education officers were current or former Club members. 'I think I was made most aware of the influence of the LBC in my days in the Army,' another activist, Norman Wiseman, later remembered. 'I became what was called an Education Sergeant, largely on the strength of my earlier well-educated political speeches made to soldiers in the unit.' In discussions, he recalled, the most articulate soldiers were often LBC readers.

LBC choices (together with the Penguin Specials) helped to make full employment, proper housing, socialised medicine and civilised town planning axioms of general expectation, not only for an increasingly politicised working class, but for residents in middle-class and suburban constituencies which had seemed beyond the reach of Labour in 1936.

Most of the electorate were determined that the harshness of Britain in the thirties – described in Wal Hannington's *Ten Lean Years*, Max Cohen's *I Was One of the Unemployed* and Ellen Wilkinson's account of Jarrow, *The Town That Was Murdered* – would never be experienced again. Other Club choices provided more specific ammunition for the hustings, notably *Tory MP* by Simon Haxey, a breakdown of the financial and industrial interests, together with the voting record, of every one of the 400 Conservative members in the Commons. Gollancz was proud, too, that Attlee's new administration included eight Club authors, among them Wing-Commander Strachey, 'Austerity' Cripps and the Prime Minister himself. When a lobby journalist was asked how he always seemed to be able to anticipate Attlee's next policy move, he replied that he had read *The Labour Party in Perspective.*

Yet it was difficult to rescue the Club's reputation. The political atmosphere that had brought Labour into power soon altered; the unusual influence exerted on the left by intellectuals and the progressive middle classes began to wane. Foreign politics changed, too, and with the onset of the Cold War, the Club was more than ever dismissed as a Communist racket. (When Arthur Miller's future wife, Inge Morath, arrived in Hollywood in 1951, she was roughed up by immigration officers because she had an LBC book in her suitcase.) Former sympathisers were the most vituperative of all. The LBC, Philip Toynbee said, was regarded with 'scorn and hatred' in later years: it 'came to represent for many people much that they wanted to forget in their lives; for other, younger people it was a symbol of all that they thought worst about the Thirties'. Strachey's view of the LBC's influence was more generous and more durable. 'It is curious', he said long after the Club had folded, 'to find in unlikely places, high and low, East and West, among law-makers and law-breakers, minds which were sparked by the Left Book Club.' Perhaps the following extracts will spark a few more.

THE ROAD TO WIGAN PIER

by George Orwell

(monthly choice, March 1937)

It was Gollancz's idea to send George Orwell (1903–50) north to report on poverty and unemployment in Britain's industrial towns: Orwell was to enter the world of the working class, as he had become a tramp and outcast to write *Down and Out in Paris and London*. A first-hand account of deprivation and difficulty – filthy rooms, perilous mines, the effect of the Means Test – would be, Gollancz hoped, a forceful piece of socialist propaganda. Orwell, still little known, was glad to accept the commission and the big advance. He gave up his job in a Hampstead bookshop, put on his old clothes and left London in the spring of 1936 to spend two months in Barnsley, Wigan and Sheffield.

He wrote a book of two halves – the first descriptive, the second autobiographical and argumentative. The second half is a coruscating attack on dogooder, sandal-wearing, intellectual left-wingers ('snob-Bolsheviks', 'Marxist prigs'), combined with a polemic on the intransigence of class divisions. True, it ends with a plea for socialist unity to fight fascism, but by 'socialism' Orwell really means the time-honoured English radicalism of 'the people' vs tyrants, at the centre of which is not a collectivist state but the individual struggling against oppression. 'We could do with a little less talk about "capitalist" and "proletarian",' he writes, 'and a little more about the robbers and the robbed.'

Orwell turned in the manuscript in December but was doubtful whether Gollancz would publish it as an LBC choice – it was 'too fragmentary and, on the whole, not very left-wing'. Gollancz was, predictably enough, delighted with the first half, horrified by the second. He tried to persuade Orwell to publish the social investigation separately; Orwell refused (though this later happened). Strachey also objected strongly to the second half, as did Harry Pollitt, who said that it deflected the reader's attention away from important social problems to the insignificant life of a 'disillusioned little middle-class boy'. Gollancz published it anyway. 'I must confess that the selectors chose the book with some trepidation,' he wrote in *Left News*, 'as there was so much in it that they personally found repugnant.'

His solution was to write a special foreword, designed for Club members, which argues – against Orwell – for 'scientific' rather than 'emotional' socialism and emphasises that Orwell's assault on socialist 'cranks' is the work of a devil's advocate. Richard Hoggart has called this foreword 'a classic minor document of English middle-class left-wing intellectualism and a striking example of much that Orwell was attacking'. For Orwell's biographer Michael Shelden it makes some valid points but is smug and condescending. At the time when Gollancz was rebuking Orwell for failing to recognise the proper way 'to defeat fascism', Shelden points out, Orwell was in a trench on a Spanish hilltop dodging sniper fire. Although he wrote to Gollancz from Barcelona thanking him for the foreword, Orwell in fact hated it – he was fast developing a contempt for the LBC and its fellow-travelling guru. The foreword came to be an embarrassment for Gollancz, too: he was furious when, years later, it was reprinted by an American publisher.

The overwhelming response to *The Road to Wigan Pier* within the Club reassured Gollancz that he had been right to publish it. It 'produced more, and more interesting letters' than any previous choice. The first part was proving, he wrote in *Left News*, 'one of the best weapons in rousing the public conscience about the ghastly conditions of so many people in England today'. Subscribers had been 'so profoundly shocked' by the conditions described that they had written to him 'by the hundreds' saying: '"Tell us, please, what can we *do?*"' Orwell's satire and soul-searching in the second part also provoked unusually animated discussions at group meetings: 'it exercises our wits,' one convenor wrote to say; 'we sit up and sharpen our brains so as to refute his erroneous notions'. Although Laski in *Left News* argued that Orwell's socialism stopped at 'a little social amelioration here and there . . . above all for the "deserving poor"', most Club adherents welcomed the call for them to face up to their class prejudices – they had nothing to lose but their aitches. 'I was often on the verge of joining a socialist party,' one enlightened member wrote to Gollancz,

> but it needed Orwell's *The Road to Wigan Pier* to make me realise that my middle-class background was no reason why I should not consider myself a convinced socialist, without heeding the taunts of my acquain-

tances to the effect that it was ridiculous for me to identify myself with an organisation which would despise me as not being working class. I think differently now, thanks to George Orwell and the Left Book Club.

FOREWORD BY VICTOR GOLLANCZ

THIS FOREWORD IS addressed to members of the Left Book Club (to whom *The Road to Wigan Pier* is being sent as the March Choice), and to them alone: members of the general public are asked to ignore it. But for technical considerations, it would have been deleted from the ordinary edition.

I have also to make it clear that, while the three selectors of the Left Book Club Choices – Strachey, Laski and myself – were all agreed that a Foreword was desirable, I alone am responsible for what is written here – though I think that Laski and Strachey would agree with me.

Why did we think that a Foreword was desirable? Because we find that many members – a surprisingly large number – have the idea that in some sort of way a Left Book Club Choice, first, represents the views of the three selectors, and, secondly, incorporates the Left Book Club 'policy'. A moment's thought should show that the first suggestion could be true only in the worst kind of Fascist State, and that the second is a contradiction in terms: but we get letters so frequently – most interesting and vital letters – which say: 'Surely you and Laski and Strachey cannot believe what So-and-So says on page so-and-so of Such-and-Such a book,' that there can be no doubt at all that the misconception exists.

The plain facts are, of course, (*a*) that the three selectors, although they have that broad general agreement without which successful committee work is impossible, differ as to shade and *nuance* of opinion in a hundred ways; (*b*) that even if they were in perfect agreement on every point, nothing could be worse than a stream of books which expressed this same point of view over and over again; and (*c*) that their only criterion for a Choice is whether or not the reading and discussion of it will be helpful for the general struggle against Fascism and war. And that brings me on to this question of Left Book Club 'policy'. The

Left Book Club has no 'policy': or rather it has no policy other than that of equipping people to fight against war and Fascism. As I have said elsewhere, it would not even be true to say that the People's Front is the 'policy' of the Left Book Club, though all three selectors are enthusiastically in favour of it. What we rather feel is that by giving a wide distribution to books which represent many shades of Left opinion (and perhaps, most of all, by providing facilities for the discussion of those books in the 300 local centres and circles that have sprung up all over the country) we are creating the mass basis without which a genuine People's Front is impossible. In other words, the People's Front is not the 'policy' of the Left Book Club, but the very existence of the Left Book Club tends towards a People's Front.

But we feel that a Foreword to *The Road to Wigan Pier* is desirable, not merely in view of the misconception to which I have referred, but also because we believe that the value of the book, for some members, can be greatly increased if just a hint is given of certain vital considerations that arise from a reading of it. The value can be *increased*: as to the positive value itself, not one of us has the smallest doubt. For myself, it is a long time since I have read so *living* a book, or one so full of a burning indignation against poverty and oppression.

The plan of the book is this. In Part I Mr Orwell gives a first-hand account of the life of the working-class population of Wigan and elsewhere. It is a terrible record of evil conditions, foul housing, wretched pay, hopeless unemployment and the villainies of the Means Test: it is also a tribute to courage and patience – patience far too great. We cannot imagine anything more likely to rouse the 'unconverted' from their apathy than a reading of this part of the book; and we are announcing in the current number of *The Left News* a scheme by means of which we hope members may make use of the book for this end. These chapters really *are* the kind of thing that makes converts.

In the second part, Mr Orwell starts with an autobiographical study, which he thinks necessary in order to explain the class feelings and prejudices of a member of 'the lower upper-middle class', as he describes himself: and he then goes on to declare his adherence to Socialism. But before doing so he comes forward as a devil's advocate, and explains, with a great deal of sympathy, why, in his opinion, so many of the best people detest Socialism; and he finds the reason to lie in the 'personal inferiority' of so many Socialists and in their mistaken methods of propaganda. His conclusion is that present methods should be thrown overboard, and that we should try to enrol everyone in the fight for Socialism and against Fascism and war (which he rightly sees to be disasters in the face of which little else is of much importance) by making the elemental appeal of 'liberty' and 'justice'. What he envisages is a great league of 'oppressed' against 'oppressors'; in this battle members of all classes may fight side by side – the private schoolmaster and the jobless Cambridge graduate with the clerk and the unemployed miner; and then, when they have so fought, 'we of the sinking middle class . . . may sink without further struggles into the working class where we belong, and probably when we get there it will not be so dreadful as we feared, for, after all, we have nothing to lose but our aitches'.

Now the whole of this second part is highly provocative, not merely in its general argument, but also in detail after detail. I had, in point of fact, marked well over a hundred minor passages about which I thought I should like to argue with Mr Orwell in this Foreword; but I find now that if I did so the space that I have set aside would be quickly used up, and I should wear out my readers' patience. It is necessary, therefore, that I should limit myself to some of the broader aspects.

In the first place, no reader must forget that Mr Orwell is throughout writing precisely as a member of the 'lower upper-middle class' or, let us say without qualification, as a member of the middle class. It may seem stupid to insist on this point, as nothing could be clearer than Mr Orwell's own insistence on it: but I can well imagine a reader coming across a remark every now and again which infuriates him even to the extent of making him forget this most important fact: *that such a remark can be made by Mr Orwell is* (if the reader follows me) *part of Mr Orwell's own case.* I have in mind in particular a lengthy passage in which Mr Orwell embroiders the theme that, in the opinion of the middle class in general, the working class smells! I believe myself that Mr Orwell is exaggerating violently: I do not myself think that more than a very small proportion of them have this quaint idea (I admit that I may be a bad judge of the question, for I am a Jew, and passed the years of my early boyhood in a fairly close Jewish community; and, among Jews of this type, class distinctions do not exist – Mr Orwell says that they do not exist among any sort of Oriental). But clearly *some* of them think like this – Mr Orwell quotes a very odd passage from one of Mr Somerset Maugham's books – and the whole of this chapter throws a most interesting light on the reality of class distinctions. I know, in fact, of no other book in which a member of the middle class exposes with such complete frankness the shameful way in which he was brought up to think of large numbers of his fellow men. This section will be, I think, of the greatest value to middle-class and working-class members of the Left Book Club alike: to the former because, if they are honest, they will search their own minds; to the latter, because it will make them understand what they are 'up against' – if they do not understand it already. In any case, the moral is that the class division of Society, economic in origin, must be superseded by the classless society (I fear Mr Orwell will regard this as a wretched and insincere cliché) in which alone the shame and indignity so vividly described by Mr Orwell – I mean of the middle class, not of the lower class – will be impossible.

Mr Orwell now proceeds to act as devil's advocate for the case against Socialism.

He looks at Socialists as a whole and finds them (with a few exceptions) a stupid, offensive and insincere lot. For my own part I find no similarity whatsoever between the picture as Mr Orwell paints it and the picture as I see it. There is an extraordinary passage in which Mr Orwell seems to suggest that almost every Socialist is a 'crank'; and it is illuminating to discover from this passage just what Mr Orwell means by the word. It appears to mean anyone holding opinions not held by the majority – for instance, any feminist, pacifist, vegetarian or advocate of birth control. This last is really startling. In the first part of the book Mr Orwell paints a most vivid picture of wretched rooms swarming with children, and clearly becoming more and more unfit for human habitation the larger the family grows: but he apparently considers anyone who wishes to enlighten people as to how they can have a normal sexual life without increasing this misery as a crank! The fact, of course, is that there is no more 'commonsensical' work than that which is being done at the present time by the birth control clinics up and down the country – and common sense, as I understand it, is the antithesis of crankiness. I have chosen this particular example, because the answer to Mr Orwell is to be found in his own first part: but the answers to Mr Orwell's sneers at pacifism and feminism are as obvious. Even about vegetarianism (I apologise to vegetarians for the 'even') Mr Orwell is astray. The majority of vegetarians are vegetarians not because 'they want to add a few miserable years to their wretched lives' (I cannot find the exact passage at the moment, but that is roughly what Mr Orwell says), but because they find something disgusting in the consumption of dead flesh. I am not saying that I agree with them: but anyone who has seen a man – or woman – eating a raw steak (*saignant*, as the French say so much more frankly) will feel a sneaking sympathy.

The fact is that in passages like that to which I have referred, and in numerous other places in this part of the book, Mr Orwell is still a victim of that early atmosphere, in his home and public school, which he himself has so eloquently exposed. His conscience, his sense of decency, his understanding of realities tell him to declare himself a Socialist: but fighting against this compulsion there is in him all the time a compulsion far less conscious but almost – though fortunately not quite – as strong: the compulsion to conform to the mental habits of his class. That is why Mr Orwell, looking at a Socialist, smells out (to use a word which we have already met in another connection) a certain crankiness in him; and he finds, as examples of this crankiness, a hatred of war (pacifism), a desire to see women no longer oppressed by men (feminism), and a refusal to withhold the knowledge which will add a little happiness to certain human lives (birth control).

This conflict of two compulsions is to be found again and again throughout the book. For instance, Mr Orwell calls himself a 'half intellectual'; but the truth is that he is at one and the same time an extreme intellectual and a violent anti-intellectual. Similarly he is a frightful snob – still (he must forgive me for saying this), and a genuine hater of every form of snobbery. For those who can read, the exhibition of this conflict is neither the least interesting nor the least valuable part of the book: for it shows the desperate struggle through which a man must go before, in our present society, his mind can really become free – if indeed that is ever possible.

I have said enough, I think, to show, by means of one example, the way in which I should venture to criticise the whole of this section of the book. But there is another topic here which cannot be passed over without a word or two. Among the grave faults which Mr Orwell finds in Socialist propaganda is the glorification of industrialism, and in particular of the triumphs of industrialisation in the Soviet Union (the words 'Magnitogorsk' and 'Dnieper' make Mr Orwell see red – or rather the reverse). I have a fairly wide acquaintance among Socialists of every colour, and I feel sure that the whole of this section is based on a misunderstanding. To leave Russia out of account for the moment, no Socialist of my acquaintance *glorifies* industrialism. What the Socialist who has advanced beyond the most elementary stage says (and I really mean what he *says*, not what he *ought to say*) is that capitalist industrialism is a certain stage which we have reached in the business of providing for our needs, comforts and luxuries: that though it may be amusing to speculate on whether or not a pre-industrialist civilisation might be a more attractive one in which to live, it is a matter of plain common sense that, whatever individuals may wish, industrialism will go on: that (if Mr Orwell will forgive the jargon) such 'contradictions' have developed in the machine of capitalist industrialism that the thing is visibly breaking down: that such break-down means poverty, unemployment and war: and that the only solution is the supersession of anarchic capitalist industrialism by planned Socialist industrialism. In other words, it is not industrialism that the Socialist advocates (a man does not advocate the sun or the moon), but Socialist industrialism as opposed to capitalist industrialism.

Mr Orwell, of course, understands this quite elementary fact perfectly well: but his understanding conflicts with his love of beauty, and the result is that, instead of pointing out that industrialism can be the parent of beauty, if at all, then only under planned Socialist industrialism, he turns to rend the mythical figure of the Socialist who thinks that gaspipe chairs are more beautiful than Chippendale chairs. (Incidentally, gaspipe chairs *are* more beautiful than the worst Chippendale chairs, though not nearly as beautiful as the best.)

As to the particular question of the Soviet Union, the insistence of Socialists on the achievements of Soviet industrialisation arises from the fact that the most frequent argument which Socialists have to face is precisely this: 'I agree with you that Socialism would be wholly admirable if it would work – but it wouldn't.' Somewhere or other Mr Orwell speaks of intelligent and unintelligent Socialists, and brushes aside people who say 'it wouldn't work' as belonging to the latter category. My own experience is that this is still the major *sincere* objection to Socialism on the part of decent people, and the major *insincere* objection on the part of indecent people who in fact are thinking of their dividends. It is true that the objection was more frequently heard in 1919 than in 1927, in 1927 than at the end of the first Five Year Plan, and at the end of the first Five Year Plan than to-day – the reason being precisely that quite so direct a *non possumus* hardly carries conviction, when the achievements of the Soviet Union are there for everyone to see. But people will go on hypnotising themselves and others with a formula, even when that formula is patently outworn: so that it is still necessary, and will be necessary for a long time yet, to show that modern methods of production *do* work under Socialism and *no longer work* under capitalism.

But Mr Orwell's attack on Socialists who are for ever singing paeans of praise to Soviet industrialisation is also connected with his general dislike of Russia – he even commits the curious indiscretion of referring to Russian commissars as 'half-gramophones, half-gangsters'. Here again the particular nature of Mr Orwell's unresolved conflict is not difficult to understand; nor is it difficult to understand why Mr Orwell states that almost all people of real sensitiveness, and in particular almost all writers and artists and the like, are hostile to Socialism – whereas the truth is that in several countries, for instance in France, a great number, and probably the majority, of writers and artists are Socialists or even Communists.

All this is not to say that (while this section gives, in my view, a distorted picture of what Socialists are like and what they say) *Socialists themselves* will not find there much that is of value to them, and many shrewd pieces of, at any rate, half-truth. In particular I think that Mr Orwell's accusation of arrogance and dogmatism is to a large extent justified: in fact as I think back on what I have already written here I am not sure that a good deal of it is not itself arrogant and dogmatic. His accusation of narrowness and of sectarianism is not so well grounded to-day as it would have been a few years ago: but here also there is still plenty of room for improvement. The whole section indeed is, when all has been said against it, a challenge to us Socialists to put our house and our characters in order.

Having criticised us in this way (for though Mr Orwell insists that he is speaking merely as devil's advocate and saying what other people say, quite often and quite obviously he is really speaking *in propria persona* – or perhaps I had better say 'in his own person', otherwise Mr Orwell will class me with 'the snobs who write in Latinised English' or words to that effect) Mr Orwell joins us generously and whole-heartedly, but begs us to drop our present methods of propaganda, to base our appeal on freedom and liberty, and to see ourselves as a league of the oppressed against the oppressors. Nothing could be more admirable as a first approach; and I agree that we shall never mobilise that vast mass of fundamentally decent opinion which undoubtedly exists (as, for instance, the Peace Ballot showed) and which we *must* mobilise if we are to defeat Fascism, unless we make our first appeal to its generous impulses. It is from a desire for liberty and justice that we must draw our militant strength; and the society which we are trying to establish is one in which that liberty and that justice will be incarnate. But between the beginning in that first impulse to fight, and the end when, the fight won, our children or our children's children will live in the achievement, there is a great deal of hard work and hard thinking to be done – less noble and more humdrum than the appeal to generosities, but no less important if a real victory is to be won, and if this very appeal is not to be used to serve ends quite opposite to those at which we aim.

It is indeed significant that so far as I can remember (he must forgive me if I am mistaken) Mr Orwell does not once define what he *means* by Socialism; nor does he explain *how* the oppressors oppress, nor even what he understands by the words 'liberty' and 'justice'. I hope he will not think I am quibbling: he will not, I think, if he remembers that the word 'Nazi' is an abbreviation of the words 'National Socialist'; that in its first phase Fascism draws its chief strength from an attack on 'oppression' – 'oppression' by capitalists, multiple stores, Jews and foreigners; that no word is commoner in German speeches to-day than 'Justice'; and that if you 'listen in' any night to Berlin or Munich, the chances are that you will hear the 'liberty' of totalitarian Germany – 'Germans have become free by becoming a united people' – compared with the misery of Stalin's slaves.

What is indeed essential, once that first appeal has been made to 'liberty' and 'justice,' is a careful and patient study of just *how* the thing works: of *why* capitalism inevitably means oppression and injustice and the horrible class society which Mr Orwell so brilliantly depicts: of *the means* of transition to a Socialist society in which there will be neither oppressor nor oppressed. In other words, *emotional* Socialism must become scientific Socialism – even if some of us have to concern ourselves with what Mr Orwell, in his extremely intellectualist anti-intellectualism, calls 'the sacred sisters': Thesis, Antithesis and Synthesis.

What I feel, in sum, is that this book, more perhaps than any that the Left Book Club has issued, clarifies – for me at least – the whole meaning and purpose of the Club. On the one hand we have to go out and rouse the apathetic by showing them the utter vileness which Mr Orwell lays bare in the first part of the book, and by appealing to the decency which is in them; on the other hand we have so to equip ourselves by thought and study that we run no danger, having once mobilised all this good will, of seeing it dispersed for lack of trained leaders – lance corporals as well as generals – or even of seeing it used as the shock troops of our enemies.

January 11th, 1937 V.G.

From CHAPTER IV

As you walk through the industrial towns you lose yourself in labyrinths of little brick houses blackened by smoke, festering in planless chaos round miry alleys and little cindered yards where there are stinking dust-bins and lines of grimy washing and half-ruinous w.c.s. The interiors of these houses are always very much the same, though the number of rooms varies between two and five. All have an almost exactly similar living-room, ten or fifteen feet square, with an open kitchen range; in the larger ones there is a scullery as well, in the smaller ones the sink and copper are in the living-room. At the back there is the yard, or part of a yard shared by a number of houses, just big enough for the dust-bin and the w.c. Not a single one has hot water laid on. You might walk, I suppose, through literally hundreds of miles of streets inhabited by miners, every one of whom, when he is in work, gets black from head to foot every day, without ever passing a house in which one could have a bath. It would have been very simple to install a hot-water system working from the kitchen range, but the builder saved perhaps ten pounds on each house by not doing so, and at the time when these houses were built no one imagined that miners wanted baths.

For it is to be noted that the majority of these houses are old, fifty or sixty years old at least, and great numbers of them are by any ordinary standard not fit for human habitation. They go on being tenanted simply because there are no others to be had. And that is the central fact about housing in the industrial areas: not that the houses are poky and ugly, and insanitary and comfortless, or that they are distributed in incredibly filthy slums round belching foundries and stinking canals and slag-heaps that deluge them with sulphurous smoke – though all this is perfectly true – but simply that there are not enough houses to go round.

'Housing shortage' is a phrase that has been bandied about pretty freely since the war, but it means very little to anyone with an income of more than £10 a week, or even £5 a week for that matter. Where rents are high the difficulty is not to find houses but to find tenants. Walk down any street in Mayfair and you will see 'To Let' boards in half the windows. But in the industrial areas the mere difficulty of getting hold of a house is one of the worst aggravations of poverty. It means that people will put up with anything – any hole and corner slum, any misery of bugs and rotting floors and cracking walls, any extortion of skinflint landlords and blackmailing agents – simply to get a roof over their heads. I have been into appalling houses, houses in which I would not live a week if you paid me, and found that the tenants had been there twenty and thirty years and only hoped they might have the luck to die there. In general these conditions are taken as a matter of course, though not always. Some people hardly seem to realise that such things as decent houses exist and look on bugs and leaking roofs as acts of God; others rail bitterly against their landlords; but all cling desperately to their houses lest worse should befall. So long as the housing shortage continues the local authorities cannot do much to make existing houses more livable. They can 'condemn' a house, but they cannot order it to be pulled down till the tenant has another house to go to; and so the condemned houses remain standing and are all the worse for being condemned, because naturally the landlord will not spend more than he can help on a house which is going to be demolished sooner or later. In a town like Wigan, for instance, there are over two thousand houses standing which have been condemned for years, and whole sections of the town would be condemned *en bloc* if there were any hope of other houses being built to replace them. Towns like Leeds and Sheffield have scores of thousands of 'back to back' houses which are all of a condemned type but will remain standing for decades.

I have inspected great numbers of houses in various mining towns and villages and made notes on their essential points. I think I can best give an idea of what conditions are like by transcribing a few extracts from my notebook, taken more or less at random. They are only brief notes and they will need certain explanations which I will give afterwards. Here are a few from Wigan:

1. House in Wallgate quarter. Blind back type. One up, one down. Living-room measures 12 ft by 10 ft, room upstairs the same. Alcove under stairs measuring 5 ft by 5 ft and serving as larder, scullery and coal

hole. Windows will open. Distance to lavatory 50 yards. Rent 4*s*. 9*d*., rates 2*s*. 6*d*., total 7*s*. 3*d*.

2. Another near by. Measurements as above, but no alcove under stairs, merely a recess two feet deep containing the sink – no room for larder, etc. Rent 3*s*. 2*d*., rates 2*s*., total 5*s*. 2*d*.

3. Another as above but with no alcove at all, merely sink in living-room just inside front door. Rent 3*s*. 9*d*., rates 3*s*., total 6*s*. 9*d*.

4. House in Scholes quarter. Condemned house. One up, one down. Rooms 15 ft by 15 ft. Sink and copper in living-room, coal hole under stairs. Floor subsiding. No windows will open. House decently dry. Landlord good. Rent 3*s*. 8*d*., rates 2*s*. 6*d*., total 6*s*. 2*d*.

5. Another near by. Two up, two down and coal hole. Walls falling absolutely to pieces. Water comes into upstairs rooms in quantities. Floor lopsided. Downstairs windows will not open. Landlord bad. Rent 6*s*., rates 3*s*. 6*d*., total 9*s*. 6*d*.

6. House in Greenough's Row. One up, two down. Living-room 13 ft by 8 ft. Walls coming apart and water comes in. Back windows will not open, front ones will. Ten in family with eight children very near together in age. Corporation are trying to evict them for overcrowding but cannot find another house to send them to. Landlord bad. Rent 4*s*., rates 2*s*. 3*d*., total 6*s*. 3*d*.

So much for Wigan. I have pages more of the same type . . .

But mere notes like these are only valuable as reminders to myself. To me as I read them they bring back what I have seen, but they cannot in themselves give much idea of what conditions are like in those fearful northern slums. Words are such feeble things. What is the use of a brief phrase like 'roof leaks' or 'four beds for eight people'? It is the kind of thing your eye slides over, registering nothing. And yet what a wealth of misery it can cover! Take the question of overcrowding, for instance. Quite often you have eight or even ten people living in a three-roomed house. One of these rooms is a living-room, and as it probably measures about a dozen feet square and contains, besides the kitchen range and the sink, a table, some chairs and a dresser, there is no room in it for a bed. So there are eight or ten people sleeping in two small rooms, probably in at most four beds. If some of these people are adults and have to go to work, so much the worse. In one house, I remember, three grown-up girls shared the same bed and all went to work at different hours, each disturbing the others when she got up or came in; in another house a young miner working on the night shift slept by day in a narrow bed in which another member of the family slept by night. There is an added difficulty when there are grown-up children, in that you cannot let adolescent youths and girls sleep in the same bed. In one family I visited there were a father and a mother and a son and daughter aged round about seventeen, and only two beds for the lot of them. The father slept with the son and the mother with the daughter; it was the only arrangement that ruled out the danger of incest. Then there is the misery of leaking roofs and oozing walls, which in winter makes some rooms almost uninhabitable. Then there are bugs. Once bugs get into a house they are in it till the crack of doom; there is no sure way of exterminating them. Then there are the windows that will not open. I need not point out what this must mean, in summer, in a tiny stuffy living-room where the fire, on which all the cooking is done, has to be kept burning more or less constantly. And there are the special miseries attendant upon back to back houses. A fifty yards' walk to the lavatory or the dust-bin is not exactly an inducement to be clean. In the front houses – at any rate in a side-street where the Corporation doesn't interfere – the women get into the habit of throwing their refuse out of the front door, so that the gutter is always littered with tea-leaves and bread crusts. And it is worth considering what it is like for a child to grow up in one of the back alleys where its gaze is bounded by a row of lavatories and a wall.

In such places as these a woman is only a poor drudge muddling among an infinity of jobs. She may keep up her spirits, but she cannot keep up her standards of cleanliness and tidiness. There is always something to be done, and no conveniences and almost literally not room to turn round. No sooner have you washed one child's face than another's is dirty; before you have washed the crocks from one meal the next is due to be cooked. I found great variation in the houses I visited. Some were as decent as one could possibly expect in the circumstances, some were so appalling that I have no hope of describing them adequately. To begin with, the smell, the dominant and essential thing, is indescribable. But the squalor and the confusion! A tub full of filthy water here, a basin full of unwashed crocks there, more crocks piled in any odd corner, torn newspaper littered everywhere, and in the middle always the same dreadful table covered with sticky oilcloth and crowded with cooking pots and irons and half-darned stockings and pieces of stale bread and bits of cheese wrapped round with greasy newspaper! And the congestion in a tiny room where getting from one side to the other is a complicated voyage between pieces of furniture, with a line of damp washing getting you in the face every time you move and the children as thick underfoot as toadstools! There are scenes that stand out vividly in my memory. The almost bare living-room of a cottage in a little mining village, where the whole family was out of work and everyone seemed to be underfed; and the big family of grown-up sons and daughters sprawling aimlessly about, all strangely alike with red hair, splendid bones and pinched faces ruined by malnutrition and idleness; and one tall son sitting by the fireplace, too listless even to notice the entry of a stranger, and slowly peeling a sticky sock from a bare foot. A dreadful room in Wigan where all the furniture seemed to be made of packing cases and barrel staves and was coming to pieces at that; and an old woman with a blackened neck and her hair coming down denouncing her landlord in a Lancashire-Irish accent; and her mother, aged well over ninety, sitting in the background on the barrel that served her as a commode and regarding us blankly with a yellow, cretinous face. I could fill up pages with memories of similar interiors.

Of course the squalor of these people's houses is sometimes their own fault. Even if you live in a back to back house and have four children and a total income of thirty-two and sixpence a week from the P.A.C., there is no *need* to have unemptied chamber-pots standing about in your living-room. But it is equally certain that their circumstances do not encourage self-respect. The determining factor is probably the number of children. The best-kept interiors I saw were always childless houses or houses where there were only one or two children; with, say, six children in a three-roomed house it is quite impossible to keep anything decent. One thing that is very noticeable is that the worst squalors are never downstairs. You might visit quite a number of houses, even among the poorest of the unemployed, and bring away a wrong impression. These people, you might reflect, cannot be so badly off if they still have a fair amount of furniture and crockery. But it is in the rooms upstairs that the gauntness of poverty really discloses itself. Whether this is because pride makes people cling to their living-room furniture to the last, or because bedding is more pawnable, I do not know, but certainly many of the bedrooms I saw were fearful places. Among people who have been unemployed for several years continuously I should say it is the exception to have anything like a full set of bedclothes. Often there is nothing that can be properly called bedclothes at all – just a heap of old overcoats and miscellaneous rags on a rusty iron bedstead. In this way overcrowding is aggravated. One family of four persons that I knew, a father and mother and two children, possessed two beds but could only use one of them because they had not enough bedding for the other.

Anyone who wants to see the effects of the housing shortage at their very worst should visit the dreadful caravan-dwellings that exist in numbers in many of the northern towns. Ever since the war, in the complete impossibility of getting houses, parts of the population have overflowed into supposedly temporary quarters in fixed caravans. Wigan, for instance, with a population of about 85,000, has round about 200 caravan-dwellings with a family in each – perhaps somewhere near 1,000 people in all. How many of these caravan-colonies exist throughout the industrial areas it would be difficult to discover with any accuracy. The local authorities are reticent about them and the census report of 1931 seems to have decided to ignore them. But so far as I can discover by enquiry they are to be found in most of the larger towns in Lancashire and Yorkshire, and perhaps further north as well. The probability is that throughout the north of England there are some thousands, perhaps tens of thousands of *families* (not individuals) who have no home except a fixed caravan.

But the word 'caravan' is very misleading. It calls up a picture of a cosy gypsy-encampment (in fine weather, of course) with wood fires crackling and children picking blackberries and many-coloured washing fluttering on the lines. The caravan-colonies in Wigan and Sheffield are not like that. I had a look at several of them, I inspected those in Wigan with considerable care, and I have never seen comparable squalor except in the Far East. Indeed when I saw them I was immediately reminded of the filthy kennels in which I have seen Indian coolies living in Burma. But, as a matter of fact, nothing in the East could ever be quite as bad, for in the East you haven't our clammy, penetrating cold to contend with, and the sun is a disinfectant . . .

I sometimes think that the price of liberty is not so much eternal vigilance as eternal dirt. There are some Corporation estates in which new tenants are systematically deloused before being allowed into their houses. All their possessions except what they stand up in are taken away from them, fumigated and sent on to the new house. This procedure has its points, for it *is* a pity that people should take bugs into brand-new houses (a bug will follow you about in your luggage if he gets half a chance), but it is the kind of thing that makes you wish that the word 'hygiene' could be dropped out of the dictionary. Bugs are bad, but a state of affairs in which men will allow themselves to be dipped like sheep is worse. Perhaps, however, when it is a case of slum clearance, one must take for granted a certain amount of restrictions and inhumanity. When all is said and done, the most important thing is that people shall live in decent houses and not in pigsties. I have seen too much of slums to go into Chestertonian raptures about them. A place where the children can breathe clean air, and women have a few conveniences to save them from drudgery, and a man has a bit of garden to dig in, *must* be better than the stinking back-streets of Leeds and Sheffield. On balance, the Corporation estates are better than the slums; but only by a small margin.

When I was looking into the housing question I visited and inspected numbers of houses, perhaps a hundred or two hundred houses altogether, in various mining towns and villages. I cannot end this chapter without remarking on the extraordinary courtesy and good nature with which I was received everywhere. I did not go alone – I always had some local friend among the unemployed to show me round – but even so, it is an impertinence to go poking into strangers' houses and asking to see the cracks in the bedroom wall. Yet everyone was astonishingly patient and seemed to understand almost without explanation why I was questioning them and what I wanted to see. If any unauthorised person walked into *my* house and began asking me whether the roof leaked and whether I was much troubled by bugs and what I thought of my landlord, I should probably tell him to go to hell. This only happened to me once, and in that case the woman was slightly deaf and took me for a Means Test nark; but even she relented after a while and gave me the information I wanted.

I am told that it is bad form for a writer to quote his own reviews, but I want here to contradict a reviewer in the *Manchester Guardian* who says apropos of one of my books:

> Set down in Wigan or Whitechapel Mr Orwell would still exercise an unerring power of closing his vision to all that is good in order to proceed with his wholehearted vilification of humanity.

Wrong. Mr Orwell was 'set down' in Wigan for quite a while and it did not inspire him with any wish to vilify humanity. He liked Wigan very much – the people, not the scenery. Indeed, he has only one fault to find with it, and that is in respect of the celebrated Wigan

Pier, which he had set his heart on seeing. Alas! Wigan Pier has been demolished, and even the spot where it used to stand is no longer certain.

From CHAPTER XI

MEANWHILE, what about Socialism?

It hardly needs pointing out that at this moment we are in a very serious mess, so serious that even the dullest-witted people find it difficult to remain unaware of it. We are living in a world in which nobody is free, in which hardly anybody is secure, in which it is almost impossible to be honest and to remain alive. For enormous blocks of the working class the conditions of life are such as I have described in the opening chapters of this book, and there is no chance of those conditions showing any fundamental improvement. The very best the English working class can hope for is an occasional temporary decrease in unemployment when this or that industry is artificially stimulated by, for instance, rearmament. Even the middle classes, for the first time in their history, are feeling the pinch. They have not known actual hunger yet, but more and more of them find themselves floundering in a sort of deadly net of frustration in which it is harder and harder to persuade yourself that you are either happy, active or useful. Even the lucky ones at the top, the real bourgeoisie, are haunted periodically by a consciousness of the miseries below, and still more by fears of the menacing future. And this is merely a preliminary stage, in a country still rich with the loot of a hundred years. Presently there may be coming God knows what horrors – horrors of which, in this sheltered island, we have not even a traditional knowledge.

And all the while everyone who uses his brain knows that Socialism, as a world-system and wholeheartedly applied, is a way out. It would at least ensure our getting enough to eat even if it deprived us of everything else. Indeed, from one point of view, Socialism is such elementary common sense that I am sometimes amazed that it has not established itself already. The world is a raft sailing through space with, potentially, plenty of provisions for everybody; the idea that we must all co-operate and see to it that everyone does his fair share of the work and gets his fair share of the provisions seems so blatantly obvious that one would say that no one could possibly fail to accept it unless he had some corrupt motive for clinging to the present system. Yet the fact that we have got to face is that Socialism is *not* establishing itself. Instead of going forward, the cause of Socialism is visibly going back. At this moment Socialists almost everywhere are in retreat before the onslaught of Fascism, and events are moving at terrible speed. As I write this the Spanish Fascist forces are bombarding Madrid, and it is quite likely that before the book is printed we shall have another Fascist country to add to the list, not to mention a Fascist control of the Mediterranean which may have the effect of delivering British foreign policy into the hands of Mussolini. I do not, however, want here to discuss the wider political issues. What I am concerned with is the fact that Socialism is losing ground exactly where it ought to be gaining it. With so much in its favour – for every empty belly is an argument for Socialism – the *idea* of Socialism is less widely accepted than it was ten years ago. The average thinking person nowadays is not merely not a Socialist, he is actively hostile to Socialism. This must be due chiefly to mistaken methods of propaganda. It means that Socialism, in the form in which it is now presented to us, has about it something inherently distasteful – something that drives away the very people who ought to be flocking to its support.

A few years ago this might have seemed unimportant. It seems only yesterday that Socialists, especially orthodox Marxists, were telling me with superior smiles that Socialism was going to arrive of its own accord by some mysterious process called 'historic necessity'. Possibly that belief still lingers, but it has been shaken, to say the least of it. Hence the sudden attempts of Communists in various countries to ally themselves with democratic forces which they have been sabotaging for years past. At a moment like this it is desperately necessary to discover just *why* Socialism has failed in its appeal. And it is no use writing off the current distaste for Socialism as the product of stupidity or corrupt motives. If you want to remove that distaste you have got to understand it, which means getting inside the mind of the ordinary objector to Socialism, or at least regarding his viewpoint sympathetically. No case is really answered until it has had a fair hearing. Therefore, rather paradoxically, in order to defend Socialism it is necessary to start by attacking it.

In the present chapter I am merely dealing with the obvious, preliminary objections – the kind of thing that the person who is not a

Socialist (I don't mean the 'Where's the money to come from?' type) always starts by saying when you tax him on the subject. Some of these objections may appear frivolous or self-contradictory, but that is beside the point; I am merely discussing symptoms. Anything is relevant which helps to make clear why Socialism is not accepted. And please notice that I am arguing *for* Socialism, not *against* it. But for the moment I am *advocatus diaboli*. I am making out a case for the sort of person who is in sympathy with the fundamental aims of Socialism, who has the brains to see that Socialism would 'work', but who in practice always takes to flight when Socialism is mentioned.

Question a person of this type, and you will often get the semi-frivolous answer: 'I don't object to Socialism, but I do object to Socialists.' Logically it is a poor argument, but it carries weight with many people. As with the Christian religion, the worst advertisement for Socialism is its adherents.

The first thing that must strike any outside observer is that Socialism in its developed form is a theory confined entirely to the middle class. The typical Socialist is not, as tremulous old ladies imagine, a ferocious-looking working man with greasy overalls and a raucous voice. He is either a youthful snob-Bolshevik who in five years' time will quite probably have made a wealthy marriage and been converted to Roman Catholicism; or, still more typically, a prim little man with a white-collar job, usually a secret teetotaller and often with vegetarian leanings, with a history of Nonconformity behind him, and, above all, with a social position which he has no intention of forfeiting. This last type is surprisingly common in Socialist parties of every shade; it has perhaps been taken over *en bloc* from the old Liberal Party. In addition to this there is the horrible – the really disquieting – prevalence of cranks wherever Socialists are gathered together. One sometimes gets the impression that the mere words 'Socialism' and 'Communism' draw towards them with magnetic force every fruit-juice drinker, nudist, sandal-wearer, sex-maniac, Quaker, 'Nature Cure' quack, pacifist and feminist in England. One day this summer I was riding through Letchworth when the bus stopped and two dreadful-looking old men got on to it. They were both about sixty, both very short, pink and chubby, and both hatless. One of them was obscenely bald, the other had long grey hair bobbed in the Lloyd George style. They were dressed in pistachio-coloured shirts and khaki shorts into which their huge bottoms were crammed so tightly that you could study every dimple. Their appearance created a mild stir of horror on the top of the bus. The man next to me, a commercial traveller I should say, glanced at me, at them, and back again at me, and murmured, 'Socialists,' as who should say, 'Red Indians.' He was probably right – the ILP were holding their summer school at Letchworth. But the point is that to him, as an ordinary man, a crank meant a Socialist and a Socialist meant a crank. Any Socialist, he probably felt, could be counted on to have *something* eccentric about him. And some such notion seems to exist even among Socialists themselves. For instance, I have here a prospectus from another summer school which states its terms per week and then asks me to say 'whether my diet is ordinary or vegetarian'. They take it for granted, you see, that it is necessary to ask this question. This kind of thing is by itself sufficient to alienate plenty of decent people. And their instinct is perfectly sound, for the food-crank is by definition a person willing to cut himself off from human society in hopes of adding five years on to the life of his carcase; that is, a person out of touch with common humanity.

To this you have got to add the ugly fact that most middle-class Socialists, while theoretically pining for a classless society, cling like glue to their miserable fragments of social prestige. I remember my sensations of horror on first attending an ILP branch meeting in London. (It might have been rather different in the North, where the bourgeoisie are less thickly scattered.) Are *these* mingy little beasts, I thought, the champions of the working class? For every person there, male and female, bore the worst stigmata of sniffish middle-class superiority. If a real working man, a miner dirty from the pit, for instance, had suddenly walked into their midst, they would have been embarrassed, angry, and disgusted; some, I should think, would have fled holding their noses. You can see the same tendency in Socialist literature, which, even when it is not openly written *de haut en bas*, is always completely removed from the working class idiom and manner of thought. The Coles, Webbs, Stracheys, etc., are not *exactly* proletarian writers. It is doubtful whether anything describable as proletarian literature now exists – even the *Daily Worker* is written in standard South English – but a good music-hall comedian comes nearer to producing it than any Socialist writer I can think of. As for the technical jargon of the Communists, it is as far removed from the common speech as the language of a mathematical textbook. I remember hearing a professional Communist speaker address a working-class audience. His speech was the usual bookish stuff, full of long sentences and parentheses and 'Notwithstanding' and 'Be that as it may', besides the usual jargon of 'ideology' and 'class-consciousness' and 'proletarian solidarity' and all the rest of it. After him a Lancashire working man got up and spoke to the crowd in their own broad lingo. There was not much doubt which of the two was nearer to his audience, but I do not suppose for a moment that the Lancashire working man was an orthodox Communist.

For it must be remembered that a working man, so long as he remains a genuine working man, is seldom or never a Socialist in the complete, logically consistent sense. Very likely he votes Labour, or even Communist if he gets the chance, but his conception of Socialism is quite different from that of the book-trained Socialist higher up. To the ordinary working man, the sort you would meet in any pub on Saturday night, Socialism does not mean much more than better wages and shorter hours and nobody bossing you about. To the more revolutionary type, the type who is a hunger-marcher and is blacklisted by employers, the word is a sort of rallying-cry against the forces of oppression, a vague threat of future violence. But, so far as my experience goes, no genuine working man grasps the deeper implications of Socialism. Often, in my opinion, he is a truer Socialist than the orthodox Marxist, because he does remember, what the other so often forgets, that Socialism means justice and common decency. But what he does not grasp is that Socialism cannot be narrowed down to mere economic justice and that a reform of that magnitude is bound to work immense changes in our civilisation and his own way of life. His vision of the Socialist future is a vision of present society with the worst abuses left out, and with interest centring round the same things as at present – family life, the pub, football, and local politics. As for the philosophic side of Marxism, the pea-and-thimble trick with those three mysterious entities, thesis, antithesis, and synthesis, I have never met a working man who had the faintest interest in it. It is of course true that plenty of people of working-class *origin* are Socialists of the theoretical bookish type. But they are never people who have *remained* working men; they don't work with their hands, that is. They belong either to the type I mentioned in the last chapter, the type who squirms into the middle class via the literary intelligentsia, or the type who becomes a Labour MP or a high-up trade-union official. This last type is one of the most desolating spectacles the world contains. He has been picked out to fight for his mates, and all it means to him is a soft job and the chance of 'bettering' himself. Not merely while but *by* fighting the bourgeoisie he becomes a bourgeois himself. And meanwhile it is quite possible that he has remained an orthodox Marxist. But I have yet to meet a *working* miner, steel-worker, cotton-weaver, docker, navvy or whatnot who was 'ideologically' sound.

One of the analogies between Communism and Roman Catholicism is that only the 'educated' are completely orthodox. The most immediately striking thing about the English Roman Catholics – I don't mean the real Catholics, I mean the converts: Ronald Knox, Arnold Lunn *et hoc genus* – is their intense self-consciousness. Apparently they never think, certainly they never write, about anything but the fact that they *are* Roman Catholics; this single fact and the self-praise resulting from it form the entire stock-in-trade of the Catholic literary man. But the really interesting thing about these people is the way in which they have worked out the supposed implications of orthodoxy until the tiniest details of life are involved. Even the liquids you drink, apparently, can be orthodox or heretical; hence the campaigns of Chesterton, 'Beachcomber', etc., against tea and in favour of beer. According to Chesterton, tea-drinking is 'pagan', while beer-drinking is 'Christian', and coffee is 'the puritan's opium'. It is unfortunate for this theory that Catholics abound in the 'Temperance' movement and the greatest tea-boozers in the world are the Catholic Irish; but what I am interested in here is the attitude of mind that can make even food and drink an occasion for religious intolerance. A working-class Catholic would never be so absurdly consistent as that. He does not spend his time in brooding on the fact that he is a Roman Catholic, and he is not particularly conscious of being different from his non-Catholic neighbours. Tell an Irish dock-labourer in the slums of Liverpool that his cup of tea is 'pagan', and he will call you a fool. And even in more serious matters he does not always grasp the implications of his faith. In the Roman Catholic homes of Lancashire you see the crucifix on the wall and the *Daily Worker* on the table. It is only the 'educated' man, especially the literary man, who knows how to be a bigot. And, *mutatis mutandis*, it is the same with Communism. The creed is never found in its pure form in a genuine proletarian . . .

The fact is that Socialism, *in the form in which it is now presented*, appeals chiefly to unsatisfactory or even inhuman types. On the one hand you have the warm-hearted unthinking Socialist, the typical working-class Socialist, who only wants to abolish poverty and does not always grasp what this implies. On the other hand, you have the intellectual, book-trained Socialist, who understands that it is necessary to throw our present civilisation down the sink and is quite willing to do so. And this type is drawn, to begin with, entirely from the middle class, and from a rootless town-bred section of the middle class at that. Still more unfortunately, it includes – so much so that to an outsider it even appears to be composed of – the kind of people I have been discussing; the foaming denouncers of the bourgeoisie, and the more-water-in-your-beer reformers of whom Shaw is the prototype, and the astute young social-literary climbers who are Communists now, as they will be Fascists five years hence, because it is all the go, and all that dreary tribe of high-minded women and sandal-wearers and bearded fruit-juice drinkers who come flocking towards the smell of 'progress' like bluebottles to a dead cat. The ordinary decent person, who is in sympathy with the *essential* aims of Socialism, is given the impression that there is no room for his kind in any Socialist party that means business. Worse, he is driven to the cynical conclusion that Socialism is a kind of doom which is probably coming but must be staved off as long as possible. Of course, as I have suggested already, it is not strictly fair to judge a movement by its adherents; but the point is that people invariably do so, and that the popular conception of Socialism is coloured by the conception of a Socialist as a dull or disagreeable person. 'Socialism' is pictured as a state of affairs in which our more vocal Socialists would feel thoroughly at home. This does great harm to the cause. The ordinary man may not flinch from a dictatorship of the proletariat, if you offer it tactfully; offer him a dictatorship of the prigs, and he gets ready to fight . . .

WALLS HAVE MOUTHS

by Wilfred Macartney

(monthly choice, September 1936)

Wilfred Macartney (1899–1970), the notorious 'Russian Spy', was tried at the Old Bailey in January 1928 and found guilty on five counts of obtaining information calculated to be useful to an enemy. He served eight years, most of them in Parkhurst (on the Isle of Wight) and wrote *Walls Have Mouths* as a revelatory account of what life was like inside. Yet it wasn't the first time he'd been in prison or in the headlines.

First, there was the 'Boy Directors' case, a favourite of the press in 1915 as light relief from war news. Years before, Macartney and his brother had been made directors of their father's successful electrical engineering company, which had contracts for laying tramways all over Europe. When Macartney's father died unexpectedly, the firm's secretary procured a share of the company, but was ousted by the brothers. The secretary sued for wrongful dismissal. During the hearing, the sixteen-year-old Macartney, who had already seen action in France, announced to an astonished judge that if he was old enough to die in the trenches, he was old enough to be in business, and that, besides, he had been attending board meetings and signing documents since he was nine.

His father's death had left Macartney very wealthy but he was desperate to get back to the war. After fighting in Malta and Egypt, he came under the command of Compton Mackenzie, novelist and head of British Intelligence in the eastern Mediterranean. Macartney – a mere 'pink-faced, cherubic, grinning youth with glasses' – found himself in charge of the island of Kythera, one of the Cyclades. The following year, back in France, he was wounded in the head and taken prisoner at Cambrai. He managed to escape from his German captors by jumping from a train.

After the Armistice, he went to Constantinople and seems to have joined the Spanish Foreign Legion in Morocco. But the prospect of making more money drew him back to London, and he started a bout of riotously heavy drinking and bad financial dealing. He quickly lost most of his fortune but, by all accounts, kept his sense of humour and was fun to be around. In 1925 he became part of a Communist set and started to write for the *Sunday Worker*, though he continued to dabble in the markets and spend his afternoons in the Café Royal. 'It's true', he later wrote, 'that my passionate belief in Communism did not greatly alter my way of living.' He was arrested for smashing the window of a jeweller's shop in Albemarle Street – probably during a drunken spree – and spent nine months in Wormwood Scrubs. A couple of fines for being drunk and disorderly followed his release; then he really got into trouble.

He was working at Lloyd's as an underwriter, a position potentially valuable to Moscow. Having been instructed by the Communist Party to obtain information about the shipment of British arms to the Baltic States, he asked a colleague, George Monckland, for copies of relevant insurance documents, slipping him twenty-five pounds for his pains. When Monckland asked him what was going on, Macartney revealed that he was working for the Russians. Monckland was a terrible choice as a co-conspirator; through him, Scotland Yard was alerted straight away. Macartney was followed and spotted handing over a questionnaire about the RAF to a member of the Russian Trade Delegation. This triggered the famous Arcos raid (Arcos stood for All-Russian Co-operative Society Ltd), which saw 150 policemen rampaging through the Delegation for four days, hunting down documents and demolishing concrete vaults. Soviet officials protested (the Delegation had diplomatic immunity), but London severed diplomatic relations with Moscow having found evidence of plans for subversive action involving the Communist Party and various trade unions. Poor Macartney was trailed around Europe for another six months, until the details of a spy ring had been established. When he was finally arrested and put on trial, the jury decided on his guilt after only fifteen minutes. His sentence of ten years of penal servitude was harsh, though *The Times* leader said he was lucky not to have been shot.

On his release from Parkhurst in 1935, Macartney was shunned by some erstwhile friends as a traitor, but Compton Mackenzie put him up and gave him a room in which to write. Mackenzie also agreed to contribute a prologue to Macartney's prison book, along with comments at the end of each chapter. It was due to Mackenzie's salesmanship that Gollancz read the manuscript of *Walls Have Mouths*. Macartney was lucky that its publication coincided with the launch of the Left Book Club, and he benefited, too, from one of Gollancz's aggressive publicity campaigns. 'Have you written to your MP about *Walls Have Mouths*?' one ad demanded. Another showed a grisly photo of the former Home Secretary J. R. Clynes, above his comment: 'I denounce this book. Better left unread.' The volume was extremely popular within the Club; it became Gollancz's model of the racy narrative which subscribers often demanded (*Our Street*, for example, was 'another book of the Macartney-type').

Macartney didn't hang around to enjoy his celebrity. Still a fervent Communist, he set off for Spain, donned leather jacket and beret and became the first commander of the British Battalion in the International Brigade. At first, he was reported to be 'a big hit with the lads', though he soon grew miserable – the combined effect of disciplinary problems and a stinking cold. He was apparently too soft-hearted and had, it was said, only 'rudimentary' abilities 'as an organiser and decision-maker'. His fellow soldiers began to describe him as not only 'irritable and querulous' but sometimes 'critical of the Party'. He then received a shot in the arm – from a pistol, held by a comrade. Whether it was accidental is impossible to say (that was the claim). Macartney was replaced as commander by Tom Wintringham and didn't return to Spain.

At least he could celebrate the fact that one of the reforms called for in *Walls Have Mouths* – a lifting of the ban on cigarettes which was imposed on most prisoners – had been announced in Parliament. 'For the Left Book Club, it is the first victory,' he wrote in *Left News*. 'True, flogging remains and many other beastly horrors, but tobacco in prison, it is almost a miracle.'

Macartney seems to have regained full faith in the Communist Party and, after the USSR had entered World War Two, was heavily involved – alongside Bevan, Michael Foot, Beaverbrook and others – in the campaign to open a second front, to help the beleaguered Red Army. The CP organised large 'Aid to Russia' meetings using the Russia Today Society as a front. 'He was a remarkable fellow and became my closest friend in the Communist Party,' Michael Foot has said. 'He used to say that he went to prison for giving information to our ally – he was just a little ahead of his time.' After the war, Macartney was arrested once more: for helping the double agent Eddie Chapman write and publish his espionage experiences. This time he got away with a fine.

From CHAPTER XVI: ESCAPES

To ESCAPE has been the dream of all captives since man began to enslave man. Yet so difficult is it to achieve in the English prisons of to-day that most prisoners become apathetic and the dream is forgotten. Perhaps the old urge to escape has been weakened, or perhaps the English prisoner makes a virtue of necessity by remaining docilely in prison, for without doubt the English locking-up system is the most efficient in the world, and this careful method of safe custody is much helped by the informer. It is true to say that over half the convicts in English gaols are informers, or potential informers. This characteristic trait in the English does not only apply to convicts. To inform – or, in official speech, 'to approve' – seems as much the nature of an Englishman as it is to kick a ball or to drink a glass of beer.

Combined against the convict anxious to escape is an almost unassailable system of security and an eager willingness on the part of half of his comrades to betray him in the hope of obtaining extra remission, in order to placate the jailors, or simply from downright jealousy, because the informer is afraid to try himself.

The modern reluctance to escape from prison is not confined to convicts. As an officer I was a prisoner of war, and I experienced the same lack of initiative among my brother officers. The number of escapes from Germany was remarkably small; less than two hundred officers escaped during the whole of the war. Compared with Parkhurst, to get away from Germany was child's play. The general attitude of a captive officer was to stay put. This is not to say that some officers did not show as much grit and as fierce a determination to escape as some convicts. The officer did not encounter the informer difficulty to anything like the extent the convict does, although it was there too.

My first attempt to get away from the Germans was made from a hospital, and I was baulked by the almost insane clumsiness of another prisoner. At the time I was hardly nineteen, and did not imagine that his action was anything except sheer obtuseness. Now, in the light of many years' experience, I am convinced that this fellow's intrusion was intended to prevent my making an escape, in case reprisals were taken against the other people in the ward. Reviewing the whole circumstances, I am convinced that this particular prisoner was the informer type, and there were plenty like him. Informers are actuated by three stimuli – fear, greed, and jealousy – and one or other of these emotions operates anywhere.

There was current in Parkhurst the legend of an escape which, if it is not true, ought to be. Two young fellows, D. and E., had made an exciting escape based on a sound judgment of the English love of sport. This escape had a perfect historical precedent: Edward I's escape from Simon de Montfort's guards.

D. and E. were working out on a farm, and not far from the prison boundary. A few minutes before pack-up time, when there is always a little relaxation in the working party, D. started an argument as to his ability to cover 100 yds in so many seconds.

'In these boots I can do the hundred in eleven and a half seconds,' he challenged.

'What? On this grub and in these boots you'd be lucky if you could do it in thirteen or fourteen seconds, let alone eleven and a half,' said E.

The screw in charge of the party was sports crazy, and the authority in the party on records, performances, and capabilities. The argument grew hot.

'I'll bet I can do it. Let's show him, governor,' begged D.

'Never mind about your doing it in eleven and a half seconds. I can't do the one hundred in that, and I can beat you,' bragged E.

'In your hat you can!'

'Let us have a race to that fence; it's just about a hundred yards,' asked D.

'Yes, and get me the sack,' replied the screw; but he looked interested.

'Don't be silly. The principal warder has gone in. There's nobody about, and the patrol is a good fellow,' E. pleaded.

'No, can't be done. Collect the tools, boxman.'

'Be a sport, guv; let 'em have a go,' the other lags joined.

'Yes, and you time 'em,' suggested another.

This suggestion did the trick. The screw fancied himself with a watch in his hand, judging races. Besides, he was genuinely interested in seeing a race between D. and E. Such a race would be good fun.

'All right, keep your eyes open, boxman, and see that no one spots us,' agreed the screw, taking out his watch and setting the two racers level.

'Ready! Go!' And away they raced over the dug field. They were both young and strong and could run like deer. Neck and neck, arms outstretched, clods of earth flying, they fairly rushed over the ground. D. won, and came to the fence just a little ahead.

'Well, they have done it in twelve and a half seconds, and that's pretty good running,' said the sporting screw, closing his watch.

But the men still went on running. Like chamois they leaped the wire fence and scorched away to the neighbouring forest.

'Hi, stop, you fools! You've done the hundred! Come back! Where are the bloody fools running to now? Hi! Hi!' the screw yelled. He could not grasp that they were escaping. It was only as they vanished into the undergrowth that he came to himself and understood what had happened. Snatching his whistle from his pocket, he blew furiously. Between blowing and swearing he got his grinning party together and marched them in. The escape hooter was going by now. The bell was tolling. Screws were running to their posts. The patrols were out after the 'racers'. The two were away for nearly a week, when they were caught, exhausted, by a farmer, who handed them over to the gaol and, no doubt, collected the £5 reward.

As for Parkhurst, the hostile population is one of the main difficulties a man encounters in attempting to escape. The islander of the Isle of Wight really has a self-righteous dislike of the convict. These unpleasant people are only too eager to catch a poor devil escaping. What grand sportsmen they are! It is strange, because most island folk are kindly, but on the Isle of Wight they are cruel and mean-minded. Besides, Parkhurst gives these people plenty of jobs and plenty of work. I compare the islanders of the Isle of Wight with other islanders I know. I remember Malta, where the convicts and prisoners are always collected for, and where the charming inhabitants regard the unfortunate with great compassion. I am sure that were there a prison on the Isle of Barra, where I am writing this, these delightful, soft-spoken folk would have the same sympathy. I cannot believe that the Barra people, with their beautiful manners, exquisite courtesy, and gentle kindness, would hound a man escaping from perhaps life imprisonment like those harsh-voiced Isle of Wight yokels, with their eternal 'yurr' and their inane grins. There are no Boy Scouts on Barra, thank goodness, but, if there were, the Barra lads would be more likely to hide and feed a fleeing prisoner than to help police and jailor in the hue and cry. Ugh! Boy Scouts, hounding with their poles like an otter some poor devil only wishing his freedom! It makes one sick! Are not the police and jailors paid enough? Yet when a man escapes on the Isle of Wight the whole population, from Royal Yacht Squadron to retired Pompey whores, turn out to catch him; they make a gala of it . . .

So far, nobody has ever got right away from Parkhurst. There is a legend that in the last century a man escaped and stayed away fifteen years. He was put up by a woman on the place, and lived and worked for her all those years. When he was old – so the story goes – and she had no further use for him in the bed or the field, she gave him up to the authorities. It may be only a legend, but it's what I'd expect from an Isle of Wight Hampshire hog – or sow in this case.

'Lag's luck' is an expression current among convicts over escapes; and certainly the ill fortune which dogs lags attempting to get away is remarkable.

On April 30th, 1926, Davies got out of a cell in hospital, got out of the hospital in the prison grounds, got over the wall by throwing a rope through the steel gate and hooked over the wall. He obtained clothes and money. He reached Ryde in time to catch the early boat to Portsmouth, where he would arrive before the prison was awake. On May 1st, 1926, the General Strike began. No boat sailed that morning. Davies could not get off the island. He was caught in a fish-and-chip shop!

Working in the cutting-room with me was a tall chap called Deakin who, a little before I arrived at the prison, had made a good attempt to get away. Deakin was a tall, merry fellow, quite irresponsible, doing three years for worthless cheques and false pretences. He had been a deserter from the Navy, and from this had gravitated to crime. He was not at all a bad chap, full of the ordinary social conventions which even a lagging had failed to upset; in short, a cheerful ass right out of P. G. Wodehouse, but gone a bit bent!

Deakin worked in the tailor's shop making naval tunics and trousers for Greenwich Hospital. Screened by a pal just before cease-labour time, he put on a pair of blue trousers and his prison trousers over them. Then, as the 'Pack up' order was given, he nipped into the lavatory with a coat, shirt, collar, and tie. In a minute he changed. Over his naval uniform (he said it felt like old times) he put his slip and buttoned it up to the neck. He then fell in with the remainder of his party to go to exercise. As they wheeled to the left and broke off, he lagged behind, avoided the screw, and got behind the corner of the shop wall. Here he swiftly divested himself of the prison clothes and strode boldly through a fence on the road along which were the jailors' houses. The prison road, which is a road within the penal settlement itself, led to the main Cowes–Ryde road. Deakin was nearing the road when a jailor approached him, and was on the point of telling the 'stranger' that the land was prison land and strictly private. The screw had not seen that the trespasser in naval uniform was a convict escaping. No whistle had blown; no hooter sounded; no bell rang. Deakin might have bluffed by politely apologising and walking quietly away. He would have had about half an hour's start, and might have made something of it, but he lost his head and began to run. The screw blew his whistle, and on principle dashed in pursuit. The whistle was taken up by the patrols, and in a few seconds the hooter was blowing and the bell tolling. In Deakin's party the screw in charge was unaware that it was one of his men missing. All parties are immediately marched in when an escape takes place, and only when Deakin's screw had lined his men up and counted them preparatory to marching them in did he discover his loss. Then he started to blow his whistle. A principal warder observed sardonically, 'A bit late, mister.' In the meantime Deakin was running here and there, over ditches and under hedges, with screws and farm labourers after him. He got as far as the Medina, a tidal river on the Isle of Wight, and plunged in and attempted to swim to the other side. The pursuing screws got a boat and rowed after him, and got up to him about three-quarters of the way across. One struck Deakin over the head with an oar while the other grabbed him with a boat-hook and pulled him into the boat. Poor Deakin was marched back, wringing wet, and slung into chokey. He got fifteen days' bread and water, and lost three months' remission for his attempt.

The first attempted escape that I experienced was a few months after I'd come to the prison, and was a humorous affair. A comic fellow – one of those jokers to be found under even the most trying conditions – was employed in painting the railing of the governor's dog-kennel. The governor was away on leave and the house empty. It was a very hot day, and the screw, being tired, 'lost observation' over Johnson, who was also a bit bored with prison and its life. Johnson was a train thief, a small man with very big feet, tow-coloured hair, and a perpetual grin. To relieve the monotony he now forced a scullery window and roamed round the governor's house. In Mrs Governor's bedroom he found a wardrobe full of women's clothes. Some of these he put on, including a large summer hat and some *chic* underwear. Alas! his feet were too big for any of the shoes, so he had to stick to his prison boots, and they resembled barges. Dressed as a lady of fashion – skirts were short that year – 'Miss Johnson', as he came to be known, set out on his great adventure. He walked boldly out of the front door, past the main gate, right under the nose of a principal warder, and began to cross the cricket-field when a screw off duty, coming in the opposite direction across the field, spotted his boots, stared, and then blew his whistle. 'Miss Johnson' took to her big heels and ran. The poor girl was soon caught and ignominiously dragged, in her borrowed finery, by harsh and unfeeling screws through the gaol gate. I saw the procession come. There was poor Johnson being frog-marched, head nearly touching the ground, hat half off, one screw at the back, one on each arm. Johnson was irrepressible. His shrill voice could be heard: 'Fancy treating an honest working-girl like this. Beasts!' The honest working-girl received very little sympathy from the visiting magistrates. Much bread and water was all Johnson got for his escapade.

Escapades are, indeed, what most attempted escapes amount to. The two escapes related were nothing much more than light-hearted pranks. None was a desperate break for liberty or a carefully planned get-away. Yet even the most elaborately planned and detailed attempt always appears to come up against 'lag's luck', and hardly ever more so than in the case of George Taylor and Billy Brain.

Billy Brain was a very remarkable man. A strongly built, shambling body supported a large, half-bald, fair-haired head. Peering eyes under heavy eyebrows were helped by thick glasses. These spectacles were the strongest I've ever seen – I don't mean the lenses, but the steel support circles and nose-piece. Billy came from Birmingham, and in him was the inherited mechanical ability of generations of skilled toolmakers. Billy could make anything. In those large, powerful hands a bit of wire and a piece of bone would become anything that Billy's mechanical mind was set on. He turned out gadgets by the score, and his ivory carvings were clearly cut and beautiful in design. Telescope-making is one of the illegal industries of prison. To an extent it is winked at. Now and again there is a general clean-up. Searchers go round the cells and seize any telescope they can find. Billy was the champion telescope-maker. For hours and hours he would grind lenses down with some specially contrived gadget. Lenses were made from any piece of glass that could be used; diminishers were made as well as magnifiers, and microscopes as well as telescopes, but, while the telescopes were frequently very good, the microscopes were usually very poor.

Billy Brain had taught himself German so that he could swot up the art of lens-making. One day he surprised me with his knowledge of the Zeiss lenses factory at Jena.

'Why, Billy, have you been over it as well? I went over it the year I was pinched.'

'No, Mac, I've just read about it.'

Billy knew a good deal more than I did of that factory, and I had been all over it.

When the lenses are finished, stout pieces of cardboard and brown paper would be stuck with paste to make the tube, and the resulting telescope would, were it Billy's manufacture, be a very fine magnifier. Parkhurst is built on hills, so that from some of the top-landing cells, and especially from the top ward in hospital, a fine view can be obtained looking right across the Medina away over the lofty downs. Men, freedom hungry, would spend hours with these telescopes, searching the countryside. Some men, over a period of years, would come to know a five- or six-mile sweep of the countryside. They learned a farmer's habits, and they would often comment on any departure from the ordinary in the routine of a farmer or a boatman on the Medina whom they'd 'adopted'. A good telescope had a value; one ounce of tobacco, perhaps two ounces for a really good one, could be obtained. Billy was fond of tobacco, so he worked extremely hard. Billy was also a very tough nut, and quite unamenable to discipline. He always lost all his remission and did a lot of bread and water. This was his second or third lagging for warehouse-breaking. He was doing six years this time, and, even before his attempted escape with George Taylor, had lost all his remission, i.e. he had to do a full six years in prison. George Taylor was doing life for a crime of non-violence, and he had nothing to lose.

The Taylor–Brain attempt was a carefully and cleverly thought-out business, while most attempts are just blind dashes. Moreover, about seven men knew that such an attempt was to be made and yet the secret was kept. Usually for so many to know was to be informed on. It failed through the worst 'lag's luck' imaginable.

The locks in Parkhurst in those days showed a white panel when locked; when unlocked the white panel disappeared. Behind the lock and in the cell is a steel lining to the door. Billy first built in his cell a cache for his tools. This was so well done that the cell searchers never found it. He then took out enough studs from the steel lining to let him prise up the lining and give him sufficient room to work behind the lock. Then above and below the lock, through the wood, he bored two holes, very small. At the right of the keyhole he bored another hole, making a triangle. He then bored into the back of the lock in direct line with the key entrance. All this took months of careful work, for, apart from the work itself, there was the puttying and painting of the door after every operation to stop the screws from noticing that the door had been tampered with. Billy then 'built' his key. It consisted of thirty-seven different pieces. Bone, steel, brass, and ebonite went to its make-up. I don't pretend to know the 'dynamics' of that key, but it could open cell doors and take hall gates off the double. Billy knew the shape of every key in the prison by heart. He had only to look at a key to remember every edge of it. One of his most important tools was a long and very strong pair of tweezers. Billy's next task was to open his door. He poked three long pieces of string, with very thin wire on the end through the three holes, which he waggled about till they reached the floor, and he could fish for them under his cell door – there is quite a gap; a folded paper can pass easily. When he'd caught these strings he pulled them into the cell, and attached his key to them. Don't imagine that the key looked anything like a key or had a handle. Then he pulled the other end of his string and of course the key travelled up the outside of the door till it reached the keyhole, where it hung. Then the top string was pulled and the bottom one held loose. This had the effect of making the key stand straight out from the door. Then the string from the hole to the right was pulled, and this brought the key to the keyhole. Some further pulling and the key was right in front of the keyhole. Then into the back of the lock, in direct line with the key-entrance, went the long and strong tweezers. They grasped firmly the nose of the key, and, gently turning, brought it sweetly into the keyhole. Then a good hard steady turn; the tumblers fell; the lock slipped back; the white signal disappeared. Billy's door was open.

George Taylor's part of the escape had been to supply clothes and money and general directions, and this he'd done with consummate care and discretion. It was thus that I came to know that the escape was planned. One Saturday afternoon, about three months after I'd been in the prison, at the end of July, the fellow in the next cell to mine, a Geordie, slung a white tailor's work-bag into my cell, saying, 'Look after this, Mac. I think I'm going to be turned over.' It was in the cell before I could say yes or no; there was no chance of giving it back without attracting a screw's attention, and in 1928 they were red hot. So I had to carry the baby; all I could hope was that the child had had plenty of Godfrey's Cordial and would keep quiet.

Of course, I opened the work-bag. I must know what I had, in case something went wrong. In it were a civilian cap, two civilian shirts and collars, a half-finished waistcoat, and a pair of striped trousers. I nearly had a fit. If I got caught with this little lot, it meant three months', perhaps six months', loss of remission, and the Lord knew how much bread and water. I was fed up. Why the devil couldn't he give it to someone else? But nothing could be done. I had to keep it till Sunday morning. Then Geordie took them back, much to my relief. He had not had a turn-over, either; it was just wind-up.

'Thanks, old man,' said Geordie, as he got the wretched bag. I grunted, and then, I suppose to soften me, he proceeded to burden me with his confidences, nearly as unwelcome as his bag.

'Old George Taylor and Billy Brain are going to have a go; that's their clobber,' he said.

'Well, keep their clobber more carefully in future. I wish 'em luck. Only don't frighten the guts out of me without warning,' I said, not at all mollified.

When Billy was sure he could open his door, a date was arranged. Certain extramural arrangements were completed, and all was set. The clothes, now completed, were left handy in the tailor's shop, which is outside the big wall.

Billy's cell and Taylor's cell were on the same landing, but on different sides. This meant that Billy would, after he got out of his, have to cross a bridge to let George out. In those days there was only one patrol for B hall, where George and Billy were located, and C hall. B and C halls were joined, and together formed a very long hall. The telephone was at the far end of C hall, through the door in the wall separating the halls – a distance of quite 150 yds. The patrol's duty was to walk about the two halls, go down to the punishment cells, keep his eyes open, and see that everything was normal.

Violence had no part in George Taylor's plan; he intended to make his escape as 'sweet as a nut'. Therefore the patrol had to be got out of the way for about five minutes, while Taylor was being let out of his cell by Billy and during the few minutes it would take them to get out of the hall into the prison yard.

A part of the top landing in B is called the B5; here were special TB cells, big windows, special beds, etc.; it was considered, for administrative purposes, as a part of the hospital. TB cases were confined there.

George arranged with one of the TBs for him to report sick at 7.30. At 7 o'clock the last lock-up takes place in prison. Two jailors come round and visit every cell. The visit is more or less perfunctory, but they see that the door is secure, and take reasonable precautions. As soon as every cell door in the prison has been examined, all the early night screws go off duty, leaving the patrols in the hall, one patrol to A hall, one patrol to B and C halls. When a man reports sick he rings the bell in his cell. This causes an indicator to drop outside his door; at the same time a bell rings over the principal warder's desk, and a signal shows on which landing the indicator has fallen. The patrol must then go to the landing and find the cell with the indicator projecting. In this case he had to go right up to the top of the hall. While he was asking the TB what was wrong with him, Billy let himself out of his cell and dodged into a lavatory.

The TB complained that he thought he was going to have a haemorrhage. 'Get a hospital screw or the doctor.' The patrol had to go the whole length of the two halls, enter the sick report in a book (everything has to go in the book!) and telephone to the hospital for a nurse. All this takes time, and he is away from B hall.

Billy waited till the patrol had passed into C, and then crossed the bridge joining the opposite side of the landing, went to George's cell, and let him out. Clad only in jersey and underpants – their clothes were left on a chair in full view, so that the dummies in the cells would look more convincing – they crept down to the ground floor, and Billy's key unlocked the gate opening into the warders' hall. Warders' hall is a large space between B and C halls formed by knocking out about thirty cells. Half of this gap is taken up by the adjudication room; the other is a bare stone-flagged square. It is called the warders' hall because years ago the screws from B and C used to assemble here before coming on and going off duty. The gate from warders' hall gives on to the main parade, and in the night is always kept on the double.

Billy got his key into this lock, gave a twist and took the lock off the single, gave it another twist and his key fell to pieces. He started swearing and searching the floor for the missing parts. Poor George in his pants was shivering with cold and fear.

'Come on, look for the bits'; and down went George on his hands and knees to search.

After three or four moments Billy got all his bits and pieces and assembled his key. This time the lock gave, they swung open the gate, and were three-quarters of the way to freedom. Billy closed the gate and put the single on it. Try as he could he was not able to get the double on. It would have been fatal to leave the gate unlocked and it was even a little risky to leave it on the single, for all outside gates must be on the double.

'Never mind,' said Billy, 'some bastard will get a half-sheet.'

A half-sheet is the document a screw gets to answer when reported to the governor: for, say, leaving a gate on the single.

Billy and George crept across the parade-ground to behind the shoe-shop and made their way down towards the artisans' yard, a section of the prison where a ladder was kept chained up. For this they had no use, but just on the other side of the wall near the artisans' yard was a sloping shed, and therefore the drop would not be so far. George had a ladder made of mail-bag canvas stitched together, at one end a strong hook. This Billy slung to the top of the wall; the hook bit into the brick and held firmly. George gave Billy a lift and away he swarmed. On arrival at the top he was to haul George up.

Up to this point the escape had worked splendidly except for leaving the warders' hall gate on the single. No mistake had been made, and this error was unimportant. Whereas the odds against a successful escape from Parkhurst had been hundreds against, it now appeared a certainty for George and Billy to get away. They would not be missed till 7 o'clock next morning, and a boat left Ryde at 9.15 p.m. – the one late boat. They had clothes and money waiting for them. A boat leaves Southampton at 12.45 for Havre. George would have caught this. He was a Levantine, at home in France. Billy would have got to Ireland, and from there to America. The impossible would have been achieved, and the plan of escape might never have been known, for Billy, neat worker, had hidden the tell-tale holes in his door pretty well.

But 'lag's luck' ran true to form. As Billy drew near the top of the wall, Howell, a screw, finished addressing an envelope in the jailors' mess, which is part of the shoe-shop building. He then walked out of the mess to go to the gate to post his letter. As he passed the end of the building he turned his head, and for a second he caught Billy's shadow against the wall. He took another look, and saw the whole picture. He stepped quickly to the gate and blew his whistle. The gatekeeper rang the big bell. The hooter went off with an angry snarl, and Billy dropped off the wall.

Screws in the dark were rushing here and there. Lags were jumping up to the windows with excited enquiries: 'What is it? Fire?' 'No, escape.' 'Who?' 'God knows.'

George's quick brain saw a ray of hope. Could they get back to the cells? Whoever had spotted them could have no idea who they were.

'Bring the rope, Billy; we might beat it.' They ran swiftly through the darkness across the parade-ground to warders' hall. Billy took the gate off the single; they slipped in, Billy carefully put the gate back on the single. They crept into B hall, where the patrol, quite unaware that all the fuss was over two men away from his hall, was standing by the desk. George and Billy actually managed to avoid him to the extent of getting as far as their landing. Just a little good luck to balance the bad, and they might have been back in their cells, with the warders' hall gate on the single as the only clue. But 'lag's luck'! As George crept by the recess leading to the lavatory the patrol lifted his head to B4 landing, and saw George. His whistle shrilled like a siren; he ran to the alarm bell, and in a couple of seconds the place was alive with screws. George was caught by his cell door and Billy a few feet from his. Thus was foiled by 'lag's luck' the best-planned attempt to escape from Parkhurst ever made, certainly not through any virtue of the administration . . .

Another attempt into which a deal of planning went was made by an ex-Army champion runner, Willis.

Willis was employed on the farm, and was a semi-trusted man; indeed, he was not the type that tries to get away. With great diligence and craft he made himself a complete running outfit. It consisted of natty shorts made from his pillow-slip, with coloured stripes made from light blue American cloth used in the bookbinding department, and a singlet, edged with blue, made from the muslin that frozen meat is wrapped in. His cell slippers, suitably faked, suggested running-shoes.

Willis's work on the farm took him out of the prison about three-quarters of an hour before the parties come out to labour. During this time, and for half an hour or so afterwards, Willis was engaged in feeding the pigs, and was generally left on his own. Next to the prison is the Victoria Barracks, where an infantry battalion is always stationed. The regimental running team often exercised along the main Cowes–Ryde road. It was over a quarter of a mile from the farm to the main road, no wall intervened, and Willis could hope that a patrol spotting him would imagine that one of the soldiers had missed his way, run on to the prison estate, and was now getting back to the main road.

Willis would have perhaps two hours' start. After that he was going to take pot-luck. He had various ideas, and he may have stood a chance; but he'd only been away five minutes before another lag who'd seen him go ran to the farm-jailor. The alarm was given, and Willis was caught after an exciting chase. He got the usual bread and water.

There was one attempted escape where a whole party co-operated to give a man a chance to get away. Freddie Harris was a fine motor-driver doing six years for a mail-bag robbery. He was a decent little fellow, straightforward and universally liked. His imprisonment had come as a result of some despicable work by an associate, and the lags were sorry for him. This was his second lagging. He was working in a party doing general odd jobs, and on this morning they were engaged in carrying chairs and forms from the warders' club to the deputy-governor's garden. The prison staff was to be photographed, and the chairs were to be placed in position. The party had to traverse the prison gate a dozen times or so, and in their walking to and fro they passed the open shed where the higher officials' cars were parked. Asking one of his mates to get 'Old Aussie's nut' – i.e. distract the screw's attention – Harris nipped into Dr Snell's car and sped away. It was some minutes before Aussie missed Freddie. He looked all over the place for him. The party kept saying, 'He's in the lav'; 'He's in the club'; 'He's under the boy's hut trying for fag-ends,' and so on. Aussie kept looking here and looking there while Freddie was on his way to Cowes. Again 'lag's luck'! Usually the patrols are temporary screws who do not know the individual lag as well as the permanent screws, who may have been years in the prison. It just happened that on that morning 'Lofty' Harding, a very popular screw, well known by, and well knowing, every lag in the gaol, had been relegated to patrol duty. He knew Freddie well, and, when Freddie, muffled up in Snell's raincoat, sitting low in the seat, shot past, Lofty recognised him and gave the alarm. A thrilling chase began. Jumbo

Ennion, the deputy-governor, and two screws with batons hanging on to the side of his car, tore at sixty miles an hour after the runaway. Freddie was a cockney car bandit, and could out-drive anybody in the Isle of Wight. Away through the farms and lanes they tore, poultry screeching to the ditches. Once Freddie turned into a cul-de-sac, backed out, shot right in front of Jumbo's car, wheeled round, and was away before Jumbo could brake. One screw flung his stick at Freddie, but missed him. He led them a fine dance all over the Isle of Wight, but lack of knowledge of the country beat him, and at last Jumbo, in a quicker car, ran him into a ditch.

The screws rushed at Freddie, and Jumbo snarled at him, 'You bloody bastard! I've smashed my car over you.' He stopped the screws from clubbing Freddie though! Freddie was hauled back to gaol and slung into chokey.

Dear old Jumbo, with his beautiful Oxford accent, went down to the punishment cells to see his captive.

'I say, Harris, I'm awfully sorry I called you a bastard, but, you know, you jolly well upset me,' he explained.

'That's all right, dep. You upset me a jolly sight more when you caught me.' Freddie was sad but magnanimous . . .

Persistent escapers were few, but Joe Conning was a modern Jack Sheppard. Joe came from the Liverpool waterfront, and was a deep-sea sailor, a good fellow with a nose like Cyrano. He was doing four years at Dartmoor for robbery, and received a further ten years for his part in the mutiny, making a consolidated sentence of fourteen years.

Joe was a type somewhat rare in prison. He was class conscious, a trade unionist, and had worked on co-operative ships, and could compare them to their advantage with some capitalist lines. He had visited Soviet ships, and was enthusiastic about the life of the Soviet sailor. He'd sailed all over the world, and his criminal career was spasmodic and sporadic. He was a collectivist, easily affected by the herd or team spirit. He hated injustice, and would go up in the air if he saw anyone getting unjustly the dirty end of the stick. He was one of the most indiscreet men I've ever listened to, and yet, by dint of trying, he did get away from prison for a time. His first attempt at Parkhurst cost me remission and stage. He attempted to cut his bar. I got him a hack-saw blade, and with this he went to work. Either he was too noisy, or some lag in a near-by cell informed on him, or the cut was noticed in his bar; anyway, he was detected. The Saturday afternoon on which he was caught I had lent him a bound copy of the *Labour Monthly*. He admired Palme Dutt, and read his 'Notes of the Month' avidly. When Joe was taken to chokey, my *Labour Monthly* was in his cell. To lend books is forbidden. I endeavoured to get it out, but an attempt to escape in prison, besides being a breach of discipline, seems to affect the jailors like a personal insult. Indeed, in the first few years of my lagging, a man escaping, and caught, usually got a hiding. Therefore I was unsuccessful in my attempts to get my book, and on Monday I was taken to chokey. Joe was already there. I had no defence. I had lent a book, so I lost a month's special stage and had to stay in prison three days longer.

About a year after this the only attempt at escape on a grand scale was made.

About six men, all on my landing, made a plot to make a desperate escape. Joe was one of them. Keys were made to fit the cell doors; iron bars and rope ladders were obtained. The idea was for one to get out of his cell by boring through the wall into a cupboard on the landing. I happened to be in the cell next to the lavatory. A chap came to me and said:

'Mac, change cells, will you? I'd like the recess cell and you can have my cell. It's all faked up, newly painted, and need not be cleaned for months.'

My hatred of char work was well known in the prison. I agreed, and the change-over took place after a little wangling. The plot proceeded.

The chap who had obtained my cell was to get out of the cell into the cupboard, and then with the key release the others. Six of them would then seize the patrol; six big powerful fellows could easily and without violence have tied him up. They then would have opened the gate, scaled the wall, made their way to Cowes, and seized a boat. Four of them were sailormen, and they might have been successful in a night escape. In a day escape all the screws are on duty, and immediately rush to various tactical points in the island. Every screw has his post, and screws are placed at the gangway of the cross-Solent boats. At night this programme is more difficult to carry out than in the daytime.

Everything was set; all the stuff was smuggled into the cells. One had a rope ladder, another had a bar and hook, another the key, and so on.

That afternoon I had obtained for my tea a large strong Spanish onion, a little vinegar, and some white cheese from the governor's house. Tea was served, cells locked, unlocked and checked, landings checked; the screws fell in, keys were handed in, and I sat down to enjoy my onion – such a big one! Suddenly I heard the deputy-chief's voice give a loud command: 'Unlock!' A second after, I heard the keys turn in several cells – all near mine – the scuffling of feet, and a general disturbance.

What can this be? A general turn-over (search)? Such searches were known, but very rare. I don't recall a general prison search in my lagging. Whatever it was, cells were being opened. The deputy-chief was in the hall. I had vinegar, white cheese, and a big onion. I swilled the vinegar and wolfed the cheese. I ran to the window to get rid of the onion, looked out, and saw six screws placed at intervals, one just beneath my cell, to catch anything that might be thrown out of the cell windows. In the ordinary course of events nothing would be said about an onion – for this was 1934, after the Dartmoor mutiny – but if the jailors were panicky, and if something special were in process, to be found with an onion would mean chokey. I just had to get rid of it. At any moment my cell might open and three screws enter to strip me naked, turn my cell upside down, and rip the bedding to pieces. I could hide it nowhere. I could not throw it out of the window. I must eat it, eat it at once, too, without a pause, eat it as one eats an apple, and this onion was as big as a big apple. I took a large bite and chewed and swallowed. My throat burned, and tears as big as marbles came into my eyes, but I went on eating. I nearly died. My whole digestive tract roared its rejection of the outrage, but down it I kept forcing the onion. At last, in about one minute – it seemed nearly as long as my lagging – I had swallowed the last morsel and sat down, out to the world. I took some water and thought I should have a heart seizure. But I was safe. I stank, but they'd have to cut me open or give me an emetic before I could lose any remission on account of the onion.

And then I was not searched at all. Only the cells of those involved in the escape were opened. They had been betrayed – by one of their own band, it was said, but nothing was known for certain. They were all severely punished, and, on completion of their long period of bread and water, they were distributed round different prisons all over the country.

Joe Conning was sent to Durham, managed to break out of prison, and got as far as Gateshead in a snowstorm. In climbing over the wall, his shoes had dropped back into the prison yard. More 'lag's luck'. He was exhausted and his feet were torn. The debility every man suffers in prison militates against the great and prolonged physical effort needful to make a good getaway. Poor Conning was dead-beat, and so was recaptured. The gaol-house has it every way!

From CHAPTER XXIII: NOTES ON PRISON SEX LIFE

A GREAT DEAL OF MY YOUTH was spent in the Levant, and very early I was aware of sex. I was not ignorant. I entered the Army at fifteen, and was a commissioned officer at sixteen. I spent very little time at an English public school, and I can affirm that masturbation and homosexuality had no part whatsoever in my adolescence. I was married when twenty-three, and my married life was a happy period during which sex took its right place, never intruding, and never repressed. My attitude to homosexuality and the more moderate forms of perversion was tolerant. From the comfort of my own sex life, I could gaze amiably upon those who for some reason or other had to seek solace in what were to me untravelled paths. Little did I dream that these paths would one day become familiar.

Not until five months after I was sentenced did the libido sufficiently intrude itself so as to push out of the way the restraint imposed upon me by the shock of a ten years' sentence. At Brixton, awaiting trial, sex occasionally tried to assert itself, but by the exigencies of the situation it was relegated to the position of an uncomfortable travelling companion.

As I have noted elsewhere, one was frequently left in a cell over the week-end for forty-four hours without anything to read, and this was one of the main incitements to masturbation. When one has nothing to read, nothing to write, and a loathing of sewing mail-bags, so monotonous is it, the thoughts inevitably turn towards sex. I decided early in my prison life to deal with sex on a scientific basis. I use the word 'scientific' to define a process whereby I classified and recorded my sex impulses so as to get a good knowledge of what really happened to me. Every manifestation of auto-erotism was entered in my calendar. Later on, with other developments, I book-kept in the same way. I was thus able to control throughout the whole of eight years the increase and decrease of the sex urge. I may state definitely that the immediate post-masturbatory period was one of nausea and of self-distaste, and that I never got over this. For a normal man it is a wretched substitute. Miss Ethel Mannin, in an article in the *New Leader* dealing with Borstal boys, says that masturbation has no ill effects. From *Confessions and Impressions* we may gather that Miss Mannin's sex life had been too healthy for her to know anything of the effects of substitution.

The only way to master auto-erotism is to direct energy away from sex; but prison is a deliberate destroyer of all energy. The long hours in the cells, the lack of books, the apathy that grows on the prisoner, the absence of all interests and all hobbies, the hopeless outlook – these weaken the resistance. Masturbation is general in prison, and it is referred to openly and indifferently. When I went to prison, the idea of becoming even temporarily homosexual never entered my head. There are many homosexuals in gaol, and for at least four years I took no interest in them. The first knowledge that the mind was being perverted by the unnatural existence of gaol came to me through my dreams. The imagery began to change. The persistent, sharply accentuated image of womanhood became clouded after about three and a half years. Even when awake I began to find that fantastic images were pushing the original normal image out of the way. Gradually a homosexual shadow obscured the normal picture, and I began to have definitely homosexual dreams. I do not propose to enlarge further upon my own sex life, but I shall assert that within my observation the beneficial effects of such contacts upon the mental and physical health were undeniable, and my experience was that of the average man. Of course, some repressed themselves terribly and never consciously entered into this life. Others went to extremes and developed perversions that would make Krafft-Ebing's hair stand upright. Through the method of control I evolved, I was able to get a good idea of the effect of different aspects of prison life upon one's sexual activity in prison. The difference between solitary confinement and association was conspicuous.

For a period of six months I was orderly in a hospital ward, always in company, and with plenty of interest, whether it was chess or the work round the ward. I was looking after a tubercular case in a side ward, and seldom got to bed before twelve o'clock. I was up at five, and had a really busy time. Not *once* during the whole of this six months did sex intrude.

There were many out-and-out homosexuals in the prison, and these men were distinct characters. None was in for sexual offences. Ordinary criminal offences had sent them to prison, and here they were among the coolest, and frequently the soundest, men in the prison. Three or four stand out – particularly Elsie and Nora. Elsie was a tall, well-built blond, always beautifully made up, with trim golden hair, plucked and pencilled eyebrows, schoolgirl complexion, and rouged lips. One day he swayed past the tally-point heavily made up. The old chief jailor gazed at him, and then roared to an assistant jailor, 'Take it to the bath-house and scrub him.' And two lusty jailors dragged poor Elsie off, protesting, and washed 'her' clean.

Cosmetics came from a variety of sources, but were mostly improvised. Rouge was got from the dye in the red mail-bags. Powder was picked from the refuse tip. Sometimes, as in the case of Nora, whose lover was one of the jailors, the real stuff was forthcoming, with scent and ribbons and silk underwear as well.

Elsie, mentioned above, was never put out. A lover of his, working in the kitchen, and distracted by Elsie's infidelities, plunged a knife into himself. Was Elsie upset? Not a bit. She watched the whole drama, and then softly breathed, 'So silly. He's so jealous.' During Elsie's time, we had a deputy-governor who set himself to check homosexuality. This was one of the finest-built men I have ever seen. Six foot three, broad-shouldered, flat-backed, slim-hipped, his upright military carriage was rendered attractive by a slight and graceful sway in his carriage. He sent for the notorious Elsie.

'Now, my man, I want to talk to you seriously.'

'Yes, sir, what about?'

'I want you to give me, in confidence, the names of the men who pester you with their homosexual attentions. I am sure that you are really a decent fellow, and that you only lend yourself to these pernicious practices through fear. Possibly you are blackmailed into it. I mean to put an end to it all. Tell me their names, and I'll protect you.'

Elsie leered at him, and then simpered sweetly, 'Well, as one girl to another, do you think that would be playing the game?'

That homosexuality should take place between convicts is inevitable, and so tense is the prison atmosphere with the vibrations of suppressed sex that the jailors themselves are affected by it, and some of these men make homosexual contacts with their captives.

Nora, a pansy of repute, gained a prestige, something like that of a great courtesan, by a long affair with a jailor known as S—, who was a very decent fellow. He was a little dull; but he never shouted or took liberties with us, and in general he was well liked by the lag. S— was in charge of the landing where Nora was located. Nora was a short well-built young fellow, not bad-looking, but disfigured by a scarred neck. Nora had been temperamental once, and years ago had attempted to commit suicide. He had got over this phase, and he was now as cold as an iceberg and as mercenary as any calculating hussy could be.

It soon became apparent to us that old S— had fallen for Nora. He was always round the man's cell, often opening the door for no reason, and talking to Nora a lot. I was a few cells away, and, with others, I watched with interest the development of the affair. The prison morality of our landing was high. There were no informers on it, and all of us were accustomed to mind our own business and not butt in on others' pursuits. S— had a long and successful affair. We looked after him, and took good care that he was never trapped while he was in Nora's cell. The affair became notorious throughout the prison, and many attempts were made to catch S—, but they were always foiled. There was a general conspiracy to defend S— and Nora from interference. That disaster overtook S— eventually was due to his getting away from our care.

Nora, under the protection of an affluent jailor, bloomed. With real rouge, lipstick, powder, and scent, his cell smelt like Yardley's. His undershirt, boiled in alkali to shade down the harsh colour, was threaded with ribbon. Real handkerchiefs with lace borders sometimes appeared, and to see Nora take his Sunday exercise with his prison mittens folded to resemble a lady's handbag was as exhilarating as a walk in Hyde Park on a Sunday morning in spring. Nora finished his three years and was released. We considered that S— was a lucky man. Unfortunately, he persisted extramurally. He met Nora outside. He also wrote letters. Nora, who was a burglar, was taken up as a suspect, and poor S—'s correspondence was found on him. It was sent by the police to the Home Office, to the Prison Commissioners, and to the governor of the prison, and S— got the sack.

It must not be assumed that this was an isolated case. It was not. I once witnessed a jailor beaten up over a pansy. It was in hospital, and George, a good old lag, employed as the dispensary runner, was successfully in love with a pansy known as Jill. Charley, a 'searching' jailor, also desired the young man. One day, George, going along the landing where Jill was located, noticed his cell door slightly open. All cells must be kept locked. Surprised, he gently pushed open the door, and caught Charley. George was furious. He dropped his basket, tore them asunder, and started in to belt hell out of Charley. I came along the landing, heard the shindy, and looked in. A fine set-to was taking place. In the corner stood Jill, frightened out of his life. I guessed at once what it was all about, and immediately stopped the fight.

'You bloody fools! Do you want the sack, Charley? And do you, George, want to lose the best job in the prison? Shut up, you pair of idiots.'

They quieted down at once, and in a few minutes George was wiping the blood off Charley and cleaning him up, for Charley was a good screw, and, notwithstanding a gross betrayal like this, good 'screws' must be looked after. At the same time, George could not help moaning, while he sponged the bloodstained and swollen nose he had inflicted on his rival:

'You should be ashamed, and you a married man as well. I've a good mind to tell your old woman the next time I take the medicine round.'

'Shut up. If the chief sees me now, I'm finished; and so's your 'bacca. Give us that lint, Mac.'

None of us took the slightest notice of Jill, who was left to clean up his cell, which looked as if a tank had passed that way.

Parkhurst and Dartmoor differ from other prisons in that they are penal settlements and not just lock-ups. Clustered round Parkhurst prison are the dwellings of the jailors. Some of these are beautiful and well kept. All the maintenance work is done by the lag – carpentry, electricity, plumbing and painting and attending to the hundred-and-one jobs consequent upon keeping sixty or eighty houses in proper repair.

Men go in twos or threes, under the charge of a jailor, to do whatever work may be necessary in a particular house, and, as the sentences are very long, these workmen-lags become well known to the women-folk of the jailors. Most of these women are extremely good and kind to the convicts. They give them meals while the job is in progress. Although this practice is officially out of order, it is more or less connived at, and is one of those cases in which the administration acts more or less sensibly and humanely. Of course, the Home Office growl now and again, but, after all, a good meal is a good craftsman's perquisite, and it is one of the silly contradictions of the prison regulations that a man is expected to work as skilfully and willingly under an irksome supervision as he would in normal circumstances. This is impossible, and either the work is botched owing to the supervision or the work is well done and the supervision lapses. Thus a freer atmosphere is engendered, and with this freedom Cupid creeps between the handcuffs and laughs at locks – real ones – and bolts and bars, so that romances, mostly frustrated, between the convicts and the wives and daughters of the screws sometimes occur.

I often wondered what special sex urge fostered these romances. Did some of the women unconsciously sympathise with the poor lag so long deprived of the life essential and develop towards him a kind of 'Maya' attitude? Was it sentiment more than sensuality? Anyhow, whatever it was, romances there were. Love or lust, whichever you like, would beat anything.

One young fellow, N—, was working as a jobber in the house of a jailor called O—. O— was an old naval man of about fifty-five, married to a young upstanding woman of thirty or thereabouts. N— was good-looking, and physically very strong; with it he was merry and amusing, and ingenious. He once made himself some fine false teeth from cement. N—'s job at O—'s lasted a long time, and the jailor's wife and the convict fell crazily in love with each other. Their love was consummated in situations that make the winter-time difficulties of 'Liza of Lambeth' and her lover seem convenient. After a week-end locked up in his cell, N— would come out to labour with a wild look in his eyes, anxious to see which screw was detailed to take him to work at O—'s house. With an 'easy' screw things were not so bad, and old N—'s face would be full of smiles. A springy walk and squared shoulders told the world of his happiness. If, on the other hand, a 'no-good swine' was detailed, poor old N— was disconsolate; but he was full of fight, and fearless. He would mess up the work and complain to the foreman of works that the 'no-good swine' was interfering, and would agitate to have him taken off the job. Sometimes he got his way, for the foreman of works was interested in output and quality, not in discipline and morals, and N— was a magnificent worker, skilful and careful. N—'s sentence was three years, and his affair lasted intermittently the whole of this time. Mrs O— used to bust up her plumbing, rip the boiler or smash the copper in some way, so that N— would have to repair the damage caused by love and longing. At last, during the summer, N—'s sentence finished, and he was released. The children of the jailors have a sports day during the summer, with tents, races, flags, and whatnot. On this particular day, O— took the children to the sports, leaving his wife at home. N— visited the Isle of Wight that day, and left, with Mrs O—, by the 5 o'clock boat. O— returned home to find his wife gone and the tea unprepared.

The vicissitudes of N— and his sweetheart can be told briefly. N— had a fair amount of money, and the pair had a good time in a Midland town till the money ran out. Then N— went to blow a safe. He put in too much dynamite, and blew the safe, himself, and the shop up. He was picked up, nearly dead, and got five years; and the woman has stuck to him like a brick. She writes to him, and she is waiting for him to come out.

SPANISH TESTAMENT

by Arthur Koestler

(monthly choice, December 1937)

Spanish Testament was the book which launched Arthur Koestler (1905–83) as a writer. He had already been a journalist in Palestine, Paris and Berlin (and joined the Graf Zeppelin expedition to the North Pole). He had also become a member of the Communist Party, taken part in various Party activities and travelled to the USSR. Following the outbreak of war in Spain, it was suggested that he use his journalistic credentials to gain access to Francoist territory. To this end, he arranged to be a special correspondent of the London *News Chronicle*. Over the following months, Koestler reported from Seville and witnessed the siege of Madrid. Then, in February 1937, he was arrested by the Nationalist Army in Malaga and imprisoned pending execution. After several months, and thanks to pressure exerted on Franco by both the British and French governments, he was released in exchange for the wife of a fascist airman. His rescue made the front pages. Koestler travelled to England, where he wrote up the story of his capture and imprisonment as *Spanish Testament*.

Alick West, organiser of the LBC Writers and Readers' Group, recalled that when he spoke at meetings about Koestler's book he 'kept silent' about a strange part of the story: 'that when Franco's forces were advancing on Malaga, Koestler, against all political reason and duty, and under a "strange and uncomfortable fascination", got out of the car that was taking him from Malaga into Republican territory and was next day arrested by the fascists'. The circumstances of Koestler's capture, described in part of the following extract, are certainly unusual. At the end of January 1937, he arrived in Malaga just as it was about to be hit by a Nationalist offensive. Having decided not to join other journalists who were leaving for Valencia, he moved from his hotel to a villa owned by Sir Peter Chalmers-Mitchell, an expat Englishman (a former secretary of the Zoological Society and the creator of Whipsnade Zoo). It offered little sanctuary. Chalmers-Mitchell had recently written to *The Times* detailing Nationalist atrocities, and the advancing rebel forces had orders to arrest him.

Spanish Testament opens with Koestler's journey to Spain, but the bulk of the first section is an historical analysis of the origins of the war, written from a Communist Party perspective, with large doses of atrocity propaganda thrown in (much of this material had appeared in his earlier book, *L'Espagne ensanglantée*). Orwell later wrote that this part of *Spanish Testament* was too coloured by Popular Front orthodoxy: 'one or two passages even look as though they had been doctored for the purposes of the Left Book Club'. The more celebrated second part – later published separately as *Dialogue with Death* – is a personal recollection of imprisonment ('the lone individual within an apocalyptic world'), which describes the psychological effects of solitary confinement and the experience of hearing fellow prisoners dragged from their cells to be shot. In one passage, he recalls his response to hearing a condemned prisoner sing 'The Internationale' – he imagined the whole prison standing, with fists clenched in the Communist salute, experiencing 'a rapturous feeling of brotherly love and oneness with the others'.

'We are engaged in a struggle between life and death,' Laski wrote in his review of the book in *Left News*; 'Mr Koestler has made inescapably plain the character of that conflict.' The Club arranged a speaking tour for Koestler in January 1938 – he raced around Britain addressing a dozen towns in as many days. Despite all that he had written in *Spanish Testament*, however, Koestler was losing faith in Communism, and he later said that this lecture tour intensified his doubts. He was asked several times by Club members about the anarchist fighters in Spain who had recently been denounced by the Comintern. Koestler's reply – that he could not regard them as traitors – was always met by a 'short, embarrassed silence' from the eager audiences who expected, and wanted, a confirmation of the Communist Party line. Koestler left the Party weeks later; *Darkness at Noon* was published in 1940.

From PART I

ON JULY 18TH, 1936, when the Franco revolt broke out, I was staying at a little seaside resort on the Belgian coast, engaged in writing a pacifist novel.

It looked at first as though the revolt had proved abortive and that the Government was master of the situation throughout Spain. Then the news grew more and more alarming. By the end of a week it was clear that there was to be a civil war of long duration, with possible European complications. We greedily devoured a preposterous number of newspapers; the pacifist novel came to a standstill and found its way into a drawer, there to moulder away forgotten. *Requiescat in pace.*

The part played by the Press in the Spanish affair was from the outset a most peculiar one. The rebels refused to allow a single correspondent of any Left-wing or even Liberal newspaper into their territory, while correspondents of newspapers with pronouncedly Right-wing views were equally unwelcome on the Government side. Thus a state of affairs was rapidly created whereby, roughly speaking, the Right-wing newspapers had correspondents only on the Franco side, and the Liberal and Left Press only on the Government side. The communiqués from the respective headquarters were grossly contradictory, and almost as great were the discrepancies between the telegrams sent by the correspondents on both sides, for whom a drastic censorship, furthermore, made it impossible to send out unbiased messages.

The Spanish Civil War had, as it were, infected the Press of Europe.

In these circumstances, as a journalist of liberal convictions and author of fragments of pacifist novels – the first was brought to an untimely end by the outbreak of the Abyssinian War, and the third I shall never dare to embark upon – I was bound to be tempted by the idea of getting into rebel territory. I arranged with the *News Chronicle* to try my luck at getting into Seville. I fancied I stood a better chance of success than many of my colleagues, since as occasional theatre and film critic of the official organ of a Central European Government I was able to exploit certain connections.

At this time, the first month of the Civil War, Seville was still the headquarters of the rebels and likewise the central clearing station for the men and arms despatched from Germany and Italy. I felt some uneasiness; but I calculated that the worst that could happen to me was that I should be expelled. Man proposes . . .

On August 20th I went to Cook's and bought a ticket to Lisbon; two days later I embarked at Southampton.

From the moment of leaving Cherbourg an oppressive atmosphere hung over the ship. The steamer was called the *Almanzora*; it had left Southampton on August 22nd and was due to arrive at Lisbon on the 25th. It was full of Spaniards travelling to rebel territory; that is to say, they were either adherents of the rebel side or were behaving as though they were, since they had no desire to be arrested and denounced immediately on their arrival. Everyone was mistrustful of everyone else; we all sat in silence reading the wireless news from the war zone posted up on the noticeboard, scrutinised our fellow passengers, and gave them a wide berth.

The general tension was noticeable even in the first-class saloon, penetrating even that armour plate of icy boredom in which the Englishman on a sea voyage is so supremely able to encase himself. The Englishmen in the first class were almost all in sympathy with the rebels; having read their *Daily Mail* thoroughly, they were firmly convinced that the rebellion was a crusade to save civilization; they took Queipo de Llano to be a kind of Richard Coeur de Lion at the microphone, Azaña an Anarchist. Any attempt to disabuse their minds of at least this last misconception only invited mistrust. A knowledge of the facts was in itself sufficient to bring one under suspicion of being a 'red'.

In the third class opinions were divided. There was a sixteen-year-old Spanish boy who played around with a little Portuguese girl of about fifteen, sang charmingly to the guitar and was given to making cheeky remarks. Five days later I saw him in Seville being taken out of a van with a number of other prisoners and escorted through a line of gaping spectators into the headquarters of the Falange Española. His face was bruised black and blue, and tears were running down his grimy cheeks.

He did not recognize me, and I avoided making myself known to him; the next day he was shot in accordance with the usual custom.

On August 24th we touched at the rebel port of Corunna. A Portuguese destroyer and a French cruiser, *Le Triomphant*, lay ill at ease in the utterly silent harbour. A motor sloop flying the flag of the Spanish Monarchy, a yellow stripe on a red ground, surmounted by the Bourbon Crown, brought on board the port officials: a commissioner of police and a representative of the Phalanx. The Phalangist, who was obviously acting as an auxiliary policeman, a fat bespectacled youth of the type who has failed in his University examinations, planted himself down in the middle of the promenade deck so that he could be admired, raised his arm frequently in the Fascist salute, announced that Madrid had fallen the day before, that all Freemasons, Jews and Communists were going to be exterminated, that then, and then only, would life in the true sense begin, and politely accepted the foreign cigarettes that were offered him.

Vigo, the second rebel port that we touched at, presented a similar picture. Side by side with an English destroyer lay two Portuguese torpedo boats, and a little distance away a German Dornier-Wal flying-boat rocked peacefully back and forth in the water. Otherwise the harbour was utterly lifeless and glowed a sullen red under the grilling rays of the sun, as though under a silent, evil spell. And in peace-time Vigo is the largest sea-port for transatlantic shipping in the whole of Spain. To-day the town, situated as it is only twenty miles from the Portuguese frontier, is the centre of operations for the smuggling of German and Italian arms to the rebels. In Vigo itself there was nothing to betray this fact; the harbour was cordoned off by a double row of sentries, who looked as though they would not hesitate to shoot at sight . . .

I had anticipated having some difficulty in getting into rebel territory, and I therefore applied to a Central European Consul in Lisbon whom I knew for advice.

'You will, of course, have to get a visa,' said the Consul.

'A visa? From whom?'

'Why,' said the Consul. 'From Señor Gil Robles, of course.'

'Where am I to find Gil Robles?'

'Why, at the Embassy.'

It transpired that there were two Spanish Embassies in Lisbon.

In the one was the legal representative of the Madrid Government,

Sánchez Alvornoz, a sick man, entirely isolated, deserted by his staff, spied upon by the Civil Police; to all intents and purposes a prisoner of the Portuguese Government.

The other, the Black Embassy, calling itself the 'Agency of the Burgos Junta', had its offices at that time in the Hotel Aviz, and was run by two people who detested each other. One was Gil Robles; the other, who went under the alias of Hernández D'Avila, was Nicholás Franco, General Franco's youngest brother.

The Central European Consul of whom I have already spoken took me on the evening of my arrival to Estoril, the 'Le Touquet' of Portugal, an hour's journey out of Lisbon. The Consul was a very nice fellow, married to a Portuguese aristocrat and therefore on friendly terms with the rebel leaders. At the Estoril Casino we came across a great number of them, some sitting at the bar, some playing bac, others trente-et-quarante. It was altogether a curious company that was gathered here in this Casino behind the front lines of the Little Iberian World War: the Ambassador of a Balkan State (Heaven knows why this state maintains an embassy in Portugal) was reeling about, obviously the worse for drink, among the dancing couples on the terrace; a Japanese and a Hungarian attaché were whispering at the bar, evidently thinking themselves terribly important; while ladies of the Portuguese aristocracy, my friend's wife among them, went to and fro among the company with collecting sheets, 'for Franco's hospitals', as they said with a flutter of their eyelids. The atmosphere was just such as one might find in Shanghai or Harbin. Most of the ladies and gentlemen were slightly tipsy and all were filled with a great sense of their own importance. It obviously gave them great satisfaction to be able to point out to a foreign journalist that so-and-so was a spy or an arms smuggler or a foreign agent. If one had taken them seriously, one might have imagined that half Estoril consisted of super-spies, all playing the part of 'The Man who was Thursday'.

This visit to the Casino as an introduction to the Civil War was to prove useful, after all. For I got to know one or two leading figures of the rebel aristocracy socially, as it were, and I even gained permission to put up at the Hotel Aviz. There I made the acquaintance of some more leading officials at the Lisbon rebel headquarters, amongst them Franco's brother, Gil Robles, the Marqués de Quintanar and the Marqués de la Vega de Anzo, both of the Falange Española, and Señor Mariano de Amadeo y Galarmendi, who posed as 'Spanish Ambassador'.

The atmosphere at rebel headquarters was completely unlike that at the Casino.

In the Hotel Aviz there prevailed a bizarre mixture of conspiratorial secrecy and court ceremonial: one had a feeling that all these black-coated gentlemen, as they discussed, in hushed whispers and in tones of exquisite courtesy, gun-running, plans for the offensive, exchange transactions, and, last but not least, the commission accruing therefrom, imagined their necks to be still encased in the starched ruffles of the Court of Philip the Second. The only exception was Gil Robles. When the Marqués de la Vega de Anzo presented me to him as an English newspaper correspondent, he flatly and abruptly turned his back on us, to the silent consternation of his assembled staff. This was a piece of luck for me, for the Marqués, his former secretary, proceeded to reproach him at such length for his undiplomatic handling of the Press that he finally gave me, in addition to my rebel passport, a letter of recommendation in his own handwriting to General Queipo de Llano in Seville (which in its turn produced the unexpected result that the latter, who was on terms of open hostility with Gil Robles, kept me waiting for four hours for an interview).

During my stay in the Hotel Aviz I had ample opportunity of collecting evidence with regard to the activities of the Portuguese rebel headquarters. Later on I had occasion to give evidence in London with regard to these activities before the Committee of Enquiry into breaches of International Law relating to Intervention in Spain.

Since that time the fact that the Portuguese Government is virtually in a state of war with Madrid has gradually become common knowledge in Europe, so that there is no longer any point in recapitulating these things.

I stayed in Lisbon only thirty-six hours . . .

My stay in Seville was very instructive and very brief.

My private hobby was tracking down the German airmen; that is to say, the secret imports of planes and pilots, which at that time was in full swing, but was not so generally known as it is to-day. It was the time when European diplomacy was just celebrating its honeymoon with the Non-Intervention Pact. Hitler was denying having despatched aircraft to Spain, and Franco was denying having received them, while there before my very eyes fat, blond German pilots, living proof to the contrary, were consuming vast quantities of Spanish fish, and, monocles clamped into their eyes, reading the *Völkischer Beobachter*.

There were four of these gentlemen in the Hotel Cristina in Seville at about lunchtime on August 28th, 1936. The Cristina is the hotel of which the porter had told me that it was full of German officers and that it was not advisable to go there, because every foreigner was liable to be taken for a spy.

I went there, nevertheless. It was, as I have said, about 2 o'clock in the afternoon. As I entered the lounge, the four pilots were sitting at a table, drinking sherry. The fish came later.

Their uniforms consisted of the white overall worn by Spanish airmen; on their breasts were two embroidered wings with a small swastika in a circle (a swastika in a circle with wings is the so-called 'Emblem of Distinction' of the German National-Socialist Party).

In addition to the four men in uniform one other gentleman was sitting at the table. He was sitting with his back to me; I could not see his face.

I took my place some tables further on. A new face in the lounge of a hotel occupied by officers always creates a stir in times of civil war. I could tell that the five men were discussing me. After some time the fifth man, the one with his back to me, got up and strolled past my table with an air of affected indifference. He had obviously been sent out to reconnoitre.

As he passed my table, I looked up quickly from my paper and hid my face even more quickly behind it again. But it was of no use; the man had recognized me, just as I had recognized him. It was Herr Strindberg, the undistinguished son of the great August Strindberg; he was a Nazi journalist, and war correspondent in Spain for the Ullstein group.

This was the most disagreeable surprise imaginable. I had known the man years previously in Germany at a time when Hitler had been still knocking at the door, and he himself had been a passionate democrat. At that time I had been on the editorial staff of the Ullstein group, and his room had been only three doors from mine. Then Hitler came to power and Strindberg became a Nazi.

We had no further truck with one another but he was perfectly aware of my views and political convictions. He knew me to be an incorrigible Left-wing Liberal, and this was quite enough to incriminate me. My appearance in this haunt of Nazi airmen must have appeared all the more suspect inasmuch as he could not have known that I was in Seville for an English newspaper.

He behaved as though he had not recognized me, and I did the same. He returned to his table.

He began to report to his friends in an excited whisper. The five gentlemen put their heads together.

Then followed a strategic manoeuvre: two of the airmen strolled towards the door – obviously to cut off my retreat; the third went to the porter's lodge and telephoned – obviously to the police; the fourth pilot and Strindberg paced up and down the room.

I felt more and more uncomfortable and every moment expected the Guardia Civil to turn up and arrest me. I thought the most sensible thing would be to put an innocent face on the whole thing, and getting up, I shouted across the two intervening tables with (badly) simulated astonishment:

'Hallo, aren't you Strindberg?'

He turned pale and became very embarrassed, for he had not expected such a piece of impudence.

'I beg your pardon, I am talking to this gentleman,' he said.

Had I still had any doubts, this behaviour on his part would in itself have made it patent to me that the fellow had denounced me. Well, I thought, the only thing that's going to get me out of this is a little more impudence. I asked him in a very loud voice, and as arrogantly as possible, what reason he had for not shaking hands with me.

He was completely bowled over at this, and literally gasped. At this point his friend, airman number four, joined in the fray. With a stiff little bow he told me his name, von Bernhardt, and demanded to see my papers.

The little scene was carried on entirely in German.

I asked by what right Herr von Bernhardt, as a foreigner, demanded to see my papers.

Herr von Bernhardt said that as an officer in the Spanish Army he had a right to ask 'every suspicious character' for his papers.

Had I not been so agitated, I should have pounced upon this statement as a toothsome morsel. That a man with a swastika on his breast should acknowledge himself in German to be an officer in Franco's army, would have been a positive tit-bit for the Non-Intervention Committee.

I merely said, however, that I was not a 'suspicious character', but an accredited correspondent of the London *News Chronicle*, that Captain Bolín would confirm this, and that I refused to show my papers.

When Strindberg heard me mention the *News Chronicle* he did something that was quite out of place: he began to scratch his head. Herr von Bernhardt too grew uncomfortable at the turn of events and sounded a retreat. We went on arguing for a while, until Captain Bolín entered the hotel. I hastened up to him and demanded that the others should apologize to me, thinking to myself that attack was the best defence and that I must manage at all costs to prevent Strindberg from having his say. Bolín was astonished at the scene and indignantly declared that he refused to have anything to do with the whole stupid business, and that in time of civil war he didn't give a damn whether two people shook hands or not.

In the meantime the Civil Guards had actually arrived on the scene, with fixed bayonets and pugnacious expressions, to arrest the 'suspicious character'. Bolín angrily told them to go to the devil. And to the devil they went.

I decamped there and then from the confounded Cristina. Arrived at my hotel, I began hurriedly to pack. I had hardly finished when a French colleague of mine came up to my room and privately advised me to leave for Gibraltar as quickly as possible. He was obviously acting as the mouthpiece of some higher authority; but he refused to say whom. He merely said that he had heard of the shindy and that the whole affair might turn out very seriously for me.

Eight hours later I was in Gibraltar.

Twenty-four hours later I learned from private sources that a warrant for my arrest had been issued in Seville.

So Strindberg junior had had his say after all.

I didn't care two hoots, I thought. Seville has seen the last of me.

There I was wrong.

* * *

Saturday, February 6th [1937, Malaga]
Several air raids during the morning. No news from London since Thursday, so feel certain my messages are not getting through. Went to Civil Governor's Residence, as I wanted to find out whether I could use radio for SOS message telling the world that Italian troops are going to capture Malaga. But at the Governor's Residence they've all lost their heads. Went to military headquarters with same object, but Villalba is invisible and has left orders that *la presse – la presse, c'est moi* – is not to be allowed to cable anything about the military situation except

optimistic propaganda stuff. Army people always imagine that if they call a defeat a victory it *is* a victory and the dead will arise. They believe in the magical effect of lying propaganda just as bushmen do in the prayers of the witch doctor.

In the meantime G.G. has got ready to leave. An official is taking her in his car to Valencia. I have just time to scribble a few words on a scrap of paper for her to phone from Valencia to the Foreign Editor of the *News Chronicle*: 'Malaga lost. K. staying. Try to obtain appointment of Sir Peter Chalmers-Mitchell as acting honorary Consul so that he may mitigate the slaughter.'

At 2 p.m. the exodus from Malaga begins. The road to Valencia is flooded with a stream of lorries, cars, mules, carriages, frightened, quarrelling people.

This flood sucks up everything and carries it along with it: civilians, deserting Militiamen, deserting officers, the Civil Governor, some of the General Staff. From the arteries of Malaga it sucks all its powers of resistance, its faith, its morale. Nothing can resist its magnetic force. The road to the east has become a road for one-way traffic. Nothing more coming through from the capital; no munitions, no food, no organizer, no saviours – although even now it is not too late.

Nobody knows the fate of this stream once it is lost beyond the first bend in the road to the east. Odd rumours go the rounds in Malaga: the rebels have already occupied Vélez, the next town to the east, about thirty miles away; the stream of refugees is flowing into a death trap. According to another rumour the road is still open, but under fire from warships and aeroplanes, which are mowing down the refugees with machine-guns. But nothing can stop the stream; it flows and flows, and is incessantly fed from the springs of mortal fear.

At 4 o'clock I decide to have a look at what is happening in Vélez. My driver, although he is a former Militiaman, is infected by the panic; he tries to persuade me to drive on through Vélez to Valencia and not to come back. To calm him I tell him that we will decide when we get to Vélez. As the car drives off I can see that all our luggage is stowed away in it, although I have given no orders for this to be done.

We let ourselves be carried along by the stream to the little fork that branches off from the coast to the north. The town of Vélez itself lies some miles inland. The road is still open. We drive into Vélez.

The Militiamen of the routed army lie sleeping on the pavements – in the cafés, in doorways, in public buildings. There is no order, no discipline – complete chaos.

Our car is immediately surrounded by a group of Anarchist Militiamen. 'This car is requisitioned.' 'What for?' 'To dynamite the bridge on the road to Ventas.' 'But I've been told that the bridge has already been blown up.' 'Shut up and get out of the car.' After a little palavering I persuade the Anarchist leader to come with me to military headquarters. It is deserted. A solitary Civil Guard is killing flies in the courtyard. 'Where is the Commandant?' 'If you want to see the Commandant you must address a written request to him.' 'Are you mad? The rebels are only three miles from the town.' 'You're joking. The rebels are fifty miles to the north, the other side of Ventas.' 'Can't you hear the machine-guns? That's the rebels.' When the man at last realizes that we are speaking the truth, he reacts in an odd way: clutching his head with both hands, he runs off and vanishes. The Anarchist, I don't know why, runs after him and also vanishes.

We ask everybody where the Commandant is; nobody knows and nobody cares. At last we find him in a restaurant – he looks dog-tired and has apparently not slept for at least two days; he is listening calmly to three Militiamen, who all speak at once, gesticulating wildly, while he carefully peels himself an orange.

'If you are a newspaperman look around you and you won't need to ask any questions.' 'What about the bridge to Ventas?' 'We blew it up an hour ago.' 'How long will it take to build a temporary bridge?' 'Twelve hours.' 'And then?' No answer. The Commandant shrugs his shoulders and peels a fresh orange very carefully. Then he asks: 'Are you going back to Malaga?'

The driver: 'No, to Valencia.'

I: 'Yes, back to Malaga.'

'Then please take my political Commissar with you to Malaga. I have no car. Maybe he can get some munitions for us.' 'No munitions in Malaga either.' 'I know. Still—'

We hurry away. The driver is completely unnerved. He complains that somebody has stolen his cigarettes out of the car while we have been talking to the Commandant. The Commissar asks him whether he has nothing better to worry about at this moment; and he answers, pale, stubborn: 'No.'

We fight our way against the stream back to Malaga.

As soon as we get back to Malaga, and stop at headquarters, the driver declares categorically that he won't stay any longer. As a matter of fact, I have neither the right nor the power to keep him; I only ask him to take my luggage from the hotel to Sir Peter Chalmers-Mitchell's house, since the critical moment seems to have arrived. Twenty minutes later driver and car disappear along the Valencia road, and with them the last chance of getting away.

It is dawn now. I feel very lonely, and abandoned, and sit down on the staircase at headquarters. Colonel Alfredo comes along and sits down beside me. After a while he says: 'This is probably our last night. The road will be cut off in a few hours, and they will kill us like rats in a trap.'

'What are you going to do if they come?'

He taps his revolver. 'I've still got five cartridges. Four for the Fascists, the fifth for myself.'

I have an uneasy feeling that he is acting a part, and the absurd idea occurs to me that Alfredo and the Commandant of Ventas and the Anarchist and the Civil Guard and all the others, including myself, are just children playing at being Walter Scott heroes and unable to visualize the stark reality of death.

It is completely dark now; uninterrupted grumbling of cannon and coughing of machine-guns behind the hill.

Alfredo takes me to the officers' canteen. I fill my pockets with dry bread and two bottles of cognac. Then I stagger through the pitch dark city to Sir Peter's house, which has the Union Jack planted on its white roof.

Sunday, February 7th

Breakfast air raid at 8 a.m. The noise of artillery and machine-guns incessant now. Later on another air raid. One of the planes, a white monoplane, swoops scarcely a hundred feet above the house, screaming and scattering bullets. Lola, Sir Peter's housemaid, has hysterics.

We climb the hill opposite to get a good view. We can hear the bombardment more clearly, here and there we can see white puffs of smoke, but it is impossible to gain a clear picture of the strategic position.

On our way back we see thick smoke pouring out of the windows of the house adjoining ours. The house, lying in the midst of a large park, belongs to a rich Spaniard, who after the outbreak of the Civil War fled abroad with the help of Sir Peter. Now it is used as a temporary hospital. After a time the smoke becomes less dense and then stops entirely. Obviously the building has not been set alight by a bomb, but by a chance conflagration.

To think that such a thing is still possible . . .

After lunch – lunch is an exaggeration – went into the town. Since yesterday the physiognomy of the town completely changed; no more trams, all shops closed, groups at every corner and every face shrouded in the grey cobweb of fear. Brilliant sunshine, the sky a glaring blue, but the wide wings of death are outspread and envelop the town. Just as I am passing Caleta Bridge a squadron of six rebel planes flies very low above our heads, sowing murder. I look for shelter beyond the bridge; there are two Militiamen drinking cognac, one singing the 'Internationale', the other, in a low voice and with a stupid smile, the hymn of the Falange. I feel the contagion of fear getting me, too.

Reach headquarters; it looks like a night refuge; inhuman-looking men asleep on desks and floors. While I wait to be received by Colonel Villalba an exhausted sergeant staggers in and is conducted straight to the Colonel. I enter with him.

'What news?' asks Vallalba.

'They are coming down the Colmenar road with fifteen tanks.'

'How far are they?'

'An hour ago they were five miles from the city.'

'Resistance?'

'None. Our people threw away their rifles and made off to the Sierra.'

'Thank you.'

The sergeant slumps down under a table and immediately falls asleep. Villalba has a short whispered conversation with some of his staff officers. An order is given to an aide-de-camp and they leave the room rather hurriedly.

I stop Villalba. 'What do you want?' he says nervously. 'Can't you see I'm in a hurry? I can give you the following statement: The situation is critical, but Malaga will put up a good fight.'

'Where are you going?' I ask him. But he is already gone.

I rush to a window and look down. Villalba and his staff officers are getting into a car. Everybody is looking rather embarrassed. The car leaves the courtyard.

'Where is he going?' I ask an officer whom I know.

'He has deserted,' the officer says calmly.

'It was his duty to leave,' says another one. 'We shall be cut off in an hour, and he is the Commanding Officer of the entire southern sector; so he had to leave.'

'How can he command if we are cut off?'

'He has deserted,' repeats the first one.

'Who is boss now?' I ask.

'Boss?' Everybody looks surprised. Nobody knows.

I go into another room. There is Colonel Alfredo sitting at a typewriter. It is all like a bad dream. I note that he is using the red half of the ribbon. I read:

> To all whom it may concern. This is to certify that Colonel Alfredo G. is leaving on an important mission to Valencia. Authorities are requested to let him pass.

'You too, Alfredo?' I ask him.

He blushes. 'And you, too. I'll take you in my car. It's all up.'

This is no longer Walter Scott. It is, rather, James Joyce.

In the courtyard we find X. a common friend. He is ill; a high temperature, coughing and spitting.

'Come,' says Alfredo, 'it is all over.'

'Go to hell. I'm staying,' said X.

'Villalba has left too. We'll take you by force,' says Alfredo, tears in his eyes.

'Go to hell,' says X. (He is dead now. Eighty per cent of the persons mentioned in this story are dead.)

We step into Alfredo's car. Alfredo's mother is in the car, and Alfredo's sister and some other women, all crying and sobbing.

When the car starts I remember Sir Peter; during the last hour I have completely forgotten him.

'We must take my English friend,' I say to Alfredo.

'Impossible,' says the driver, 'the Fascists are on the New Road; his house is cut off.'

'But I only left him an hour ago!'

'They've entered the town since. Can't you hear the machine-guns?'

I hesitate. We reach the city barrier. The crowd of refugees stares at us, privileged owners of a car, with envy and hatred.

A feeling of deep disgust suddenly comes over me; my nerves are all to pieces.

'Stop,' I say to the driver. 'I want to go back.'

'Don't stop,' says Alfredo.

I jump out of the car. Alfredo gesticulates wildly. The car disappears in the crowd.

It is dusk again. I walk back slowly to Sir Peter's house. The rebels are not yet here.

They came the next day.

From PART II

DIALOGUE WITH DEATH

THEY CAME ON Monday afternoon.

But as yet it is only Sunday. There is yet time to get away. It is dusk, and the sombre, flaccid shadows of the Andalusian night are rapidly closing in round the dying Malaga. No electric light. No trams. No policemen at the corners of the streets. Nothing but darkness, no sound but the death-rattle of a strangled city: a shot, a drunken, muttering cry, a whimpering somewhere in the next street.

Militiamen run through the streets, demented, aimless. Women in black mantillas flit along like bats in the shadows of the houses. From somewhere or other comes the sound of splintering glass – the window of a car . . .

There is still time to get away . . .

Sir Peter's house is on a hill half a mile outside the town. I wander across the dark fields and find myself outside the park gate of a large, villa-like building. I assume it is the hospital we saw burning early this morning. Now it is dark and deserted, an enchanted castle. I knock for a long time on the door of the porter's lodge; after a while the porter appears, grasping a revolver. His whole body trembles and the revolver trembles with it . . .

Sir Peter is sitting at his writing desk in the light of an oil lamp, apparently oblivious of what is going on outside – a perfect Victorian idyll in the midst of the apocalyptic flood. I feel rather like a Job's comforter; moreover, quite absurdly, I feel conscience-stricken because I am late for dinner and my clothes are dirty – on the way here there was another air raid and I had to grovel among the furrows.

At dinner – two sardines, some jam, and two bottles of excellent Spanish white wine – I tried once more to persuade Sir Peter to leave the town. Looked at objectively, it was downright crazy to stay. Sir Peter had published a letter in *The Times* attacking the rebels, and had engaged in open propaganda in favour of the Spanish Government in England; while I myself, since my Seville adventure and the publication of the book that I wrote following upon it, had become one of the best-hated journalists at rebel headquarters.

'Look here, I am not going to run away,' said Sir Peter in his dry fashion. 'To-morrow, when the rebels come, they may possibly shoot fifty thousand people. All the consuls have gone, and there are no foreigners left. If they know that I, a "distinguished observer", am here, perhaps they'll only shoot forty thousand. And even if my presence makes no difference, I want to stay. Never yet, either in Badajoz or in Toledo, has a journalist been a witness of what happens when the rebels enter a town. I think it is worth while staying for that.'

Then he tried to persuade me to leave him alone, since I was far more compromised than he.

Whereupon I tried to make him see that I could not possibly leave him alone – after all, he was a man of seventy-three and I a man of thirty-two. Despite the solemnity of the occasion, this was an argument that was not to dear Sir Peter's taste.

In the intervals of conversation we sipped Spanish white wine, and it was all rather like the last days of Pompeii.

Then we went out on to the terrace and saw in the distance beyond the dark hills a row of shining points of light, like a chain of fairy lamps at a fête, which seemed scarcely to move; they were the rebel tanks coming down the mountains from Colmenar. The sight of them sobered us a little. Sir Peter went to his room and came back with two small metal cases, that looked like Gillette razor sets. Each contained a hypodermic syringe, with a reserve needle and a tube of morphine tablets.

'Look here,' said Sir Peter, 'I have seen the illustrations in your book' – he meant the photographs of Franco's tortured and mutilated victims – 'and I don't like the thought of it. I don't want them to get me alive.'

Then he explained to me with scientific thoroughness how to use a hypodermic syringe. The tube contained sufficient tablets to enable one to escape from all the horrors of all wars, civil and otherwise.

'One must disinfect the needle over a flame, of course, before giving oneself an injection,' explained Sir Peter, 'or one may get an abscess.'

I remarked that in the present situation an abscess more or less was of no great consequence. Sir Peter said that my remark was logically unassailable.

I went straight into the bathroom and practised giving myself subcutaneous injections. Through the window I could see the fairy lights of the tanks slowly drawing nearer, and yet I had a feeling that I was carrying out a perfectly absurd and nonsensical experiment, the sort of thing for which my father used to threaten to spank me.

Afterwards we switched over to gin and vermouth and wise and philosophic conversation. From the town isolated shots rang out, and we heard the occasional abrupt bark of a machine-gun. Our great ambition was to ignore these disturbing sounds and refuse to allow them to spoil our chat. There was obviously a certain element of snobbishness in our attitude, and I think Sir Peter was as aware of this as I; but we both probably felt that in our present situation a little snobbishness was excusable.

I have a profound horror of all melodrama, and that is why I dwell on these psychological details. Were every instance of so-called heroic behaviour to be examined under the microscope there would be fewer heroes and less hero-worship in the world, and I believe it would be to the world's advantage. Psychology is the *bête-noir* of dictators.

THE THEORY AND PRACTICE OF SOCIALISM

by John Strachey

(monthly choice, November 1936)

This book was the LBC 'bible'. Gollancz claimed that its popularity among subscribers rivalled that of *Walls Have Mouths*. In the months after its publication, the local Club branches ran four-week study courses structured around the book; lectures amplifying its message were given by John Strachey (1901–63) himself and other LBC regulars. According to John Lewis, the co-ordinator of the groups,

> no single book more completely filled the basic aim of the Club: to provide that disciplined study, rooted in fact and illuminated by theory, which was what the Club wanted to give its members. It stiffened the fibres of a Club whose sympathetic feeling and genuine passion needed precisely this basic *understanding* of the forces at work in capitalist civilisation.

Many LBC subscribers would have encountered Strachey's ideas before, if only in his regular and long articles for *Left News*. His Marxist interpretation of contemporary politics became something of a mantra: declining rates of profit under capitalism were leading to ever deeper economic crises, one of the manifestations of which was mass unemployment. The political oppression required to cope with this situation was, sooner or later, ending in fascism, built around existing state structures. Declining profits at home were also stimulating the search for outlets overseas, encouraging an intense competition to grab new territories. The inevitable result was war between the fascist, imperialist states. There was no way out, Strachey insisted, except Soviet-style Communism: social democracy had simply led a passive working class to defeat after defeat.

What follows is taken from the Introduction to *The Theory and Practice of Socialism.*

THIS BOOK ATTEMPTS to say plainly what the working-class movement of the world is striving for.

Such general re-statements of socialism and communism become necessary from time to time. For socialism and communism are living, growing concepts. Moreover, there are to-day special reasons for attempting to say exactly what socialism and communism are, and are not. Socialism has now been established in one of the major countries of the world. Hence a more positive, descriptive, constructive, and a less analytical, negative, and critical, approach to the subject is now possible. Formerly socialism existed only as a doctrine, a critique of things as they are, and an aspiration towards things as they might be. To-day it exists as the institutions of a great state. Before this incarnation the positive approach attempted in these pages was impossible; it would have led to no more than fantasy-building and dreaming. Then it was necessary to put almost all the emphasis on the analysis of capitalism; now it is possible to shift the emphasis to the elucidation of socialism.

But the capitalist five-sixths of the world also supply urgent reasons for making an attempt to re-define the goal of socialists and communists. In the highly developed capitalist empires, in Britain for example and to a lesser extent in America, there exist long-established movements, based upon the working class, which have the abolition of capitalism and the establishment of socialism as their objective. These movements possess an enormous literature and a rich tradition of socialism. But some of the events of the last two decades have tended to blur the conception of socialism as the sole possible solution for the world's present agony. By a tragic paradox, at the very moment when socialism has been securely established on the face of the earth for the first time in history, and when the conditions of human life in the rest of the world cry aloud for the socialist solution, some of the oldest and most powerful socialist movements, such as the British, have allowed themselves to become confused, to lose direction and so to slacken their efforts to produce a living realization of the necessity of social change in the minds of men . . .

The British labour and socialist movement has suffered severe defeats in the last fifteen years because its comprehension of both the socialist objective and of the methods necessary to social change was inadequate. This inadequacy resulted in an attempt to go forward towards socialism along a road which could only lead, and which did lead, to temporary defeat. But already it is clear that the effect of the setbacks to the British labour movement which culminated in the political defeat of 1931 could not, in contemporary conditions, last long. In 1848 the defeat of Chartism, which was the first wave of British working-class revolt against capitalism, set our movement back by nearly fifty years; the equally severe defeats of 1926 and 1931 could delay the rising of the tide by a decade at most. For the tide of British working-class resistance to capitalism is once more rising. But what is not yet decided is the vital question of the degree of political and economic clarity to which the British workers will attain in this new phase of their century-old struggle. They can only win if this time not only the leaders, but every active member of the British working-class movement, attains to a higher consciousness of the goal for which he is struggling, and of the necessary methods of struggle.

There has appeared in the last five years in Britain a quite unprecedented volume of literature, both in books and in periodicals, aiming at the achievement of this higher level of political consciousness and clarity in the working-class movement. This literature is symptomatic of the fact that the events of the last fifteen years have not been in vain. Now that once again life itself is forcing the British workers to feel that socialism is their only way out, they are coming to realize also the need for the adoption of new methods and new principles of political struggle. And this is doubly necessary. For not only did the old methods prove totally inadequate but also the new wave of working-class activity is rising in conditions which are far more complex and far more stormy than any which have ever before faced our movement. The first aim of this book is to make a contribution to the creation of that sharp, clear, passionate realization both of what socialism is and of how it may be established, without which the British working-class movement cannot triumph in the struggles that lie before it.

In America the situation is very different. There the economic and social forces capable of creating a working-class movement determined on the abolition of capitalism and the establishment of socialism only came to maturity with the 1929 crisis. But already such a movement is beginning to take shape. That America will possess, within the next decade, a powerful labour movement is not in doubt. Moreover, that movement will almost certainly be in some sense and degree anti-capitalist and pro-socialist. But what is not decided, and what is all-important, is the quality of the socialism of the coming American labour movement. Hence in America, even more than in Britain, though for different reasons, the need of the hour is the unceasing definition, re-statement and popularization of the basic principles of socialism and communism. The second, and equally important, purpose of this book is to make a contribution to this work.

In this connection it may be well to define at the outset how the words socialism and communism are used in these pages. For the history of both the working-class movement and of the social science which that movement has evolved out of its struggles may be unfamiliar to some readers. Throughout the last century Marx and Engels used the words socialism and communism almost indifferently. Moreover, up till 1917 Lenin referred to himself as a Socialist or Social Democrat. It was not until the April of that year that he proposed to change the name of the Party which he led. He made his proposal in these words: 'I am coming to the last point, the name of our party. We must call ourselves the Communist party – just as Marx and Engels called themselves Communists . . . Mankind can pass directly from Capitalism only into Socialism, i.e. into social ownership of the means of production and the distribution of products according to the work of the individual. Our party looks farther ahead than that: Socialism is bound sooner or later to ripen into Communism, whose banner bears the motto, "From each according to his ability, to each according to his needs."' (the 'April Theses') . . .

Lenin states that communists are persons who work for the establishment of socialism and that they call themselves communists rather than socialists for certain historical reasons, and also because they look forward to a state of human society beyond socialism for which they reserve the word communism.

It is true, however, that there are important differences within the working-class movement as to the proper methods, policies, and forms of organization by means of which capitalism may be replaced by socialism.

The problems with which this book attempts to grapple seem to me to be worthy of the attention not only of the British and American workers but also of those whose economic existence is relatively satisfactory. For some of this fortunate minority such questions as the comparative merits of economic systems, based respectively on production for profit and production for use, may seem remote from the daily business of their lives. But they are not. Those of us to whom fate has been comparatively kind would like to ignore these problems, for they put into question the very foundations of our contemporary society. We inevitably long to be allowed to lead our own personal lives against the background of a society which, however imperfect, is at any rate stable. But the society in which we live is not stable. We can no more escape its perturbations by refusing to take part in the social struggles of our times, than a frightened passenger can escape from a shipwreck by locking himself up in his cabin.

Thus ever-increasing numbers of relatively well-circumstanced men and women are now finding themselves impelled to examine the basis of contemporary society. A growing number of them are beginning to find that they cannot live lives which yield them an adequate degree of either mental or physical satisfaction in the existing world. Amongst the economically privileged there are, as there always have been, men and women who find it impossible to bear in silent complacency the sufferings, which they now see to be totally unnecessary, of by far the greater number of their fellow men. But it is the peculiar characteristic of our times that the property-owning members of society are themselves beginning to experience the effects of a contracting economic system.

In Britain and America the greater number of them have as yet maintained their incomes fairly well. But to an ever-increasing extent they find, and will find, that there are no constructive tasks left for them within the framework of capitalism. They will find that no longer can they, as did the fathers and grandfathers of the contemporary capitalist class, create both a fortune for themselves and some major productive enterprise (some new railway, some great plant, or the like) for the community. For the remaining roads to wealth lie increasingly through a mere manipulation of the ownership of existing enterprises, the merging of companies, the pushing of stocks, the shuffling and reshuffling of shares. Gambling, and the cheating which always goes with it, become more and more the essential occupations of the top layer of contemporary society. To such lengths has this prostitution of the older types of economic incentive now gone that the foremost theorists of the capitalist world are themselves profoundly disturbed by it. Mr Maynard Keynes in his most recent book, for example, complains that 'the capital development of a country' has become the 'byproduct of the activities of a casino'.

Moreover, even in these purely financial fields, as well as in productive industry and in Imperial Government, the positions of power tend more and more to become hereditary. The directors' sons, and sons-in-law, and nephews, fill the avenues to promotion. They sit in the Parliaments, the bank parlours, the managing directors' rooms, and in the headquarters staffs of the imperial apparatus of administration and coercion. Capitalist imperialism ossifies. With every decade the order of its hierarchy comes to have less and less relation to merit. The able serve the dull. The insensitive, the foolish, and the brutal command; the intelligent and the humane obey.

It is true that in the vast apparatus of the British and American systems many relatively important posts are still open to the claims of talent. Thousands of able architects, scientists, doctors, and civil servants are still employed on interesting and apparently constructive tasks by the great corporations and by the governmental agencies. And as yet many of these fortunate men and women feel satisfied with their work. But one by one even these workers will be unable to prevent themselves from realizing that the decay of the economic system within which they work is bringing to naught, or turning to vile uses, their most brilliant and devoted activities.

The frustration of the contemporary scientist, however well paid and well employed, is now a familiar theme. A notorious example is afforded by the chemist, bio-chemist, or physicist, who sees his work used more and more exclusively to perfect the technique of slaughter. But the technical inventor who produces a device which will enable a hundred men to produce the current supply of some article, where a thousand were required before, is in a similar case. For nothing is now more frequent than that the end result of his invention should be no net increase in the wealth of the world, and the ruin, by unemployment and destitution, of nine hundred of his fellow men. Or, again, the contemporary scientist, having developed some unquestionably useful device, may take it to market and may find a buyer; but his device is now often bought by some great Trust, not for use, but in order to prevent its use – so that existing plant and machinery may not be made obsolete.

The young doctor often finds that at the end of his training he must buy the right to attend to the medical needs of the small class of persons who can afford to pay him. If he (or she) cannot afford to buy a practice, he may well be forced into idleness, surrounded by men and women who suffer and die for lack of his services. For the invisible restraints of the economic system bar the way between his skill and their suffering. Slowly but surely the intolerable irrationality of such an arrangement must break through the formidable conditioning to an acceptance of the world as it is, which the young doctor (like every other young professional man) undergoes in the process of his training.

The situation of members of the other professions is in some ways less obviously affected by their social environment. At certain times and in certain places particular professions still enjoy periods of prosperity. In Britain, for example, the architectural profession, after some years of severe depression, is now (1936) well employed – just as were the architects of America before 1929. But even in these periods of intermittent, if intense, activity the modern architect must surely sometimes experience disgust at the use to which his talents are put? For example, the American architects in the boom period often derived the utmost satisfaction from solving the technical problems presented by new types of buildings, such as the skyscraper. But, after all, the ultimate purpose of a building is to serve, not as an exercise in statics, but as a place in which to live or work. Hence the architect must in the end be frustrated if his building remains forever empty.

Again, modern architects can, and do, produce elaborate and technically excellent plans for the rehousing of the population on modern standards. And as yet the majority of British and American architects suppose that this is a technical problem. They cannot conceive what communists and socialists can mean when they say that the existing economic system makes the rehousing of the population economically and politically impossible. They believe that the fact that capitalism has never yet anywhere been able to undertake such an enterprise, and that the soviets, in spite of their inferior technical and material resources, actually are doing so, must be due to some peculiar accident. And yet in this field, too, the sheer force of experience will in the end drive one architect after another to look into the question of whether the frustration of the purpose of a growing proportion of his work is no accident, but an inherent and predicable effect of the existing social and economic system.

Another category of intellectual workers whose devotion to and enthusiasm for their work attest their earnest sense of its social importance are the teachers. And no doubt many British and American teachers still feel that they can constructively contribute to human welfare. This introduction is written soon after the series of teachers' conferences which are held in Britain during the Easter holidays. In the 1936 conferences teacher after teacher from the great distressed areas of Britain rose to report that their pupils were too undernourished to learn much. (In America during recent years there have been states and cities – as, for instance, Chicago – where the teacher was as hungry as the pupil; for during many months they received no pay.) It must surely begin to occur to the teaching profession that the first thing which it is necessary for us, and for them, to learn is how to arrange our economic life in such a way that we do not keep our children's minds in the numbness of semi-starvation.

In a very few, and relatively very small, fields of human activity (of which the book publishing trade is a good example) the able and enterprising, *if they are equipped with or can command the necessary capital*, can still find their way to success and independence in free competition with their fellows. How relatively narrow those remaining fields of genuinely competitive endeavour now are can only be envisaged by recalling that once the whole field was of this character. Once it was true that for those who had, or could obtain access to, a relatively moderate sum of capital (*but only for them*) there were great opportunities of independent success. But in one sphere after another the process of trustification and monopolization has gone forward.

It is true that the great privately owned corporations in banking, industry, commerce, and newspaper publication, which have now largely taken the place of the freely competing individual firms, offer young men attractive careers as their officers. But these are the careers of well-paid subordinates. The ownership and control remain in the hands of a more and more hereditary hierarchy of families. The broad purposes of these controlling families cannot be even questioned by the best-paid employee. If they should be anti-social, he will be as powerless to affect them as the worker at the bench.

The higher officers of the state form another large group of relatively well-paid and secure workers. Such skilled civil servants may, and often do, feel that they are performing an invaluable function. A British civil servant may help to build up a system of unemployment insurance administration which undeniably saves whole districts from starvation. He may, and often does, derive great satisfaction from such work. But in the end the fact that the decay of the present economic system has alone produced the irrational problem of unemployment, which he spends his life in alleviating, should penetrate to his consciousness. Or, again, the imperial administrator may help to operate, often with devoted labours, the administrative machine which maintains peace and order in a sub-continent. Many Indian civil servants have up till now felt satisfied by such a life work. But can they ultimately fail to notice that the net effect of their work for the Indian people has been a steady, and now steep, decline in the Indian standard of life?

The truth is that a contracting economic system brings to naught the best efforts of every type of intellectual worker. If society is confined within ever narrower limits; if the opportunities for constructive work grow more and more meagre, then the community must needs show those dreadful symptoms of decay which Shakespeare catalogued in his sixty-sixth sonnet:

And art made tongue-tied by authority,
And folly – doctor like – controlling skill,
And simple truth miscalled simplicity,
And captive good attending captain ill.

The frustrations of our epoch, although not yet universal, are growing. Of those who already experience them, communists and socialists ask only that they should not rest till they have satisfied themselves as to their cause. Of those who can still feel that their work is fruitful, we ask them only to notice the prediction that sooner or later their province, too, will be invaded by the symptoms of social decay. They may not believe us now. But we believe that experience can, and will, convince them.

Moreover, over us all, the employed and the unemployed, the prosperous and the destitute, there now hangs the prospect of war. This prospect as it advances must tend to prevent all constructive effort. For why should we build targets for the bombs, prevent the tubercle bacillus from destroying lungs destined for the poison gas, or administer with sterling probity the affairs of a city which may soon be uninhabited? If men do not succeed in realizing that there is an alternative social order ready for their construction, they will despair when they realize the general frustration which is involved in the decay of the present order. If the best men and women of every class would save themselves from this despair, and from the personal degeneration which such despair brings with it, they must turn their attention to social science. For a science of society has now been evolved which can enable us to be rid of capitalism, and then to lay down social foundations upon which constructive work for the individual will once more be possible.

The best men and women of every class in Britain and America will come to the conclusion that they cannot find a worthy purpose for their lives except by participation in the organized movement to change the world.

WAITING FOR LEFTY

by CLIFFORD ODETS

(supplementary book, June 1937)

The first performance of *Waiting for Lefty* – in New York, in 1934 – became legendary: there were twenty-eight curtain calls before finally the audience rushed the stage. Clifford Odets (1903–63) was a member of the US Communist Party and an actor in the influential Group Theater. He had written the play in three evenings and entered it for a competition for a short drama on a labour subject (there had been a cab drivers' strike in the city earlier that year).

The extract includes the first and final scenes of the forty-five-minute play. Colin Chambers, historian of the Unity Theatre, has described its structure and setting:

> *Waiting for Lefty* is played on a bare stage with a committee of New York cabbies sitting in a semi-circle discussing strike action 'to get a living wage'. The members of the audience are cast as if they were also taxi drivers at the same meeting being asked to vote on the strike call. The strike is opposed by a tough, corrupt union boss, Harry Fatt, who is accompanied by his gunman. The meeting is waiting for its leader, Lefty Costello. In the meantime, five of the committee step forward in turn, to tell through short, realistic scenes, a crucial personal story which explains why each of them is backing the strike. Odets described this moving back and forth, from and to the meeting in cinematic flashback, as being like a minstrel show in which performers present their own special acts one after the other. A chair is left empty for Costello while the other members of the committee, young and new to union affairs, act like a chorus commenting on the scenes.

The first story is that of a driver, Joe, whose furniture is taken away because he can't pay the instalments. In 'The Young Hack and his Girl' (also extracted), Sid is too poor to marry Flo. Other episodes feature a scientist, Miller, who is sacked for refusing to spy on a colleague and make poison gas; a young actor who is rejected by a Broadway producer; and a doctor who loses his job because he is a Jew. In the final scene, Agate Keller challenges Fatt – who represents the capitalist system – and calls for a strike.

The play was so popular partly because the cinematic technique of flashback and intercutting scenes hadn't been seen on stage before, but mostly because of its simplicity and emotionalism. John Allen, the LBC Theatre Guild organiser, said that the first time he saw *Lefty* it knocked him 'upside down and sideways': the play was full of the political commitment he felt was lacking in professional theatre. It was put on hundreds of times in Britain before the Second World War, mostly under the auspices of LBC groups and the Unity Theatre. At one performance, at the Royalty Theatre in Chester, the theatre manager lowered the curtain while the play was still running and ordered the orchestra to play 'God Save the King'. On another occasion, when the play was being staged in a Mosleyite area of London, the innovation of an actor coming through the audience caused the theatre stewards to raise the alarm that a disruption by Blackshirts was imminent.

Odets wrote a number of other plays in the mid-thirties; with his friend Elia Kazan he became a spokesman for the necessary relationship between theatre and political struggle. In the fifties, however, he 'named names' before the McCarthyite UnAmerican Activities Committee and was eager to make it clear that he had nothing to do with the 1934 cab strike.

As the curtain goes up we see a bare stage. On it are sitting six or seven men in a semicircle. Lolling against the proscenium down left is a young man chewing a tooth-pick: a gunman. A fat man of porcine appearance is talking directly to the audience. In other words he is the head of a union and the men ranged behind him are a committee of workers. They are now seated in interesting different attitudes and present a wide diversity of type, as we shall soon see. The fat man is hot and heavy under the collar, near the end of a long talk, but not too hot: he is well fed and confident. His name is HARRY FATT.

FATT: You're so wrong I ain't laughing. Any guy with eyes to read knows it. Look at the textile strike – out like lions and in like lambs. Take the San Francisco tie-up – starvation and broken heads. The steel boys wanted to walk out too, but they changed their minds. It's the trend of the times, that's what it is. All we workers got a good man behind us now. He's top man of the country – looking out for our interests – the man in the White House is the one I'm referrin' to. That's why the times ain't ripe for a strike. He's working day and night—

VOICE (*from the audience*): For who? (*The* GUNMAN *stirs himself.*)

FATT: For you! The records prove it. If this was the Hoover regime, would I say don't go out, boys? Not on your tintype! But things is different now. You read the papers as well as me. You know it. And that's why I'm against the strike. Because we gotta stand behind the man who's standin' behind us! The whole country—

ANOTHER VOICE: Is on the blink! (*The* GUNMAN *looks grave.*)

FATT: Stand up and show yourself, you damn red! Be a man, let's see what you look like! (*Waits in vain.*) Yellow from the word go! Red and yellow makes a dirty colour, boys. I got my eyes on four or five of them in the union here. What the hell'll they do for you? Pull you out and run away when trouble starts. Give those birds a chance and they'll have your sisters and wives in the whore houses, like they done in Russia. They'll tear Christ off his bleeding cross. They'll wreck your homes and throw your babies in the river. You think that's bunk? Read the papers! Now listen, we can't stay here all night. I gave you the facts in the case. You boys got hot suppers to go to and—

ANOTHER VOICE: Says you!

GUNMAN: Sit down, Punk!

ANOTHER VOICE: Where's Lefty? (*Now this question is taken up by the others in unison.* FATT *pounds with gavel.*)

FATT: That's what I wanna know. Where's your pal, Lefty? You elected him chairman – where the hell did he disappear?

VOICES: We want Lefty! Lefty! Lefty!

FATT (*pounding*): What the hell is this – a circus? You got the committee here. This bunch of cowboys you elected. (*Pointing to man on extreme right end.*)

MAN: Benjamin.

FATT: Yeah, Doc Benjamin. (*Pointing to other men in circle in seated order.*) Benjamin, Miller, Stein, Mitchell, Phillips, Keller. It ain't my fault Lefty took a run-out powder. If you guys—

A GOOD VOICE: What's the committee say?

OTHERS: The committee! Let's hear from the committee! (FATT *tries to quiet the crowd, but one of the seated men suddenly comes to the front. The* GUNMAN *moves over to centre stage, but* FATT *says:*)

FATT: Sure, let him talk. Let's hear what the red boy's gotta say!

Various shouts are coming from the audience. FATT *insolently goes back to his seat in the middle of the circle. He sits on his raised platform and relights his cigar. The* GUNMAN *goes back to his post.* JOE, *the new speaker, raises his hand for quiet. Gets it quickly. He is sore.*

JOE: You boys know me. I ain't a red boy one bit! Here I'm carryin' a shrapnel that big I picked up in the war. And maybe I don't know it when it rains! Don't tell me red! You know what we are? The black and blue boys! We been kicked around so long we're black and blue from head to toes. But I guess anyone who says straight out he don't like it, he's a red boy to the leaders of the union. What's this crap about goin' home to hot suppers? I'm asking to your faces how many's got hot suppers to go home to? Anyone who's sure of his next meal, raise your hand! A certain gent sitting behind me can raise them both. But not in front here! And that's why we're talking strike – to get a living wage!

VOICE: Where's Lefty?

JOE: I honest to God don't know, but he didn't take no run-out powder. That Wop's got more guts than a slaughter house. Maybe a traffic jam got him, but he'll be here. But don't let this red stuff scare you. Unless fighting for a living scares you. We gotta make up our minds. My wife made up my mind last week, if you want the truth. It's plain as the nose on Sol Feinberg's face we need a strike. There's us comin' home every night – eight, ten hours on the cab. 'God,' the wife says, 'eighty cents ain't money – don't buy beans almost. You're workin' for the company,' she says to me, 'Joe! you ain't workin' for me or the family no more!' She says to me, 'If you don't start . . .'

EPISODE III:
THE YOUNG HACK AND HIS GIRL

Opens with girl and brother. FLORENCE *waiting for* SID *to take her to a dance.*

FLOR: I gotta right to have something out of life. I don't smoke, I don't drink. So if Sid wants to take me to a dance, I'll go. Maybe if you was in love you wouldn't talk so hard.

IRV: I'm saying it for your good.

FLOR: Don't be so good to me.

IRV: Mom's sick in bed and you'll be worryin' her to the grave. She don't want that boy hanging around the house and she don't want you meeting him in Crotona Park.

FLOR: I'll meet him any time I like!

IRV: If you do, yours truly'll take care of it in his own way. With just one hand, too!

FLOR: Why are you all so set against him?

IRV: Mom told you ten times – it ain't him. It's that he ain't got nothing. Sure, we know he's serious, that he's stuck on you. But that don't cut no ice.

FLOR: Taxi drivers used to make good money.

IRV: Today they're makin' five and six dollars a week. Maybe you wanta raise a family on that. Then you'll be back here living with us again and I'll be supporting two families in one. Well . . . over my dead body.

FLOR: Irv, I don't care – I love him!

IRV: You're a little kid with half-baked ideas!

FLOR: I stand there behind the counter the whole day. I think about him—

IRV: If you thought more about Mom it would be better.

FLOR: Don't I take care of her every night when I come home? Don't I cook supper and iron your shirts and . . . you give me a pain in the neck, too. Don't try to shut me up! I bring a few dollars in the house, too. Don't you see I want something else out of life. Sure, I want romance, love, babies. I want everything in life I can get.

IRV: You take care of Mom and watch your step!

FLOR: And if I don't?

IRV: Yours truly'll watch it for you!

FLOR: You can talk that way to a girl . . .

IRV: I'll talk that way to your boy friend, too, and it won't be with words! Florrie, if you had a pair of eyes you'd see it's for your own good we're talking. This ain't no time to get married. Maybe later—

FLOR: 'Maybe later' never comes for me, though. Why don't we send Mom to a hospital? She can die in peace there instead of looking at the clock on the mantelpiece all day.

IRV: That needs money. Which we don't have!

FLOR: Money, money, money!

IRV: Don't change the subject.

FLOR: This is the subject!

IRV: You gonna stop seeing him? (*She turns away.*) Jesus, kiddie, I remember when you were a baby with curls down your back. Now I gotta stand here yellin' at you like this.

FLOR: I'll talk to him, Irv.

IRV: When?

FLOR: I asked him to come here tonight. We'll talk it over.

IRV: Don't get soft with him. Nowadays is no time to be soft. You gotta be hard as a rock or go under.

FLOR: I found that out. There's the bell. Take the egg off the stove I boiled for Mom. Leave us alone, Irv.

SID *comes in – the two men look at each other for a second.* IRV *exits.*

SID (*enters*): Hello, Florrie.

FLOR: Hello, honey. You're looking tired.

SID: Naw, I just need a shave.

FLOR: Well, draw your chair up to the fire and I'll ring for brandy and soda . . . like in the movies.

SID: If this was the movies I'd bring a big bunch of roses.

FLOR: How big?

SID: Fifty or sixty dozen – the kind with long, long stems – big as that . . .

FLOR: You dope . . .

SID: Your Paris gown is beautiful.

FLOR (*acting grandly*): Yes, Percy, velvet panels are coming back again. Madame La Farge told me today that Queen Fanny herself designed it.

SID: Gee . . . !

FLOR: Every princess in the Balkans is wearing one like this. (*Poses grandly.*)

SID: Hold it. (*Does a nose camera – thumbing nose and imitating grinding of camera with other hand.*)

Suddenly she falls out of the posture and swiftly goes to him, to embrace him, to kiss him with love. Finally:

You look tired, Florrie.

FLOR: Naw, I just need a shave. (*She laughs tremorously.*)

SID: You worried about your mother?

FLOR: No.

SID: What's on your mind?

FLOR: The French and Indian War.

SID: What's on your mind?

FLOR: I got us on my mind, Sid. Night and day, Sid!

SID: I smacked a beer truck today. Did I get hell! I was driving along thinking of us, too. You don't have to say it – I know what's on your mind. I'm rat poison around here.

FLOR: Not to me . . .

SID: I know to who . . . and I know why. I don't blame them. We're engaged now for three years . . .

FLOR: That's a long time . . .

SID: My brother Sam joined the navy this morning – get a break that way. They'll send him down to Cuba with the hootchy-kootchy girls. He don't know from nothing, that dumb basketball player!

FLOR: Don't you do that.

SID: Don't you worry, I'm not the kind who runs away. But I'm so tired of being a dog, baby, I could choke. I don't even have to ask what's going on in your mind. I know from the word go, 'cause I'm thinking the same things, too.

FLOR: It's yes or no – nothing in between.

SID: The answer is no – a big electric sign looking down on Broadway!

FLOR: We wanted to have kids . . .

SID: But that sort of life ain't for the dogs which is us. Christ, baby! I get like thunder in my chest when we're together. If we went off together I could maybe look the world straight in the face, spit in its eye like a man should do. Goddamit, it's trying to be a man on the earth. Two in life together.

FLOR: But something wants us to be lonely like that – crawling alone in the dark. Or they want us trapped.

SID: Sure, the big shot money men want us like that.

FLOR: Highly insulting us—

SID: Keeping us in the dark about what is wrong with us in the money sense. They got the power an' mean to be damn sure they keep it. They know if they give in just an inch, all the dogs like us will be down on them together – an ocean knocking them to hell and back and each singing cuckoo with stars coming from their nose and ears. I'm not raving, Florrie—

FLOR: I know you're not, I know.

SID: I don't have the words to tell you what I feel. I never finished school . . .

FLOR: I know . . .

SID: But it's relative, like the professors say. We worked like hell to send him to college – my kid brother Sam, I mean – and look what he done – joined the Navy! The damn fool don't see the cards is stacked for all of us. The money man dealing himself a hot royal flush. Then giving you and me a phoney hand like a pair of tens or something. Then keep on losing the pots 'cause the cards is stacked against you. Then he says, what's the matter you can't win – no stuff on the ball, he says to you. And kids like my brother believe it 'cause they don't know better. For all their education, they don't know from nothing.

But wait a minute! Don't he come around and say to you – this millionaire with a jazz band – listen Sam or Sid or what's-your-name, you're no good, but here's a chance. The whole world'll know who you are. Yes, sir, he says, get up on that ship and fight those bastards who's making the world a lousy place to live in. The Japs, the Turks, the Greeks. Take this gun – kill the slobs like a real hero, he says, a real American. Be a hero!

And the guy you're poking at? A real louse, just like you, 'cause they don't let him catch more than a pair of tens, too. On that foreign soil he's a guy like me and Sam, a guy who wants his baby like you and hot sun on his face! They'll teach Sam to point the guns the wrong way, that dumb basketball player!

FLOR: I got a lump in my throat, honey.

SID: You and me – we never even had a room to sit in somewhere.

FLOR: The park was nice . . .

SID: In winter? The hallways . . . I'm glad we never got together. This way we don't know what we missed.

FLOR (*in a burst*): Sid, I'll go with you – we'll get a room somewhere.

SID: Naw . . . they're right. If we can't climb higher than this together – we better stay apart.

FLOR: I swear to God I wouldn't care.

SID: You would, you would – in a year, two years, you'd curse the day. I seen it happen.

FLOR: Oh, Sid . . .

SID: Sure, I know. We got the blues, babe – the 1935 blues. I'm talkin' this way 'cause I love you. If I didn't, I wouldn't care . . .

FLOR: We'll work together, we'll—

SID: How about the backwash? Your family needs your nine bucks. My family—

FLOR: I don't care for them!

SID: You're making it up, Florrie. Little Florrie Canary in a cage.

FLOR: Don't make fun of me.

SID: I'm not, baby.

FLOR: Yes, you're laughing at me.

SID: I'm not.

They stand looking at each other, unable to speak. Finally, he turns to a small portable phonograph and plays a cheap, sad, dance tune. He makes a motion with his hand: she comes to him. They begin to dance slowly. They hold each other tightly, almost as though they would merge into each other. The music stops, but the scratching record continues to the end of the scene. They stop dancing. He finally unlooses her clutch and seats her on the couch, where she sits, tense and expectant.

Hello, babe.

FLOR: Hello. (*For a brief time they stand as though in a dream.*)

SID (*finally*): Good-bye, babe.

He waits for an answer, but she is silent. They look at each other.

Did you ever see my Pat Rooney imitation? (*He whistles Rosy O'Grady and soft shoes to it. Stops. He asks:*)
Don't you like it?
FLOR (*finally*): No. (*Buries her face in her hands.*)

Suddenly he falls on his knees and buries his face in her lap.

BLACKOUT

AGATE [KELLER]: LADIES AND GENTLEMEN, and don't let anyone tell you we ain't got some ladies in this sea of upturned faces! Only they're wearin' pants. Well, maybe I don't know a thing; maybe I fell outa the cradle when I was a kid and ain't been right since – you can't tell!

VOICE: Sit down, cockeye!

AGATE: Who's paying you for those remarks, Buddy? – Moscow Gold? Maybe I got a *glass eye*, but it come from working in a factory at the age of eleven. They hooked it out because they didn't have a shield on the works. But I wear it like a medal 'cause it tells the world where I belong – deep down in the working class! We had delegates in the union there – all kinds of secretaries and treasurers . . . walkin' delegates, but not with blisters on their feet! Oh no! On their fat little ass from sitting on cushions and raking in mazuma. (SECRETARY *and* GUNMAN *remonstrate in words and actions here.*) Sit down, boys, I'm just sayin' that about unions in general. I know it ain't true here! Why no, our officers is all aces. Why, I seen our own secretary Fatt walk outa his way not to step on a cockroach. No boys, don't think—

FATT (*breaking in*): You're out of order!

AGATE (*to audience*): Am I outa order?

ALL: No, no. Speak. Go on, etc.

AGATE: Yes, our officers is all aces. But I'm a member here – and no experience in Philly either! Today I couldn't wear my union button. The damnest thing happened. When I take the old coat off the wall, I see she's smoking. I'm a sonovagun if the old union button isn't on fire! Yep, the old celluloid was makin' the most god-awful stink: the landlady come up and give me hell! You know what happened? – that old union button just blushed itself to death! Ashamed! Can you beat it?

FATT: Sit down, Keller! Nobody's interested!
AGATE: Yes they are!
GUNMAN: Sit down like he tells you!
AGATE (*continuing to audience*): And when I finish—

His speech is broken by FATT *and* GUNMAN *who physically handle him. He breaks away and gets to other side of stage. The two are about to make for him when some of the committee men come forward and get in between the struggling parties.* AGATE*'s shirt has been torn.*

(*to audience*): What's the answer, boys? The answer is, if we're reds because we wanna strike, then we take over their salute too! Know how they do it? (*Makes Communist salute.*) What is it? An uppercut! The good old uppercut to the chin! Hell, some of us boys ain't even got a shirt to our backs. What's the boss class tryin' to do – make a nudist colony outa us?

The audience laughs and suddenly AGATE *comes to the middle of the stage so that the other cabmen back him up in a strong clump.*

Don't laugh! Nothing's funny! This is your life and mine! It's skull and bones every incha the road! Christ, we're dyin' by inches! For what? For the debutant-ees to have their sweet comin' out parties in the Ritz! Poppa's got a daughter she's gotta get her picture in the papers. Christ, they make 'em with our blood. Joe said it. Slow death or fight. It's war!

Throughout this whole speech AGATE *is backed up by the other six workers, so that from their activity it is plain that the whole group of them are saying these things. Several of them may take alternate lines out of this long last speech.*

You Edna, God love your mouth! Sid and Florrie, the other boys, old Doc Barnes – fight with us for right! It's war! Working class, unite and fight! Tear down the slaughter house of our old lives! Let freedom really ring.

These slick slobs stand here telling us about bogeymen. That's a new one for the kids – the reds is bogeymen! But the man who got me food in 1932, he called me Comrade! The one who picked me up where I bled – he called me Comrade too! What are we waiting for . . . Don't wait for Lefty! He might never come. Every minute—

This is broken into by a man who has dashed up the centre aisle from the back of the house. He runs up on stage, says:

MAN: Boys, they just found Lefty!

OTHERS: What? What? What?

SOME: Shhh . . . Shhh . . .

MAN: They found Lefty . . .

AGATE: Where?

MAN: Behind the car barns with a bullet in his head!

AGATE (*crying*): Hear it, boys, hear it? Hell, listen to me! Coast to coast! HELLO AMERICA! HELLO. WE'RE STORMBIRDS OF THE WORKING CLASS. WORKERS OF THE WORLD . . . OUR BONES AND BLOOD! And when we die they'll know what we did to make a new world! Christ, cut us up to little pieces. We'll die for what is right! put fruit trees where our ashes are! (*to audience*) Well, what's the answer?

ALL: STRIKE!

AGATE: LOUDER!

ALL: STRIKE!

AGATE (*and others on stage*): AGAIN!

ALL: STRIKE, STRIKE, STRIKE!!!

OUR STREET

by Jan Petersen

(supplementary book, February 1938)

Our Street is an account of left-wing resistance to Nazism in the Charlottenburg district of Berlin – a first-person narrative, rather than straight political history. It covers a period of eighteen months, from just before Hitler's appointment as Chancellor to the autumn of 1934. During this time, socialists and Communists who had spoken and agitated against the Nazis were searched out and silenced with maximum publicity (the Reichstag fire, blamed on Communists, took place in February 1933). The street in question is Wallstrasse, a centre of Red resistance, which was targeted by the Nazis after a skirmish there ended in the killing of a Stormtrooper. 'The residents of Wallstrasse paid over and over again for the death of Stormtrooper Maikowski,' Gollancz wrote in his notice of the book. It is the reason given for the execution of Richard Huttig, a prominent activist whose funeral is the last event described in *Our Street*.

Jan Petersen, a Communist, led a resistance group of German anti-fascist writers between 1933 and 1935. The book is, in effect, his semi-fictionalised memoir (some names and places were changed). The narrator describes the struggle to keep opposition to Hitler alive after it has been driven underground. Communication between the secret groups of socialists and Communists is difficult; almost everyone is suspected of spying. The protagonist lives in constant fear of exposure and arrest by the Nazis, and is prevented from meeting Käthe, his lover, because her brother has been murdered – to see her is to invite suspicion.

Petersen dedicated *Our Street* to his dead comrades from Charlottenburg – eighteen names were listed at the front of the volume. His was perhaps the only book critical of the Nazis to have made it out of Hitler's Germany and been published overseas. The story of its transit is remarkable.

The manuscript was typed in Petersen's small room just a few minutes' walk from Wallstrasse. Once a week, he motorbiked into the centre of Berlin, carrying a few recently written pages in a rucksack. He gave these to a friend to hide. When the manuscript was finished, two copies were made. A sailor-comrade was entrusted to ship one copy to England, but it had to be thrown overboard to escape detection. The second was taken to Dresden en route to Czechoslovakia, but Petersen received no confirmation that it had arrived. Finally, he decided that he should personally take the original manuscript – unearthed from under a fir tree – to Prague. His cover was a skiing holiday with a friend, and he smuggled the manuscript past customs by baking it inside a cake. He later learned that the second copy had made it to Prague, too, packed in a basket under a stack of sandwiches.

Our Street was translated into English by Betty Rensen in 1938 (the German edition had to wait until the end of the war). Gollancz called it 'vivid and exciting'; *Left News* defended its romanticism. 'If it is as widely read as it deserves to be,' Sylvia Townsend Warner wrote, 'we may realise with adequate indignation to what sort of government, to what sort of iniquity, the Chamberlain Government would ally us.' Petersen emigrated to Switzerland, France and then England during the late thirties and was deprived of German citizenship by the Nazis. He returned to the GDR after the war and was awarded a number of literary prizes.

. . . WE HAVE AGAIN been struck a heavy blow.

Franz Zander, our Franz has been arrested. Yesterday evening in our street. Franz – in our street! We know now how it happened. We made careful enquiries everywhere. We had to discover the details because we did not know whether the Thirty-threes came for him alone, or whether other comrades are soon to be arrested too. We know Franz was with comrades in the neighbouring district. In Moabit. He went to discuss a new method for printing papers, one which has been used for some time in his district. It is much cheaper and more copies can be printed. We know now that Franz came to our street for a few minutes to see his old mother. He learnt from Hilde that she has been ill for months . His sister Käthe had not mentioned it to him. He was less than half an hour away from our street. The temptation to visit his mother would be natural. He must have struggled with himself a long time. It would be all right just for once; he would stay only a few minutes, and who would see him anyway, as it was already dark? We can guess this now. But we still can't understand how Franz, who had trained us all to be so very cautious, could have come to our street. He knew that the SA had been looking for him here for a year.

The loud speaker was grinding martial music into the bar of the pub Africander, which is just opposite Franz's house. The fat landlady was sitting behind the bar knitting. Three men were playing cards at one of the round tables on her right. In the other corner, on her extreme left, sat a lonely customer. He was staring into his half-empty beer glass. His bald head rested on his hands. The cauliflower ears protruded above his thumbs. It was Kranz, a regular customer. The landlady mentally reckoned up his bill. Three whiskies, four beers, two cigars.

Kranz stood up suddenly, took the cold cigar out of his mouth, and glanced round searchingly. The landlady threw her sock down on to the bar and went up to him. She struck a match. 'Here you are.'

Kranz looked at her glassily. He took the match from her, turned the flame to the window, and puffed at his cigar. A second later he let the match fall. The cigar slithered down from the corner of his mouth. He stood there with his mouth wide open and stared across. The landlady looked at him in surprise. The other three were attracted by Kranz's curious behaviour. Then he pulled himself together and ran to the door.

'I'll pay afterwards . . . coming back later,' he stuttered.

The landlady ran after him, wanting to protest, but Kranz was already outside; had not even stopped to close the door. Meanwhile one of the three men stood up. He saw Kranz running off in the direction of the Rosinenstrasse. As there was nothing unusual to be seen in our street they were unable to account for Kranz's peculiar behaviour. (Franz must have disappeared into his house a second ago. The customer who had gone to the door knew him. He told us that he had not seen him.)

'He gets crazier every day. Still, he'll pay his bill for sure,' the landlady remarked to the others.

Soon afterwards SA men came running along our street. The mob of brown uniforms soon split up and formed a chain which stretched from the last two corner houses at the bend in the street right up to the narrow path between the Power Works and the Relief Barracks. A group of SA then entered Franz's house and occupied all the staircases and the doors on to the yard.

Nothing unusual had been noticed in Franz's house. But the quiet street was stirred up in the few minutes. The long rows of windows were packed with faces. Groups stood in the doorways and glanced across to the brown cordon with hate in their eyes. They were all standing a good way off, but it seemed that their silent protest had its effect on the Brown Shirts. The SA men felt it quite obviously. They turned their heads nervously, looked along the rows of houses and windows. The business people peeped timidly through their shop windows, all except the fruiterer, who stood full square in his shop doorway. The same anxious thought was shared by all. Who is it for? . . . They've come so suddenly . . . who is in danger? Who? . . . Who?

Franz rang at the door of his home. No one opened. Käthe was still at the office and his mother was in bed, unable to get up. The neighbour, Frau Schulze, heard him ringing. She was astonished when she saw

Franz. Yes, she had a key to the flat; she looked after his mother during the day, she explained. She refused to go to the hospital and Käthe was away all day. Käthe ought to have told him that ages ago, Franz replied. He had only just heard it from his girl. At first she had only hinted at things, but he had kept at her until she told him everything. He wanted to see and speak to his mother for a couple of minutes; he would leave almost at once. He soon came out of the flat, but stopped to tell the neighbour that he had attempted to persuade his mother to go to the hospital. That was the best thing for her. She was even worse than he had imagined, was so terribly thin and weak. Then he took the stairs in flying leaps. A second later the neighbour heard a crash on the steps below.

A voice was shouting, hoarse with rage:

'We've caught you at last! We've got you now, you son-of-a-bitch!'

When the Brown Shirts came out into the street, a sudden movement was noticeable among the people in the doorways; the heads at the windows jerked up with fear. A choking feeling came to their throats. It was Franz Zander – their Franz! Everyone in the street knew him very well.

The street remained silent. The men stood in front of the doors. But their pockets bulged with their clenched fists. All the windows were crowded out with spectators. Our street took leave of Franz in dead silence. It seemed that arms were outstretched from all sides, wanting to shake hands once more.

Franz must have felt that too. His face was calm. A smile even flickered on his lips. He nodded across the streets, up to the windows.

The SA pushed him along with quick steps. To the Maikowski Barracks, to the Rosinenstrasse. Children ran alongside the procession. That was the last time that Franz saw our street – that our street saw Franz.

My first thought when I heard the news the same evening was that Teichert must be warned. Teichert, because he lives in the same house as Franz. And because we do not know which of us the Thirty-threes might still want to arrest.

The trams from Siemensstadt run along at short intervals. They are all packed. At this time of the day, knocking off time at Siemens Works, many extra cars can hardly cope with the rush. I stand at the stop and cast flying glances at all the passengers getting off. Where is Teichert? Perhaps he got out at an earlier stop today in order to buy something?

Would it be better to wait for him at the top of our street? Too conspicuous. And if he comes from the other end he'll run unprepared into his flat.

Car after car comes along, stops, rolls off, empty.

Not there – and not in the next one. Ten minutes drag tormentingly.

I pace up and down – for hours, it seems to me.

Another tram rolls along. And in it, at last – Teichert!

He is surprised, fidgets with his dinner basket.

'You here?' is all that he says.

It seems that the question 'Why?' is about to follow. But he walks along at my side without saying another word. I feel very depressed. Steal a quick glance at him. There is a deep furrow between his eyebrows. He has become even paler the last few days, the cheek-bones more prominent. Seems to have aged years since Richard's verdict was pronounced. And now I must tell him this too.

'Why . . . ? It's sure not to be anything pleasant.' he says at last.

I don't look at him. Each step seems to hammer at my head.

'They've arrested Franz!'

Teichert stops.

'Fraaanz?' He draws the word out, as if he had not heard the name properly. 'Has his district been caught, or what – how . . . ?'

He grips my arm.

'In our street – an hour ago!'

Teichert wipes his brow with his hand.

'In our . . . in our . . .' he says uncomprehendingly.

I drag him away. We daren't excite attention.

'The neighbour opened the flat for him – she said he wanted to see his mother.'

Teichert does not answer; stares fixedly ahead.

'They surrounded the house quite suddenly – perhaps—'

I falter, but Teichert has already understood. He nods dejectedly.

'That's why I wanted to catch you.'

We walk about. Teichert still remains silent. He presses his lips together, breathes heavily.

'We got someone to tell the neighbour to stop Käthe. It's too dangerous for one of us. Her mother mustn't get to know anything – not now . . .'

'Jan,' is all that Teichert says. He presses my hand.

I avoid his glance. Käthe – she must get over it on her own. I dare not – not now –

'I'm going. Let's get it over. And if I'm – well, we'll see what happens.'

He shakes hands again. I gaze after him, then walk round the block of houses in the opposite direction.

We'll arrive from different directions. But that won't save us either – if it's our turn now as well.

Käthe had not been able to get much sleep while her mother had been ill. The old woman usually went off to sleep in the early hours of the morning. She had almost agreed to be taken to the hospital before Franz came. But since Franz had been to see her she keeps on refusing to leave the flat. With the obstinacy of the sick she repeated that she was waiting at home for his next visit. Käthe explained that Franz would be able to visit her just as often in the hospital. But no, she insisted on remaining at home. The days since then have been not only a physical strain for Käthe, but also days of mental torture. Her mother talks such a lot about Franz now. What he looked like, how he promised to come back again soon. Käthe dare not let her suspect, by the slightest sign of her real feelings, how things really stand with Franz.

Where is Franz now, and how is he being treated? Käthe has tried to make enquiries about him everywhere. At the local police station, which disclaimed all responsibility; at the Politische Polizei in the Alexanderplatz Police Headquarters; at the Geheime Staatspolizei (Gestapo) in the Prinz-Albrecht-Strasse, and in the Columbiahaus. They all dismissed her curtly. Franz Zander? The name was unknown there. No they could not undertake enquiries; had enough to do as it was. We could not help Käthe either; it would only excite suspicion if we started making enquiries about him. We advised Käthe to tell Hilde that Franz had been arrested by the police and not by the SA. For Hilde would only have blamed herself all the more because she had been the one to tell Franz about his mother. Hilde is quite desperate since Franz's arrest. She only talks about trying to do something for him. Käthe tells her every time that she does not know where he is. Hilde would only be dragged into the affair if she made enquiries about Franz. And if Hilde got to know that the Thirty-threes had arrested Franz she would have been sure to try to obtain information from her brother. We have to prevent her from betraying herself to her brother, the SA troop leader.

The Thirty-threes! Is Franz still in the Maikowski Barracks? The SA have not let Käthe enter the barracks. She could report to him after hours, the officer on duty had remarked mockingly. Where, where, is Franz? This 'where' is Käthe's first thought when she wakes up in the morning.

She rises early one morning. Dresses hastily and then fetches the basin and towel for her mother from the kitchen. On her way back across the hall her glance falls on the wire letter-box on the front door. Something white is lying there. A letter. At this time, so early in the morning? It must have come by the last post yesterday evening, and remained unnoticed in the dark. There is a printed stamp on the envelope. An official communication? – For Frau Elise Zander. Käthe does not know why, but the letter suddenly feels as heavy as lead in her hand. An official communication! She turns the letter undecidedly about in her hand, then tears the perforated edge.

> Died in hospital . . . Death caused by a weak heart . . . Will be released for burial on . . .

Käthe reads the lines again and again. She whispers them softly to herself, without realising that she is doing so. Died – but who? Died . . . But the letter isn't for her at all. She turns it round mechanically. For Frau Elise Zander . . .

Elise Zander . . . Elise . . . for her mother. She stares fixedly at the sheet . . . Died . . . Above is written – a name; Franz Zander.

Franz – Franz.

'Kä . . . the, Kä . . . the!'

Her mother is calling her in her weak, trembling voice. Käthe stands up. She stands there for a second with limp arms, still holding the crumpled letter in her hand. She raises her arm; it feels stiff and heavy, as if it did not belong to her. She looks at the letter again.

'Kä . . . the! Kä . . . the! Where . . . are you?'

Käthe pulls herself together. Her mother! She has not dared to let her mother know anything so far; this is an additional reason for keeping things from her. She hides the letter away in a drawer. Her mother is resting on her elbows. She must have vainly attempted to stand up. Her face is yellow, the cheek-bones protrude.

She looks at Käthe reproachfully.

'I keep on calling . . . and calling . . . and you don't come,' she says.

She points to the wash-basin, the towel. Käthe brings everything to the bed.

'Don't . . . you have . . . to go to . . . work soon?' Frau Zander asks.

Yes, she has to go to the office. She won't go; she does not care about anything any more now.

'We've got – we've got a holiday today,' she answers.

She is herself surprised to hear herself telling her mother that. The latter puts the flannel down, looks at her searchingly.

'Why are you talking like that? . . . Don't you feel well?' she asks. 'You're so pale.'

'There's nothing wrong with me – we've got a holiday today,' Käthe repeats.

She must allay her mother's suspicions at all costs.

The news that Franz is dead spreads from house to house in our street like lightning during the morning. The street is in mourning. No black is to be seen, but the death of our comrade is shown on everyone's face. His presence is felt in the talks, in the silent glances. Franz is taking leave of his street. He comes into the houses. He does not knock anywhere; no door opens, but he steps in everywhere.

An old woman is crying. He had often helped her, the young chap had. Carried things, fetched coal.

A comrade thinks.

'Do you still remember? . . . the fight at the meeting in Neukölln . . . Friedrichshain, the free fight in the hall? Do you still remember? Good luck, Franz. You were one of the best . . .'

They are taking leave of Franz everywhere, for ever.

Our street is long.

There are many houses.

I walk slowly down the Berliner Strasse. Hilde lives across the way. Mustn't forget to ask Teichert this evening whether he knows how she is. We must look after her more now that she has lost Franz. My glance falls on the electric clock in a watchmaker's shop. Plenty of time; I don't have to be there before twelve. I sit down on a nearby seat. The traffic goes past in never-ending streams. The sun is already quite warm. The trees! A few days ago yellow buds were still on the twigs. They have now unfolded to form tiny leaves. The change comes so quickly that one can almost watch it happening. How pleasant to lie in a green meadow – insects swarming . . . Franz! He won't ever see all that again – won't ever come for a picnic with us again. It all suddenly comes back to me. I have seen Käthe only once since then, out in the Grunewald. She had gone to the Charlottenburg SA Standard doctor. He lives in the Kaiserdamm, in a luxurious flat. 'The strongest man can die from heart failure,' he had remarked ironically. She had received permission for herself alone to see Franz in the mortuary. They allowed her just to look through a window; the body lay some yards away, wrapped in white sheets. Only a small portion of the face was left uncovered, and that was thickly powdered. She had been unable to recognise him, had not known whether it was him at all. She told me all this between sobs. I could not utter a word; could only stroke her hair. I could not find anything to say which would help to console her. Franz won't ever return.

We shall not be able to meet at all after this; she is sure to be watched. It was difficult enough recently.

My thoughts go back again to the large Wald cemetery. The hundreds of workers who disrupted the traffic on their way, and then stood round the grave. Many had sacrificed their only coppers for the fare, for a few flowers. The faces filled with hate and sorrow appear before me again. The women weep; dead silence apart from that. A silence enforced by the threatening faces of the Gestapo guards. The young comrade from the Youth League rushes forward to the open grave, starts speaking. The arms of the Gestapo drag him away before he can say more than a few sentences. Yet hundreds of voices cry: 'Revenge! Red Front!' . . .

I open my eyes. It is broad daylight.

You are no longer with us, Franz, my best friend and comrade . . .

The Zoological Gardens are across the way. People are standing in front of the huge iron gate. They are all looking across at the elephants. Right in front, Jumbo, the oldest elephant, is receiving lumps of sugar with his trunk. Then he throws sand over his massive body, blows a jet of water into the air. The others near me are enjoying the scene. The grown-ups as well as the children. I pull my paper, the *Nachtausgabe*, from my pocket. Hold it in my right hand, keeping a good look-out. The hands of the station clock are exactly on twelve. The comrade will be arriving any minute now. He can't be here yet. No one else is holding a paper. I don't know the comrade, but he has been described in detail to me. He will also be holding a paper, and is to approach me with the passwords. I seem to be looking across to the elephants playing about, like all the others here, but I am watching my surroundings all the time. A small pale man wearing gold-rimmed glasses soon comes along. He also joins the others at the cage. That's him! I have developed extreme sensitiveness to this kind of work. The description fits – he has the *Berliner Börsenzeitung* in his hand. I notice him stealing quick glances at the people round him. But it's better to wait a bit; it might still be a coincidence. I continue looking at the elephants, but turn the title-page of my paper more noticeably outward. A few minutes pass. Then the woman near me leaves. The little man takes her place afterwards.

Good guess; be careful.

'How old do you think the fellow'll be?' the little man immediately asks in a thin falsetto voice.

The question seems to have been carelessly uttered. No one answers; they are all looking across.

'Difficult to say. Eighty, perhaps even a hundred years,' I say calmly.

But even now! It might have been a random question. The answer – the answer now!

He laughed. A gold tooth gleams between his lips.

'If you wanted to make sure, you would have to keep a colossal animal like that as a pet. Like an Indian rajah, eh?' he jokes.

The woman next to me laughs.

The answer was correct – especially 'Indian rajah'. So it's all right.

We meet a few seconds later a short way off. The little man gives me his paper.

'It's in there,' he says curtly.

His voice is now deep. Quite a different person is walking at my side.

'Have you any news for us from your district?'

'No. Our comrades are rather depressed after our last death. Things have got to get right again soon, though.'

And, after a pause:

'He was one of our best.'

The little man nods earnestly, shakes hands.

'Well, in a week, the same time,' he says. 'But we'll meet somewhere else. I have been detailed for you now.'

We then decide where to meet, and separate at once . . .

I jump up in bed. Someone is knocking at the door of my room. There it is again! I have a buzzing feeling in my head. It aches so. My pyjama jacket sticks wetly to my back. I press my hands to my temples, force myself to wake – stand up. The alarm clock shows it is only four o'clock – and knocking!

House search – police! I am paralysed with fright. My hands tremble; I can't hold them still. I've still got the report here – the report! Anything else? No. The report is well hidden! I go slowly to the door, open it. My landlady is standing in the corridor outside. She has pulled a dressing gown on over her nightgown; the plait of thin, white hair hangs over her shoulder.

'For the dear Lord's sake, Herr Petersen, what's wrong? You've been shouting so loudly!' she said worriedly.

'With me? Nothing. I'm sorry I disturbed you!' I force myself to say.

The old woman goes back to her room, shaking her head. But I stand staring out of the window.

The street is veiled in a dim greyness.

This has been going on for weeks. At night, in my sleep, the Browns chase me; during the day I listen to each step on the stairs, to every ring of the bell. My nerves. I must relax for a while soon. What had I been shouting about? I don't remember very clearly; must have been something about Baker Voss. Does the landlady often hear my shouting during these nightmares? I might even betray myself to her by this.

I stare at the rumpled sheets, at the eiderdown on the floor, for a long time. I shiver; my teeth chatter; the jacket sticks clammily to my body.

X, the SA reserve man, reported to Ernst Schwiebus two days ago. At his job, in the perfumery. X, who had told me about Kurgel's torture in the Maikowski Barracks. (Kurgel was only arrested by the Thirty-threes because they wanted to know where Franz Zander was. Franz is dead – but Kurgel is still in the Oranienburg Concentration Camp.)

X is now sitting in front of me, drawing at his cigarette, without saying a word. I don't urge him, yet the thought comes: he used to belong to one of our mass organisations, has remained the same, has known me for years, and yet finds it so difficult to unburden himself.

'Altogether a hundred and twenty SA men have been arrested from the Charlottenburg Storms. For grumbling and lack of discipline. They are in the Charlottenburg police barracks, in the Königin-Elisabeth-Strasse. They are treated as "privileged prisoners"! Are allowed to talk to each other, play cards, smoke. But they get their heads screwed on for them all right a couple of hours in the day. Have to exercise in the yard.'

'Hundred and twenty. Are you sure?'

'Yes! I even heard from a few what for.'

X extinguishes his cigarette end.

'One of the "old guard". Had taken an active part in founding his Storm. The Storm had found work for him. He had been unemployed for years. At the end of the second week he kicked up a row in his factory – he only earned a dog's wage. And the slavery was worse than ever before!'

(Teichert had told me about a similar incident at his factory, too.)

'And another one. It was the other way round with him. He had a good job; joined the SA in March 1933 because he didn't want to lose it. The continual marches got on his nerves. His girl left him because he never had any time for her Sundays. He just didn't turn up any more. Got two doses of eight days' arrest for that. Alexanderplatz, police headquarters. Then he shirked duty again. They're supposed to be treating him as one of the "March converts" in the police barracks now.'

X crosses his legs; his fingers tap nervously at his heavy trench boot.

'But they arrested the majority because they were conducting propaganda for the second revolution.'

'We've heard about that. Do you know any details?'

'Only what they say among themselves: "The SA snatched the chestnuts out of the fire all right but we've been deceived. The bosses have our Socialism; they've climbed into all the soft jobs on our backs, that's all they've changed in Germany," and such talk.'

He takes a piece of paper from the table, tears it into narrow slips.

'Did you have a share in that?'

'Perhaps. I don't know anything about it,' I answer noncommittally.

X twists the strip of paper about in his hand. Keeps his gaze fixed on it.

'Hm! Well, yes. I heard the following tale too. One of the men they afterwards arrested came into the Storm premises with a cyclostyled paper in his hand. "The Red SA Man." Someone had stuck it into his letter-box. He read a few extracts. An article on the "leaders" swell way of living. Names were mentioned. The Reds had also said a number of good things in the old days too, he had remarked. "But that was not their reason for suppressing the Communists. Oh, no, not because of that!"'

(Of course I know the paper. It is published by SA men who already sympathise with us.)

He is silent for a long time.

'Do you know Director Thomas?' is his sudden question.

'No. Why?'

'His case caused a lot of excitement in the SA. A few of the "old guard" are in the police barracks because of that too!'

He plays with the paper again. What a time it takes until he says anything!

'Director Thomas was a Nazi commissioner. Appointed on the Berlin Transport Co. He disappeared suddenly. A few days later the papers printed the announcement that Director Thomas had been drowned in the Havel. It soon came out that he had inserted the notice in the papers himself. The police arrested him. In a seaport. He had the benevolent funds of the Berlin Transport Co. on him; only a couple of hundred thousand marks . . .'

'And the SA men, why were they arrested?'

'They were tram conductors. A notice appeared in their plant station that Director Thomas had died, the funeral was on such and such a date, but none of the workers were allowed to go. And of course this surprised them. The Nazi bosses usually have such swell funerals . . .'

'Well! Carry on.'

'It's coming. The embezzlement tale soon got round. The SA talked about it at work; they even went to their Nazi superiors and asked for an explanation. They considered it their duty, as old SA men – and then they had their mouths closed. "Rotten grumblers"; off with them to the police barracks . . .'

X's opinion was that it was these arrests which had been the cause of making the incidents the topic of conversation among the SA. There were whole groups which were dissatisfied, and could only be held together under severe compulsion. The Nazi leaders knew that too.

I asked X whether he wouldn't try to talk to these opposition SA men about our ideas now and again. It is our job to make the most of this dissatisfaction. We must direct it along our channels. He should at least tell us the names of the SA grumblers. We would send them papers, might even try to get into touch with them ourselves later on. X refused. It was too risky for him; he had a family to consider. He would be sure to hear more details and would then pass them on. But we could not expect more from him. I told him how important these reports about the feeling among the SA were for us. (Preuss had also told me that there were SA prisoners in the Brandenburg Concentration Camp and in the field police barracks in General-Pape-Strasse. Comrades from other districts report the same.)

X is our group's contact with the SA. This was the first time that we heard details about the disintegration among the Charlottenburg SA. The comrade in charge of our district committee told me that they also had other connections with the Charlottenburg SA.

We must induce X to speak more openly with disillusioned SA men in the future, and see that he later introduces them to us.

Frau Zander closed the door of her flat. Her neighbour was standing in her doorway. She went up to the old woman, laid her arm on her shoulder.

'Now, now! You're surely not wanting to go down, when you've only been up for a few days! You've still got to take care of yourself, you know,' she said reproachfully.

She supported Frau Zander, who seemed to have shrunk since her illness. The months in bed had told on her. Her cheeks were sunken.

'You're all so kind to me – I only want to buy something,' she answered.

'But Käthe can do that when she comes home. And if you need it at once I can go for you,' the kindly neighbour protested.

Frau Zander shook her head.

'It's time I started again; must get accustomed to things again. What would Franz say if he saw me like this?'

Franz, always Franz, thought Frau Schulze. We've kept it from her for weeks that Franz is dead. All the tenants in the house. But what'll happen when the old woman gets to know things in the end?

'You were the last one to see him. What did Franz say? When did he want to come again?' Frau Zander asked.

'He said he'd be back soon,' she answered hesitatingly. 'Yes, quite soon.'

'Soon, soon,' Frau Zander repeated; 'but it's such a long time ago.'

She went to the banisters, supported herself heavily against the railing.

'But you shouldn't go out, you really shouldn't!' the neighbour repeated.

'But I want to – and I must.'

The neighbour looked after her, shaking her head disapprovingly.

The old woman took one step at a time, her hand slipping down from rail to rail.

There was only one other woman with a market-bag on her arm in the dairy. She was talking to the shop woman, who was cutting thin slices of cheese. As the door opened the latter quickly put the knife down and ran round the counter.

'Frau Zander, you here!' she said, astonished. 'But you're getting up much too soon, really!'

She supported the old woman, then pulled a chair out for her.

'Now do sit down, just rest yourself, do.'

Frau Zander sat down.

'I've got to start again, you know.' She was breathing heavily.

The dairy woman started cutting her cheese again; the customer went up to the old woman.

'So you're Frau Zander?' she said thoughtfully. And then pityingly: 'Then Franz was your son?'

'Yes. Do you know him, my Franz?' Frau Zander asked.

'I knew him well. I often used to see him. I remember him quite well,' the woman replied.

'Frau Meier! Frau Meier! Do you want anything else?' the woman interrupted from the counter. Frau Meier turned round. She wondered why the dairy woman was shouting so. The latter was standing behind the glass case in which different kinds of food were displayed, and nodding across, shaking her head, and holding her finger warningly to her mouth. But Frau Meier did not understand the signs. The dairy woman kept on nodding across, tapping her finger against her mouth.

'What's the matter?' Frau Meier asked at last. 'Yes, let me have a quarter of salami, and a quarter of tongue sausage!'

She pointed to the glass case.

'You know him?' Frau Zander asked her softly.

'Yes, I knew him. He was a good sort. It's a great pity,' Frau Meier said.

At that the dairy woman called out again, 'Frau Meier! Frau Meier!'

The latter was beginning to get angry.

'Yes, of course that's right – that one there!' she said, vexed. The dairy woman continued making signs, but her customer did not bother herself with them any more.

'He hasn't been here for ages – and yet he wanted to come back soon,' Frau Zander confided. She smiled secretly to herself.

'Who?' asked the other woman doubtfully.

'Why, Franz, my son,' answered the old woman quietly, as if she were talking to herself.

Frau Meier then walked right up to the old woman and looked her straight in the eyes. She took no notice of the dairy woman hammering away on the counter with the handle of her knife.

'Your Franz?' she said quickly. 'He can't come any more. Why, we buried him six weeks ago!'

Dead silence in the shop. The dairy woman stood with her mouth open and drooping shoulders; the knife had slipped out of her hand. Frau Zander made a convulsive movement at her heart; her fingers plucked at her blouse. She sat like that for long seconds. Stiffly, with staring eyes. (In these few seconds she must have understood a lot that had happened during the last weeks; the neighbours ever ready to help, the compassionate faces of the other tenants, Käthe's nervous manner, the reason for her being so pale and sad.)

All of a sudden the old woman jumped up from her chair. Her face became distorted; she shrieked at the top of her voice. The other customer ran off to fetch help. But Frau Zander was still shrieking when they carried her out of the shop. In the yard, on the stairs. Then the whole house became quiet.

With sullen faces, with their lips pressed together, the people stood at their doors and windows.

I stand in front of the advertisement pillar. It is an advertisement pillar like all the others. A huge poster is pasted on the upper half. A woman is depicted; the body is formed by a cigarette. 'The Berlinerin', 'The big round Juno', is written in large letters underneath. And near it the bright cinema posters, *Love and Kisses, Veronika, Annemarie, the Bride of the Company.*

I read and read that. I can't keep on reading the yellow poster in the centre. I can't do that.

PUBLIC NOTICE

The judicial Press service announces that Richard Hüttig, of Berlin, born on March 18th, 1908, in Bottendorf, was sentenced to death by the legal verdict of the special court of the Berlin Tribunal on February 16th, 1934. The death sentence was executed this morning in the courtyard of the penal prison at Plötzensee.

Berlin, June 14th, 1934.

I do not know how long I have been standing in front of the notice, but I cannot stay here any longer.

Left foot, right foot, left foot, right foot, the movement is mechanical, independent of my will. The people rush past; the traffic noises seem to come from a long way off.

I slowly return to our street.

FORWARD FROM LIBERALISM

by STEPHEN SPENDER

(monthly choice, January 1937)

Forward from Liberalism was supposed to be written jointly with A. J. Ayer. Stephen Spender (1909–95) and Ayer spent the autumn of 1936 reading for and discussing the book, which Gollancz had told them would be an LBC choice. But when, in December, Spender married the beautiful Communist Inez Pearn, he learned that not only had she had a recent fling with Philip Toynbee but one with Ayer, too. Peeved, he decided to write the book on his own.

Both Spender and Ayer, presumably, were attracted by the idea of explaining why Communism was the natural home for liberal idealists, now that the shortcomings of the old liberal democracies were all too evident. The initial idea for the book had come from Gollancz, who had himself toyed with writing something about the limited extent of freedom in capitalist societies. 'I am a Communist,' Gollancz was in the habit of saying, 'because I am a liberal.' Spender was asked to 'write a book on my approach to Communism'; his aim was less to 'develop a thesis' than to 'portray an attitude of mind'. The LBC touted the book as marking 'a definite step in the breakdown of the traditional isolation of the creative writer from politics'. As a fashionable poet who had a 'semi-deified' status among Oxford undergraduates, Spender held out the promise of converting a legion of young progressives to Communism, especially as his conception of Communism was one which entered all areas of life. The book discussed both political freedom – 'I strayed into realms of historical analysis and political ratiocination,' he later wrote, 'a task for which almost any university student of history was better equipped than I' – and artistic freedom, attained by joining the class struggle and moving outside 'the private worlds of romanticism'.

It seemed to work. 'There is a possibility', the reviewer in the *New Statesman* said, 'that this book may, and I hope it will, exercise a greater influence over the political opinions of the younger generation than any one publication since the war.' Young Communists did indeed cite the book as one which had formed their opinions. The *Manchester Guardian* was less kind, describing it as 'a characteristic product of English parlour Bolshevism', while E. H. Carr said that Spender, 'a young poet and open-hearted', had 'marched forward from liberalism into a mass of illusions'.

The review in the *Daily Worker*, by Randall Swingler, criticised Spender for his refusal to admit the 'irrefutable logic of Zinoviev's guilt'. This was because in the book's final chapter – on the whole a hymn of praise to Stalin and the Webbs' *Soviet Communism* – Spender called for the introduction of a democratic constitution and the legalisation of political criticism in the USSR (he was writing as the first news of the show trials was coming in). Harry Pollitt, who, having read *Forward*, called Spender into his office in King Street in the hope of persuading him to visit (or fight in) Spain, managed to persuade him of the authenticity of the trial confessions, and Spender became an enthusiastic Communist Party representative, if only for a while. He soon made the journey back to liberalism, and this time he stayed there, retelling the story of his flirtation with Marxism many times, in increasingly self-exonerating versions. The text of *Forward from Liberalism* cuts through these deceiving memories and makes clear that Spender fully believed traditional liberal politics to be doomed; it is this which makes it such an interesting document.

From CHAPTER I:
THE GOAL OF AN UNPOLITICAL AGE

'Religion is politics, and politics is Brotherhood,' wrote William Blake. These words take us back to the time when Thomas Paine, his friend William Blake, Godwin, and later the romantics, inspired by events in France and America, believed that their political faith, interpreted in action, would overthrow kings and tyrants and make all men brothers. Politics became a religion without God, that is to say, a way of life. Godwin believed that when men had seen the light of political reason, the advantages of equality and of a free individuality enjoyed by everyone, even the aristocratic and the rich would be willing to resign their superior positions and their wealth to the common good.

Thomas Paine was certain, writing at the end of the eighteenth century, that all the monarchies of Europe were doomed to fall before long. Shelley postulated an age of political justice which would be the background of a new classicism: his own poetry is incomplete, a voice in the wilderness prophesying that greater age which would come after him, fulfilling conditions which might have made him a tragedian of Hellenic stature. Byron hated everything that meant 'politics' to the aristocracy, the governing class into which he was born: the politics of George III, Lord Castlereagh, Wellington, Bob Southey, even Wordsworth. This hatred was the subject of his greatest poetry.

The link between communists to-day and the political idealists of a hundred and fifty years ago is not one of method, not even of the 'blood shed like water and tears like mist', which must precede the overthrow of monarchies; it is the understanding they both share that 'politics is Brotherhood', upheld against the accepted political practice of their times.

Between us and the idealist revolutionaries of the early nineteenth century lies the 'liberal experiment' of the past hundred years, reaching forward to our own day. Liberal democracy certainly means political freedom, free elections, equality before the law, freedom of assembly, habeas corpus; yet these genuine political rights are undermined by the doctrine of *laissez faire* which has left economic power in the hands of a small class owning the greater part of the whole wealth of the country. The legal and political systems of liberal democracy are built up to protect private ownership by putting it outside the range of political interference. Freedom of trade and *laissez faire* have come to mean the protection of the individual proprietor from the political system. Liberal governments made themselves powerless against the great capitalist interests which guided the state. But, to the communist, politics begin with the abolition of the system of private property, which is exactly where, for the liberal, they end.

Thus in our day although the politics of democratic government mean something very different from the aristocratic system of government which Byron raged against, they are no nearer to Blake's epigram.

In the last hundred years, reformist democratic politics have meant administration by government departments: reforms – factory acts, education, health insurance, old age pensions – which do not restore the balance of an increasing inequality between the classes; budgets which are the chief perennial event of the financial year, with their small adjustments of 2*d.* off tea, 3*d.* on or off income tax; debates, speeches, scenes in Parliament which occasionally precede other sensations in the attention which the press pays them; foreign politics acted out on the shores of Lake Leman; secret treaties signed behind closed doors; tactfully worded claims sent from prime minister to foreign chancellor; declarations of war.

When the English two-party system was at its parliamentary zenith, politics dramatized a clash between personalities. For nearly a generation, the conflict between Disraeli and Gladstone dominated all other issues. Parliamentary debates between these two captains and their teams were followed by the Victorians with an interest which people now give to football matches. The contest towered up with a baroque extravagance so important to the chief actors themselves that the reader of Morley's *Life of Gladstone* is bound to admit that Gladstone – a great figure in many respects, not to be jibed at, but worthy to be portrayed by a Cervantes – at certain moments regarded Disraeli as the devil in person: and the devil was very real to Mr Gladstone. Although he was a humble man, the very blackness of his opponent made an election in which Disraeli's party was licked a revelation of 'the great hand of God, so evidently displayed'.

That great parliamentary era is over. To-day there is so strong a reaction from the politics of personal ambition, vacillation, parliamentary debate and delay, that to many people the very word 'politics' has become associated with these worst features of democratic government. If one analyses this reaction one finds that it can nearly always be summed up in the phrase 'politicians can't do anything but talk'; behind this phrase is an awareness that within the present democratic system, Labour, Liberal and Conservative are all very much alike. Whatever the more radical leaders say in opposition, experience shows that when in power they grapple like the former government with events quite outside their control – world crisis, the approaching war. It is true that democracy puts through reforms, but a hundred years of such reforms show that a reformist policy only scratches the surface of the real forces that govern our lives. In fact, political questions that most deeply concern us are not decided by Parliament at all but by the industrial interests which control the liberal democratic state.

For example, the pretence that an English parliamentary government creates employment or prevents war, rings hollow. The phrase used by the National Government speakers that they are 'creating confidence' describes with perfect frankness all that democratic government can do. It can satisfy business interests with the assurance that Parliament will not interfere with private enterprise. Indeed, in the name of 'employment' it will subsidize private enterprise with money raised from public taxation. It can rearm, but must on no account nationalize the armaments industry. Above all, it can obstruct the path to power of any socialist government which might strain the machinery of democracy to take government out of the hands of industry and govern in the interests of the workers.

Democracies are passing through a stage of acute disappointment with the very limited and ineffective political power which they enjoy. In England this disappointment takes the form of apathy, on the Continent, of despair. It is apathy and despair, not enthusiasm, which produce, or rather permit, fascism and war, although, when they are whipped up by propaganda, these tired emotions can be raised to an angry vehemence. The mood of the Germany which allowed Hitler to seize power was: 'Things can't be worse than they now are, so we might as well try Hitler.' Those people who said or felt this were so disillusioned with the quarrels of their twenty-seven German political parties and with the emergency decrees of the Bruening government, that they wanted any government which would meet crisis with a display of effectual political power.

So despair and apathy, negative emotions, have reactionary political effects of the first importance. People associate the word 'politics' with the particular system of government which they know. When they say that they are sick of politics, they mean that they are in the mood to overthrow this system, and that is a far-reaching political action, leading to nationalism and war. In this mood people do not set up a better political system of their own: they have grown so used to thinking of parliamentary government as ineffectual that such a democracy seems to them outside the possibilities of 'politics' altogether. On the contrary, they wish only to throw back the responsibility of power on to rulers whom they have recognized in the past – kings, generals, priests, dictators. It is the mood in which a *coup d'état* is possible. In the capitalist countries, some form of fascism is the inevitable coup: the seizure of power by a minority which represents capital, the force which has already made liberal democratic government almost impotent to work against its interests. The small military, industrial, monarchical, clerical oligarchy (it may have any or all of these attributes), instead of directing affairs through or against a democratically elected parliament, suddenly dictates them. 'Freedom does not give us work or bread,' the German *Lumpenproletariat* and the impoverished bureaucratic middle class cried. 'All right, then, you need have no freedom: and as for bread, if you are not free you will not have the chance to ask for it,' answered the bankers, industrialists, Junkers, generals: and they produced their puppet, Hitler.

To-day the world is witnessing a struggle between three different political systems, different conceptions of the meaning of politics. As the competition between the fundamental capitalist and imperialist interests of the separate nations grows intenser, the ineffective liberal democracies are being discarded or remodelled, whilst the party representing the real centre of nationalist power sets up a naked or a veiled dictatorship. This intensified competition leads to war, whilst the very threat of war produces a reaction towards nationalism even in those countries that are still called democratic, just as during the Great War the English Liberal coalition government set up a dictatorship which served as a precedent for Hitler and Mussolini.

The only politics which is opposed not merely to actual war but to the competitive system which produces the conditions of want and fear which lead to war is a politics directed in the interests of the workers and not of those who exploit them, of the peoples of the whole world and not of the directors of nationalist commercial rivalry.

For the real political problems are not those which go by the name of politics when people say that they are sick of parliamentary debates and governmental vacillation; they are the fight of the ordinary man for bare existence in a world of natural abundance and mechanical over-production; the climax of the competition between the different capitalist national groups in a war more terrible than the last. Any political system which does not grapple with these questions is bound to be superseded. Brutal realities expose the weakness of liberal democracy, the flimsiness of our illusions of freedom in a world where one man is free to make huge profits from selling armaments that will be used against his countrymen, another only to die on the battle-field. Yet if we restrict or abandon the genuine though limited rights of liberal democracy, we are confronted with the fact that there are only two political ways left: that of the exploiters or the exploited, that of the capitalist rivals and rulers or the 'Brotherhood of man'.

In such a world, with such unprecedented possibilities of happiness and justice, with such actuality of misery and fear, politics is not an abstract argument, nor even questions of administration and reform, but of the life or death of our civilization. If it is death, nothing that we do matters, even if our lives are concerned with artistic creation or scientific inquiries that seem far more important than any political question: for all our activities will be destroyed or repressed. For the sake of civilization, which is, as an end, more important than the means by which it is achieved, it is necessary that we should live, just as for the sake of one's country, which is more important than the war by which it was saved, it has been held necessary to die. Everything which we do to fight for life, to extend knowledge and understanding, to create beauty, must be bound up with the political will to make impossible war, hatred and public misery which destroy these values.

People living in democracies find that the power called politics and centred in their system of government can resolve none of the problems which confront themselves, their country or the world. They are forced then to resign that power into other autocratic hands – as it has been resigned before – or to compel a politics conducted in the interests of the whole people to mean power and be effective.

So, to explain what the meaning of the word 'politics' is to me is to declare my political attitude. Politics to me is the effort to 'assimilate the treasures of knowledge accumulated by humanity as a whole'; to make this knowledge available to the greatest number of human beings, so that it may be the widely distributed basis of a better society. Politics means making democracy effective instead of destroying it: to do this, it is necessary to have not merely a political but also an economic and a cultural democracy of those who 'give according to their ability and receive according to their need'.

The alternative to this is the fascist state where the political freedom of the liberal constitution is withdrawn altogether from the democracy. Capitalism is then the revealed centre of power. The measures taken by the dictator – suppression of all who stand for political freedom, re-armament, propaganda for the increase of population, lowering of the standard of life of the workers – are exactly those required by an over-producing industrialism which must fight for expanding markets. No doubt the capitalists themselves have to pay a heavy price for the dictatorship; their reward is the complete suppression of the working-class movements. In the fascist state all the political ardour of the people is concentrated on nationalist and imperialist aims – ultimately, on war. Thus every tendency of capitalism to drift towards war is increased a hundredfold.

One might compare politics in the totalitarian state to a single dazzling light concentrated on the dictator, but controlled by the forces of capital and the army, which have put him into power. Liberal democracy is like a dishonest pair of scales heavily weighted in favour of industry, which has the real power, the knowledge, the self-interest to make and unmake governments and control their policies when they are made: nevertheless, the scales do work, and with great resolution, energy, and an enormous popular increase of political realism, it would be possible for socialism to tip the scales, as the French and Spanish Popular Fronts have recently shown. In a communist state, political power is a light diffused throughout the whole state, for the essential political fact is that all property is public socialist property. It is true that during the period of transition from the capitalist to the socialist state, the carriers of this idea are the Communist party members directing the dictatorship; yet experience of liberal democracy shows that without this transitional period, economic freedom cannot be achieved within the weighted democratic system. Therefore the transitional dictatorship is a dictatorship against capitalism; it is essentially the dictatorship of an idea by the guardians of that idea during a period of reorganization when it is impossible to put the democracy into force.

The propertyless nature of the classless society is a political fact at the very centre of communist life, shared by the whole people. This gives the communist faith a significance which so far has only derived from the ways of life laid down by religion. Yet it is a mistake to call communism a religion, for whereas the very essence of religion is that its aims are unrealizable in this life, communist faith is inseparable from the action that will achieve the classless society. Religion is not the name for a movement which refuses to entertain any aims that are not realizable, that does not make a God of humanity, but the equal rights of human beings a realizable goal. If you require a phrase, it would be better to call communist morality a 'way of life' than a religion.

Instead of abandoning the idealist achievements of the liberal state, communism would make them real. It would provide the equal economic basis for freedom, make democracy effective, states international. It is evident that the liberal democratic state cannot survive in its present form; the pressure of war, economic crisis, public disappointment, is too great; its leaders must choose between the interests of the financial oligarchy and the disinterested ideal of democratic freedom. Since liberal democracy is pledged to protect the sanctity of private property, it is fairly evident which path the liberal democracies will choose. So that whether there is a world war or an intensification of the present armaments race and desperate commercial competition, democracy, in either case, is likely to be superseded by a repressive form of nationalism. Fascism means two things: an intensification of nationalist government in the interests of industry, and the effective removal of all power of political choice from the electorate. The repressive methods adopted by fascist countries are only matters of degree. The reality behind the barrage of government propaganda, the electoral farces, the system of spying and political violence, is that the people do not will: they are the willed.

Communism is the struggle to inspire the standards of our civilization with the political will not only to survive the attacks of a barbarism growing up in our midst, but also to go forward and create a more extensive civilization which will grow from the roots of a classless society. The life of the past does not depend on our deaths, our apathy, our disgust; but upon our life and our will to extend culture into further times and amongst broad masses of people. When a civilization, instead of going forward, turns back to imitate its own past, the greatness of the past exists in the present as though it were preserved in a museum, or else as a destructive violence of reaction.

Thus, when the very existence of civilization is threatened by war and oppression, politics become either an affirmation of life or an alliance with death. More than this, in innumerable ways, even when men are unaware of it, the activities of their lives assume a political aspect. Although they may be indifferent to politics and politicians, they cannot ignore the contemporary history which feeds or starves them, breeds and shoots them. They cannot avoid taking sides; if they are apathetic, the democratic government which they might support is swept aside without a protest, to be replaced with tyranny. If they live a life of private sensations, personal relationships, cultivated sensibilities, they will come to set a value on the economic arrangements of a society which have made these self-centred, amoral experiences possible to them. They will allow others to suffer, the whole of the society to be ruined even, sooner than lose the privilege of their individualism, which has become, not a way of life, but a drug. The lover of past traditions who cannot relate the life of the past to the future, will direct his thoughts backward to some more fortunate niche of history; in his life he will take the side of forces that are fighting against the future. The past rises up, greets him, assumes the robes of Roman imperialism and destroys him with weapons which Rome never dreamed of.

To die is easier than to live. For to live, in the fullest sense, in our society, requires not merely the ability to exist, whilst the conditions that will make even existence possible for our children are being removed or violently destroyed; whilst half the population of capitalist countries lives in a state of semi-starvation; but also the will to remove material evils that are at present choking civilized life.

All the moral and aesthetic standards of the present and the past, even the memories of the greatness of past times, spring from and are affected by the contemporary environment. We only experience that tradition of the past which still lives in the present. The isolated individualist may imagine that he escapes from his environment, that he can preserve and create values of life out of a vacuum of surrounding fear and death. It is not true. He cannot escape from his own consciousness: and consciousness is never completely isolated. He cannot reject every impression of his senses: and every impression is imperceptibly coloured with the time in which he lives.

It is true that the great creative works of civilization are achieved, not during periods of war and political stress, but of equilibrium. Yet we cannot, by denying the present and by isolating ourselves mentally and physically, create these conditions. At most we can only create thus a culture and an art of the isolated, which ignores dangers threatening the whole of humanity.

What we can do is to work towards an age in which deep political class and nationalist divisions no longer exist. The final aim of civilized men must be an unpolitical age, where conditions of peace and security are conducive to a classical art, rooted not in a small oligarchy but in the lives of the whole people.

And the only true equilibrium which the modern world can achieve must cut across all national boundaries and capitalist interests, since the present distribution can achieve no equilibrium, but at best a balance of imperialist interests: a balance which is always precarious, allowing men to starve amidst plenty, and leaving civilization permanently under the shadow of war. Science, invention, art, the cultural standards of our time, in all their implications strive towards the equilibrium of a new classical period, the achievement of a new and stable democracy . . .

RED STAR OVER CHINA

by Edgar Snow

(monthly choice, October 1937)

Edgar Snow (1905–72), a journalist from Kansas City, first began reporting from China in 1928. Based in Beijing, he wrote for the *Saturday Evening Post* and sometimes for *Life*. He cultivated friendships with Chinese radicals, students and secret sympathisers with the Communists. In 1936, he was told that there was a chance he could visit the Red Army in north-west China, its base following the Long March. Very little was known about the Chinese Communists in Europe or the States; no foreign journalist had got in detail the story of their 6,000-mile fighting retreat from Chiang Kai-shek's Nationalist forces. So Snow set off – in his luggage was a letter of introduction to Mao Tse-tung written in invisible ink. He travelled by train to Sian and by truck to Yenan, still in Nationalist territory. A day later, in a town called Pai Chia Ping, a young Communist officer with a black beard walked up to him and said in English: 'Hello. Are you looking for somebody?' It was Chou En-lai. *Red Star over China* reports Snow's encounters and conversations with the leaders and the rank-and-file of the Red Army. He gives a generous, admiring account of the Long March and paints an idyllic picture of life in the Communist soviets of the north-west. The culmination of Snow's journey is his series of conversations with Mao – the first ever in-depth interview with the Communist leader. It was a gigantic scoop, wrapped inside what *Left News* called a 'magnificent adventure story'.

Red Star over China was, Gollancz said, 'one of those rarely opportune books for which every publisher prays'. Enthusiastic letters 'poured in' from LBC members; it was 'infinitely the finest "recruiter"' the Club had ever had. Its publication coincided with a sharp increase in interest in China, attendant on the massive Japanese invasion in 1937 and the formation of a United Front between the Chinese Communists and Nationalists to wage the 'Great Patriotic War'. When the book appeared in October, Nanking was being raided by Japanese warplanes;

Japan was making inroads into Chinese territory and stories of atrocities were beginning to emerge. That month's issue of *Left News* was devoted to China, focusing subscribers' thoughts on the 'cold and calculated murder' committed by the Japanese Army. 'While our minds are still so full of Spain that it might seem that they could hold no further thought,' Gollancz wrote, 'the agony of a whole continent has put in its claim.' The 'ineffable sufferings of the Spaniards and the Chinese should,' he said, 'be as real to us as our own'. A new people were adopted, a new cause taken up. Within months, hundreds of LBC meetings and marches for China had been held. Mrs Sellars describes one in Pamela Hansford Johnson's novel *The Monument*: 'Young men and women paraded in the street, bearing Chinese lanterns, flapping posters, and shouting in giant voices their fury against murder and aggression.'

Snow expressed gratitude to his 'enterprising and brilliant publisher' and collected messages of support for the LBC from Mao and Madam Chiang (they were read out at the Club's second national rally). Gollancz embraced the Chinese cause wholeheartedly. He helped set up the China Campaign Committee – to supply information and attract public support for the United Front – and was later awarded the Glorious Star of China. Snow's book, which was published in the United States in 1938 and translated into many languages, soon became world famous. He continued to enjoy privileged access to Mao, and although copies of *Red Star over China* were thrown on to bonfires by Red Guards during the Cultural Revolution, it was in an interview with Snow in December 1970 that Mao signalled to Nixon that he would be welcome to visit China.

From PARTS I, II, X, XI

DURING MY SEVEN years in China, hundreds of questions had been asked about the Chinese Red Army, the Soviets, and the Communist movement. Eager partisans could supply you with a stock of ready answers, but these remained highly unsatisfactory. How did they *know*? They had never been to Red China.

The fact was that there had been perhaps no greater mystery among nations, no more confused an epic, than the story of Red China. Fighting in the very heart of the most populous nation on earth, the Celestial Reds had for nine years been isolated by a news blockade as effective as a stone fortress. A mobile Great Wall of thousands of enemy troops constantly surrounded them; their territory was more inaccessible than Tibet. No one had voluntarily penetrated that wall and returned to write of his experiences since the first Chinese Soviet was established at Ch'alin in south-eastern Hunan, in November 1927.

Even the simplest points were disputed. Some people denied that there was such a thing as a Red Army. There were only thousands of hungry brigands. Some denied even the existence of Soviets. They were an invention of Communist propaganda. Yet Red sympathizers extolled both as the only salvation for all the ills of China. In the midst of this propaganda and counter-propaganda, credible evidence was lacking for dispassionate observers seeking the truth. Here are some of the unanswered questions that interested everyone concerned with politics and the quickening history of the Orient:

Was or was not this Red Army of China a mass of conscious Marxist revolutionaries, disciplined by and adhering to a centralized programme, a unified command under the Chinese Communist Party? If so, what was that programme? The Communists claimed to be fighting for agrarian revolution, and against imperialism, and for Soviet democracy and national emancipation. Nanking said that the Reds were only a new type of vandals and marauders led by 'intellectual bandits'. Who was right? Or was either one?

Before 1927, members of the Communist Party were admitted to the Kuomintang, but in April of that year began the famous 'purgation'. Communists, as well as unorganized radical intellectuals, and thousands of organized workers and peasants, were executed on an extensive scale under Chiang Kai-shek, the leader of a Right *coup d'état* which seized power at Nanking. Since then it had been a crime punishable by death to be a Communist or a Communist sympathizer, and thousands had paid that penalty. Yet thousands more continued to run the risk. Thousands of peasants, workers, students and soldiers joined the Red Army in its struggle against the military dictatorship of the Nanking regime. Why? . . .

We all knew that the only way to learn anything about Red China was to go there. We excused ourselves by saying, '*Mei yu fa-tzu*' – 'It can't be done.' A few had tried and failed. It was believed impossible. People thought that nobody could enter Red territory and come out alive. Such was the strength of years of anti-Communist propaganda in a country whose Press is as rigidly censored and regimented as that of Italy or Germany.

Then, in June 1936, a close Chinese friend of mine brought me news of an amazing political situation in north-west China – a situation which was later to culminate in the sensational arrest of Generalissimo Chiang Kai-shek, and to change the current of Chinese history. More important to me then, however, I learned, with this news, of a possible method of entry to Red territory. It necessitated leaving at once. The opportunity was unique and not to be missed. I decided to take it, and attempt to break a news blockade nine years old.

It is true there were risks involved, though the reports later published of my death – 'killed by bandits' – were probably exaggerated. But, against a torrent of horror-stories about Red atrocities that had for many years filled the subsidized vernacular and foreign Press of China, I had little to cheer me on my way. Nothing, in truth, but a letter of introduction to Mao Tse-tung, chairman of the Soviet Government. All I had to do was to find him. Through what adventures? I did not know. But thousands of lives had been sacrificed in these years of Kuomintang–Communist warfare. Could one foreign neck be better hazarded than in an effort to discover why? I found myself somewhat attached to the neck in question, but I concluded that the price was not too high to pay.

In this melodramatic mood I set out . . .

* * *

'Down with the landlords who eat our flesh!'

'Down with the militarists who drink our blood!'

'Down with the traitors who sell China to Japan!'

'Welcome the United Front with all anti-Japanese armies!'

'Long live the Chinese Revolution!'

'Long live the Chinese Red Army!'

It was under these somewhat disturbing exhortations, emblazoned in bold black characters, that I was destined to spend my first night in Red territory.

But it was not in An Tsai and not under the protection of any Red soldiers. For, as I had feared, we did not reach An Tsai that day, but by sunset had arrived only at a little village that lay nestled in the curve of a river, with hills brooding darkly on every side. Several layers of slate-roofed houses rose up from the lip of the stream, and it was on their mud walls that the slogans were chalked. Fifty or sixty peasants and staring children poured out to greet my caravan of one donkey.

My young guide – an emissary of the Poor People's League – decided to deposit me here. One of his cows had recently calved, he said; there were wolves in the neighbourhood, and he had to get back to his charges. An Tsai was still ten miles distant and we could not get there easily in the dark. He turned me over for safe-keeping to the chairman of the local branch of the Poor People's League. Both guide and muleteer refused any compensation for their services – either in White money or Red.

The chairman was a youth in his early twenties who wore a faded blue cotton jacket under a brown open face, and a pair of white trousers above a pair of leathery bare feet. He welcomed me and was very kind. He offered me a room in the village meeting-house, and had hot water brought to me, and a bowl of millet. But I declined the dark evil-smelling room, and petitioned for the use of two dismantled doors. Laying these on a couple of benches, I unrolled my blankets and made my bed in the open. It was a gorgeous night, with a clear sky spangled with northern stars, and the waters in a little falls below me murmured of peace and tranquillity. Exhausted from the long walk I feel asleep immediately.

When I opened my eyes again dawn was just breaking. The chairman was standing over me, shaking my shoulder. Of course I was startled, and I sat up at once, fully awake.

'What is it?' I demanded.

'You had better leave a little early. There are bandits near here, and you ought to get to An Tsai quickly.'

Bandits? It was on my tongue to reply that I had in fact come precisely to meet these co-called bandits, when I suddenly realized what he meant. He was not talking about Reds, he meant 'White-bandits'. I got up without further persuasion. I did not want anything to happen to me so ridiculous as being kidnapped by White-bandits in Soviet China . . .

Hastily swallowing some hot tea and wheat cakes I set off with another guide and muleteer contributed by the chairman. For an hour we followed the bed of the stream, occasionally passing small cave-villages, where heavy-furred native dogs growled menacingly at me and child sentinels came out to demand our road pass. Then we reached a lovely pool of still water set in a natural basin hollowed from great rocks, and there I saw my first Red warrior.

He was alone except for a pretty white pony which stood grazing beside the stream, and wearing a vivid silky-blue saddle-blanket with a yellow star on it. The young man had been bathing, and at our approach he jumped up quickly, pulling on a sky-blue coat and a turban of white towelling, on which was fixed a red star. A mauser hung at his hip, with a red tassel dangling bravely from its wooden combination holster-stock. With his hand on his gun he waited for us to come up to him, and demanded our business from the guide. The latter having produced his road pass, and briefly explained how I had been cast upon him, the warrior looked at me curiously for further elucidation.

'I have come to interview Mao Tse-tung,' I offered; 'I understand he is at An Tsai. How much farther have we to go?'

'Chairman Mao?' he inquired slowly. 'No, he is not at An Tsai.' Then he peered behind us and asked if I were alone. Having convinced himself that I was, his reserve dropped from him, he smiled as if at some secret amusement, and said, 'I am going to An Tsai. I'll just go along with you to the district Government.'

He walked his pony beside me and I volunteered more details about myself, and ventured some inquiries about him. I learned that he was in the Political Defence Bureau (Gaypayoo), and was on patrol duty along this frontier. And the horse? It was a 'gift' from Young Marshal Chang Hsueh-liang. He told me that the Reds had captured over 1,000 horses from Chang's troops in recent battles in north Shensi. I learned further that he was called Yao, that he was twenty-two years old, and that he had been a Red for six years. Six years! What tales he must have to tell!

I liked him. He was an honest-looking youth, rather well made, with a shock of glistening black hair under his red star. Meeting him in the lonely valley was reassuring. In fact I even neglected to question him about the bandits, for we were soon discussing the Red Army's spring march into Shansi. In return for my account of the effect it had produced in Peking, he told me of his own experiences in that astonishing 'Anti-Japanese Expedition', in which the Red Army column had collected 15,000 new followers in a single month.

In a couple of hours we had reached An Tsai, which lay opposite the Fu Ho, a sub-tributary of the Yellow River. A big town on the map, An Tsai turned out to be little but the pretty shell of its wall. The streets were completely deserted and everything stood in crumbling ruins. My first thought was that these were the evidences of pillage and vandalism. But closer inspection showed no signs of burning and it was clear enough that the ruins were ancient and could not have been made by the Reds.

'The town was completely destroyed over a decade ago by a great flood,' Yao explained. 'The whole city went swimming.'

An Tsai's inhabitants had not rebuilt the city, but lived now in the face of a great stone cliff, honey-combed with *yao-fang*, a little beyond the walls. Upon arrival we discovered, however, that the Red Army detachment stationed there had been dispatched to chase bandits, while members of the district Soviet had gone to Pai Chia P'ing, a nearby hamlet, to render a report to a provincial commissioner. Yao volunteered to escort me to Pai Chia P'ing – 'Hundred Family Peace' – which we reached at dusk.

I had already been in Soviet territory a day and a half, yet I had seen no signs of war-time distress, had met but one Red soldier, and a populace that universally seemed to be pursuing its agrarian tasks in complete composure. Yet I was not to be misled by appearances. I remembered how, during the Sino-Japanese war at Shanghai in 1932, Chinese peasants had gone on tilling their fields in the very midst of battle, with apparent unconcern. So that when, just as we rounded a corner to enter 'Hundred Family Peace', and I heard the most awful and blood-curdling yells directly above me, I was not entirely unprepared.

Looking towards the sound of the fierce battle-cries, I saw, standing on a ledge above the road, in front of a row of barrack-like houses, a dozen peasants brandishing spears, pikes and a few rifles in the most uncompromising of attitudes. It seemed that the question of my fate as a blockade-runner – whether I was to be given the firing squad as an imperialist, or to be welcomed as an honest inquirer – was about to be settled without further delay.

I must have turned a comical face towards Yao, for he burst into laughter. '*Pu p'a!*' he chuckled. 'Don't be afraid. They are only some partisans – *practising*. There is a Red partisan school here. Don't be alarmed!'

Later on I learned that the curriculum for partisans includes this rehearsal of ancient Chinese war-cries, just as in the days of feudal tourneys described in *All Men Are Brothers*. And having experienced a certain frigidity of spine as an unwitting subject of the technique, I can testify that it is still very effective in intimidating an enemy. Shouted during a surprise attack in the dark, when partisans prefer to act, these cries must be utterly terrifying.

I had just sat down and begun an interview with a Soviet functionary to whom Yao had introduced me in Pai Chia P'ing, when a young commander, wearing a Sam Browne belt, stumbled up on a sweating horse, and plunged to the ground. He looked curiously at me. And it was from him that I heard the full details of my own adventure.

The new arrival was named Pien, and he was commandant of the An Tsai Red Guard. He announced that he had just returned from an encounter with a force of about a hundred *min-t'uan*. A little peasant boy – a 'Young Vanguard' – had run several miles and arrived almost exhausted at An Tsai, to warn them that *min-t'uan* had invaded the district. And that their leader was a really *white* bandit! – a foreign devil – *myself*!

'I at once took a mounted detachment over a mountain short-cut, and in an hour we sighted the bandits,' Pien recounted. 'They were following you' – he pointed at me – 'only about two *li*. But we surrounded them, attacked in a valley, and captured some, including two of their leaders, and several horses. The rest escaped toward the frontier.' As he concluded his brief report, some of his command filed into the courtyard, leading several of the captured mounts.

I began to wonder if he really thought I *was* leading the *min-t'uan*. Had I escaped from Whites – who, had they seized me in no-man's-land, undoubtedly would have called me a Red – only to be captured by the Reds and accused of being a White?

But presently a slender young officer appeared, ornamented with a heavy black beard. He came up and addressed me in a soft cultured voice. 'Hello,' he said, 'are you looking for somebody?'

He had spoken in *English*!

And in a moment I learned that he was Chou En-lai, the 'notorious' Red commander, who had once been an honours student in a missionary school. Here at last my reception was decided

* * *

North Shensi was one of the poorest parts of China I had seen, not excluding western Yunnan. There was no real land scarcity, but there was in many places a serious scarcity of real land – at least real farming land. Here in Shensi a peasant may own as much as 100 *mou* (about a sixth of an acre) of land and yet be a poor man. A landlord in this country has to possess at least several hundred *mou* of land, and even on a Chinese scale he cannot be considered rich unless his holdings are part of the limited and fertile valley land, where rice and other valued crops can be grown.

The farms of Shensi may be described as slanting, and many of them also as slipping, for landslides are frequent. The fields are mostly patches laid on the serried landscape, between crevices and small streams. The land seems rich enough in many places, but the crops grown are strictly limited by the steep gradients, both in quantity and quality. There are few genuine mountains, only endless broken hills, hills as interminable as a sentence by James Joyce, and even more tiresome. Yet the effect is often strikingly like Picasso, the sharp-angled shadowing and colouring changing miraculously with the sun's wheel, and towards dusk it becomes a magnificent sea of purpled hilltops with dark velvety folds running down, like the pleats on a mandarin skirt, to ravines that seem bottomless.

After the first day I rode little, not so much out of pity for the languishing nag, but because everyone else marched. Li Chiang-lin was the oldest warrior of the company. Most of the others were lads in their teens, hardly more than children. One of these was nicknamed 'Lao Kou', the Old Dog, and walking with him I asked why he had joined the Reds.

He was a southerner and had come all the way from the Fukien Soviet districts, on the Red Army's 6,000-mile expedition which foreign military experts refused to believe possible. Yet here was Old Dog, seventeen years old, and actually looking fourteen. He had made that march and thought nothing of it. He said that he was prepared to walk another 25,000 *li* if the Red Army did.

With him was a lad nicknamed Local Cousin, and he had walked, almost as far, from Kiangsi. Local Cousin was sixteen.

Did they like the Red Army? I asked. They looked at me in genuine amazement. It had evidently never occurred to either of them that anyone could not like the Red Army.

'The Red Army has taught me to read and to write,' said Old Dog. 'Here I have learned to operate a radio, and how to aim a rifle straight. The Red Army helps the poor.'

'Is that all?'

'It is good to us and we are never beaten,' added Local Cousin. 'Here everybody is the same. It is not like the White districts, where poor people are slaves of the landlords and the Kuomintang. Here everybody fights to help the poor, and to save China. The Red Army fights the landlords and the White-bandits and the Red Army is anti-Japanese. Why should anyone not like such an army as this?'

There was a peasant lad who had joined the Reds in Szechuan, and I asked him why he had done so. He told me that his parents were poor farmers, with only four *mou* of land (less than an acre), which wasn't enough to feed him and his two sisters. When the Reds came to his village, he said, all the peasants welcomed them, brought them hot tea and made sweets for them. The Red dramatists gave plays. It was a happy time. Only the landlords ran. When the land was redistributed his parents received their share. So they were not sorry, but very glad, when he joined the poor people's army.

Another youth, about nineteen, had formerly been an ironsmith's apprentice in Hunan, and he was nicknamed 'T'ieh Lao-hu', the Iron Tiger. The Reds arrived in his district, and he dropped bellows, pans and apprenticeship, and, clad only in a pair of sandals and trousers, he hurried off to enlist. Why? Because he wanted to fight the masters who starved their apprentices, and to fight the landlords who robbed his parents. He was fighting for the revolution, which would free the poor. The Red Army was good to people and did not rob them and beat them like the White armies. He pulled up his trouser leg and displayed a long, white scar, his souvenir of battle.

There was another youth from Fukien, one from Chekiang, several more from Kiangsi and Szechuan, but the majority were natives of Shensi and Kansu. Some had 'graduated' from the Young Vanguards, and (though they looked like infants) had already been Reds for years. Some had joined the Red Army to fight Japan, two had enlisted to escape from slavery, three had deserted from the Kuomintang troops, but most of them had joined 'because the Red Army was a revolutionary army, fighting landlords and imperialism'.

Then I talked to a squad commander, who was an 'older' man, of twenty-four. He had been in the Red Army since 1931. In that year his father and mother were killed by a Nanking bomber, which also destroyed his house, in Kiangsi. When he had gone home from the fields and found both his parents dead he had at once thrown down his hoe, bade his wife good-bye, and enlisted with the Communists. One of his brothers, a Red partisan, was killed in Kiangsi in 1935.

They were a heterogeneous lot, but more truly 'national' in composition than ordinary Chinese armies, usually carefully segregated according to provinces. Their different provincial backgrounds and dialects did not seem to divide them, but became the subject of constant good-natured raillery. I never saw a serious quarrel among them. In fact, during all my travel in the Red districts, I was not to see a single fist-fight between Red soldiers, and among young men I thought that remarkable.

Though tragedy had touched the lives of nearly all of them, they were perhaps too young for it to have depressed them much. They seemed to me fairly happy, and perhaps the first consciously happy group of Chinese proletarians I had seen. Passive contentment is the common phenomenon in China, but the higher emotion of happiness, which implies a feeling of positiveness about existence, is rare indeed.

They sang nearly all day on the road, and their supply of songs was endless. Their singing was not done at a command, but was spontaneous, and they sang well. Whenever the spirit moved him, or he thought of an appropriate song, one of them would suddenly burst forth, and commanders and men joined in. They sang at night, too, and learned new folk-tunes from the peasants, who brought out their Shensi guitars.

What discipline they had seemed almost entirely self-imposed. When we passed wild apricot-trees on the hills there was an abrupt dispersal until everyone had filled his pockets, and somebody always brought me back a handful. Then, leaving the trees looking as if a great wind had struck through them, they moved back into order and quick-timed to make up for the loss. But, when we passed private orchards, nobody touched the fruit in them, and the grain and vegetables we consumed in the village were paid for in full.

As far as I could see, the peasants bore no resentment towards my Red companions. Instead they seemed on close terms of friendship, and very loyal – a fact probably not unconnected with a recent redivision of land and the abolition of taxes. They freely offered for sale what edibles they had, and accepted Soviet money without hesitation. When we reached a village at noon or sunset the chairman of the local Soviet promptly provided quarters, and designated ovens for our use. I frequently saw peasant women or their daughters volunteer to pull the bellows of the fire of our ovens, and laugh and joke with the Red warriors; in a very emancipated way for Chinese women – especially Shensi women.

On the last day, we stopped for lunch at a village in a green valley, and here all the children came round to examine the first foreign devil many of them had seen. I decided to catechize them.

'What is a Communist?' I asked.

'He is a citizen who helps the Red Army fight the White-bandits and the Japanese,' one youngster of nine or ten piped up.

'What else?'

'He helps fight the landlords and the capitalists!'

'But what is a capitalist?' That silenced one child, but another came forward: 'A capitalist is a man who does not work, but makes others work for him.' Over-simplification, perhaps, but I went on:

'Are there any landlords or capitalists here?'

'No!' they all shrieked together. 'They've all run away!'

'Run away? From what?'

'From our RED ARMY!'

'Our' army, a peasant child talking about 'his' army? Well, obviously it wasn't China, but, if not, what was it? I decided it was incredible. Who could have taught them all this?

Later on I was to discover who it was, when I examined the textbooks of Red China, and met old Santa-Claus Hsu Teh-lih, once president of a normal college in Hunan, now Soviet Commissioner of Education . . .

* * * *

I rode with the Red cavalry several days in Kansu – or more correctly, I walked with it. They lent me a fine horse with a captured Western saddle, but at the end of each day I felt that I had been giving the horse a good time instead of the contrary. This was because our battalion commander was so anxious not to tire his four-legged charges that we two-legged ones had to lead a horse three or four *li* for every one we rode. He treated his horses as if they had been Dionne quintuplets, and I concluded that any one who qualified for this man's cavalry had to be a nurse, not a *mafoo*, and an even better walker than rider. I paid them due respect for kindness to animals – no common phenomenon in China – but I was glad to disengage myself and get back to free-lance movement of my own, in which occasionally I could actually ride a horse.

I had been grumbling about this mildly to Hsü Hai-tung, and I suspect he decided to play a joke on me. To return to Yu Wang Pao he lent me a splendid Ninghsia pony, strong as a bull, that gave me one of the wildest rides of my life. My road parted with the 15th Army Corps near a big fort in the grassland. There I bade Hsü and his staff good-bye. Shortly afterwards I got on my borrowed steed, and from then on it was touch and go to see which of us reached Yu Wang Pao alive.

The road lay level across the plain for over fifty *li*. In that whole distance we got down to a walk just once. He raced at a steady gallop for the last five miles, and at the finish I swept up the main street of Yu Wang Pao with my companions trailing far behind. Before Peng's headquarters I slithered off and examined my mount, expecting him to topple over in a faint. He was puffing very slightly and had a few beads of sweat on him, but was otherwise quite unruffled, the beast.

The real trouble with the ride had been the wooden Chinese saddle. It was so narrow that I could not sit in the seat, but literally had to ride on my inner thighs the whole distance. The short, heavy iron stirrups had cramped my legs, which now felt like logs. All I wanted was rest and sleep . . .

* * *

One morning I climbed the wide, thick, yellow wall of Yu Wang Pao, from the top of which you could look down thirty feet and see at a glance a score of different and somehow incongruously prosaic and intimate tasks being pursued below. It was as if you had prized off the lid of the city. A big section of the wall was being demolished, in fact, for this is one act of destruction the Reds do carry out. Walls are impediments to guerrilla warriors like the Reds, who endeavour to come to battle with an enemy in open country, and if they fail there, they do not waste men in an exhausting defence of the walled city, where they can be endangered by blockade or annihilation, but withdraw and let the enemy put himself in that position if he likes. In any case, the broken wall simplifies their work if and when they are strong enough to attempt a reoccupation of the city.

Half-way round the crenellated battlement I came upon a squad of buglers – at rest for once, I was glad to observe, for their plangent calls had been ringing incessantly for days. They were all Young Vanguards, mere children, and I assumed a somewhat fatherly air towards one to whom I stopped and talked. He wore tennis shoes, grey shorts, and a faded grey cap with a dim red star on it. But there was nothing faded about the bugler under the cap; he was rosy-faced and had bright shining eyes, a lad towards whom your heart naturally warmed as towards a plucky waif in need of affection and a friend. How homesick he must be! I thought. But I was soon disillusioned. He was no mama's boy, but already a veteran Red. He told me he was fifteen, and that he had joined the Reds in the south four years ago.

'Four years!' I exclaimed incredulously. 'Then you must have been only eleven when you became a Red? And you made the Long March?'

'Right,' he responded with comical swagger. 'I have been a *hung-chun* for four years.'

'Why did you join?' I asked.

'My family lived near Changchow, in Fukien. I used to cut wood in the mountains, and in the winter I went there to collect bark. I often heard the villagers talk about the Red Army. They said it helped the poor people, and I liked that. Our house was very poor. We were six people, my parents and three brothers, older than I. We owned no land. Rent ate more than half our crop, so we never had enough. In the winter we cooked bark for soup and saved our grain for planting in the spring. I was always hungry.

'One year the Reds came very close to Changchow. I climbed over the mountains and went to ask them to help our house because we were very poor. They were good to me. They sent me to school for a while, and I had plenty to eat. After a few months the Red Army captured Changchow, and went to my village. All the landlords and moneylenders and officials were driven out. My family was given land and did not have to pay the tax-collectors and landlords any more. They were happy and they were proud of me. Two of my brothers joined the Red Army.'

'Where are they now?'

'Now? I don't know. When we left Kiangsi they were with the Red Army in Fukien; they were with Fang Chih-min. Now, I don't know.'

'Did the peasants like the Red Army?'

'Like the Red Army, eh? Of course they liked it. The Red Army gave them land and drove away the landlords, the tax-collectors, and the exploiters.' (These 'little devils' all had their Marxist vocabulary!)

'But, really, how do you *know* they liked the Reds?'

'They made us a thousand, ten thousands, of shoes, with their own hands. The women made uniforms for us, and the men spied on the enemy. Every home sent sons to our Red Army. That is how the *lao-pai-hsing* treated us!'

No need to ask him whether *he* liked his comrades: no lad of thirteen would tramp 6,000 miles with an army he hated.

Scores of youngsters like him were with the Reds. The Young Vanguards were organized by the Communist Youth League, and altogether, according to the claims of Fang Wen-ping, secretary of the CY, there were some 40,000 in the north-west Soviet districts. There must have been several hundred with the Red Army alone: a 'model company' of them was in every Red encampment. They were youths between twelve and seventeen (really eleven to sixteen by foreign count), and they came from all over China. Many of them, like this little bugler, survived the hardships of the march from the south. Many joined the Red Army during its expedition to Shansi.

The Young Vanguards worked as orderlies, mess-boys, buglers, spies, radio-operators, water-carriers, propagandists, actors, *mafoos*, nurses, secretaries, and even teachers! I once saw such a youngster, before a big map, lecturing a class of new recruits on world geography. Two of the most graceful child dancers I have ever seen were Young Vanguards in the dramatic society of the 1st Army Corps, and had marched from Kiangsi.

You might wonder how they stood such a life. Hundreds must have died or been killed. There were over 200 of them in the filthy jail in Sianfu, who had been captured doing espionage or propaganda, or as stragglers unable to keep up with the army on its march. But their fortitude was amazing, and their loyalty to the Red Army was the intense and unquestioning loyalty of the very young.

Most of them wore uniforms too big for them, with sleeves dangling to their knees and coats dragging nearly to the ground. They washed their hands and faces three times a day, they claimed, but they were always dirty, their noses were usually running, and they were often wiping them with a sleeve, and grinning. The world nevertheless was theirs: they had enough to eat, they had a blanket each, the leaders even had a pistol, and they wore red bars, and a broken-peaked cap a size or more too large, but with a red star on it. They were often of uncertain origin: many could not remember their parents, many were escaped apprentices, some had been slaves, most of them were runaways from huts with too many mouths to feed, and all of them had made their own decisions to join, sometimes a whole group of youngsters running off to the Reds together . . .

I met a youth of fourteen who had been an apprentice in a Shanghai machine-shop, and with three companions had found his way, through various adventures, to the north-west. He was a student in the radio school in Pao An when I saw him. I asked whether he missed Shanghai, but he said no, he had left nothing in Shanghai, and that the only fun he had ever had there was looking into the shop-windows at good things to eat – which of course he could not buy.

But best of all I liked the 'little devil' in Pao An, who served as orderly to Li Ko-nung, chief of the communications department of the Foreign Office. This *hsiao-kuei* was a Shansi lad of about thirteen or fourteen, and he had joined the Reds I know not how. He was the Beau Brummell of the Vanguards, and he took his role with utmost gravity. He had inherited a Sam Browne belt from somebody, he had a neat little uniform tailored to a good fit, and a cap whose peak he regularly refilled with new cardboard whenever it broke. Underneath the collar of his well-brushed coat he always managed to have a strip of white linen showing. He was easily the snappiest-looking soldier in town. Beside him Mao Tse-tung looked a tramp.

But this *wa-wa*'s name happened by some thoughtlessness of his parents to be Shang Chi-pang. There is nothing wrong with that, except that Chi-pang sounds very much like *chi-pa*, and so, to his unending mortification, he was often called *chi-pa*, which simply means 'penis'. One day Chi-pang came into my little room in the Foreign Office with his usual quota of dignity, clicked his heels together, gave me the most Prussian-like salute I had seen in the Red districts, and addressed me as 'Comrade Snow'. He then proceeded to unburden his small heart of certain apprehensions. What he wanted to do was to make it perfectly clear to me that his name was not Chi-pa, but Chi-pang, and that between these two there was all the difference in the world. He had his name carefully scrawled down on a scrap of paper, and this he deposited before me.

Astonished, I responded in all seriousness that I had never called him anything but Chi-pang, and had no thought of doing otherwise. I half expected him to offer me the choice of swords or pistols.

But he thanked me, made a grave bow, and once more gave that preposterous salute. 'I wanted to be sure', he said, 'that when you write about me for the foreign papers you won't make a mistake in my name. It would give a bad impression to the foreign comrades if they thought a Red soldier was named Chi-pa!' Until then I had had no notion of introducing Chi-pang into this strange book, but with that remark I had no choice in the matter, and he walked into it right beside the Generalissimo, the dignity of history notwithstanding.

One of the duties of the Young Vanguards in the Soviets was to examine travellers on roads behind the front, and see that they had their road passes. They executed this duty quite determinedly, and marched anyone without his papers to the local Soviet for examination. Peng Teh-huai told me of being stopped once and being asked for his *lu-t'iao* by some Young Vanguards, who threatened to arrest him.

'But I am Peng Teh-huai,' he said. 'I write those passes myself.'

'We don't care if you are Commander Che Teh,' said the young sceptics; 'you must have a road pass.' They signalled for assistance, and several boys came running from the fields to reinforce them.

Peng had to write out his *lu-t'iao* and sign it himself before they allowed him to proceed.

Altogether, as you may have gathered, the 'little devils' were one thing in Red China with which it was hard to find anything seriously wrong. Their spirit was superb. I suspect that more than once an older man, looking at them, forgot his pessimism and was heartened to think that he was fighting for the future of lads like those. They were invariably cheerful and optimistic, and they had a ready '*hao!*' for every how-are-you, regardless of the weariness of the day's march. They were patient, hard-working, bright, and eager to learn, and seeing them made you feel that China was not hopeless, that no nation was more hopeless than its youth. Here in the Vanguards was the future of China, if only this youth could be freed, shaped, made aware, and given a role to perform in the building of a new world. It sounds somewhat evangelical, I suppose, but nobody could see these heroic young lives without feeling that man in China is not born rotten, but with infinite possibilities of personality.

* * *

In the middle of October 1936, after I had been with the Reds nearly four months, arrangements were finally completed for my return to the White world. It had not been easy. Chang Hsueh-liang's friendly Tungpei troops had been withdrawn from nearly every front, and replaced by Nanking or other hostile forces. There was only one outlet then, through a Tungpei division which still had a front with the Reds near Lochuan, a walled city a day's motor-trip north of Sian.

I walked down the main street of Defended Peace for the last time, and the farther I got towards the gate, the more reluctantly I moved. People popped their heads out of offices to shout last remarks. My poker club turned out *en masse* to bid the *maestro* good-bye, and some 'little devils' trudged with me to the walls of Pao An. I stopped to take a picture of Old Hsü and Old Hsieh, their arms thrown around each other's shoulders like schoolboys. Only Mao Tse-tung failed to appear; he was still asleep.

'Don't forget my artificial arm!' called out Tsai.

'Don't forget my films!' urged Lo Ting-yi.

'We'll be waiting for the air-fleet!' laughed Yang Shang-k'un.

'Send me in a wife!' demanded Li Ke-nung.

'And send back those four ounces of cocoa,' chided Po Ku.

The whole Red Academy was seated out in the open, under a great tree, listening to a lecture by Lo Fu, when I went past. They all came over, and we shook hands, and I mumbled a few words. Then I turned and forded the stream, waved them a farewell, and rode up quickly with my little caravan. I might be the last foreigner to see any of them alive, I thought. It was very depressing. I felt that I was not going home, but leaving it.

In five days we reached the southern frontier, and I waited there for three days, staying in a tiny village and eating black beans and wild pig. It was a beautiful wooded country, alive with game, and I spent the days in the hills with some farmers and Red soldiers, hunting pig and deer. The bush was crowded with huge pheasants, and one day we even saw, far out of range, two tigers streaking across a clearing in a valley drenched with the purple-gold of autumn. The front was absolutely peaceful, and the Reds had only one battalion stationed here.

On the 20th I got through no man's land safely and behind the Tungpei lines, and on a borrowed horse next day I rode into Lochuan, where a lorry was waiting for me. A day later I was in Sianfu. At the Drum Tower I jumped down from the driver's seat and asked one of the Reds (who were wearing Tungpei uniforms) to toss me my bag. A long search, and then a longer search, while my fears increased. Finally there was no doubt about it. My bag was not there. In that bag were a dozen diaries and notebooks, thirty rolls of film – the first pictures ever taken of the Chinese Red Army – and several pounds of Red magazines, newspapers, and documents. It had to be found!

Excitement under the Drum Tower, while traffic policemen curiously gazed on a short distance away. Whispered consultations. Finally it was realized what had happened. The lorry had been loaded with gunny sacks full of broken Tungpei rifles and guns being sent for repairs, and my bag, in case of any search, had been stuffed into such a sack also. But back at Hsienyang, on the opposite shore of the Wei River, twenty miles behind us, the missing object had been thrown off with the other loads! The driver stared ruefully at the lorry. '*T'a ma-ti*,' he offered in consolation. 'Rape its mother.'

It was already dusk, and the driver suggested that he wait till morning to go back and hunt for it. Morning! Something warned me that morning would be too late. I insisted, and I finally won the argument. The lorry reversed and returned, and I stayed awake all night in a friend's house in Sianfu wondering whether I would ever see that priceless bag again. If it were opened at Hsienyang, not only would all my things be lost for ever, but that 'Tungpei' lorry and all its occupants would be *huai-la* – finished. There were Nanking gendarmes at Hsienyang.

Luckily . . . the bag was found. But my hunch about the urgency of the search had been absolutely correct, for early next morning all traffic was completely swept from the streets, and all roads leading into the city were lined with gendarmes and troops. Peasants were cleared out of their homes along the road. Some of the more unsightly huts were simply demolished, so that there would be nothing offensive to the eye.

Generalissimo Chiang Kai-shek was paying a sudden call on Sianfu. It would have been impossible then for our lorry to return over that road to the Wei River, for it skirted the heavily guarded aerodrome.

This arrival of the Generalissimo made an unforgettable contrast with the scenes still fresh in my mind – of Mao Tse-tung, or Hsü Hai-tung, or Lin Piao, or Peng Teh-huai nonchalantly strolling down a street in Red China. And the Generalissimo did not even have a price on his head. It vividly suggested who really feared the people and who trusted them. But even all the precautions taken to protect the Generalissimo's life in Sian were to prove inadequate. He had too many enemies among the very troops who were guarding him . . .

THE LEFT SONG BOOK

edited by ALAN BUSH AND RANDALL SWINGLER

(supplementary book, March 1938)

'We must sing what we really mean and sing it as though we meant it, or else singing is only a pleasant way of passing the time.'

Randall Swingler (1909–67), godson of an Archbishop of Canterbury, Wykehamist, Oxford Blue, poet and sometime LSO flautist, joined the Communist Party in 1934. He moved to London two years later, edited the *Left Review*, and championed all forms of radical culture. Alan Bush (1900–95), a student of the Royal Academy and Berlin University, joined the Party in 1935. He had already written the music for a 'Pageant of Labour' held at Crystal Palace (Michael Tippett assisted with the conducting). Bush helped found the Workers' Music Association and became a central figure in the LBC Musicians' Group (which brought together members of the LSO and the BBC Orchestra, dance band leaders, composers and solo artists). At the Club summer school in 1937, Swingler and Bush formed a scratch choir which gave a performance on the final evening. Convinced that amateur choirs could be formed around the country, they began – with comrades from the WMA and the Musicians' Group – to assemble a repertoire of suitable songs.

'Music has been one of the banners at the head of every great progressive movement,' the short introduction to *The Left Song Book* begins:

> For music has the faculty of binding together in a single emotion all those who are united by a common interest and a common purpose. Men marching in unison, riding in buses on an excursion, sitting in public bars, often are moved spontaneously to sing, in expression of their feeling of community. The socialist movement then, that movement which aims to make an equal community the basis of social life, is the only movement today capable of restoring to music a concrete

> social basis for its development and of utilising the power of music to the full.

The book aimed to 'do no more than provide a basis for a repertoire of songs which can be of use on any occasion, public or private, at which people . . . may feel the impulse to utter their unity of purpose in the traditional way of singing'.

Among the songs in the book are – naturally – 'The Internationale', 'The Red Flag' and 'The Marseillaise'. There are a number of 'Traditional Songs of Revolt from the British Isles', including 'England, Arise' – reprinted here – and 'Scots Wha Hae'. (Swingler and Bush shared an interest in the radical, dissenting tradition: it informed much of Swingler's poetry, and in 1949 the Arts Council commissioned Bush to write an opera based on the life of Wat Tyler.) Another section comprised 'Topical Workers' Songs'. Randall Swingler's lyrics are reproduced here – Bush composed the music. (When the Jarrow Crusade was approaching London, Bush used to visit the ramshackle and weary men during their evening rests and exhort them to give a rousing rendition of 'Song of the Hunger Marchers'. By all accounts, he didn't have much luck.) Finally, there are 'Five Famous Rounds with New Words'. 'Prices Rise', for example, is sung to the tune of 'Three Blind Mice':

Prices rise, Prices rise
See how they mount, See how they mount
They've raised the price of your daily bread
And given you cruisers and guns instead
For they know it won't trouble you when you're dead
That prices rise.

Meetings of the Labour Party, the League of Nations Union and the Communist Party used the book to sing for socialism; LBC choirs were formed in Nottingham, Leicester, Aberystwyth and Hounslow.

Swingler and Bush continued to collaborate. The Left Book Club 'Theatre Festival and Cultural Week' in May 1938, for example, began with a performance at the Scale Theatre of their adaptation of Handel's oratorio 'Belshazzar' as a three-act opera. Amateur choirs sang from *The Left Song Book* throughout the week.

'SONG OF THE HUNGER MARCHERS'

(Words by Randall Swingler)

We march from a stricken country,
From broken hill and vale,
Where factory yards are empty,
And the rusty gear for sale.
Our country will not thrive again,
Our strength is not for use,
The bubble of prosperity
Has never come to us.

Chorus *Then rouse to our tread*
When you hear us marching by;
For servility is dead
And the Means Test too shall die!
Though they think our spirit's broken,
Because we're underfed,
We will stamp the Starvation Government
Beneath the workers' tread!
Stamp, stamp, stamp, stamp.

We pass through sleeping villages
And poor and struggling farms,
We pass through towns where factories
Are forging war and arms.
In towns and fields and villages
We see it more and more,
How the boss exploits the worker
And drives him into war.

Chorus *Then rouse to our tread* etc.

And this Employers' Government
Is hoping for the best,

To set one against another
By the grading of the Test.
They would train us in their Labour Camps
For action against you,
But we march for the working class,
For we are workers too.

Chorus *Then rouse to our tread* etc.

Remember, fellow workers,
Who earn a wage to-day,
That they'll throw you on the scrapheap,
When they find it doesn't pay.
All you who are employed,
Making cartridges and bombs,
We'll be marching side by side,
When the final crisis comes.

Chorus *Then rouse to our tread* etc.

'QUESTION AND ANSWER'

(Words by Randall Swingler)

Q. Are the workers badly fed?
A. Yes! most of 'em.
Q. Are the workers badly housed?
A. Yes! most of 'em.
Q. Do their children ever feel the pinch?
A. Yes! most of 'em.
Q. Aren't they always being robbed?
A. Yes! Yes! Yes! all of 'em.

Q. Do the bosses ever starve?
A. No! none of 'em.
Q. Do the bosses live in slums?
A. No! none of 'em.
Q. Do their children ever go in rags?
A. No! none of 'em.
Q. Don't they get the juiciest plums?
A. Yes! Yes! Yes! all of 'em.

Q. Do the workers ever think?
A. Yes! some of them.
Q. Are they conscious of their class?
A. Yes! some of them.
Q. Do they fight for power to rule the state?
A. Yes! some of them.
Q. If they get together can they win?
A. Yes! Yes! Yes! Yes! all of them.

'ENGLAND, ARISE!'
(Words by Edward Carpenter)

England arise! the long long night is over.
Faint in the east behold the dawn appear;
Out of your evil dream of toil and sorrow—
Arise, O England, for the day is here;
From your fields and hills,
Hark! the answer swells—
Arise, O England, for the day is here!

By your young children's eyes so red with weeping,
By their white faces aged with want and fear,
By the dark cities where your babes are creeping
Naked of joy and all that makes life dear;
From each wretched slum
Let the loud cry come;
Arise, O England, for the day is here!

People of England! all your valleys call you,
High in the rising sun the lark sings clear,
Will you dream on, let shameful slumber thrall you?
Will you disown your native land so dear?
Shall it die unheard—
That sweet pleading word?
Arise, O England, for the day is here!

Over your face a web of lies is woven,
Laws that are falsehoods pin you to the ground,
Labour is mocked, its just reward is stolen,
On its bent back sits Idleness encrowned.
How long, while you sleep,
Your harvest shall it reap?
Arise, O England, for the day is here!

Forth, then, ye heroes, patriots, and lovers!
Comrades of danger, poverty, and scorn!
Mighty in faith of Freedom, your great Mother!
Giants refreshed in Joy's new-rising morn!
Come and swell the song,
Silent now so long;
England is risen! – and the day is here.

OUT OF THE NIGHT

by H. J. Muller

(monthly choice, May 1936)

In 1933 Hermann Joseph Muller (1890–1967) left the University of Texas to join the Institute of Genetics of the Academy of Sciences of the USSR (first in Leningrad, then in Moscow). A socialist, he embraced the Soviet Union as a progressive, experimental society which would welcome radical research: 'there the march of progress proceeds apace,' he wrote, 'while elsewhere discouragement and decadence admittedly deepen'. *Out of the Night* was written during the heyday of eugenics, as an attempt to rescue eugenic thinking from the 'perverted form' it had taken in the hands of 'Hitlerites'. The biological improvement of the human race, Muller argued – and the necessity of having 'children of choice' – was dependent on the existence of an equal, co-operative society.

Man, he declared, was mastering the material world – 'deserts will be flooded and irrigated, jungles subjugated . . . the climate modified'. Attempts were similarly being made to organise the social world. The next challenge was to control man's 'genetic thread'. The starting point of Muller's book is the recognition that some people are genetically superior to others, for example in intelligence – the aim, he says, is to maximise the number of 'excellent' genes so that the human race improves. A quality such as intelligence can properly be measured, he argues, only in a society which enjoys real equality of opportunity – otherwise it is masked by the effects of education, racial prejudice and similar forms of social conditioning. When a socialist society is finally realised, people with 'excellent' genes will be accurately identified. By enabling such people to have more children, the biological progress of the human race can be ensured.

In order that the lives of these people with 'excellent' genes aren't unduly disturbed, Muller proposes using artificial insemination and ectogenesis (raising the embryo outside the womb). The sperm of gifted men could be frozen and preserved as part of a purposeful eugenics programme, while 'excellent' eggs could be taken out of superwomen and put inside ordinary women. The usual determinants of having children – romantic love, for instance – would then be replaced by a more scientific method of ensuring the spread of good genes. 'Make personal love master over reproduction,' he argues, 'and you degrade the germ plasm of future generations.' The basis of Muller's brave new world is highly selective breeding using the genes of supermen: 'we may confidently leave it to the Darwins, Engelses, and Einsteins composing future generations not to botch the job and, with each progressing generation, the increasing intelligence and comradeliness of men will make further progress ever surer'. Muller's ideas today seem an intriguing combination of the enlightened and the laughably dated; they are certainly testimony to the breathtaking optimism and assuredness of left-wing science in the thirties.

In Moscow, Muller defended genetic theory against the ideas of T. D. Lysenko (who followed Lamarck in emphasising the inheritance of acquired characteristics), but his position became untenable and in 1937 he left for Edinburgh, before returning to the States in 1940. Six years later, he won a Nobel Prize for his work on genetic mutation caused by X-rays.

From CHAPTER VII: BIRTH AND REBIRTH

THE INTELLIGENT WOMAN who can realise some of the opportunities that life may otherwise afford, will, it is to be hoped, always refuse to make of herself either a queen-bee or a galley-slave. If one of these two courses of life for women were always to be necessary for progress, then there could be no excuse for men's desiring progress, for themselves alone. It is true that some women, through special circumstances and favourable constitution, are even to-day in a position to bear and rear a family of the old-fashioned size, but for the majority, especially of the more idealistic and capable, who are struggling to emerge from their slave-psychology of yesterday, this is a form of martyrdom too protracted and repeated to be endured: one quick burning at the stake would be much easier. On the part of a host of intelligent women, therefore, there is a growing mass strike against child-bearing. May the strike prosper until the dire, age-old grievances have been removed!

Only by lightening the physiological, the psychological, the economic, and the social burdens on the mother now caused by child-bearing and child-rearing can we attain to a state in which real eugenics is feasible.

In the first place, there must be a completely legalised and universal dissemination of knowledge about the means of birth control found to be most suitable from both the physical and the psychological standpoints. Effective education in this matter calls for free utilisation of the means of public enlightenment and propaganda, as well as active and unrestricted clinical instruction and aid. Abortion as a second line of defence must also be legalised and regulated, while at the same time its widespread exploitation by quacks must be suppressed . . .

In the second place, very little has been done (though very much can be done) to banish the unimaginable torture of childbirth – this because the doctors have been mostly men, who regard such pains in woman as obligatory, or even sadistically look upon them as desirable . . .

Thirdly, very little has been done, though very much can be, to make available the information and the means for doing away with the chronic illnesses which afflict so many children in their first six months of life . . .

Fourthly, very little has been done, though much can be done, to develop public utility organisations which will help in food-preparation, laundering, and other services necessary for infants and young children – work which commonly takes nearly all the mother's energy and time, but which could be accomplished in a much more expert fashion, and as economically as bread baking, thus releasing the mother for whatever work she is best fitted . . .

Fifthly, we find that to-day even those mothers who through fortunate circumstances would have a portion of their time left over from the deadening treadmill of domestic routine can find no place for themselves in the present organisation of work, which demands all or nothing . . .

The penalties must be removed; nay more, the very opposite policy must be embarked upon, so that instead of pushing the head of struggling woman still further beneath the swirling current, we actively raise and support it, and give her air, nourishment, and encouragement in her at best none too agreeable task. Aim to re-adapt it to her so as to give her a dignified place, to amend our attitude towards pregnancy, to reorganise our medical outlook and practices – else it is folly and brutality to talk eugenics. Though the eugenic motive to-day cannot have the driving power to work such industrial, social, and medical changes, they are coming none the less, with the change in our industrial methods. These, even under our profit system, call more and more for the labour of women, take over more and more the functions of home industry, drive women out of the home by giving their husbands inadequate means of supporting the family, and, by thus giving woman greater economic independence, unwittingly bring her into a position where she has more desire and ability to make and enforce her own demands. And with the change from the profit system to socialisation, the emancipation of women will of course be greatly hastened, both directly and also as a response to the more rationally and actively developed industrialisation process.

These are the social forces which are inevitably working to bring women into a position where it will be possible for them to let remoter considerations influence their decisions concerning the bearing of children.

. . . the discoveries and inventions of advancing biology in the fields of reproduction and development must sooner or later give us radical powers of control over what has hitherto been the female's role in child-production, which will greatly extend both the possibilities of eugenics and our ability to order these processes in the interests of mother and child. The making of such inventions will be favoured when we have a system in which their value will be duly appreciated.

Even to-day only a relatively slight advance in technique would be needed to enable us safely and without incision to transplant the mature or fertilised egg from one female into another, and have it develop. This has already been done in the rodent, but by operation, and no one has been sufficiently interested as yet to develop the technique further. It is conceivable that the fertilised egg would develop properly even if placed in the uterus of some other species of animals, though it probably would not do so in any animals that can be readily domesticated, because of the unsuitable conformation of their placentas, not to speak of the chances that antagonism may develop between the embryonic and the maternal tissues in some of their chemical reactions. The possibilities of transplanting portions of ovaries from one person into others has also received inadequate attention.

. . . Whether or not human eggs could be caused to develop without fertilisation – without a father – it would at present be impossible to predict, as no serious attempt has yet been made along this line, although the feat may easily be performed with some invertebrate animals, whose eggs are more convenient to obtain and to grow. Few biologists of our age seem to realise the social and eugenic significance of such work, and other persons are not aware of the biological potentialities.

All such accomplishments as the above would greatly extend the reproductive potencies of females possessing characters particularly excellent, without thereby necessarily interfering with their personal lives – or even, we may add, with their theologies, since the latter did not anticipate any such contingencies when they were framed and as yet contain no injunctions against them. In such ways, and by otherwise controlling the development, the twinning, the size, etc., of the embryo, and the duration and other conditions of pregnancy and labour, considerable changes may be wrought in our methods and customs concerned with the production of children – changes permitting a much greater degree of control over our choice of these children, even before we reach that ideal condition of complete ectogenesis, or development of the egg entirely outside the mother's body . . .

Most of the preceding has been concerned with the conditions affecting our selection of maternal protoplasm in the production of the next generation. But the conditions affecting paternity are, for the child, vastly more important; not that the father contributes more than the mother to the child's characteristics – for he shares almost equally with her in the determination of its inheritance – but because, on account of the enormous number of reproductive cells which each male produces (many billions in all), it is biologically possible for the selection of male germs (sperm) to be incomparably more rigorous than that of female germs (eggs). Thus it would even now be possible by means already tried and proved – that is, by artificial insemination – to determine that a vast number of children of the future generation should inherit the characteristics of some transcendently estimable man, without either of the parents concerned ever having come in contact with or even seen each other, or having been in any way disturbed in their separate personal and family lives – beyond the very important disturbance of the entrance of the child. Only social inertia and popular ignorance now hold us back from putting into effect (at least in a limited experimental way) such a severance of the function of reproduction from the personal love-life of the individual. This separation cannot be indefinitely postponed, because social inertia has its limits, and, when it comes, it must react to the emancipation and mutual advantage of both these all-important phases of life. To claim that we must wait for ectogenesis first is only to admit that we do not really have the courage of our convictions.

Personal love, on the one hand, which is largely a matter of imperative emotions, that do not readily wait for the approval of expedience and foresight – or, if they do, tend thereby to become thwarted, perverted, and cankerous – has in the past never been a willing and efficient slave to the needs of reproduction. Make considerations of reproduction dictate the expression of personal love, and you not infrequently destroy the individual at his spiritual core; thus 'eugenic marriages' cannot as a whole be successful, so far as the parents are concerned. On the other hand, make personal love master over reproduction, under conditions of civilisation, and you degrade the germ plasm of the future generations. Compromise between these two policies, and you cripple both spirit and germ. There is only one solution – unyoke the two, sunder the fetters that from time immemorial have made them so nearly inseparable, and let each go its own best way, fulfilling its already distinct function. The physical means for this emancipation are now known for the first time in history.

When we consider what the recognition of this principle would mean for the children – for those future men and women the character of whose lives we cannot in any event escape the responsibility of predetermining – our obligation becomes clear and compelling. The child on the average stands half-way, in its inherited constitution, between its father and the average of the general population, and so it would be theoretically possible even now – were it not for the shackles upon human wills in our society – so to order our reproduction that a considerable part of the very next generation might average, in its hereditary physical and mental constitution, half-way between the average of the present population and that of our greatest living men of mind, body, or 'spirit' (as we choose). At the same time, it can be reckoned, the number of men and women of great, though not supreme, ability would thereby be increased several hundredfold. It is easy to show that in the course of a paltry century or two (paltry, considering the advance in question) it would be possible for the majority of the population to become of the innate quality of such men as Lenin, Newton, Leonardo, Pasteur, Beethoven, Omar Khayyám, Pushkin, Sun Yat Sen, Marx (I purposely mention men of different fields and races), or even to possess their varied faculties combined.

We do not wish to imply that these men owed their greatness entirely to genetic causes, but certainly they must have stood exceptionally high genetically; and if, as now seems certain, we can in the future make the social and material environment favourable for the development of the latent powers of men in general, then, by securing for them the favourable genes at the same time, we should be able to raise virtually all mankind to or beyond levels heretofore attained only by the most remarkably gifted.

Do not imagine that the obligation is one that can be escaped. With such means at our command, the conscious withholding of these gifts from the people at large, by continuing our present completely *laissez-faire* methods, would in itself be a decision, a course of action – and an anti-social one – directed against the well-being of humanity. Mankind has a right to the best genes attainable, as well as to the best environment, and eventually our children will blame us for our dereliction if we have deliberately failed to take the necessary steps for providing them with the best that was available, squandering their rightful heritage only to feed our heedless egotism.

But just in proportion to the importance of this far-reaching revolution in human biological affairs would be its danger if misused. Such a system – if it could somehow be put into full effect at once in our country to-day, and directed (as it eventually would be) by the same forces as direct our Press and general propaganda – would undoubtedly lead to a population to-morrow composed of a maximum number of Billy Sundays, Valentinos, John L. Sullivans, Huey Longs, even Al Capones (and I should like to name, besides, various prominent characters in our military, financial, and university circles!). Of course we must recognise that the development of these types has required our specific social environment, yet in so far as any genes may lay a favourable basis for such development in given individuals, these are the genes that would be most highly prized in our community, and our artificial selection would hence tend to work in these directions. It would be disastrous, therefore, to attempt such reproductive methods on a grand scale so long as the present ideology of individualism, careerism, charlatanism, unscrupulous aggression, and shallow hypocrisy prevails.

Little fear need be entertained, however, that society in its present form will set itself to any such *coup de grâce*. In the first place, its present form is even now in process of disintegration. In the second place, a sufficiently deep-seated change in the attitude of the population in general in regard to reproduction can come about only after the unequivocal establishment of economic and social transformations which will bring more dignity and rationality, and less superstition, into the relations between the partners in love. These changes, by socialising our attitude in general, will socialise also our conception of our duty towards the coming generation. Moreover, an essential feature of the process of socialisation is its effect in spreading the knowledge and technique of science. The workers of the world are the only class with the economic incentive, the ethical background, and the force to accomplish this general transformation; and so when they come into their own it will be they, primarily, who will have the desire and the opportunity to reap the fruits of the victory in genetic as in other respects. By that time the old standards, formed under the combined influence of the predatory principles of the leisure class and the partial slave psychology of the workers, will have been largely swept away . . .

It should be needless to point out that in the new society participation in the type of reproduction in question, designed for the sake of the children, will be entirely voluntary. It is to be anticipated that, with the realisation of the possibilities of such procedure and with the making available of the means of carrying it out, more and more individual mothers as well as couples will become eager to participate in it. No doubt many of the participants will wish also to continue in the old method of reproduction – to some extent at least – but will wish to add to their natural family one or more 'children of choice'. Such a dual course would in some cases present psychological and social advantages and it would at the same time meet the genetic desiderata sufficiently well. The selection of genetic material will also be voluntary. We may trust the members of future society not only to have, in general, sound ideals in this matter, and a fair capacity of recognising merit within their own line of work, but also to be guided by the advice of combinations of publicists, geneticists, medical men, psychologists, and (above all) of critics from the fields especially involved – in short, by the best thought of the age. Compulsion need enter, if at all, only in a negative role, as a potential force standing ready only to prevent exploitation of the enhanced possibilities of multiplication by unduly egoistic, aggressive, or paranoid individuals.

The question may now be asked: what are the most important ideal characters, the genetic portion of whose bases we must strive to make as favourable as possible? It is these ideals which are the all-important consideration in the first place since, as we have seen, eugenics in the wrong direction would present a far more abhorrent picture than no eugenics at all. What should these ideals be, and how are they to be made acceptable? The whole course of human prehistory and history makes the necessary ideals obvious and unmistakable; they are (aside from physical well-being) primarily two: highly developed social feeling – call it fraternal love, or sympathy, or comradeliness, as you prefer; and the highest possible intelligence – call it analytical ability, or depth of understanding, or 'reason'. Each of these two traits is of course the resultant of a complex system of more elementary factors, and the development of each is highly responsive to environmental influences, as well as affected by genes. Now these two traits, when active and well organised, issue in the 'co-operation' and 'knowledge' by which mankind has advanced, is advancing, and must advance for a long time yet to come. Other desirable traits, bodily and mental, may be regarded as simply accessory to the effectiveness of these (for instance, that series of special proclivities whereby we, unlike apes, can learn to speak); and many systems of such biological accessories are probably still to come in the distant future, even as in the distant past the lower animals developed through natural selection many systems accessory to dextrous motion – such as special muscles, bones, circulation, nervous system, sense organs, etc.

The paramount position of these two ideal characters – comradeliness and intelligence – is not generally recognised to-day, but its recognition is bound to come with the coming changes in the structure of society which will put the latter on a more consciously co-operative basis. Then, but not before, will it be possible for people in general to awaken to the true ideals of humanity, and then only will they even *desire* such genes as would be of aid in working towards these ideals. Then will they see that positive advance in these directions is incomparably to be preferred to the attainment of a supposedly perfect mediocrity. Then too, and not before, will there be fair means of recognising most of the individuals in whom an exceptional concentration of such desirable genes lies, since before then the majority of these genes must be buried beneath the weight of economic and social oppression. Meanwhile – at present – a false premium is attached to gifts of the 'upper' classes, gifts which may be connected with dangerous unrecognised failings. Associated, too, with these class prejudices and artificial class inequalities of to-day there are equally unjust race prejudices and artificially created race inequalities. In regard to really important characteristics, the natural differences between the races pale into insignificance beside the natural differences between individuals – so much so that an impartial science of genetic improvement could not afford to take the former into account at all in its procedure. Thus we see that only the eugenics of the new society, freed of the traditions of caste, of slavery, and of colonialism, can be a thoroughgoing and a true eugenics.

The judgment of genetic merit, as distinguished from environmental good fortune (which can of course never be completely equalised), will become increasingly exact as time goes on, and it will be desirable, in this matter, to use methods as objective and as little susceptible to being influenced by the 'personal equation' as possible. And although, as previously stated, achievement offers one of the most important criteria for the judgment of all-round worth – there being no doubt that in the great majority of cases very eminent individuals have capabilities considerably above the average, particularly in communities established on the principles of real equality of opportunity and thoroughgoing co-operation – nevertheless it will have to be recognised that the amount of worldly acclaim given a man in his own generation furnishes by itself no sure or exact measure of this intrinsic greatness. This emphasises the need for the further development of objective criteria. Of course we cannot hope ever to obtain 'perfect' measures, nor is anything approaching perfection of judgment really necessary for our purposes, since any degree of genetic betterment, in any trait, is advantageous to the next generation, and it will be a step in the right direction, provided our method does not systematically tend to produce at the same time a decline in other, more important particulars.

Although we need not fear the likelihood of the contingency just suggested, it would be very helpful, both for the meeting of such problems and also from more purely genetic considerations, if our biological technique could be advanced to the point of enabling us to make living laboratory cultures of the male reproductive tissues, in which the male germ cells could multiply and come to maturity. There is no reason to believe that this would necessarily be a very difficult matter. Cells of other organs can be cultivated outside the body, though certain special conditions, as yet unknown, must be reproduced in order to enable the germ cells to mature. There has been little or no research as yet to determine what these conditions are. No doubt if these cultures could be made at all, they could be maintained for an indefinite period of time, long after the death of the individual from whom they had been taken, just as has been found feasible in cultures from the skin, heart, and other tissues; and so they could eventually supply an indefinitely large amount of material. If this could be done, it might be a salutary rule, eventually, not to make use of such material in any considerable way until say, twenty-five years after the death of the donor. After this length of time society would often be in a far better position to judge fairly of a man's achievements and his general worth, than during the heat and struggle, and the possible intrigue and bias, of his own personal life; there would also, by then, have been some opportunity to judge of his genes by observations on the character of a limited number of his progeny. How fortunate we should be had such a method been in existence in time to have enabled us to secure living cultures of some of our departed great! How many women, in an enlightened community devoid of superstitious taboos and of sex slavery, would be eager and proud to bear and rear a child of Lenin or Darwin! Is it not obvious that restraint, rather than compulsion, would be called for?

THESE POOR HANDS

by B. L. Coombes

(monthly choice, June 1939)

Bert Lewis Coombes (1893–1974) was one of the outstanding working-class writers in mid-twentieth-century Britain. The best description of him is that given by John Lehmann, who had published Coombes in *New Writing*:

> This small, hard-bitten miner, with his small, square head, his pale, rough hewn, serious face, was the son of a Herefordshire farmer; he had set off for Wales at the age of 17 to work in the mines, and in his thirties had decided to take up his pen and describe, for the world to know, the life in the lost country of the coal-face.
>
> He had worked in almost every type of mine, had narrowly escaped death or mutilation many times himself, had seen others escaping – and some fail to escape. He had been in charge of the installation and working of the new coal-cutting machinery, and when I first came into contact with him was responsible for dealing with accidents underground.

Lehmann speculated that the 'gift of imagination . . . perhaps worked so freshly and vividly in him because he had come as a young countryman to the mines, his senses attuned to the clean air and green fields and slow, natural rhythms of the Herefordshire farmlands'.

Coombes's memoir *These Poor Hands* is noted for its concision and lack of sentimentality. It is also an autobiography which gives away very little about the author, concentrating instead on the configuration of life in the South Wales mining towns from pre-war years to the thirties. Nor is Coombes interested in drawing any simple political lessons: the need to modernise the mines and to improve conditions underground requires no spelling out. Lehmann admired Coombes's 'sensitive, unhysterical truth with a just perceptible undercurrent of stolid bitterness'. He also believed that Coombes's writing 'had much to do with the great stirring of national conscience which eventually made the nationalisation of the mines a priority no party could withstand'.

The selection of *These Poor Hands* as an LBC choice, its favourable reviews – by V. S. Pritchett, J. B. Priestley and Cyril Connolly, among others – and its sales (80,000 copies in the first year) would have enabled Coombes to become a full-time journalist and author. Instead, he bought a decent-sized farm for his wife to run and carried on working in the mines. He now possessed a room in which to write, however, and produced numerous radio plays, short stories, articles and semi-autobiographical books over the following twenty years. He remained an important unofficial spokesman for miners into the fifties and sixties. *These Poor Hands* was reissued after his death.

From CHAPTER III

ABOUT NINE-THIRTY that night I started to dress for my first night underground. There are no rules as to what you shall wear, only an unwritten one that you must not bring good clothes unless you do not mind being teased about what you are going to do for Sunday or 'How's it looking for the old 'uns?' Clothes must be tough and not too tight; dirtiness is no bar, because they will soon be much dirtier than they have ever been before. The usual wear is a cloth cap, old scarf, worn jacket and waistcoat, old stockings, flannel shirt, singlet, and pants. Thick moleskin trousers must be worn to bear the strain of kneeling and dragging along the ground, and strong boots are needed because of the sharp stones in the roadways and the other stones that fall. Food must be protected by a tin box, for the rats are hungry and daring; also plenty of tea or water is necessary to replace the sweat that is lost.

John was waiting for me near the colliery screens at ten o'clock. I was silent, and on edge for what the night would teach me. We climbed uphill between a double set of narrow rails, and the woods shut us in on either side. It took us half an hour of steady climbing before we halted on top of a grey pile that was the rubbish-tip and we could look back on the lights in the village below. The fire from the steelworks was like a red moonlight that night; we could see the expression on one another's faces by it . . .

There were about fifty men sitting in the dark near the mouth of the level. We went inside a rough cabin that had closely printed extracts from the Mines Act and the Explosives Order nailed near the door. A youngish man was sitting on a box inside. I noticed that he was holding some pencilled notes to the left side of his face so that he could read them, and found out later that a piece of stone had knocked out his right eye some months before. He was the fireman, in charge of that shift because the colliery was not large enough to employ a night overman.

He seemed decent and intelligent. We handed in the 'starting-slip' to explain my presence, and he told John that he had found a strong-looking mate, and told me that I had got a good butty – one of the best in the valley. I am convinced the latter statement was correct.

At five minutes to eleven we started to walk inside. Each of us carried a 'naked light' or oil lamp that had no glass or gauze to restrict the light, because there was no danger of gas in that level.

As soon as we entered under the mountain I was aware of the damp atmosphere. Black, oily water was flowing continually along the roadway and out to the tip. It was up to the height of a man's knees, and to avoid it we had to balance carefully and walk along the narrow rails. I slipped several times, and then tried crouching up on the side and swinging myself along by the timber that was placed upright on either side. Suddenly I remembered that this timber was supposed to be holding the roof up and that I might pull it out of place and bring the mountain down on to us. I did not touch the timber after that.

We were not more than ten minutes reaching the coal-face – that is the name given to the exact part where coal is being cut. This was a new level, so it had not gone far into the mountain. This seam was a small one, not a yard thick, and was a mixture of steam- and house-coal.

When I had been shown where to hang my clothes I went to see our working place. It was known as the Deep. We were the lowest place of all, because this Deep was heading into the virgin coal to open work. Every fifty yards on each side of our heading other headings opened left and right, but they would be working across the slope, and so were running level. From these level headings the stalls were opening to work all the coal off.

Our place was going continually downhill. Every three yards forward took us downward another yard. It was heavy climbing to go back, and every shovelful of coal or stone had to be thrown uphill. Water was running down the roadway to us and an electric pump was gurgling away on our right side. We were always working in about six inches of water, and if the pump stopped or choked for ten minutes the coal was covered with water. There is nothing pleasant about water underground. It looks so black and sinister. It makes every move uncomfortable and every stroke with the mandril splashes the water about your body.

It takes some time to be able to tell coal from the stone that is in layers above and below it. Everything is black, only the coal is a more shining black and the stone greyer. It is difficult to tell one from the other, especially when water is about, but the penalty for putting stone – miners call it 'muck' – into a coal-tram is severe.

I tried very hard to be useful that night, but was not successful, nor do I believe that any beginner ever has been. Things are so different and there is so much to learn. For several weeks lads of nowhere near my size and strength could make me look foolish when it came to doing the work they had been brought up in. I had used a shovel before, but found that skill was needed to force its round nose under a pile of rough stones on the uneven bottom, turn in that narrow space, and throw the shovelful some distance and to the exact inch.

The need to watch where you step, the difficulty of breathing in the confined space, the necessity to watch how high you move your head, and the trouble of seeing under these strange conditions are all confusing until one has learned to do them automatically. It takes a while to learn that you must first take a light to a thing before you can find it. I started several times to fetch tools, then found myself in the solid darkness and had to return to get my lamp.

My mate lay on his side and cut under the coal. It took me weeks to learn the way of swinging elbows and twisting wrists without moving my shoulders. This holing under the coal was deadly monotonous work. We – or rather my mate – had to chip the solid coal away fraction by fraction until we had a groove under it of an inch, then six inches, then a foot. Then we threw water in the groove and moved along to a fresh place while the water softened where we had worked.

John hammered continually for nearly three hours at the bottom of the coal. He cut under it until he was reaching the full length of his arms and the pick-handle. At last he slid back and sat on his heels while he sounded the front of the coal with the mandril blade and looked closely at where the coal touched the roof to see if there showed the least sign of a parting.

'Keep away from this slip,' he warned me as he moved farther along, 'it'll be falling just now.'

It did, in less than five minutes, and after I had recovered from my alarm and most of the dust had passed I did my best to throw the coal into the tram. I soon found that a different kind of strength was needed than the one I had developed. My legs became cramped, my arms ached, and the back of my hands had the skin rubbed off by pressing my knee against them to force the shovel under the coal. The dust compelled me to cough and sneeze, while it collected inside my eyes and made them burn and feel sore. My skin was smarting because of the dust and flying bits of coal. The end of that eight hours was very soon my fondest wish.

After working for a while John went away to search for a post. About that time one of the hauliers – I never heard him called anything but Will Nosey – decided to go and see how this new starter was getting on. I was alone, and pretty nervous, when he arrived. His nickname came partly from his interest in the concerns of other people and partly because of his long nose, which curved downward as if it meant to get inside his mouth.

Our lighting was feeble, and his face showed a grey white in colour. His voice was always loud, and the hollow passage amplified it. He had a different type of lamp from mine. His was one with an open wick and it was worn on his cap. The ventilation was good, so that the flame blew back over his head. I had reason to be alarmed, for his eyes were sunken alongside that hooked nose and there was a queer grin on his grey features, while above his head the oil flame hissed and crackled. He was exactly like one of those pictures we see of the Devil.

I did not speak, but stood and stared. He did exactly the same thing. Then someone not far away fired a shot to blow the roof down. In that confined space the noise and vibration were terrific. The whole mountain seemed to shake with the powder-charge. I could not hear for some seconds after.

I had never before heard such a crash, nor had I had any warning to prepare me. I could only imagine that an explosion must have happened and that this other being with flame over his head was there to capture me.

Then the haulier, who had finished his scrutiny, and had been delighted to see how startled I had been, started to laugh. It was intended for laughter, but it sounded most sinister to me.

'He, he,' he chuckled, and when I realised that he used earthly words I became more at ease. 'He, he. Made you jump, did it? That was a shot for ripping top, that was. Oughter have warned us, they did; but I s'pose they was on the watch. Don't half shake things up, do it? Like to be here, hey?'

I had still enough determination left to say the lie that I did like being there. I was discovering still another new pain. My knees, unused to the hard rubbing against the stone bottom, had become like those of a

Yorkshire miner whom I met later and who insisted that his knees had become 'b— red hot'.

As we were anxious to open work, we only cut the width of the roadway, about nine feet. The top coal was about one foot thick. We holed that off, then wedged up the lower coal. Altogether we filled three trams of coal, and the heading had gone forward about one yard. Then John rammed a bore-hole with powder and they lit the fuse. We went away to have food while the smoke from the shot was clearing.

We had a quarter of an hour for food. For the first time that I could remember I had no appetite, and the rats that ran about outside the circle of our lights had my food and squealed a lot while eating it.

The shot had ripped the top down, and we had to clear the stones so that the tram could be brought closer. Before that shot was fired we did not have more than a yard of height at the coal-face, and as I was clumsy I rubbed my back against the slime of the roof. My shirt-back was soon covered with a thick coat of clay and my back was getting as sore as my knees.

By four o'clock in the morning the shovel felt to be quite a hundredweight and I winced every time I touched my knees or back against anything. I got sleepy too, and felt myself swaying forward on my feet. I dropped some water in my eyes and revived for awhile, then I pinched my finger between two stones and was wide awake for some time after.

I had thought that night and day were alike underground, but it was not so. It is always dark, but Nature cannot be deceived, and when the time is night man craves for sleep. When the morning comes to the outside world he revives again, as I did.

Even the earth sleeps in the night and wakens with perceptible movement about two o'clock in the morning. With its waking shudders it dislodges all stones that are loose in the workings. It is about that time that most falls occur, at the time when man's energy is at its lowest.

Somehow that shift did end, although I felt it lasted the time of two. Then we had to lock our tools for the day. Holes are bored in the handles of the tools and they are pushed on a thin steel bar with a locking-clip fitted in the end.

John had a pile of tools, and they were all needed. Shovels, mandrils of different sizes, prising-bars, hatchet, powder-tin and coal-boxes, boring-machine and drills and several other things. He valued them at eight pounds' worth, and he was forced to buy them himself. He knew they might be buried by a fall any day and was not hopeful of getting any compensation for them. Nearly every week he had to buy a new handle of some sort and fit it into the tool at his home, so that his wages were not all clear benefit, and his work not always finished when he left the colliery.

How glad I was to drag my aching body towards that circle of daylight! I had sore knees and was wet from the waist down. The back of my right hand was raw and my back felt the same. My eyes were half closed because of the dust and my head was aching where I had hit it against the top, but I had been eight hours in a strange, new world.

The outside world had slept while we worked, and the dew of the morning sparkled from a thousand leaves when I looked down on the valley. It was beautiful after that wet blackness to see the sun, and the brown mountain, and the picture that the church tower made peeping out over the trees.

As we went down the incline, the day-shift came up. They called their 'Good morning' or 'Shu mai?' as they hurried past with their tea-jacks in their hands.

My landlord worked nights that week, as well, and they were all ready at the lodgings. We drank a cup of warm tea by holding the handle with a piece of paper so that we should not dirty it, then prepared to bath. We used a wooden tub, made by sawing one of the company's oil-casks in half.

My landlord gave me the benefit of his experience in getting all the dirt out of my eyes and ears. This was not so easy a task. After some days my skin seemed to get used to the dust and washing was easier after. Nowadays if anything interrupts the routine of a daily bath I begin to feel scruffy and to itch all over.

The landlady warned us against splashing, then left us to it. We washed to the waist, and he washed my back and I did likewise to him. We threw towels over our shoulders, then carried the tub out to empty it at the drain. Then filled the tub with fresh water that had been warming and stripped ourselves to complete our washing. After we called out that we were dressed, the rest of the family returned and we had breakfast.

I forgot my shyness over bathing in a few days, but it was not so with Jack. He did not wash under the same conditions, either. They were much more crowded at his lodgings than we were. Another family occupied the front room there – as was the case in almost every house in that street – and Jack was miserable because some of the women came into the room while he was washing, and stayed. It was torture to Jack to wash all over in the sight of anyone, but the people there were used to that sort of thing from childhood and thought nothing of it. No doubt they noticed Jack's shyness, and had a bit of fun over it.

I knew a Welshman who went to work in the Yorkshire mines and stayed there some years. When he returned to South Wales he brought the new accent with him and settled in a fresh place. Everyone thought he was an Englishman. The women where he lodged and some female neighbours always stayed indoors while he bathed, and amongst sly glances they had a lot to say concerning his physical capabilities and shortcomings. They spoke freely to one another in Welsh and became more personal as the days passed and he showed no sign of understanding. One day they annoyed him too much and he started to abuse them in fluent Welsh. There was consternation in that circle after that and a definite silence until he found other lodgings.

It was quite half an hour after my arrival home before I was properly clean and ready for food. This time used to get rid of dirt has always seemed to me to be part of the working day. Apart from that we had more than a half-hour's walk to work each day, so that I was away from home about nine and a half hours.

Life is complicated when one works by night. I went to work one day and returned the next. We started work on a Monday night, and one hour later it was Tuesday morning and the date was one day later. I had to watch this question of dates very carefully years afterwards when I had to report a lot of accidents, as the wrong date might lose a compensation claim.

Then again, I went to bed on Tuesday morning, stayed there for eight hours, and it was still Tuesday. It seemed strange that a night had not passed while I was in bed. There were no roaring loud-speakers in those days, but there were children playing in the street and hawkers with voices that sounded to be shaking the bed I tossed about on. The wind was the right way that morning, so that the dust of the colliery screens blew away from the village. So all the women were busy doing their washing. Tubs were bumped and washing-boards banged right underneath my window. All the water had to be carried from taps which were set at various spots throughout the village and a crowd of women were usually near these taps waiting for their water-vessels to be filled. These taps were great places for gossip, and every now and then I would hear a sharp voice calling, 'Our Lizzie Ann! D'you know I'm waiting for that water?' or 'Gwennie! Gwennie! You've been up at that tap all the morning.'

When the wind was the wrong way I had the choice of stewing in a bedroom with a tightly closed window or swallowing coal dust while I slept on bedclothes that became blacker every minute.

That first day I dozed and awoke until I could stay there no longer – and got up. My head ached as badly as the rest of my body and my mind decided that one week would be six days too long at that job.

Jack consoled me by saying that the aching of my body would get better in a few days but that there was little hope that I would ever sleep properly by day. He was quite right, and even to-day I notice that the beginning of each night-shift shows the men to be weary and disheartened by the lack of proper rest and that all are hoping the week-end will come soon so that they can have a real night's sleep.

I remember an old Welshman who detested night work as much as I did. He came to me one day and told me that 'that undermanager, mun, he did ask me to work nights for a couple of day, aye he did'.

'What did you tell him?' I asked, and tried not to smile at his confusion.

'That'll be the day, I did tell him,' he replied, 'that'll be the day – when I do work nights.'

An owl hooted at us when we walked through the woods to work on the third night. Whether it was in sympathy or derision I have never been sure. I thought so much about that combination of third night and hooting owl that I would have turned back gladly, only I was ashamed to do so.

From CHAPTER XIII

I HAVE HAD a shock to-day. Of course, we expect shocks on Friday, because it is our pay-day, but this one was not the usual 'day-short' or 'extra-deduction' sort of surprise; it was the reappearance of one of my old mates – Billy Ward.

I was dressed and ready by one o'clock on that Friday because I had to draw my pay for the previous week's work. That meant that I had to sacrifice some of the broken sleep that I manage to get during the day, and probably accounts for the bad humour that I usually have when I come downstairs. I feel very grumpy, and have little to say to anyone.

The colliery where I work is about four miles from this village, so I have quite a journey to get my money. I could travel by train or motor bus, but usually I prefer to walk on a Friday, so that I shall be sure of being by myself.

It is a grand day, and this valley is beautiful, with the glitter of the slow-moving river down the centre and the several shades of green among the trees that shade the mountain on each side. The sun is warm; some pigeons wheel above the village, and their white undersides show like puffs of steam; the polish shows on the laurel leaves when they move slowly with the warm wind; and the steam that rises from the turf has the smell of rain that has fallen to good purpose. I draw in the beauty of it all, slowly and gratefully, for I feel the wonder of such a day right into my bones. I am not often out in the fresh air, and so I enjoy every moment of it; yet I cannot help that feeling of regret that my mates should be shut away from it all.

Underneath the mountain that is over to my right more than a thousand of my mates are shut away from the sight of this day. They are swallowing dust with each gasping breath; they are knocking pieces out of their hands or bodies because of the feeble light; they are sweating their insides away so that they, and those dear to them, may live.

My home is on the outskirts of the village, and I am soon on the main road. There I walk quickly, so that I can get to the pay-office before the crowd arrives. The road is wide, and a lot of traffic travels along it. The many cars that pass throw out a spray of small stones and grit towards me, for they have been tarring recently. When I have walked over two miles I pass under a bridge that carries the coal-trams from one of the collieries. Just past this bridge, alongside the road, are the screens. The trams are tipped on the moving riddles of these screens, then the coal is sifted until the largest lumps are carried over to the outside row of trucks. There are six rows of trucks; each row is for a different size of coal, graded from the very small to the large lumps; but the colliers are not paid anything for the three smaller sizes. A large pointer on a clock-face shows the amount of small coal that is in each tram, and a weigher books it down so that it can be deducted from the total weight. Whilst these screens are working, a thick haze of dust covers all around. It is difficult to see the way along the main road, and one feels that evening has come suddenly.

The car-drivers rush through this cloud of coal-dust as quickly as they dare, but I have often thought that they should be compelled to stop and made to get out to stand for some time in that dust, so that they could taste it and enjoy a few sneezes. Some lumps of coal could be dropped from that bridge on to them, too, so that they might realise how hard they can hit. These people might then value the men more who get the coal, or, if they had to be with me this afternoon, they might discover some of the misery that is caused by that black mineral which comforts them with its heat.

About two o'clock I arrive at the next village. Here another colliery screen is at work. It shakes the dust into the lower atmosphere, and the sets of coal-trams rattle down towards it between the rows of houses. The dust shaken from the loaded trams covers the windows of the houses, but sometimes a lump rolls off into one of the gardens as some little compensation. The soil in these gardens is coal-dust; cabbages are grey in colour, and are loaded with dust between their leaves; and everywhere one puts a finger, a print is left in that dust. The higher atmosphere is no clearer, because a tall stack gives out a continual smudge of black smoke, which soon releases more soot to fall on the houses. I have heard it stated that nearly 20 per cent. of all the air breathed in this village contains the dust that causes silicosis. Children in the school yard breathe that dust; people in bed inhale it as they sleep; the posters outside the newsagents' are covered with soot, and a dress or collar is not clean for ten minutes.

The colliery office is near the main road. I bend to the window and shout my name and number. When the slip is handed to me I sign it, then get a large envelope in return. The size of that envelope is not a good guide to what it contains. Before I move away I make sure that the pay is right, for no mistake will be rectified after the man has gone from that window.

I shake out my money – two pound-notes, two half-crowns, three shillings and sixpence; two pounds eight and sixpence. That's all correct, so I move past the doorway. A bag of bolts is on one side and a steel rope coiled on the other. There must have been a wall-covering on that passage once – green, I should imagine – but now it is all grey-black, with a thicker coating of coal-dust where the colliers have leaned their bodies against it.

In the room on the left about twenty men are seated on plank forms waiting for the compensation doctors to come and examine them. The signs of injury are plain on most of them, for several have their arms slung, and four are on crutches. It resembles the dressing-station after a battle. Across the passage is another group waiting in a line for the clerk to pay them some compensation. He counts some money out, and calls each man forward to sign for his payment. They will receive not more than thirty shillings, usually less, for a week's compensation, but they are easier in their minds than those in the opposite room, because their claims have been admitted.

Soon afterwards I move away, and walk along the main street. Here, again, the shops are in most cases the front rooms of houses. About fifty yards along this street is a public-house. Somehow I crave for a stimulant to-day. My nerves are upset, and I know there will not be many men inside at this time. I am a poor drinker; sometimes I do not enter a public-house for six months at a stretch, and even then I usually hurry over my drink and get outside as quickly as I can. I do not like the atmosphere of these places, and often wish that the beer-garden method was in favour in this country. About here the drinkers talk so much of their work; probably because they have no other interests. They argue about trams they have filled or driven; about timber they have notched and placed in position; about this yardage and that tonnage, whilst I have always been determined that I will forget the drudgery once the shift is completed. To-day, however, I feel so shaky that I must have a drink, so I push the door back, order a small Guinness, then enter a room on the left. This is a large room, probably the most cheerful in that village. It is clean because no man in collier's clothes is allowed in there; they have their rooms at the back.

The four men who are playing bagatelle are not acquaintances of mine, neither are the two who watch them. I sip my drink slowly. When it is finished I order another, then sit with it before me because two drinks are my limit – I never take more. Whilst I am watching the froth sink, another man comes in, notices me, and comes to sit alongside. He is about my age, but wears spectacles. He has a good trilby on his head, and the crease on his grey trousers is exact. We have worked together and know one another's habits, so when I tell him it is my second drink, he does not bother me to drink again.

I am looking through the window above the bagatelle table when I hear my companion whistle to himself. I turn to see what has surprised him.

Another man has come in – with the silence of a ghost. His features, too, are ghost-like in their pallor. His skin stretches tightly across his cheek-bones, and his eyes are like two large drops of water in holes that have shrivelled into his face. This newcomer is closing the door when I look towards him, so I can see the trembling of every muscle when he moves. He is hardly strong enough to close the door, then when he succeeds, he sinks into the nearest chair, and his sigh sounds clearly across that quiet room. The barman brings him half-a-pint of beer, takes the coppers from that trembling hand, hesitates near him as if he wishes to ask this customer something, but finally decides to say nothing and walks back to the bar.

The drink is not used. I doubt if the trembling hand could lift it or that slobbering mouth contain it. The man sits alongside the table and trembles, with his cap going back and forth with each shake of his head. He is like a man who is very old, but there is something about his figure that refutes this idea of age.

One of the bagatelle players makes a stroke, then looks around for our appreciation. He notices the newcomer for the first time; the words of banter are choked in his throat. He stares for some seconds, then whispers to his neighbour, and I hear the words he uses:

'God in heaven, Jack! What's the matter with that chap, eh? He looks devilish bad, that he do. Didn't ought to be about in that state. Took bad in the street, I s'pose, and thought as a drink would liven him up, I expect.'

'Where've you been living lately?' his mate asks. 'Don't you know a chap as have got silicosis when you sees him?'

'Silicosis? Phew!' the other gasped. 'His face looks like a dead man's face, that it do.'

'Won't be long first,' his mate replied. 'I've seen enough of it to know as he can't last long.'

I glanced at the man near the door, then quickly away again. He had not touched that drink; his head was still nodding continually. When I look again at the window I feel my companion touching me on the arm.

'I think that chap signalled to you when you looked that way,' he said. 'You didn't notice him. D'you know him?'

I look again, for I had not seen any signal.

The newcomer notices me as I look, so he tries to smile at me. He does manage a queer kind of grin, but that alters his expression, and in those altered features something that is familiar touches my memory. I look at him steadily – and wonder. It isn't? – no, it can't be? – and yet, somehow he does resemble. Then he gives me that wistful travesty of a smile once again, and I am sure it is.

I move across that room quickly, so that I shall sit next to that trembling figure. 'Dai?' I question, then I check myself, because I cannot let him see that he is so altered that I did not recognise him; yet I am still not quite convinced that this shadow of a man can be the well-built and healthy friend I knew less than two years ago. Then he nods – just a more emphatic shake between his constant trembling – to confirm the name. I do not know what I can say next. I am not so foolish as to ask a dying man if he feels ill.

'Have a drink,' I suggest, because it is the only thing I can think of at that moment. 'Put that one inside you, and I'll get you another. It'll buck you up a bit.'

'No, thanks.' He mumbles the refusal, and I can see his chest lifting with every breath. 'I had to get this one – as – as excuse, see.' He paused to gain more strength before he continued, 'Because I wanted to sell – some of these – tickets.'

Slowly, by being very patient, I learn about his trouble. It is more than twelve months since he staggered home after his last working shift and had to realise that his usefulness was over. The stone-dust had got inside his lungs, then every respiration had damaged and torn the delicate lining of the chest – as if rough stones were being rubbed inside a silken pocket handkerchief. This dust accumulated in his breathing-organs, then closed together like cement. When the lungs were torn they were no longer air-tight. Every day his breathing became more difficult; soon it would be impossible. He is a long time telling me about this, and he goes through the details minutely, as would a man who has studied his own disease.

Dai was an intelligent type, and he must know what has happened to so many others, and that his time must be short. I do not attempt to hurry him, and I listen to the record of his visits to the doctors and their methods. As he talks I recall the others that I know who are in a similar state. There are two who are not yet so bad but that they can mount the steps to the Welfare Library if someone helps them; that other who struggles early to evening chapel and totters behind the door to hide his clothes, for he has started listening to a sermon for the first time when he realised that he would not live many more weeks, and that he would never see his thirtieth birthday; and that other of whom they said that the doctors blunted a chisel on his lungs when they held the post-mortem.

Dai is gasping to me that the Federation is fighting his case, and that meanwhile he is living on 'the parish'. He is hopeful that his case will be won, for he will then receive about twenty-five shillings a week regularly. I am not so sure about that winning, and I am fairly confident that he will not be alive to see the winning, anyway. I know that these silicosis cases are difficult ones to fight, because the men who are the most frequent sufferers are the workmen who open out the hard-headings through the solid rock to get at the coal.

These headings are completed when the coal is reached, and then the colliers develop the coal-seam. The hard-ground men, as those who drive these hard headings are termed, then move on to another district, or perhaps another colliery, to open more work; so they are moving about every few months, and no company will admit that they contracted the disease whilst at their work. It is sometimes necessary to produce samples of dust from the strata where the men have worked. Often this is practically impossible owing to that part of the mine having closed down, or the continual movement of the workings has hidden it so that it would be a costly matter to expose it again.

Masks are usually provided, but when a man is working to his limit to keep up to the pace set for him, how can he do so if he is handicapped by a mask, for air is nearly always scarce in these new headings? Many men know the danger of this dust-inhalation, but, as they have the choice of this work or none, they choose the course that will shorten their own lives but will give their families food for awhile and a lump sum in a few years – if they are lucky. Of course, every man who goes in these headings hopes that he will be luckier than his fellows, and that he will either avoid the dust, or that it will not affect him. Almost always this hope is vain. Man seems to be very sure that he can beat the mountain, but Nature nearly always wins. I knew six young men who came direct from the farming areas to this part less than ten years ago. They were fine specimens of manhood, and a hard-heading contractor gave each of them a few extra shillings to work with his gang as labourers. All have been taken back to that village churchyard except one, who was saved because he had his back injured in an accident. I once complained to a manager that the dust was affecting my throat. He advised me to drink more beer. Earn a little more money so that one shall drink more beer to wash the dust away – it might appeal to some, but not to me.

By slow stages Dai comes to the object of his call. In his more prosperous days he bought a gramophone – 'a good 'un it is, with thirty records'. Now he is trying to raffle it so that he can get a little ready money for his wife. He has a bundle of tickets – the sort of tickets one can buy in Woolworth's, that have a perforated centre and a corresponding number on each side. I notice that he has not sold any as yet, because the number one is showing on top; he is shy and does not like asking strangers.

Dai looks at me so hopefully, wondering if I will start this thing going and take that ticket from which the number mocks him. I decide to take a shilling's worth, and to explain things to the wife when I return home. My mate with the glasses takes another shilling's worth after I have explained to him. We approach the others, and the three who are miners buy without any hesitation. The two railwaymen are not so agreeable, but they do buy eventually. That is the thing that I have always noticed in these areas: if a man has a job that is comfortable and secure, he has not the same sympathy for others as the man who is in the midst of it – you will never see a miner refuse help to another who is sick or injured, for it may be his own turn next; but the others who make up the mining communities may live with them for years and yet not take any interest in the problems of those who create the industry on which they live.

Dai cannot rip the tickets for them or sign the names. He holds the tickets out, then they follow the shaking of his hand and do the rest. My mate with the glasses has much more cheek than either Dai or myself. He is a salesman who helps his brother in a market at week-ends. He offers to take Dai around the other rooms and help to sell the tickets. I know he will get rid of a good number, and I want to catch the train home. I follow them to the next room to watch Dai swaying alongside the table whilst my mate sells the tickets. The men there are buying after one glance at Dai; they do not ask what the prize is, they would not claim it in any case . . .

Crowds of black-faced men were coming from the pay-office when I passed back. Some beggars were holding out their caps to them as they passed. A splendidly built girl was selling flags near the entrance. The falling dust was settling on the cream she had used and was making a grey mask of her features. Her light dress was becoming more dingy every minute. A cheap-jack was offering bargains in working trousers, and an ice-cream man was raising the lid off his cream just long enough to lift a spoonful, then dabbing it down hard again. Several children peered eagerly at the features of the men as they came along, for it is difficult to tell one's own father when he comes home from colliery work; and there was apparently an urgent connection between those children, their pay-bearing fathers, and that ice-cream man . . .

We had a visitor at our house when I got there. I should have known that it was Billy Ward by that habit of rubbing his finger along his chin, even if I had not seen his face. His face would not have guided me so well, for he was altered very much. I had the affection for Billy that every workman feels for a mate who has shared years at a dangerous job with him. I remember when we were working a lot of overtime and Billy came to work displaying a packet of Player's cigarettes.

'Have a fag?' he asked. 'It ain't a Woodbine, either. It won't last for long, I'll bet – these good times when a chap can have a decent smoke.'

Obviously the times have not been good lately for Billy; he is smoking Woodbines now. He has a cup of tea with us, and tells us that things are 'middling'. He still has that habit of starting to laugh when telling you something, then breaking off to chuckle, as if he were finishing the enjoyment on his own. He was always rather sensitive and shy, so that, as I know him so well, I realise that he has something he wants to tell me – alone. Under the pretence of seeing round the old place, we go out.

'Just as dreary as it was, like, ain't it?' Billy looks at the grey streets and sees no change in them.

'Aye, just about the same,' I agree. 'Let's go up the mountain side. You didn't have mountains like this to climb at that place you went to.'

'No.' He shakes his head.

Purposely I walk towards the cottage where he used to live. As we walk I recall the times when he used to be waiting for us in his working clothes. Sometimes he had that old cornet at his mouth and we could hear him practising as we climbed upwards. He had been an Army bandsman in his youth, and was a fine player. When we get above the village we pass along a path bordered by stunted trees. I have to push the ferns aside as I walk. We pull a few of them in a heap, then sit on them.

'How's the work going now?' Billy asks.

'It's dragging on,' I answer, 'and that's about all. We don't lose much time. We don't need to if we're going to live at all. What sort of a show was that where you went?'

'Middling.' Billy looks down at the village, seems to be swallowing something hard, then adds: 'Hutch is dead. Did you hear?'

'Hutch!' For a minute I cannot believe him. I suddenly remember that Hutch had gone with Billy when he went north to work a machine in a colliery that was installing them. I had the same offer, only I had got work earlier.

'Good Lord!' I continue. 'That's a staggerer. Why, he wasn't more than thirty-five, and he was as strong as a horse. Couldn't think of him dying so young.'

'Killed he was,' Billy muttered, 'right by me, and he ought to be alive now.'

'Oh!' I answer. 'What was it – a fall or what?'

'Aye, a fall it was. A big one.'

I let him go on with his story. It is obvious that he has been longing to tell it to someone who would sympathise. As he used to tell me his worries about payments, or children's illnesses, in the past, so now he tells me about this new trouble. I visualise Hutch again. He was broad in build and fastidious about dress. He was fond of a buttonhole and a pipe that smelled of good tobacco. He had a boy's mischievous ways, yet he was a fine man in appearance . . .

'And this day,' Billy continued, 'we'd been ripping some top down and hurrying to clear it for the haulier to pass. Our singlets was soaking, and we was thinking it was time to have a bite of food, when the fireman comes running and bawling to us: "Bring them tools with you, and shape your blasted selves. Come on."

'A fall it was,' Billy explained, 'on one of the headings. Nasty it was, too; it had fell up to about eighteen feet, and the top above was like that black pan as you sees about here. You know, it drops without warning. The place was all alive; it was pinching up above and back along the sides, but that fireman wouldn't listen. "Settling down," he said it was. And there was six trams of coal the other side of it as he wanted to get out.'

'The fall was blocking the rails, was it?' I asked.

'Aye, it was' – Billy nodded – 'must have been about eight trams, but he reckoned there wasn't more'n five.'

'Same old game,' I commented.

'Aye, that's it. And we had the wind up. Hutch was afraid too, and he wasn't often frightened. Honest, it wasn't safe for a cat to be there. Hutch climbed up on top of the fall and sounded the upper top; it was like a drum. It was shaking when he touched it. Hutch started to argue, and wanted to put something under it before we started to work, but the fireman said he was going to have that coal out before the end of the shift whatever happened. I said it wasn't safe to work under it, and he started to rave at us. "Repairers, you calls yourselves," he said, "I'll bring you a couple of kids' suckers to play with. Get on at the job or take your tools out." '

'Wonder Hutch didn't land him one,' I said: 'he didn't like being roughed about.'

'You know how it is,' Billy explained; 'we'll always get the worst of it, no matter who's fault it is. We asked him if we should put a long post in the middle of the road so as to shelter us a bit, but he shouted, "You knows damn well that we couldn't get that coal by if a post was put in the middle, and anyway it'll take half an hour to get timber here. For Christ's sake," he said, "get on with it, or get to hell out of here." Well, we had to start, and we was all on edge with little bits a'falling around us all the time. We pitched in for all we was worth to get from under it all as soon as we could. After we had walled all as we could on the sides, he went to fetch a haulier and a tram. He'd been standing by us and shouting at us all the time.'

'It upsets me always, when I'm under a bad piece, to have a boss standing near me,' I stated.

'I should think it do upset everybody,' Billy agreed; 'and it was like that with us. We didn't know which was the worst, the fireman or that bad top. We had a tram, and whilst we was filling it, he went off to see as the haulier was back quick. We was about half full, and Hutch asked me to give him the sledge. I give it into his hand, then turned round to chuck a stone into the tram, and as I was doing that I felt the air going by me face, and something clouted me in the back – like a kick it was. Sort of unconscious I must have been for a bit, but I'm sure I heard Hutch squeal and give like a gasp and a long groan. I didn't know what was up, 'cos it was all so dark.'

'Lamps knocked out, I suppose,' I asked quietly.

'Smashed, they was,' he explained. 'They found 'em afterwards. I felt like as fire was in front of me eyes, and blood was running down me back. Hit me in the back it had, but not so hard, else I'd ha' been like Hutch was. Was too much small coal in my mouth to shout for a bit, and me eyes was clogged, but as soon as I could I shouted for Hutch, but he didn't answer. Then I knew as it was all over, 'cos Hutch was one who would squeeze through if there was any chance.'

'Aye, he was! Poor old Hutch!' I agreed.

'And I felt about me, but only the big stones I could feel, so I started to crawl for help. I felt me way along the rail. Could hardly drag me legs, and I had to go a good way afore I met the haulier a'coming back with the fireman. They was trotting the horse, and they nearly run over me. He sent the haulier back to get help when I told him, and he comes on with me. There was no sign of Hutch. Dozens of trams of muck was on top of him. Big stuff, too.'

'What did the fireman say then?' I asked. 'Was he upset?'

'He looks at the fall, then he say to me, "What have you got to say about this?" I says, "I've got a lot to say about it." "If you're wise," he says, "you'll say as your mate was scraping a place to put a post, and I'd gone to see about one being brought, when this fell and caught him. Don't forget." I didn't say much. I was pretty bad meself.'

'How long before they got him out?'

'Sure to be nearly an hour. Had to use posts and rails to get the stones up. They was a time before they could find him, and when they did – his head was flat almost, and only a bit of skin was holding his leg.'

Billy was biting his lip to help his control, and I had no way of soothing him.

'See,' he continued, 'I wanted to wash him, because it seemed the last

I could do, and he was my butty, but when I saw his face by daylight, it finished me. It fetched me guts up, and I ain't been able to look at food since. And we had to put him in the front room because there was only two rooms down. His wife and the two girls lived in the kitchen with us.'

'How are they now?' I asked gently.

Billy did not answer for a minute. He looked down on the village, from which the cries of the hawkers and the calls of children came faintly up to us. A coal-train was moving out from the siding. Hardly a trace of smoke showed amongst the heat haze of that afternoon; it seemed that the loaded trucks were pushing an unwilling engine along the line . . .

FALLEN BASTIONS

by G. E. R. Gedye

(monthly choice, February 1939)

The entry for *Fallen Bastions* in the Gollancz catalogue ran to 5,500 words – perhaps the longest in publishing history. The book is a first-hand account of the impact of the Nazi movement on Austria and Czechoslovakia, and their eventual seizure by Hitler's troops. George Eric Rowe Gedye (1890–1970) had been a journalist in Central Europe since the twenties. In the first years of the LBC he was based in Vienna as the correspondent of the *Daily Telegraph* and the *New York Times*. During this time he caught Gollancz's eye with his vivid and far from impartial dispatches – he was a staunch anti-appeaser who was also concerned to document the socialist opposition to the Nazis. John Lehmann recounted his memories of Gedye in pre-Anschluss Vienna:

> His personal sympathies had been strongly with the Social Democrats, and in his dispatches after the February rising he had made little effort to conceal either his contempt for the clerical-fascist regime or his hatred of the Nazis. Gedye's truculent wit and sanguine temperament were a tonic in the darkest days of foreboding and dismay. He took to a fight with the zest of a street-urchin, and had a terrier's nose for any dirty secret smooth politicians were trying to conceal. He was probably the best-informed of all the members of the Anglo-American Press Association in Vienna about the underground activities of the Social-Democrat partisans. Dollfuss and Schuschnigg had handled foreign journalists with considerable caution, and left him alone, though they knew perfectly well where his sympathies lay. He had no reason to expect such respect from the Nazis.

On the morning of the Anschluss, Lehmann writes, 'smoke from innumerable compromising letters, reports and records [was] pouring out of the chimneys of politicians, journalists and secret agents'. He went to see his friend: Gedye's face 'emerged from dense smoke as he cautiously opened a few inches of door in response to my ring at his bell . . . his stove was roaring more furiously than any other in Vienna.'

Gedye moved his office to Prague in March 1938, only to encounter an invasion there a year later; he left Czechoslovakia in the spring of 1939 to avoid arrest under Gestapo warrant. *Fallen Bastions* sold a huge number of copies, both within the LBC and to the general public. But the *Telegraph* disagreed with the book's political line – that abandoning Czechoslovakia was morally reprehensible and militarily foolish – and would not allow Gedye's connection with the paper to be mentioned in Gollancz's publicity campaign. The publication of *Fallen Bastions* led to Gedye's departure from the *Telegraph*. After the war he reported for the *Daily Herald*, the *Manchester Guardian* and the *Observer*, and became the Vienna correspondent of Radio Free Europe.

From CHAPTERS XXVIII, XXXIII, XXXIX

FROM THE MOMENT of hearing the end of Schuschnigg's farewell broadcast on March 11th, I had known that I personally had a choice between two courses. Either I suppressed all the worst features of the Nazi terror in the hope of finding sufficient favour with the new masters of Austria to be able to stay on indefinitely, or I gave the full truth without the least modification, in which case my days in Vienna would be very few. There are many cases where it may become the journalist's duty to his employers to adopt, at least for a while, the policy of tempering the wind to the unshorn wolf, but I was happy to find that this was not one of them. The Vienna post had never been one for covering Austria alone. All the staff correspondents there – at any rate of English and American newspapers – had the duty of covering the whole of the Succession States of the Austro-Hungarian Monarchy – Czechoslovakia, Austria, Hungary, Jugoslavia and Rumania – except Poland, which was too much out of the picture – and in many cases Bulgaria, Albania and Greece as well. This was done with the aid of local correspondents in each capital, part-time 'string men', who were usually natives of the country themselves and often spoke no English – and with the aid of the network of small news-agencies which grew up for the purpose. With the arrival of Nazi censorship, distortion, faking and manipulation of all news at the source, the departure of all Legations, most of which had maintained special officers to make contact with the Vienna correspondents of great newspapers, and the reduction of the former capital of the Habsburg Monarchy to the status of a German provincial city, Vienna's day as a news-gathering and transmitting centre had ended. Furthermore, I at once anticipated what in a week proved to be the case: that the Nazis would bring pressure to bear to secure the removal of all foreign staff correspondents from the former Austrian capital, where no publicity was desired for what was going to be done. My view met with approval at home, and I was authorised to start to move my offices to Prague (which, as the only remaining democratic capital in central and south-eastern Europe, was the next most suitable centre of operations) as soon as I wished, remaining myself in Austria only as long as I thought the story worthwhile. I decided that I would like to stay and see through the farce of the forthcoming Nazi plebiscite on April 10th, but that to secure this melancholy personal experience it was certainly not worthwhile to suppress or modify any aspect of the truth about Austria. In sending the facts about the German threat to fire on the Austrian staff officers in the Chancellery, I was naturally fully aware of the risks I took. I realised, further, that in giving all the details of the armed Nazi raid and plundering of the Swedish Mission to the Jews – almost the only case, owing to the diplomatic protection accorded to the Mission by the Swedish Government, where one could quote chapter and verse without endangering the life of the victim – I had taken another step towards filling up the cup.

I therefore knew exactly what was afoot when, on the afternoon of March 18th, I received a telephone call asking me to visit the headquarters of the Press Police between seven and eight that evening. The head of the section, a handsome Austrian official of the old type, Hofrat Zoffal, received me very courteously, and said that he was sorry to have to put before me an order received from the Gestapo in Berlin instructing him to request me 'politely' to leave 'Vienna' within three days. I asked him the reason of the expulsion, and, as I expected, was told none had been given. I expressed a little surprise that the famous Prussian efficiency of the Gestapo had not prevented them from writing 'Vienna' where they obviously meant 'Austria', but assured him that I would not embarrass him or his new masters by merely removing myself to Baden near Vienna. The Police Chief seemed to be expecting some protest on my part at being turned out of the country at three days' notice, after thirteen years' residence, but if so he was disappointed. I only reminded him that during these thirteen years I had not had difficulties with the Austrian police on a single occasion, despite my constant and extremely outspoken criticism of the Clerico-Fascist regime, but had proved unable to survive a single week of the Nazi regime. To this, of course, he could do no more than shrug his shoulders and point to his orders. He did, however, tell me that for the present critical state of Europe the prime responsibility lay, not with

Germany, but with the policy followed by the Entente Powers immediately after the War. I think he was surprised to find that I cordially agreed with him. I promised to send him the German translation of my book, *The Revolver Republic*, in which I had said so emphatically many years before. I told him that I did not intend to make any effort to obtain diplomatic protection against this expulsion without reason given, realising after a recent declaration in the House of Commons concerning the rights of foreign governments to expel British journalists, that this would be a waste of time. (As my colleague, Douglas Reed, late of the London *Times*, and now of the *News Chronicle*, has just written in his book *Insanity Fair*: 'Not even the domiciliary rights guaranteed to the British citizen under the treaties with foreign Powers are upheld for British journalists. They can be kicked out at will, without any specific charge, just as a propagandist stunt. Doing the job for which they are sent out, they are coming to be treated rather like spies in war time.') I therefore told the Herr Hofrat that I knew of a quite good train for Prague on Monday evening and proposed to take it. We parted on amicable terms.

I was a little pained, therefore, when he rang me up late that night and told me that I was to report myself to the head of the Gestapo for Vienna, the Prussian SS leader Oberregierungsrat Klein, in Gestapo Headquarters, No. 7 Herrengasse, at eleven the following morning. I knew of quite a number of cases where people who had reported to Klein in this way had left the headquarters in a prison van. I told Zoffal that it seemed a little harsh to be given an order of expulsion at seven and to have to report for arrest at eleven the following morning.

'There is no intention to arrest you,' Zoffal replied, 'but it is for your own advantage to obey the order promptly.'

What would have happened had I the privilege of having Jewish blood in my veins when I presented myself next day at the Gestapo I do not know, as the first question asked me by the guard at the entrance was: 'Are you an "Aryan"?' I told him that in my country we had not yet begun to ask one another these riddles, but that 'Aryan' or 'non-Aryan', I had to be in Klein's office within ten minutes, and that if he detained me playing guessing games about grandmothers he would presumably hear the answer from the Oberregierungsrat himself. On that the question of my ancestry was left in abeyance and I was given a guide to the Presence. The huge building was one great beehive of Germans in black uniforms with skull-and-crossbone badges, buzzing with their activities in arranging the arrests of Austrian citizens. Klein left me in his anteroom on the approved principle to cool my heels for nearly two hours.

'Last night you were given an order of expulsion,' he began when I was at last sent in. 'You know, of course, the reason.'

I told him that I knew of a great many causes I had given the Nazis to dislike me during the past five years, but was quite unaware what specific incident had caused the present move. The big Prussian soldier stared at me intently, his eyes glittering with the 'we-know-all-your-secrets-so-you-may-as-well-come-clean' look of the police inquisitor and said:

'You were among the journalists confined in the Chancellery on the day of the Führer's visit. On that occasion you sent a message that a German officer had threatened to give an order to fire on Austrian staff officers unless they retreated into the building. What impression do you imagine the publication of such a message made in Berlin?'

'I should imagine an even more unpleasant one than the spectacle of distinguished Austrian officers being treated in this way by a German comrade-in-arms and "liberator" made on me,' I told him. 'Not even the fact that these officers had – in my view – dishonoured their uniforms by putting on your Swastika badge and had prepared themselves to take part in the parade of your Führer saved them from this public humiliation before foreign journalists. I realised at the time that your Government would be furious at publicity being given to such a shameful incident, but my duty is to my newspaper, not to the rulers of the Third Reich.'

At this he stared at me harder than ever.

'Was not the real reason for your sending the story just resentment, due to a suspicion that our authorities had deliberately imprisoned you in the Chancellery to prevent you from seeing the Führer?'

'Although some of my colleagues expressed such suspicion,' I told him, 'I did not agree with them, and never imagined for a minute that that was the explanation. I think you were all much keener on our seeing the Führer than I for one was on seeing him. I have had that privilege more than once, and I was not curious. My reason for sending the story was that it was far too illuminating an illustration of the real position to be either modified or suppressed.'

'And what in your view,' he asked sarcastically, 'was the real position in the Chancellery that morning?'

I told him that if I gave it I should only add to my offence in his eyes.

'Never mind about that,' he retorted. 'I am interested to hear what you thought, and perhaps I will give you some indication of whether you were right.'

'I imagine', I told him, 'that your people felt unsure of themselves and of the willingness of the Austrian army officers to acquiesce in your seizure of the country. Probably there was a suspicion, rightly or wrongly, that these officers were preparing a protest or a revolt, and the officer who gave these orders took the very natural military precaution for anyone in the position of an officer of an invading army unsure of its ground and surrounded by hostility of threatening to shoot anyone who left the building. Had the threat merely been made to the journalists, it would have been worth recording, but of secondary importance only. The fact that it was made to Austrian officers in uniform threw a very valuable light for the world on the actual position between the German and the Austrian armies, which were supposed to be celebrating a fraternal reunion. That is why I sent it; the story was true, and I stand by every word of it.'

'It was not quite true,' Klein replied. 'In a way you are right as to background – a sudden emergency arose, there was reason to suspect sudden danger, and immediate and ruthless measures had to be undertaken to counteract it. Someone perhaps went too far in detaining foreign correspondents so long in the building. What is untrue, according to the investigations I had made, is that the order was given by an officer. It was given by an ordinary SS guard wearing a black uniform like mine.'

'There I must contradict you, Herr Oberregierungsrat,' I told him. 'I saw and heard the order given quite distinctly. What formation the person responsible belonged to I cannot tell you, although I tried to read the number on his shoulder-straps. He certainly had not a black uniform like yours, but military field-grey with officer's badges of rank; he was wearing a sword and holding a revolver.'

Klein asked whether I could swear to this, and I told him I could.

At this moment we were interrupted by the ringing of a telephone bell. My inquisitor picked up the receiver.

'Headquarters of the Gestapo for the City of Vienna, Oberregierungsrat Klein! What, you've got him – the publisher himself? *Einsperren! Einsperren! Alles beschlagnahmen! Meldung!*' ('Lock him up! Lock him up! Confiscate everything! Report to me!') '*Heil Hitler!*'

Then, turning to me, he fired an abrupt question:

'Were you old enough to be in the War? Officer? *Man merkt's.*' ('One sees it.') 'I am inclined to cancel the order of expulsion against you.'

This was a shock. I suspected some trap and said: 'On what conditions? I cannot agree to suppress any facts which I observe myself or can ascertain to be true.'

'I don't require that. I require that in reporting any such incidents as that in the Chancellery which you may run across, you make it clear to your readers that the circumstances are unusual here – times of violent change. Quite abnormal.'

I told him that I had never failed to make clear in all my dispatches how very far from normal conditions were and that one had only to look out of the window at the Jewish cleaning squads to realise that.

'Very well. On those conditions I cancel the order of expulsion.'

'Thank you.'

The Gestapo Chief banged the table with his fist as I let my curtness match his own.

'Don't you give a damn whether you are expelled or not?'

'Oh, yes,' I told him. 'Although it is, of course, quite impossible to stay on in this country permanently, I should be quite glad to remain until after the plebiscite.'

The Gestapo Chief told me that I could stay as long as I liked. We shook hands, clicked heels, and I went home to stop my trunks being packed.

It proved hardly worthwhile. Immediately after the interview with Klein a new campaign started from Berlin to force me out of the country without the unpleasant publicity attaching to an expulsion. Exactly why Klein cancelled the order – if the responsibility was his – and why a fresh one was issued a week later, I have never been able to ascertain definitely. Apparently the cancellation of the order, however, was only due to some bureaucratic jealousy. Dr Goebbels' Press Bureau had ordered my expulsion without the concurrence of Herr Himmler or vice versa. At any rate, it was the Press Bureau which was responsible for the ensuing series of hints conveyed to Berlin colleagues that they really thought it will be better for me to leave Austria, that 'the news centre for Greater Germany is now Berlin, not Vienna', and over and over again, when *did* I intend to go? Already the list of my colleagues who had been forced out of the country was a pretty long one – Christopher Holme of Reuter's would never again in Vienna sing to us '*Tira la bomba*';

Douglas Reed of *The Times* had been dragged out of his train and plundered while getting away to Switzerland; M. W. Fodor of the *Manchester Guardian* and his wife had been brought to safety in Prague in the car of a kindly diplomat; Alfred Tyrnauer of the International News Service and his wife had been arrested at the Journalists' Room in the Main Telegraph Office by armed Nazis on the night of the fall of Schuschnigg, and although released within a few hours, both were unable to leave the country as their passports had been confiscated. (Only the personal influence of W. R. Hearst with Hitler enabled them to go later; Mrs Tyrnauer never recovered from the shock, and died a couple of months later in Paris.) Dr Friedl Scheu of the *Daily Herald* had been transferred to Prague, and the Nazis had let him know that his two-year-old daughter would be kept in Austria as a hostage – as I write she is still so held – until he came back to fetch her. Ernst, the staff photographer of the Wide World Photo Service, and Jacobson, of the Associated Press Photo Service, were both among the many Press photographers in prison. (Later the Associated Press office was simply shut up by the Nazis.) Clearly my days were numbered; when I finally got to Prague, one of my colleagues greeted me with: 'Here comes the boy who stood on the burning deck!' . . .

* * *

. . . No summer can ever be the same to me again as every summer was before this of 1938 spent in Prague. Summer has for me always, particularly since I came twelve years ago to Vienna, and Vienna taught me her great lesson of how to live each leisure moment as intensely as every hour of work, been the season for which the three others were but the preparation. Summer has meant for me half-hours snatched from work to soak up reserves of energy from the hot Central European sun, to stretch one's limbs and muscles in and under water, to hide for a few hours on calmer week-ends from the dictatorship of the telephone bell which dominates every foreign correspondent's life, beside some rippling mountain stream and pit one's cunning against that of wily, orange-spotted trout. In this sad summer of 1938 I forgot all these lessons of Vienna, absorbed in watching the superhuman efforts of the last stronghold of democracy in Central Europe to hold out against the devilish ingenuity of those who never ceased day or night to plot its destruction and seemed untiring in finding some new point of attack. And the real danger came never from the open enemy, but from the false friend, for that was the attack to which no resistance could be offered, since it came always in the subtle guise of warnings and of good counsel. And all of it – open attack, false friendship and (carefully concealed) pressure to disastrous surrender – centred on one little, iron-nerved man, born a schoolmaster and brought from a professor's chair into public life, Edouard Beneš, co-founder with Masaryk of the democratic Republic of Czechoslovakia. And this was no sudden strain to which a man strengthened by years of ease was subjected, but the culmination of attacks which had never really ceased since the end of the strain of war and conspiratorial activities had brought the wiry little ex-schoolmaster into the limelight as his new-founded country's Foreign Minister.

After twelve years spent in the very heart of Vienna, I had taken a flat in a villa on the outskirts of Prague, not far from the airport and not far from the Hradshin, the palace of the old kings of Bohemia, now the official residence of the President of the Republic, hoping for a peaceful summer to enable me to learn a new and difficult language and to study at ease all details of a complicated situation with the outlines of which I was already familiar. Instead, I found myself plunged into a whirl of work under new, unfamiliar and difficult conditions which hardly left me time to eat and sleep. Yet when, after getting to bed at 4 a.m. night after night, I got up still tired but rested at 9 or 10 a.m., my first news was often that of all-night conferences at the Hradshin on the most vital questions for the country, followed by a reception at 9 a.m. – sometimes at 7.30 – by Beneš of some cold-blooded and bullying diplomat presenting a whole sheaf of new, nerve-racking problems. I realised that in comparison with my distinguished neighbour I was living the idle life of a pasha.

The President's steadiness and endurance were but the reflection of that shown by all his people. They, too, were subjected to the daily bullying of a powerful neighbour carried out over a radio which they could all hear and a Press the echoes of which they were compelled in their own papers to read. They it was who on May 21st went so gladly and so gallantly to man the defences of their frontiers against frightful odds. One day, lunching with someone connected with the Runciman Mission who pumped me hard as to my views of the situation here, giving nothing in return, I was asked about the general spirit of the people. I expressed my conviction that they were utterly fearless and utterly determined to defend with all the strength of a small but highly efficient and wonderfully equipped little army the independence which for twenty years they had enjoyed to the very last, aided or not. And I was told, 'Yes, I am afraid you are right. There seems to be something rather primitive, barbaric, about the Czechs, something uncivilised. Apparently they think of war and self-defence as something which has to be reckoned with in the last resort, and, as you say, they seem to be determined to fight, even against hopeless odds. That is a notion which, thank God, we have grown out of in England, where we regard war as something so unspeakably beastly that we would accept any alternative rather than face that.' I choked for a moment, swallowed half a glass of wine and collected myself enough to ask:

'Then England would never under any circumstances defend herself against aggression again?'

'England', I was told, 'would, thank God, never allow herself to be led into the beastliness of war again under any circumstances.' Then, as though allowing me a debating point, my vis-à-vis said, 'Perhaps if the country's actual independence was threatened and there were no alternative between the loss of it and resistance.'

'And do you not think that this is the case with Czechoslovakia today? Do you not see that for this country there is no choice but resistance or utter and final downfall?'

'That', I was told coldly, 'is altogether different. How can you compare this country with the British Empire?'

After the moving proofs of Czechoslovak courage – not of blind courage, but of serious, fully comprehending, anxious but quite irreducible courage which I was receiving daily, almost hourly, I really did not see how I could, and quietly subsided.

Throughout the summer there hung over Prague the shadow of war. Morning after morning I watched as I worked on my sunny balcony the aeroplanes providing target practice for the anti-aircraft batteries. As the little white puffs of smoke in the sky marked the aim of the gunners and the 'pop!' of the explosion, so reminiscent of wartime 'Archies', made my Schnauzer, a soundly Red Floridsdorf mongrel, born in the Arbeiterstrandbadgasse in Vienna during the February 1934 shelling of the workers' homes, and consequently mildly shell-shocked from birth, take cover with gallant efforts to conceal his trembling beneath my chair, I wondered how many weeks it would be before I saw real shells fired at really hostile aeroplanes. Night after night I motored home in the small hours from my office in the heart of Prague to see the long, accusing fingers of searchlights concentrating in spinster-like scorn on a detected sinning plane. Day after day I had to cope with the intricacies of new 'plans' of the Government to appease the unappeasable. The 'Second Hodza Plan' succeeded the first, the third the second, the fourth the third and the fifth the fourth. Each one was stillborn, as the Czechs knew all the time in their hearts that they would be, because there was only one plan which Henlein would ever accept: the plan demanded by his master – destruction of the democratic bastion of Czechoslovakia, whose very existence endangered his totalitarian dictatorship at home, whose military power stood between him and the oil-wells of Rumania, the granaries of Hungary. But unceasingly came the pressure from London, coupled with the hint: 'You must gain time for us all by yielding again.'

Somewhere I saw someone in a letter to the editor of some British or American newspaper writing about 'Czechoslovakia's Calvary' and 'Czechoslovakia's Crucifixion', and noticed the next day some Colonel Blimp or Councillor Blimp getting very hot under the collar about it in print. It was not the sort of comparison which would spring very easily to my own lips, but during this tragic summer it constantly forced itself into my consciousness. I have called the Czechs the Yorkshiremen or the Prussians among the Slavs. They are that – but only among the Slavs. And there is a childlike – if you will, a Christlike – quality which cannot be eradicated in all of the Slavonic peoples. The leaders of Czechoslovakia did, of course, know that all these carefully worked-out 'Plans' were foredoomed to failure before, or rather at the very moment when they were put on paper, because the fiat had gone forth from Berlin to accept nothing. Yet the Czechs produced them to satisfy the repeated demands made on them from London by the Chamberlain Government, and here I think they let the childlike quality of their race lead them into folly. I talked to Cabinet Ministers, high officials and army officers, and they were all inspired by an evident distrust of the Chamberlain policy. Yet they could not, did not want to believe in the baseness of the betrayal which was being prepared for them. If they made yet another concession, they argued, Britain would be morally bound to stand by them in the last extremity. And always they were misled by the argument of Britain's self-interest, not appreciating that the interests of Britain as a World Power were one thing, and the fears entertained by Mr Chamberlain as to what might happen to the Haves if Hitler's bluff were called or if Hitler forced himself into a disastrous war quite another. So their leaders produced 'Plans' to the *n*th degree – and with each concession of what had been declared last week to be inconcedable, they undermined the national morale, and insinuated into the astounding national determination to resist another hint that, after all, it might also be possible to surrender.

And what would I have done? I don't know – probably collapsed under British pressure early in May. But I know what I should have done – taken my stand on the May mobilisation position and refused either to demobilise or to budge in any respect. And, above all, I ought to have defied the Franco-British efforts to bully me into destroying my country after Berchtesgaden, declared that I would hold my fortifications *und es darauf kommen lassen* – and have let come what might come. To be quite honest, I often let myself be persuaded by the Czechs that perhaps the successive 'Plans' produced under British pressure might conceivably help by securing British support, although in my heart I knew it was not so. But Berchtesgaden – never. I knew, and said at once, that with the acceptance of that, Czechoslovakia had committed suicide. Yet there came resurrection – and one more chance. Czechoslovakia dismissed the 'Surrender Government' which had agreed to give up the Sudeten areas and the forts. Their successors should have at once disowned the surrender and defied the oppressor. For a few hours they intended to do so. Came another Anglo-French *démarche*, and all was over. It was over because the ally who did not rat – Russia – had made it clear that she was willing to fulfil her obligations to the letter, to defend Czechoslovakia against unprovoked aggression after France had begun to fulfil her own obligations in this respect, and to go beyond them – to defend Czechoslovakia even if France ratted: but one condition. This was that not a yard of fortifications were voluntarily surrendered.

The reactionary wing of the Czech Agrarians, Germany and reactionaries in many other countries busily circulated the story that Russia had said she was too weak to fulfil her obligations. It was even stated in a broadcast from Prague given under reactionary official influences. I have the best of reasons for knowing that it was not merely a lie, but the precise opposite of the truth.

Here is the story, as told me by a friend of Dr Beneš, of what actually happened. On the Sunday immediately before Britain and France forced Beneš to agree to the surrender of the Sudeten districts, after Berchtesgaden, Beneš sent for the Russian Minister to Czechoslovakia, Alexandrovsky, to see him in the Hradschin. Russia had already been unofficially sounded as to whether, if asked formally, she would be prepared to defend Czechoslovakia if France should let her down, and had indicated that the answer would be favourable. To Alexandrovsky Beneš formally put the following two questions:

'If we are attacked and France comes to our assistance in accordance with the terms of our two treaties, will Russia also fulfil her obligations and furnish military aid to France and Czechoslovakia?'

Alexandrovsky replied without hesitation, 'Instantly, and with all her strength. Why do you ask?'

Then Beneš said, 'If France dishonours her signature and refuses to help, what would be Russia's advice to this country as to the right course to pursue?'

Alexandrovsky replied, 'Denounce Germany immediately as the aggressor before the League and call for League support. Germany will automatically be branded as aggressor by refusing to obey the League's summons to state a case, as of course she will refuse. Russia will then fulfil her obligations under the League Covenant, and come to your assistance regardless of what the other League Powers may do.'

After this there was a long silence between the two, broken at last by Alexandrovsky saying:

'M. le President, is there not another question you wish to ask me regarding Russia's action should an appeal to the League be made impossible by some trickery or other?'

Beneš looked at him for a long time very steadily, but did not open his mouth. Silently Alexandrovsky rose, shook his head sadly, bowed and left.

Thus did the man whom the Goebbels propaganda machine was denouncing daily as a 'Red' refrain from calling in the direct aid of Russia which he knew was available to him and which might have saved his country's independence.

Throughout this long, tragic summer the vultures gathered around Czechoslovakia – vultures of the breed to which I belong myself as a foreign correspondent. The Czechs noticed grimly in their Press that they were mostly war correspondents such as Knickerbocker and Harrison, of the *News Chronicle*, who had been through the wars in Manchuria, Abyssinia or Spain. Came great bankers, anxious about invested capital. Came Right-wing conspirators from many countries, anxious to lend Hitler a hand in the game of dismembering Czechoslovakia. Came Left-wing enquirers, anxious to lend a hand in 'debunking' the plotted betrayal. Prominent among the latter was

Claude Cockburn, whom the Americans call the '*enfant terrible* of British journalism', who from so staid a background as foreign correspondent of *The Times* has become in his mimeographed news sheet the *Week* the supreme debunker of British and international politics, the uncomfortable revealer of skeletons in the British cupboard, on lines familiar to Americans from various publications, but otherwise unknown in Britain. Came representatives of the Socialist twopenny weekly, the *Tribune* – which incidentally in its own rude way I found, to my surprise, more consistently right about what was really going on in Central Europe than any other weekly published in London. Came parties of the Left Book Club of Victor Gollancz, eager for first-hand information about this incredible betrayal of a democracy which was progressing so blandly under their very noses. Came Members of Parliament, some of course with their minds made up on the basis of no information at all, most of them with open if sometimes naïve minds, determined to get at the facts. Came political quacks and cranks, pushing every kind of political nostrum. Came – gee, how they came! – the 'TWs' – the Time-Wasters . . . Schoolmasters from the Midlands, leaders of 'Y's – YMCAs – from the Middle West, lady lecturers, occasional writers, sociologists, criminologists and entomologists – social-credit prophets, pacifists and the reverse – all eager to have 'just an hour or so with you to ask you *all about* Czechoslovakia, because I do admire your messages so'. It was flattering, no doubt, but in the terrific rush of work, the impossibility to find enough time to eat proper meals and to sleep through to a refreshed awakening, one would have gladly dispensed with the compliments in order to be able to work undisturbed. After all, the foreign correspondent's job is to acquire information and to impart it in print, not to act as Public Relations Counsellor, Cook's Guide and Volume 'CZE' of the *Encyclopaedia Britannica* to all and sundry. I took what defensive measures I could to escape the onslaught – avoided my office as far as possible and worked at home, having had my home telephone number put on the 'very secret' list and threatened the direst penalties to anyone in my office who revealed it. I established a heavy 'outer-office' barrage to protect myself from interruptions, but of course I was 'landed' in nine cases out of ten. There were days when I reached my office to find four cards lying on my desk from complete strangers whose cross-questioning I had escaped. I was just five short of a pack of these when the second Czech mobilisation and the war scare scattered abruptly all those who had no professional business in Prague. To them all if they read these lines I apologise for all my subterfuges – but I had somehow to get through my work.

Among the stream of visitors there was one surprising blank. While British Cabinet Ministers were scurrying back and forth to Germany and France, not one visited Czechoslovakia, the country whose life was at stake in all these conferences. Not one found it necessary to hear from Beneš his views on the problems of his country which he was defending so gallantly, his back against the wall. Nor was it thought worthwhile to invite any Czechoslovak Minister to London. From start to finish, Czechoslovakia was treated as the ball to be tossed to and fro between London, Paris and Berlin . . .

* * *

On a warm day this summer I was sitting on the lovely flower-banked terrace of the Richmond Park Hotel at Karlsbad – now seized by the Germans, for the owner was a Jew – with a man whom I am glad to be able to call my friend, although he moves in a world of wealth and influence far removed from mine. We talked of Austria. I told him of how a month before I had seen the menacing head of Nazi Fascism raised here too, as fanatic columns of Henleinists streamed past this very spot with the old dervish incantations of Vienna – '*Sieg Heil! Sieg Heil! Sieg Heil! – Ein Volk, ein Reich, ein Führer!*'

'Yes,' he said, 'this horrid thing is on the march, and against it there seems to be only one active force – militant Socialism. As you know, I am not and never could be a Socialist. I belong to the town-house, country-mansion, automobile and dinner-jacket class. Socialism probably – Communism certainly – would deprive me of most of the good things of life which I now enjoy – not, I hope, selfishly. But this other thing – Nazism, Fascism – call it what you will – is too hideous to contemplate. The other night I was talking all this over with my wife, who is a very wise woman, and she said:

' "We of the well-to-do classes with cultured and liberal minds must always fight against the danger of either Socialism or Fascism putting an end to our pleasant and useful existences. But if the choice – which God forbid – should ever be forced upon us, I should feel that we were being compelled to choose between perishing in the drought of Fascism and the flood of Socialism – perhaps of Communism. Both, drought and flood, destroy, and either way, our sort of life would come to an end.

But when the drought has passed, it leaves behind it an arid desert where nothing new can live. After the flood subsides, new forms of life spring up, some monstrous, some young, vigorous and healthy – we see it in this world of ours to-day. I think, dear, that you and I could never choose the drought."'

And you?

THE BETRAYAL OF THE LEFT

edited by VICTOR GOLLANCZ

(additional book, February 1941)

'I saw Gollancz recently,' Orwell wrote in 1940 to his friend Geoffrey Gorer; 'he is furious with his Communist late-friends, owing to their lies etc, so perhaps the Left Book Club may become quite a power for good again, if it manages to survive.'

The Communist Party's decision to oppose British intervention in the Second World War marked the termination of its influence on the LBC. For a while, the Party could be dismissed as an irrelevance to the British public. During the summer of 1940, however, it began to gather support for the dual policy of a socialist government and a negotiated peace with Germany, using as a front the 'People's Convention Movement'. In January 1941, the PCM held a conference, attended by two hundred delegates claiming to represent a million people. Gollancz was determined to expose it as a cover for Communist revolutionary defeatism – the idea that a defeat of Churchill's Government was more important than the defeat of Hitler, and that a socialist revolution in Britain would be the inspiration for uprisings by the German and the Italian people against their (own) fascist leaders. To this end, he assembled and edited *The Betrayal of the Left.*

The book is for the most part a compilation of articles from *Left News.* A piece by Strachey, who had by this time abandoned the Communist Party, presents the case for American aid (which was opposed by the Party); a 'Labour Candidate' – Konni Zilliacus – contrasts a pro-intervention pamphlet written by Harry Pollitt just after the outbreak of war with Palme Dutt's defeatist *We Fight for Life.* Orwell is represented by two essays: in 'Fascism for Democracy' he presents a critique of the argument used by both fascists and Communists that bourgeois democracy is a figleaf for class power; he also calls for the formation of a 'real English socialist movement' which will respect national democratic traditions. 'Patriots and Revolutionaries', reprinted here, argues similarly that a new socialist Britain – the language of which could be heard in pubs up and down the country – could be realised only if the left embraced patriotism.

Gollancz's most important contribution is the 'Epilogue on Political Morality', a reflection on the impact of the Communist Party on the LBC:

> Looking back I erred more as a publisher than as a writer or speaker. I accepted manuscripts about Russia, good or bad, because they were 'orthodox'; I rejected others, by bona fide socialists and honest men, because they were not . . . I am as sure as a man can be . . . that all this was wrong.

Betrayal of the Left became – as Gollancz's biographer, Ruth Dudley Edwards, has commented – 'a critical volume in left-wing historiography'. It was 'far and away the most devastating indictment anyone had produced on the CP, precisely because the majority of its contributors understood the compulsiveness of that reassuring creed'.

Gollancz and Orwell had never much liked each other and their reconciliation didn't last long. The publisher turned down *Animal Farm* because it was an attack on one of Britain's wartime allies; and he later dismissed Orwell – the writer of the best of the 260 Left Book Club monthly choices – as 'enormously overrated'.

PATRIOTS AND REVOLUTIONARIES

by George Orwell

THE FACT THAT there has been no general election or other major political event in England during the past twelve months ought not to hide from us the swing of opinion that is taking place beneath the surface. England is on the road to revolution, a process that started, in my opinion, about the end of 1938. But *what kind* of revolution depends partly on our recognising in time the real forces at work and not using phrases out of nineteenth-century textbooks as a substitute for thought.

England spent the first eight months of war in almost the same state of twilight sleep as it had spent the eight preceding years. There was widespread vague discontent, but no active defeatism, as the votes at the by-elections showed. In so far as it thought about the war the nation comforted itself with two completely false strategic theories, one of them official, the other peculiar to the Left. The first was that Hitler would be driven by the British blockade to smash himself to pieces against the Maginot Line; the other was that by agreeing to partition Poland, Stalin had in some mysterious manner 'stopped' Hitler, who would thereafter be unable to perpetrate further conquests. Both have been utterly falsified by events. Hitler simply walked around the Maginot Line and entered Rumania via Hungary, as could have been foreseen from the start by anyone able to read a map. But the acceptance of these geographical absurdities was a reflection of the general apathy. So long as France stood, the nation did not feel itself in danger of conquest, and on the other hand the easy victory which was supposedly to be brought about by 'economic' means, leaving Chamberlain in power and everything just as it had been before, did not inspire much enthusiasm. No doubt most of us would have preferred a victory for the British businessmen to a victory for Hitler, but it was not a thing to grow lyrical about. The notion that England *could only win the war by passing through revolution* had barely been mooted.

Then came the startling disasters of May and June. Although there was no political upheaval to mark it, no one who used his ears and eyes at the time could mistake the leftward swing of public opinion. The British people had had the jolt that they had been needing for years past. There had been demonstrated to them in a way that could not be mistaken the decay of their ruling class, the inefficiency of private capitalism, the urgent need for economic reorganisation and the destruction of privilege. Had any real leadership existed on the Left, there is little doubt that the return of the troops from Dunkirk could have been the beginning of the end of British capitalism. It was a moment at which the willingness for sacrifice and drastic changes extended not only to the working class but to nearly the whole of the middle class, whose patriotism, when it comes to the pinch, is stronger than their sense of self-interest. There was apparent, sometimes in the most unexpected people, a feeling of being on the edge of a new society in which much of the greed, apathy, injustice and corruption of the past would have disappeared. But no adequate leadership existed, the strategic moment passed, the pendulum swung back. The expected invasion failed to take place, and terrible though the air-raids have been, they were nothing to what had been feared. Since about October confidence has come back, and with confidence, apathy. The forces of reaction promptly counter-attacked and began to consolidate their position, which had been badly shaken in the summer days when it looked as though they would have to turn to the common people for help. The fact that, against all expectation, England had not been conquered had vindicated the ruling classes to some extent, and the matter was clinched by Wavell's victory in Egypt. Following promptly on Sidi Barrani came Margesson's entry into the Cabinet – an open, unmistakable slap in the face for all shades of progressive opinion. It was not possible to bring Chamberlain out of his grave, but Margesson's appointment was the nearest approach to it.

However, the defeats of the summer had brought out something more important than the tendency, normal to nearly all regimes, to swing to the Left in moments of disaster and to the Right in moments of security. What it had brought out was the integrity of British national feeling. After all, and in spite of all, the common people were patriotic. It is of the profoundest importance to face this fact and not try to dispose of it with easy formulae. It may possibly be true that 'the proletarian has no country'. What concerns us, however, is the fact that the proletarian, at any rate in England, *feels* that he has a country, and will act accordingly. The conventional Marxist notion that 'the workers' don't care twopence whether or not their country is conquered is as false as the *Daily Telegraph* notion that every Englishman chokes with emotion on hearing 'Rule Britannia'. It is quite true that the working class, unlike the middle class, have no imperialist feeling and dislike patriotic bombast. Almost any working man sees promptly the equivocal meaning of 'YOUR Courage, YOUR Cheerfulness, YOUR Resolution will bring US Victory'. But let it appear that England is about to be conquered by a foreign Power, and the case is altered. There was a moment in the summer when our Allies had deserted us, our army had been heavily defeated and had barely escaped with the loss of all its equipment, and England, internally, was all but defenceless. Then, if ever, was the moment for a stop-the-war movement to arise, to the tune of 'The enemy is in your own country', etc., etc. Well, that was exactly the moment at which the British working class flung itself into a huge effort to increase armaments-production and prevent invasion. Eden's appeal for Local Defence Volunteers got a quarter of a million recruits in the first day and another million in the next few weeks; I have reason to believe that a larger number could have been obtained. Let it be remembered that at that moment the invasion was expected to happen immediately and that the men who enrolled themselves believed that they would have to fight the German army with shotguns and bottles of petrol. It is perhaps more significant that in the six months since that date the Home Guard – a spare-time, practically unpaid organisation – has barely fallen off in numbers, except through the calling-up of the younger members. And now let anyone compare the membership of the Home Guard with those of the political parties which assume that the common man is not patriotic. The Communist Party, the ILP, Mosley's organisation and the PPU may perhaps have between them an unstable membership of 150,000. In by-elections held since the war, only one stop-the-war candidate has even saved his election deposit. Is not the conclusion obvious, except to those who are unable to face facts?

But the revelation of working-class patriotism coincided with the swing of opinion that I have spoken of earlier, the sudden perception that the existing social order was rotten. People dimly grasped – and not always so dimly, to judge from certain conversations I listened to in pubs at the time – that it was our duty both to defend England and to turn it into a genuine democracy. England is in some ways politically backward, extremist slogans are not bandied to and fro as they are in Continental countries, but the feeling of all true patriots and all true Socialists is at bottom reducible to the 'Trotskyist' slogan: 'The war and the revolution are inseparable.' We cannot beat Hitler without passing through revolution, nor consolidate our revolution without beating Hitler. Useless to pretend, with the Communists, that you can somehow get rid of Hitler by surrendering to him. Useless to imagine, with the *Daily Telegraph*, that you can defeat Hitler without disturbing the status quo. A capitalist Britain cannot defeat Hitler; its potential resources and its potential allies cannot be mobilised. Hitler can only be defeated by an England which can bring to its aid the progressive forces of the world – an England, therefore, which is fighting against the sins of its own past. The Communists and others profess to believe that the defeat of Hitler means no more than a renewed stabilisation of British capitalism. This is merely a lie designed to spread disaffection in the Nazi interest. Actually, as the Communists themselves would have pointed out a year ago, the opposite is the truth: British capitalism can only survive by coming to terms with fascism. Either we turn England into a Socialist democracy or by one route or another we become part of the Nazi empire; there is no third alternative.

But part of the process of turning England into a Socialist democracy is to avoid conquest from without. We cannot, as some people appear to imagine, call off the war by arrangement and then proceed to have a private revolution with no outside interference. Something rather of this kind happened in the Russian Revolution, partly because Russia is a difficult country to invade, partly because the chief European Powers were at the time engaged in fighting one another. For England, 'revolutionary defeatism' would only be a thinkable policy if the chief centres of population and industry in the British Empire were in, say, Australia. Any attempt to overthrow our ruling class *without* defending our shores would simply lead to the prompt occupation of Britain by the Nazis, and the setting-up of a reactionary puppet Government, as in France. In the social revolution that we have got to carry through there can be no such gap in our defences as existed, potentially, in the Russia of 1917–1918. A country within gunshot of the Continent and dependent on imports for its food is not in a position to make a Brest-Litovsk peace. Our revolution can only be a revolution behind the British fleet. But that is another way of saying that we must do the thing that British extremist parties have always failed to do, the thing they have alternately declared to be unnecessary and impossible – to win over the middle classes.

Economically there are in England two main dividing lines. One is – at the present standard of living – at £5 a week, the other at £2,000 a year. The class that lies between, though not numerous compared with the working class, holds a key position, because in it is included practically the whole of the technocracy (engineers, chemists, doctors, airmen, etc., etc.) without which a modern industrial country could not exist for a week. It is a fact that these people benefit very little from the existing order of society and that their way of life would not be very profoundly altered by the change-over to a Socialist economy. It is also a fact that they have always tended to side with the capitalist class and against their natural allies, the manual workers, partly because of an educational system designed to have just that effect, partly because of the out-of-dateness of Socialist propaganda. Nearly all Socialists who even *sounded* as though they meant business have always talked in terms of the old-fashioned 'proletarian revolution', a conception which was formed before the modern technical middle class came into being. To the middle-class man, 'revolution' has been presented as a process by which he and his kind are killed off or exiled, and the entire control of the State is handed over to manual workers, who, he is well aware, would be unable to run a modern industrial country unaided. The concept of revolution as a more or less voluntary act of the majority of the people – the only kind of revolution that is conceivable under modern Western conditions – has always been regarded as heretical.

But how, when you aim at any fundamental change, can you get the majority of the people on your side? The position is that a few people are actively for you, a few actively against you, and the great mass are capable of being pushed one way or the other. The capitalist class, as a whole, *must* be against you. No hope that these people will see the error of their ways, or abdicate gracefully. Our job is not to try to win them over, but to isolate them, expose them, make the mass of the people see their reactionary and semi-treacherous nature. But how about the indispensable middle class that I have spoken of above? Can you really bring them over to your side? Is there any chance of turning an airman, a naval officer, a railway engineer or what-not into a convinced Socialist? The answer is that a revolution which waited for the full conversion of the entire population would never happen. The question is not so much whether the men in key positions are fully on your side as whether they are sufficiently against you to sabotage. It is no use hoping that the airmen, destroyer-commanders, etc. on whom our very existence depends will all turn into orthodox Marxists; but we can hope, if we approach them rightly, that they will continue to do their jobs when they see behind their backs a Labour Government putting through Socialist legislation. The approach to these people is through their patriotism. 'Sophisticated' Socialists may laugh at the patriotism of the middle classes, but let no one imagine that it is a sham. Nothing that makes men willing to die in battle – and relative to numbers more of the middle class than of the working class are killed in war – is a sham. These people will be with us if they can be made to see that a victory over Hitler demands the destruction of capitalism; they will be against us if we let it appear that we are indifferent to England's independence. We have got to make far clearer than it has been made hitherto the fact that at this moment of time a revolutionary has to be a patriot, and a patriot has to be a revolutionary. 'Do you want to defeat Hitler? Then you must be ready to sacrifice your social prestige. Do you want to establish Socialism? Then you must be ready to defend your country.' That is a crude way of putting it, but it is along those lines that our propaganda must move. That is the thing that we missed the chance to say in the summer months, when the rottenness of private capitalism was already partly clear to people who a year earlier would have described themselves as Conservatives, and when people who all their lives had laughed at the very notion of patriotism discovered that they did not want to be ruled by foreigners after all.

At the moment we are in a period of backwash, when the forces of reaction, reassured by a partial victory, are regaining the ground they lost earlier. Margesson goes into the Cabinet, the army is bidden to polish its buttons, the Home Guard is brought more and more under the control of Blimps, there is talk of suppressing this newspaper and that, the Government bargains with Pétain and Franco – big and small, these things are indications of the general trend. But presently, in the spring perhaps, or even earlier, there will come another moment of crisis. And that, quite possibly, will be our final chance. At that moment it may be decided once and for all whether the issues of this war are to be made clear and who is to control the great middling mass of people, working class and middle class, who are capable of being pushed in either one direction or the other.

Much of the failure of the English Left is traceable to the tendency of

Socialists to criticise current movements from the outside instead of trying to influence them from within. When the Home Guard was formed, it was impossible not to be struck by the lack of political instinct which led Socialists of nearly all shades to stand aloof from the whole business, not seeing in this sudden spontaneous movement any opportunity for themselves. Here were a million men springing, as it were, out of the ground, asking for arms to defend their country against a possible invader and organising themselves into a military body almost without direction from above. Would one not have expected those Socialists who had talked for years about 'democratising the army', etc., etc. to do their utmost to guide this new force along the right political lines? Instead of which the vast majority of Socialists paid no attention, or, in the case of the doctrinaires, said weakly, 'This is fascism.' It apparently did not occur to them that the political colour of such a force, compelled by the circumstances of the time to organise itself independently, would be determined by the people who were in it. Only a handful of Spanish War veterans like Tom Wintringham and Hugh Slater saw the danger and the opportunity and have since done their best, in the face of discouragement from several quarters, to form the Home Guard into a real People's Army. At the moment the Home Guard stands at the crossroads. It is patriotic, the bulk of its members are definitely anti-fascist, but it is politically undirected. A year hence, if it still exists, it may be a democratic army capable of having a strong political influence on the regular forces, or it may be a sort of SA officered by the worst sections of the middle class. A few thousand Socialists within its ranks, energetic and knowing what they want, could prevent the second development. But they can only do so *from within*. And what I have said of the Home Guard applies to the whole war effort and the steady tendency of Socialists to hand executive power to their enemies. In pre-war days, when the appeasement policy still ruled, it was an ironical thing to read through a membership list of the House of Commons. It was Labour and Communist members who clamoured for a 'firm stand against Germany', but it was Conservative members who were members of the RNVR or RAFVR.

It is only if we associate ourselves with the war effort, by acts as well as words, that we have any chance of influencing national policy; it is only if we have some sort of control over national policy that the war can be won. If we simply stand aside, make no effort to permeate the armed forces with our ideas or to influence those who are patriotic but politically neutral, if we allow the pro-Nazi utterances of the Communists to be taken as representative of 'Left' opinion, events will pass us by. We shall have failed to use the lever which the patriotism of the common man has put into our hands. The 'politically unreliable' will be elbowed out of positions of power, the Blimps will settle themselves tighter in the saddle, the governing classes will continue the war in their own way. And their way can only lead to ultimate defeat. To believe that, it is not necessary to believe that the British governing class are consciously pro-Nazi. But so long as they are in control the British war-effort is running on one cylinder. Since they will not – *cannot*, without destroying themselves – put through the necessary social and economic changes, they cannot alter the balance of forces, which is at present heavily against us. While our social system is what it is, how can they set free the enormous energies of the English people? How can they turn the coloured peoples from exploited coolies into willing allies? How (even if they wanted to) can they mobilise the revolutionary forces of Europe? Does anyone suppose that the conquered populations are going to rebel on behalf of the British dividend-drawers? Either we turn this war into a revolutionary war or we lose it. And we can only turn it into a revolutionary war if we can bring into being a revolutionary movement capable of appealing to a majority of the people; a movement, therefore, not sectarian, not defeatist, not 'anti-British', not resembling in any way the petty fractions of the extreme Left, with their heresy-hunting and their Graeco-Latin jargon. The alternative is to leave the conduct of the war to the British ruling class and to go gradually down through exhaustion into defeat – called, no doubt, not 'defeat' but 'negotiated peace' – leaving Hitler in secure control of Europe. And does anyone in his senses feel much doubt as to what that will mean? Does anyone except a handful of Blackshirts and pacifists pay any attention to Hitler's claims to be 'the friend of the poor man', the 'enemy of plutocracy', etc.? Are such claims credible, after the past seven years? Do not his deeds speak louder than his words?

At George V's Silver Jubilee there occurred a popular demonstration which was 'spontaneous' in a different sense from the organised loyalty-parades of totalitarian countries. In the south of England, at any rate, the response was big enough to surprise the authorities and lead them to prolong the celebrations for an extra week. In certain very poor London streets, which the people had decorated of their own accord, I saw chalked across the asphalt two slogans: 'Poor, but loyal' and 'Landlords, keep away' (or 'No landlord wanted'). It is most improbable that these slogans had been suggested by any political party. Most doctrinaire Socialists were furious at the time, and not wrongly. Certainly it is appalling that people living in the London slums should describe themselves as 'poor, but loyal'. But there would have been far more reason for despair if the other slogan had been 'Three cheers for the landlord' (or words to that effect). For was there not something significant, something we might have noticed at the time, in that instinctive antithesis between the King and the landlord? Up to the death of George V the King probably stood for a majority of English people as the symbol of national unity. These people believed – quite mistakenly, of course – in the King as someone who was on their side against the monied class. They were patriotic, but they were not Conservative. And did they not show a sounder instinct than those who tell us that patriotism is something disgraceful and national liberty a matter of indifference? Although the circumstances were far more dramatic, was it not the same impulse that moved the Paris workers in 1793, the Communards in 1871, the Madrid trade unionists in 1936 – the impulse to defend one's country, and to make it a place worth living in?

SOURCES

The starting point for anyone interested in the Left Book Club is Ruth Dudley Edwards's excellent *Victor Gollancz: A Biography* (London, 1987); it was a great help in writing the introduction to this anthology. John Lewis's *The Left Book Club: An Historical Record* (London, 1970) is also worth looking at, perhaps especially because his Communist Party perspective is pretty much unaltered from the time of his departure from the Club. Sheila Hodges's *Gollancz: The Story of a Publishing House 1928–78* (London, 1978) provides original information, too.

There are several essays and articles devoted to the LBC, among them: Gary McCulloch, '"Teachers and Missionairies": The Left Book Club as an educational agency', *History of Education*, 14 (1985); Gordon B. Neavill, 'Victor Gollancz and the Left Book Club', *Library Quarterly*, 41 (1971); Betty Reid, 'The Left Book Club in the Thirties' in John Clark, Margot Heinemann et al (eds.), *Culture and Crisis in Britain in the Thirties* (London, 1979); Stuart Samuels, 'The Left Book Club', *Journal of Contemporary History*, 1 (1966); and Alfred Sherman, 'The Days of the Left Book Club', *Survey: A Journal of Soviet and East European Studies*, 41 (1962).

The following books were also useful to me:

Beckett, Francis, *Enemy Within: The Rise and Fall of the British Communist Party* (London, 1995).

Chambers, Colin, *The Story of Unity Theatre* (London, 1989).

Croft, Andy (ed.), *Randall Swingler: Selected Poems* (Nottingham, 2000)

Graves, Robert and Hodge, Alan, *The Long Weekend* (London, 1940).

Hopkins, James K., *Into the Heart of Fire: The British in the Spanish Civil War* (Stanford, Cal., 1998)

Hynes, Samuel, *The Auden Generation* London, 1976)

Jones, Bill and Williams, Chris (eds.), *With Dust Still in His Throat: A B. L. Coombes Anthology* (Cardiff, 1999)

Lehmann, John, *The Whispering Gallery* (London, 1955).

Lucas, John (ed.), *The 1930s: A Challenge to Orthodoxy* (Hassocks, 1978) – especially the contributions by Arnold Rattenbury.

McKibbin, Ross, *Class and Cultures: England 1918–1951* (Oxford, 1998).

Pimlott, Ben, *Labour and the Left in the 1930s* (Cambridge, 1977).

Shelden, Michael, *Orwell: The Authorised Biography* (New York, 1991).

Strachey, John, *The Strangled Cry* (London, 1962).

Symons, Julian, *The Thirties* (London, 1960).

Toynbee, Philip, *Friends Apart* (London, 1954).